Praise for *She Gets That from Me*

"An intense, emotionally charged novel that deals with the issues of modern relationships while asking age-old questions of what it means to be a family. Provocative, engaging, and impossible to put down."

—Jayne Ann Krentz,
New York Times bestselling author of *The Vanishing*

"A lovely story of friendship and family. Perfect for fans of contemporary women's fiction. I enjoyed every word."

—Susan Elizabeth Phillips,
New York Times bestselling author of *Dance Away with Me*

"As captivating as it is witty and wise. Wells's beautiful prose brings us so close to the characters' hearts that we feel as if we've known them for all our lives. A book that reveals the importance and impact of family, as well as the transcendent power of love. Robin Wells breathes wondrous life into a deeply moving story."

—Patti Callahan Henry,
New York Times bestselling author of *The Favorite Daughter*

"Chock-full of conflict and brimming with heart. I couldn't put this book down! If you're looking for a fresh twist on a beautiful love story, sky-high stakes, and a fresh and compelling hook, look no further. A tender love story that captured my heart, *She Gets That from Me* is one of those rare books that, when I'd turned the last page, left me simultaneously satisfied and yearning for more. A gorgeous book of love and loss, family and friendship, hope and second chances."

—Lori Nelson Spielman,
New York Times bestselling author of *The Star-Crossed Sisters of Tuscany*

"Witty and wise. A loving glimpse into the families we choose and the friendships that define us."

—Wendy Wax,
USA Today bestselling author of *My Ex-Best Friend's Wedding*

"With richly drawn characters and a lovely sense of place, *She Gets That from Me* is a compelling look at how we build our tribes. A beautifully woven tale about the many paths life can take as we find our way to family."

—Victoria Schade,
author of *Who Rescued Who*

Berkley titles by Robin Wells

The Wedding Tree

The French War Bride

She Gets That from Me

She Gets That from Me

ROBIN WELLS

BERKLEY
New York

BERKLEY
An imprint of Penguin Random House LLC
penguinrandomhouse.com

Library of Congress Cataloging-in-Publication Data

Names: Wells, Robin (Robin Rouse), author.
Title: She gets that from me / Robin Wells.
Description: First edition. | New York: Berkley, 2020.
Identifiers: LCCN 2020012720 (print) | LCCN 2020012721 (ebook) |
ISBN 9781984802002 (trade paperback) | ISBN 9781984802019 (ebook)
Subjects: LCSH: Domestic fiction. | GSAFD: Love stories.
Classification: LCC PS3623.E4768 S54 2020 (print) |
LCC PS3623.E4768 (ebook) | DDC 813/.6--dc23
LC record available at https://lccn.loc.gov/2020012720
LC ebook record available at https://lccn.loc.gov/2020012721

First Edition: September 2020

Printed in the United States of America
1 3 5 7 9 10 8 6 4 2

Cover art by Sarah Oberrender
Cover image by Peopleimages / Getty Images
Book design by Katy Riegel

To Ken,

the love of my life

and the heart of my heart

CHAPTER ONE

Quinn

Tuesday, March 26

I DO THREE things really well, but saying no isn't one of them. I'm too susceptible to begging—especially from young children, small dogs, and good-looking men.

"Read me another story, Auntie Quinn."

My goddaughter, Lily, is a case in point. It's forty minutes past her bedtime, and I've already read her five books. A request from the adorable three-year-old—it's hard to believe she'll be four in just four months!—is nearly impossible for me to turn down.

I close the cover of *The Velveteen Rabbit*, ruffle Lily's honey-colored hair, and make a weak attempt. "It's late, sweetie." We're both reclining against pillows on her low four-poster bed. She and her favorite stuffed animal, Sugar Bear, are tucked under her white duvet, and I'm lying on top of it, my sandals kicked off, my arm looped around her. My black-and-white Maltipoo, Ruffles, is curled on the covers beside us.

"Just one more. Pleeeease?" Lily's eyes are fringed with ridiculously long eyelashes, and when she turns them on me with that pleading look, my insides go as soft and gooey as a campfire marshmallow.

I'm staying overnight with Lily as I do every other month or so when Brooke has to leave New Orleans for a business trip. Brooke is an absolutely amazing single mother. She's also a high-powered logistics executive at a major corporation and the most organized person I've ever met, and she runs as tight a ship at home as she does at work.

Whenever I babysit, I try to keep Lily on her schedule, but my willpower is no match for the child's swimming pool–blue eyes.

"Just one more teensy-tiny book. Please, please, please?"

Resistance is futile. "Okay, one more, but only if you promise to go right to sleep afterward, with no fuss."

"I promise."

"All right, then." I search my mind for the name of a book that's short. "How about *Goodnight Moon*?"

"Yay!" Lily scrambles out of bed and scurries to her bookcase, her blond curls bouncing. Ruffles jumps down, scampers to her side, and positions herself to get petted.

I wonder if the way I consistently cave to Lily's wishes means I won't be a good mother. I hope not. More than anything, I want to have a child and be a loving, supportive mom like Brooke. It's the deepest desire of my heart.

My mind darts to the future, and a little thrill starts to quiver through my chest. If things go the way I hope, then maybe soon I'll . . .

Keep your thoughts in the here and now, I caution myself. *Manage your expectations and you'll manage your disappointments.* This is a directive from one of the many self-improvement books I've read lately, because I'm working very hard right now on becoming the best person I can be. Managing disappointment is a concept I should have learned as a girl—heaven only knows I had ample opportunity—but I never quite got the knack of it, at least not when it comes to my personal life.

Especially when it comes to men. On two separate occasions, I've deluded myself into thinking I found Mr. Right, only to discover that the object of my affections was Mr. Wasting My Fertile Years. One relationship lasted six years and the other ate up four, adding up to a solid decade of squandered time—time when I should have been out there, meeting a man who really and truly wants the same things I do. A man who—and this is the important part, the part I keep missing—is really as wonderful as I think he is.

Brooke says I put too much stock in fairy tales. She thinks I have a bad habit of looking at men through rose-colored glasses, imagining positive traits that don't exist and ignoring negatives that are all too real. I hate to admit it, but she's right. Both times, I fooled myself into thinking that I'd found Prince Charming because that's what I so desperately wanted.

Well, I'm on a new track now. I'm all about facing reality, dealing with the stone-cold truth, and pulling up my big-girl pants. I'm determined to live life on my own terms and according to my own timeline. Instead of imagining that a man is going to come along and complete me, I'm working on completing myself.

One of the books I'm reading, *Reparenting Your Inner Child with Compassion and Mindfulness*, instructs readers to find three things they're really good at, and to appreciate and nurture those strengths every day. I love this exercise because the Rule of Three is one of my favorite design principles. The three strengths I've identified are being a good friend, finding the silver lining, and designing homes that people love to live in.

While Lily crouches in front of her bookcase, I look around the room and try to appreciate my design handiwork. I decorated the nursery when Brooke was expecting—I was actually living in Atlanta at the time—and I updated it after I moved to New Orleans, when Lily outgrew her convertible crib/toddler bed. I specialize in creating children's rooms that easily change as their occupants grow.

I feel a sense of satisfaction, because Lily's room is one of my all-time favorite little-girl spaces ever. It features pale grayish-green walls, pink silk draperies, and a matching faux canopy spilling from a crown-shaped cornice near the ceiling. The furniture is a whimsical mix of modern, antique, and art deco styles, tied together with touches of distressed white paint.

"Here it is!" Lily grabs the small board book from the shelf. Her bare feet pad whippet-fast across the thick white rug that covers the wide oak planks, her tiny toenails the same shade of aqua as her Elsa nightgown (I'd painted them for her earlier in the evening).

She jumps on the mattress, dives under the covers, and curls up beside me as I open the well-worn book. Ruffles bounds up and settles on top of both of us. Lily giggles and snuggles close, her little body warm against mine.

When I finish reading aloud and close the book, Lily and I kneel by her bed, and she says her prayers. "Thank you, God, for all that's good, an' help me do the things I should. Bless Mommy an' Grams an' Auntie Quinn an' Ruffles. An' give me a little sister. Amen."

I smile as she scrambles back under the covers while I put all six books back on the bookshelf. I tuck in Lily and Sugar Bear yet again, smoothing the pink-and-white-striped sheet over the top of the white duvet, and drop a kiss on her forehead. "Nighty night, sweet princess."

"G'night, Auntie Quinn. I love you!"

Lily's arms curl around my neck. She smells like bubblegum-flavored toothpaste and baby shampoo, and the scent makes my eyes unexpectedly fill with tears. "Love you, too, darling girl."

I turn out her bedside lamp. Ruffles pads into the hallway. I pull Lily's door closed behind me and head down the hall, my heart as warm and soft as a just-baked cinnamon roll.

Brooke's decision to become a single mother had shocked me at first, but she says it's the best thing she ever did, and knowing Lily, I have to agree. But then, Brooke has always known her own mind and been fearless about pursuing what she wants. She's my role model that way. She's just a couple of years older than me, but she's always seemed a lot further ahead in life.

We met eighteen years ago at Louisiana State University when we sat beside each other in a beginning interior design course. Brooke was a computer science junior taking the class as an elective; I was an interior design freshman having trouble loading the design software on my computer. She offered to do it for me, and I, in turn, offered to help her decorate her student apartment on a shoestring budget.

We hit it off right away. We shared the same sense of humor, we liked the same novels and movies, and we were both passionate about our fields of study. We both have dark blond hair and we're both medium height and build, so we're often asked if we're sisters.

"Yes," we always reply, usually in chorus.

"We're compensation sisters," Brooke once said.

"What?" I asked.

"We're each other's compensation for losing our families."

It's another thing we have in common. Brooke lost both parents and her little brother in a deadly car accident when she was twelve. I lost my family when my parents divorced and I became the extra baggage in their new relationships and lifestyles.

I think Brooke's loss is greater because it was so final, but she thinks mine is worse because it wasn't. Sometimes I think she's right; she, at least, always felt wanted.

Thinking about this makes my chest grow tight as I walk down the hall toward the stairs. I recall another piece of self-help instruction: *Don't allow negative thoughts to control your feelings. When you become aware of them, breathe deeply, pick a focal point, and concentrate on the present moment.*

I draw in a long breath and focus my attention on the photos grouped on the wall above the staircase wainscoting. A picture of Brooke and me dressed up as bumblebees for a Halloween party at my first apartment in Atlanta makes me smile. After college, I went to work at a high-end design firm there, and Brooke went to work for an international conglomerate in New York. We stayed in close touch despite the distance, visiting each other a couple of times a year and spending the holidays together in Louisiana at her grandmother's house in Alexandria.

I move another step down the stairs and look at a photo of Brooke's silver-haired grandmother sitting in her front porch swing. Miss Margaret is a remarkably spry and fit septuagenarian who raised Brooke after her family's tragic accident. She's a true Southern lady, genteel and gracious and unfailingly polite—although from time to time, she can come out with an old-fashioned saying that will, as she puts it, "starch your shorts." In the next photo, she's holding two-year-old Lily on a carousel horse at New Orleans City Park, glowing with great-grandmotherly pride.

I descend two more steps and gaze at a photo of Brooke cuddling newborn Lily, her face shining with such love it looks like she's sprinkled with fairy dust. I reach out and softly touch the gilt frame, wishing some of that joy would rub off. Like me, Brooke dreamed of having not only a career, but a husband and a family. Like me, she'd had a couple of serious relationships, then hit her thirties without meeting the man of her dreams. Unlike me, however, she'd had the added complication of severe endometriosis.

When Brooke was thirty-three, she learned that endometrial tissue was scarring her ovaries and uterus. "If you want to have a baby, you'd better do it soon," her doctor had told her.

Just like that, she decided to become a single mother. And then, with her typical hyperefficiency, she created a plan and put it into action.

This is where Brooke and I are not alike—not at all. It takes me a long time to make major decisions. When I have to decide something, I'll waffle back and forth, weighing advantages and disadvantages, reevaluating and second-guessing and stalling. Brooke minored in psychology and says I don't really trust myself because I couldn't trust my parents.

I suppose this is true, because I tend to look for signs. I want confirmation that something beyond my own hopefulness is informing my choices. I believe that coincidences are miracles where God chooses to remain anonymous, so I look for a coincidence—a song playing on the radio, two people mentioning the same topic, winning two consecutive games of solitaire . . . or getting goose bumps. I put a lot of weight on goose bumps. If I get goosy and I'm not cold, I take it as a sign.

I don't tell many people about this, because I know it sounds idiotic. Brooke is the only person who seems to understand, and even she will tease me about it. "What's the goose bump factor?" she asked last week when I couldn't decide between shrimp or chicken on my salad.

I'm getting better at trusting myself, though. A couple of years ago, I moved to New Orleans and started my own business. That was an uncharacteristically bold move—especially opening a retail home-furnishings shop, Verve!, to drive my design business. It's turned out to be one of the best decisions of my life; I love New Orleans, I love being close to Brooke and Lily, and my business is booming. In fact, I'm giving more and more design responsibilities to my assistant, I'm trying to hire an additional part-time manager for the store, and I often have to work nights to get everything done.

Tonight is one of those evenings. I head to the kitchen, open my laptop, and settle at the kitchen table to plot out the furniture placement of a master bedroom for a client I'm meeting with tomorrow morning.

I'm engrossed in the project when a sharp rap sounds on the front door. Ruffles barks. I glance at the time on my computer screen. It's nine thirty-seven—too late for social calls or most deliveries. My instinct is to ignore it and hope that whoever is there will go away. To my consternation, the knock sounds again, louder this time. Ruffles barks again. I rise from the chair and scoop up the little dog, hushing her.

The lights outside are on and the living room lights are off, so I step to the window and peek through the blinds. I don't know whether to feel alarmed or reassured that a police car is parked by the curb.

The door knocker clunks, thunderous brass against brass, and Ruffles once more sounds off. I'm afraid the racket will wake Lily, so I go to the door and peer out the sidelight.

Two police officers in full uniform stand on the porch. I flip on the light to the foyer and crack the door, keeping the chain on.

"Yes?"

"Good evening, ma'am. Is this the residence of Brooke Adams?" asks the taller officer.

Alarm crawls up my spine. "Yes, but she's not here."

"Are you a relative?"

"I'm a good friend staying with her daughter."

"May we come in?" asks the shorter officer, an older man with gray eyebrows. His hat sits further back on his head, and I can see that his eyes behind his wire-rimmed glasses are kind.

"Well, uh . . ." I'm flummoxed by the request. My palm grows damp on the edge of the door.

The younger officer holds out a badge.

New Orleans Police Department, I read. It matches their uniforms and the car at the curb, so it's unlikely they're anything other than what they appear to be, but I'm scared to let them inside. Whatever it is that brought them here needs to stay out of Brooke's house. "What's this about?"

"We'd prefer to discuss it inside, if you don't mind," the older officer says.

"O-okay." My hands shake as I close the door to unfasten the chain, then open it again. "Has something happened to Miss Margaret?"

"Miss Margaret?" the tall officer asks.

"Brooke's grandmother. In Alexandria."

He pulls out a notebook and jots something down.

"Wh-what's going on?" I'm running through the plots of all the TV shows and movies I've ever seen, trying to come up with an acceptable reason for them to be here, a reason that won't open a sinkhole beneath this household. Maybe they're questioning everyone in the neighborhood about a crime or something.

"I think it would be better if we come in to talk," the kind-eyed officer repeats.

"Of—of course." I step back, letting them in, still clutching Ruffles. They take off their hats and follow me into the living room. I gesture to two armchairs by the fireplace. "I have to say, you're really getting me worried."

"We apologize for that." He gives me a sympathetic smile and walks to one of the chairs. His partner goes to the other. "And we apologize for coming by at this hour and disrupting your evening." He holds out his hand, indicating the sofa, as if he were the host and I were the guest. "Please—have a seat."

I sink to the sofa, Ruffles in my lap. It seems to take forever for the two men to lower themselves into the chairs.

"What's this about?" I ask.

The gray-haired officer adjusts his glasses on his nose. "I'm afraid we have some bad news."

My heart slams hard against my rib cage. I've already figured out that much.

"It's about Brooke Adams," he continues.

My breath freezes halfway through an inhalation. "Wh-what's happened?"

"I really regret having to tell you this," he says, "but Ms. Adams is dead."

CHAPTER TWO

Margaret

Wednesday, April 3

I JUST LEFT Brooke at the cemetery, so I know she's gone, yet it doesn't seem real. I feel dazed and addlepated, like those prizefighters my late husband, Henry, used to watch on black-and-white TV, back when Muhammad Ali was still Cassius Clay—like I'm staggering around in circles, moving but not going anywhere. I feel pummeled and stunned and numb. Just when I think my head might be clearing, grief packs another wallop, sending me reeling again.

I'd forgotten this about fresh grief—how it hits, then hits again, drubbing you over and over. I'd forgotten how physical it is—how impossible it is to eat or sleep, how it makes you ache all over, how difficult it is to make decisions or conversation. And, oh, mercy—there are so many decisions, so many conversations that have to take place after a loved one dies.

"Can I get you something, Miss Margaret?" A petite brunette—why, she's no bigger than a minute—appears in front of me, her brown eyes warm behind her large black-plastic-rimmed glasses. I don't remember her name—maybe Amie, or was it Annie?—but I know she's one of Brooke's friends from that single-parent-by-choice club. They've been angels, really. They've brought food and arranged everything for this postfuneral reception at Brooke's house. One of them took Lily to preschool the past few mornings because Quinn was helping me make funeral arrangements. Lily's too young to understand what's going on and it seemed best to just keep her on her regular routine. They're lovely young women, despite the fact they're all so misguided.

"Why don't you have a seat and let me fix a plate for you," the sweet gal with the *A* name says.

"Thank you, but I don't think I could eat a bite."

"How about some iced tea, then? Or a glass of wine?"

I hesitate. I'm not much of one for day drinking, but wine has some appeal.

She puts her hand on my arm. "Let's get you settled over here by the window, then I'll bring you some wine."

Glad to be absolved of the decision, I let her lead me to the armchair as if I'm incapacitated.

I sit down, lean back, and close my eyes after she scurries off. I've been through the loss of loved ones enough times that I should be used to it, but the truth is, it never gets easier. I lost my mother, my father, my sister, and my husband. That was bad enough, but then I lost my only child and her husband and my grandson, all at once, in one terrible accident. I thought nothing could ever be as bad as that, but pain is apparently not measured by body counts or lessened by the number of times one has suffered it.

In many ways, tragedy is a matter of survivors. I'm old enough that most of my life is behind me, and it doesn't much matter to me personally if I slog my way through this or abandon all hope, but there's Lily to think about. Because of her, I can't give up. It's unbelievably horrible that my sweet great-granddaughter has lost her mother, especially at such a tender age.

Not that there's ever a good age to lose a mother—my grandmother told me that she was sixty-nine when she lost hers, and she still felt orphaned. My mother died when I was eight and it felt like the end of the world, but thank heavens I still had my father. Poor Brooke was twelve when she lost both parents.

That was truly catastrophic. Twelve is such a terrible, awkward age anyway—an age when everything wonderful about childhood is ending, but the excitement of the teen years hasn't yet arrived. Twelve-year-old minds and bodies are gangly and green and unevenly growing, prone to hormone storms and mood squalls. Twelve-year-olds really need their parents, if only to pull away from later.

At three, Lily will hopefully be more resilient. I sit for a moment, mentally checking my math. Yes, she's still three. Dear God—she's three, and I'm seventy-nine. I'll be ninety when she's fourteen!

Before Lily was born, Brooke had tactfully broached the subject of setting up her will. "You know how I love you, Grams, and you know there's no one I'd rather raise my baby if I were in an accident or something, but I'm worried about the age difference. I'm wondering if perhaps I should name Quinn as the baby's guardian if anything happens to me."

"If anything happens to you, the child's father should be named as guardian," I'd told her.

Brooke's eyebrows had lowered. "Grams, we've been over this. You know that's not what he signed up for."

"How many men in the history of the world have had children they didn't 'sign up for'? Half of the earth's population got here that way, I'd wager."

"This is different, and you know it," she'd said. "The donor signed a contract waiving all parental rights and responsibilities. I don't know his identity and he doesn't know mine, and the cryobank will keep it that way."

"Yes, yes, yes. So you've told me." I'd sighed. I knew I wasn't going to change her mind by arguing with her, but nothing would change my mind, either.

When Brooke first told me she was pregnant by an anonymous sperm donor, I tried to talk her into locating and contacting the father. She'd unpacked all these official-sounding words—cryobanks, contracts, anonymity—that should have nothing to do with parenthood. She told me that her child's father had no rights or responsibilities, and explained that the terms of the contract were binding morally as well as legally. We'd argued about it—quite vehemently, in fact. I realized then that I'd have to accept the situation on Brooke's terms if I didn't want to risk alienating her, but I'd held out hopes that she might change her mind as the child grew older. "I just think that every child should have two parents," I'd said yet again when we discussed her will.

"That's ideal, I agree, but it's not always an option," Brooke had replied. "And my child will be very blessed to have you and Quinn in her life."

Quinn is a lovely young woman, to be sure, and I'm very fond of her, but she isn't a blood relative. I believe that family should raise family. I knew this argument wouldn't hold weight with Brooke, who often said Quinn was like a sister, so I focused on the fact that Quinn was living in Atlanta at the time.

"If something were to happen to you, God forbid, it'll be best for the child to be with someone she knows well. I'll be visiting all the time since I live in Louisiana," I'd said. "Quinn will only be able to see the child occasionally. Besides, I'm remarkably sound for my age." I take great pride in my physical fitness. I walk two miles almost every day and I volunteer three days a week at the library. Everyone, including my doctor, says my physiological age is at least ten years younger than the calendar indicates. "Are you saying I'm too feeble to care for a baby?"

"I wouldn't dare!" Brooke had laughed. "You might pin me to the floor."

I'd smiled. "That's more like it."

Brooke had shaken her head, then held up her hands in surrender. "Here's what I'll do: I'll put you as the primary guardian and Quinn as the backup for now, but we'll revisit this in a few years. I'll make a note to talk to my attorney again when you're eighty and Lily's four."

She'd given me a copy of the will. Both Quinn and I already had letters of temporary guardianship for the times when Lily was in our care.

"Miss Margaret, are you okay?"

I open my eyes now to see Quinn standing in front of me. I'm embarrassed that she's caught me with my eyes closed, like a doddering old woman napping in a chair.

"Yes, yes. I'm just . . . regrouping."

"Here you go." The petite woman with the glasses reappears and hands me a glass of wine. Again, I feel a bit sheepish about Quinn watching me. I hope she doesn't think I make a habit of drinking in the middle of the day.

The thought irritates me. She's not the judge of whether or not I'm fit to raise Lily. Although, I have to say, it bothers me a bit, how close she is to the child since she moved to New Orleans. She lives just a couple of blocks over, which means she sees Lily all the time. I'm still a three-and-a-half-hour drive away in Alexandria, so my argument about why I should have guardianship of Lily no longer holds water.

Quinn and Lily are very attached to each other. I feel a little twinge of—what? Guilt? Jealousy? I don't know, but it's an unpleasant and shameful emotion—that Brooke hadn't called me to come stay with Lily when she went out of town, the way she used to before Quinn moved to New Orleans. Of course, it's a long drive for me, and I can see how much easier it was to just have Quinn pop over, but still. I feel a little . . . displaced.

Well, that's not Quinn's fault. And I'm very grateful for the way she's handled things since Brooke's death. She's been most considerate and respectful of my feelings.

After the police visited her that awful night, she phoned my minister—she knows my church because she's attended Christmas Eve services with Brooke and me for the last eighteen years—and she asked him to come to my house to break the news to me. Afterward, he put me on the phone with Quinn, and she told me everything she knew. She offered to handle the arrangements for getting Brooke's body back to New Orleans. She realized it was my place to break the news to Lily, so she waited for me to arrive from Alexandria.

The memory makes my chest hurt again. I hope I did an adequate job with that. How does one tell a child her mother is dead? I've had to do it twice, which is twice more than anyone should ever have to do such a horrific thing in a lifetime. My minister—a man with a short graying beard, caring brown eyes, and a rock-solid faith—had driven me down to New Orleans early the next morning, his wife following in their car. They and Quinn were with me when I'd told Lily the tragic news, and the support had been a tremendous help.

"Just tell Lily what happened," my minister had advised when we discussed it on the drive. "Put it in simple terms that she can understand."

How was I supposed to do that, when I didn't understand it myself?

Here's what I knew about what had happened:

Brooke had been at a business dinner in Chicago. It was at a nice restaurant downtown, one with white linens and a skyline view. She'd been wearing a black dress and her mother's pearls. Everyone at the table had been eating their main course—Brooke was having the tiger shrimp; I'd asked Quinn to find out, because for some reason, I wanted to know—when she abruptly put her hand to her head, murmured something about a headache, and tried to leave the table. She'd halfway risen from her chair, then keeled over onto the restaurant floor.

I'd asked Quinn to find out if the floor was carpeted. Thankfully, it was. I felt a little better knowing that her fall had been softened.

Everyone at Brooke's table had jumped up in concern. Someone called 911, and a doctor dining with his wife across the room gave Brooke CPR. Medics arrived and transported her by ambulance to a hospital that supposedly has a world-class reputation, but when she arrived at the emergency room, she was pronounced dead.

Because she was only thirty-eight and seemingly in perfect health, the coroner had conducted an autopsy. The cause of death: an aneurysm had burst in her brain.

It was a fluke, one of those things nobody can predict or explain. There was no way Brooke could have known it was about to occur and nothing she could have done to prevent it. She had been the picture of perfect health. There was absolutely no reason that it should have happened.

So how was I supposed to explain that to a child who's only been out of diapers a year?

"Well, honey," I'd ended up saying, "your mommy had a problem in her head that no one knew about. The problem is called an aneurysm, and it's very unusual. It got very bad very fast, and it killed her."

Lily, bless her heart, hadn't really understood. She'd been sitting on my lap on the sofa, hugging her stuffed bear. She'd turned solemn eyes up to me.

"So Mommy got sick?"

"Yes."

"But she'll get better."

In Lily's world, that's what always happens. I blinked hard, my vision blurred. "Not here on earth," I'd said. "But she's in heaven now, and she's all well there." I'd glanced over at my minister to check my theology. He'd nodded encouragingly.

"When will she come home?" Lily had persisted.

"She can't, honey. But one day we'll all be together again," I'd said.

"Where?"

"In heaven."

"Well, then, I wanna go to heaven to see her."

"You can't, honey. Not for a long time."

Lily's face had twisted. She'd turned to Quinn, as if she didn't trust me. "I don' want to wait a long time to see Mommy."

"I know, sweetie," Quinn had said. "I don't, either, but we don't get a choice."

"Why not?"

"That's just how the world is."

"I don' like it." Tears had streaked down her face. "It's not fair."

"No, it's not, but life's like that sometimes." Quinn had reached over and taken Lily's hand.

"Everyone's life has parts that seem unfair," the minister had said. "When someone we love dies, it's normal to feel sad and mad and confused, and it's normal to cry. That's when friends and family can help the most. That's when we understand how important is it to love each other and to take special care of each other."

"Mommy an' I always takes special care of each other."

Quinn and I had looked at each other. I'd had trouble seeing her through my misty eyes, but I could tell she was fighting back tears, too.

"Jesus is taking very good care of her now," I'd finally said.

Quinn nodded. "And Miss Margaret and I are going to take very good care of *you*."

Lily had stuck her thumb in her mouth and hugged her bear. Fat tears had coursed down her still-babyishly-round cheeks. "But I want my mommy."

"I know," I'd said. "I know." I'd rocked her and stroked her hair, not knowing what else to do, until her tears stopped and she looked up.

"Am I goin' to school today?" she asked.

"Do you want to go?"

Her head bobbed up and down. "It's picture show-an'-tell. I'm taking a picture of Auntie Quinn an' Mommy an' me at the zoo. An' Auntie Quinn said I could take the cookies we made yesterday afternoon."

"It's probably best to keep her on her regular routine as much as possible," my minister had murmured.

Oh, how wonderful, that Lily's mind is so young and forward-looking that it holds distressing thoughts for only short spurts of time. Even in grief, sadness isn't her default emotion. It comes and goes like summer rain, but doesn't entirely overshadow her sunny disposition.

Quinn has been a huge help these past few days. She made sure Lily went to preschool and on playdates. She coordinated which of Brooke's many friends brought us dinner, and she helped with Lily's meltdowns. She sat with me in the evenings as Brooke's friends came by, all of them bearing food, and she helped with decisions about the funeral arrangements. We decided to have a reception at Brooke's house after the service instead of a wake the night before.

I'd thought that perhaps Lily should go to school on the day of the funeral, but one of the women in Brooke's single-parent club, a salt-and-pepper-haired woman in her early forties named Sarah, was a psychologist, and she suggested Lily attend.

"She needs to be a part of the ceremony honoring her mother's life," Sarah had said. "Even if she doesn't fully understand it now, it'll be important to her when she's older."

It made as much sense as anything, so Lily had accompanied us. I was surprised at how well she'd behaved, sitting between Quinn and me during the service. Quinn had arranged for Lily to go play at a friend's house shortly after we got home.

"When is Lily due back?" I ask Quinn now.

"Anytime we want her. Her friend's house is less than a block away."

It occurs to me that I'll have to make all kinds of arrangements—find children for her to become friends with, coordinate playdates, enroll her in dance lessons. It all seems rather daunting.

"Alicia and Lily have known each other since they were infants," Quinn says. "They met in a mommy-and-me exercise class."

I feel a moment of panic. I don't participate in many things—anything, really—that attract young mothers. I'll have to build a network. "I suppose I'll have to find a good preschool for Lily in Alexandria."

Quinn's eyebrows rise, then pull together. "I thought you'd move here, into Brooke's house."

The remark startles me. "Why would I do that?"

"Well, because it—it's Lily's home."

I'm taken aback by the very thought, and my answer comes out sounding more curt than I intend. "Children live in the home of their guardian."

Quinn's mouth opens. I think she's about to say something more, but then she abruptly closes it. She blinks rapidly, and I realize she's fighting back tears.

"You're welcome to come visit anytime you want," I tell her.

"Thank you," she says. Her hands link together over her stomach, so tightly that her knuckles turn white. "Can Lily come visit me, as well?"

"Certainly. But not right away; she'll need some time to settle in."

I am, after all, Lily's family. Blood belongs with blood. I have reasons for knowing this that I'd just as soon not think about, but I know it for a fact. Friends are wonderful, but there's no substitute for true family.

Which is why, when Quinn took Lily to preschool that first day after Brooke's death and I was left all alone in Brooke's home, I went into her office and looked through her files. I didn't know how it would be labeled and I didn't know if it would be in the file cabinet or on her computer, but I knew she would have kept information about Lily's father.

I decided to look for paper first. Paper is so much easier to manage, although I'm quite good on computers, much better than most people my age. I used to work at the public library and I still volunteer there, so I know all about Google—and I've already used it to research how to track down an anonymous sperm donor.

It's still a long shot, but the anonymous nature of sperm donations is rapidly disappearing, and the odds of locating a donor are steadily getting better. Many cryobanks are developing more-open policies regarding contact between donors and recipients and children. Some are offering donor-sibling registries and message boards where children of the same donor can meet and stay in touch. Some have sent notices to former donors, offering them the opportunity to be notified if their offspring reaches out to them. Others refer all parties to organizations that forward messages from donors, siblings, and recipients to one another.

The key piece of information needed for any of this is the donor number. That's the golden ticket for making contact—the number that identifies the father. You must have it, as well as the name of the cryobank.

I'd discussed all of these findings with Brooke as I uncovered them, but she'd wanted nothing to do with it. She'd insisted on raising Lily as a single mother and abiding by the terms of the original donor agreement.

But Brooke was no longer here. I was now Lily's guardian, and I needed to do what I thought was best for her. And I was completely convinced that Lily's father should be a part of her life—now more than ever.

It took me a while, but I found a folder labeled *New Orleans Cryobank* in Brooke's file cabinet. I pulled it out, my heart fluttering as I opened it. Taped to the inside of the folder was a photo. I stared at it, and my hands began to shake. It was a picture of a young boy who looked so much like Lily that I nearly dropped the file. He even had the same dimple in his left cheek.

This was it—the file about Lily's father! I quickly riffled through the contents. There were brochures about the cryobank and a three-page form about the donor. I rapidly scanned them. Apparently he has blue eyes and brown hair and he's six foot two. He's of English, French, and Scandinavian descent, with no history of heart disease or cancer in his immediate family at the time of his donation. As Brooke had said, there was no name, phone number, or address. No picture of him as a man—just the photo of him as a child.

I pumped my fist in the air—I learned about fist pumps when Brooke taught Lily how to do one when she first ate broccoli. I'd read the rest of the information more carefully later, but I already found what I was looking for, right there at the top of the page: "Donor 17677."

That's it—the donor number for Lily's father! I'd found the golden ticket.

CHAPTER THREE

Zack

Thursday, May 9

KANSAS CITY DAN had come to New Orleans to get some nookie.

The realization dawned on me about three-quarters through the unnecessary meeting.

I'd wondered why the beefy-faced client insisted on traveling to our law offices with his assistant, when the corporate merger negotiations were basically finished and all that remained was a tedious last-draft slog through minutiae, a task better suited to email.

And then I stretched out my legs and ran smack into the reason: Dan was playing footsie with his blond assistant under the long oak conference table. I quickly pulled back my feet, straightened in my chair, and put on my best poker face.

"There you have it," I say now as I flip over the final page of the document. "Any questions?"

"I think that wraps things up," Dan says. "Just wanted to make sure we touched all the bases."

My guess is you'll do that tonight. "Well, then, I believe we're all done." I turn to the lawyer representing the selling party. "Unless you have anything to add?"

"Nope." He'd told me beforehand that he thought the meeting was a waste of time. *But, hey,* he'd said, *it'll accomplish my two key goals—keeping my clients happy and accruing billable hours.* He closes his laptop now and pushes back his chair. "I'm good."

"Well, it's been great doing business with you," I tell Dan. We all stand, shake hands, and exchange the expected pleasantries. I take my time gathering up my things until the conference room empties.

I'm not opposed to mixing business with pleasure, but Dan and his assistant are both wearing wedding rings, and I know from previous conversations that they're not married to each other. I try not to be judgmental, but I don't like the concept of cheating. I don't like the idea of a boss having an affair with an employee, either; the power differential makes things lopsided.

Come to think of it, I don't like much of anything about Dan. He's an executive with a national chain of funeral homes, and he makes his money from charging grieving people exorbitant prices. Plus he exhibited zero sympathy for the local businessman who's selling his family-operated mortuaries because he has a terminal illness. I give Dan plenty of time to clear out before I step into the hallway so I don't have to interact with him any further.

Steve Schoen, the senior partner at my firm, approaches the conference room as I'm leaving. He's a fit, silver-haired man who looks like an older version of Anderson Cooper. He greets me with a broad smile. "Great job on the Shipman Energy contract, Zack. That was partner-level work."

I get a rush of satisfaction, like I used to feel in high school when I nailed a long pass. "Thanks."

"I mean it. Are you sure we can't persuade you to stay?"

I blow out a sigh. I've worked at Schoen, Roberts, Moreau, and Associates for ten years, ever since I graduated from law school. Up until about a year ago, I would have given my eyeteeth to make partner, but I recently notified them I'd be leaving.

"If it were just me, I'd be all over it," I say, "but Jessica has a great opportunity in Seattle, and her family lives out there."

"I hate to see you go, but I understand." Steve gives a rueful grin. "Happy wife, happy life, right? Especially for a two-career couple who're probably ready to start a family. It's hard to beat doting grandparents who live nearby."

I smile and nod. It's funny, how everyone assumes you can have a child anytime you want. But then, I haven't said anything about the infertility problem Jessica and I have been dealing with for the last couple of years. What the hell would I have said? *We're going through a soul-sucking black hole of disappointment that's bled all the joy out of our marriage*?

"You'll do great in Seattle," Steve says. "The firm you're going to is stellar." He shoots me a thumbs-up. "I appreciate that you're staying here through the Henson merger and the Tripp acquisition."

"No problem." I'd brought in the two pieces of business, and I wanted to see them through—plus I'm working on a pro bono case for a seventeen-year-old from a disadvantaged background that I want to get settled.

The truth is, I hate leaving New Orleans, but Jessica needs a change. She's the one who's had to deal with hormone shots and mood swings and invasive procedures, and it's really taken a toll on her.

After six months of trying to conceive a child on our own, Jessica had gone to a fertility specialist, who'd diagnosed her with low ovarian reserves. Who knew you could be practically out of eggs at age thirty-six? After two years of hormone treatments and five failed IVF attempts—punctuated by one miscarriage, a mere week after a positive pregnancy test—her doctor had said he couldn't recommend further treatment unless we used donor eggs.

Jess had responded with anger, denial, and despair. She wants a baby that's biologically her own. I was fine with donor eggs or adoption, but now, quite frankly, all I want is a break. Jess had insisted on going to another specialist. After reading her medical records and examining her, the second one had concurred with the first. The new guy agreed to do another round of ovarian stimulation so Brooke could freeze any eggs that might be harvested, but he only did it because Jess refused to take no for an answer. "The quantity and quality of your eggs doesn't really justify it," he said, "but it's your money."

The amount of money we've already spent is astronomical, but I try not to think about that. With her eggs in the bank, the doctor insisted she take at least a six-month sabbatical from any further treatments. I want to be done with them altogether. Some things just aren't meant to be, and at some point, a person has to accept that.

I'd hoped that Jessica would get back to her old self, but the truth is, I don't even know what that is anymore. She still looks like the smart, gorgeous woman I fell for, but she doesn't want to discuss anything or go anywhere. Her feelings get hurt over the least little thing, she's irritable and remote, and she has no interest—none at all—in sex.

They warned us when we started IVF that the hormones could suppress libido, but it completely erased hers, and that pretty much killed mine, too. It got to the point that I didn't try to initiate anything because when she did agree, it felt like she was just obliging me.

She's been off the hormones for a couple of months now, but nothing has changed. If anything, we've fallen even deeper into the no-sex, no-real-communication rut. I'm worried that Jess is depressed. I've asked her repeatedly to see a doctor about it, but she says there's no point; she doesn't want to do talk therapy and she refuses to take medication.

The only thing she wants to do is work. She's the controller at a large hotel on Canal Street, and this transfer to Seattle is the first non-baby thing that's really interested her in . . . jeez. How long has it been since she's cared about anything but getting pregnant? I can't even remember.

Anyway, she wants to move to Seattle, so we've flown there twice in the last month—once so I could interview at a law firm, and another time to look at neighborhoods. Both times we visited her parents, her brother, and her sister, and that seemed to perk her up.

I think it'll be good for her to live close to her family, so I've agreed to leave this city I've grown to love. We already have the condo under contract; we close on the sale in two months. Jessica's heading back to Seattle tonight for another long weekend to look at houses. She likes to take an evening flight so she can sleep on the plane and make up the two-hour time difference.

She has an old school chum out there who's in real estate, and she thinks he can help find us a place. She's scheduled to start her new job in three weeks, but she may take a week off between positions. I'll follow four weeks or so later.

As I walk down the hall toward my office, I pull my phone out of my pocket and check my text messages. There's one from my pal Hayden—*Are you running in the 5K Saturday?*—and one from Jessica—*Can you make it home by five thirty for an early dinner before my flight? I'm leaving work at three so I can fix my special chicken cacciatore.*

My stomach does a weird flip. It's strange that she'd want to fix a meal the night she leaves town. She doesn't cook much. In fact, the last few times she cooked a meal from scratch, she was trying to talk me into another round of IVF. Surely she's not thinking . . .

Nah. We're getting ready to move, the doctor told her to give it a rest, and she knows I'm done with the whole thing. I stifle the thought and sit at my desk to check my business emails. I read a couple, then look at my personal messages. I scroll past a few I should probably set to spam, then freeze as I see a message from the New Orleans Cryobank. The subject line reads, *In response to your recent request.*

I haven't made a recent request. Hell, I haven't had any contact with the cryobank in . . . what? Seventeen, eighteen years?

I briefly donated sperm while I was a freshman scholarship student at Tulane University. Dad's business had run into trouble, and I wanted to pay my own freight. I only did it for a short while; I stopped when a long-legged blonde I had a huge crush on refused to go on a second date when I told her about it.

"I don't want to date a sperm donor," she'd said.

"Why not?" I'd asked, completely clueless.

"If you don't date someone, you won't fall in love with him."

"Huh?"

"I don't want to risk falling in love, getting married, and having children with someone who already has twenty kids out there," she'd explained. "I especially don't want to have them showing up on my doorstep in eighteen years and vying with my kids for their father's affections. So the best policy is just don't date anyone who's ever been a donor."

"Hey, I was only asking you out for a beer," I'd said as casually as I could, but the truth was, I'd been thunderstruck. Until she'd said that, I hadn't been concerned about how being a donor might affect a future partner. I'd just thought, *Hey, I can make up to $1,200 a month and I won't need to hit up Dad for money.* What little further thought I might have given it had been along the lines of, *I've been through a lot of testing so I have proof I'm healthy* and *I'm providing a valuable service for infertile couples.*

It's nuts, how stupid a nineteen-year-old kid can be. Once I'd realized the implications of being a donor, I'd called the cryobank and resigned. I even asked about getting my swimmers back, but they told me they'd already been processed. They reminded me I'd signed a contract, and that it was past the one-month deadline for changing my mind. The best they could do was list me as a "limited donor"—meaning my data wouldn't be actively promoted on their website, and they'd move my info to the end of their donor list, where it would be buried under more than five hundred other names. Since I hadn't produced a lot of "product," I suppose I wasn't worth advertising.

I'd told Jessica about my brief foray into sperm donorship early in our dating relationship. It felt like an ethical necessity, like letting potential partners know about an STD or a stalker ex-girlfriend.

At first, Jessica acted like it wasn't a big deal, but apparently she did some research, and a few of months later, she asked me about it. She wanted to know if I'd always remain anonymous or if I'd agreed to let donor offspring contact me when they became adults. I said I'd agreed to let them contact me when they turned eighteen.

"So do you know if you have any kids out there?"

"No."

"Don't you want to find out?"

"No," I'd said. "I waived all parental rights and responsibilities. I'm nobody's father; I'm just a donor who contributed biological material, like a kidney or skin tissue or something."

She'd dropped the subject, the relationship progressed, and a year later, we married in a big to-do in Seattle. I thought we were done with the topic, but then she'd brought it up again about a year ago, when we were in the hellhole of IVF treatments.

We were sitting at Café du Monde and a woman came in, pushing a baby in a carriage. At that point, with the hormones and constant disappointments, just the sight of a baby could make Jess cry. Sure enough, her eyes had welled up.

"Do you ever look at a child and wonder if it's yours?" she asked.

The question hit me like pigeon poop—unexpected, messy, unpleasant. "No."

"Sometimes I do," she said. "Especially if they look like you, like that one."

I squinted at the baby. I wasn't not bald, red-faced, or dressed in a onesie sailor outfit, and I was sure as hell not sucking on a Binky. He didn't look anything like me. Hell, he didn't look like anyone, except maybe another baby. "That's flat-out crazy."

"No, it's not. You were a sperm donor in New Orleans, so it's likely you have children here." Her voice is tear-choked and aggrieved.

I feel unfairly accused of deliberately hurting her. I've tried to be nothing but supportive, but this whole infertility thing hasn't been easy on me, either. "You knew I was a donor when you married me," I said.

"Yeah. But I didn't know we'd have trouble conceiving our own baby." She brushed away a tear with her forefinger. "It eats me up inside to think that you may have children with another woman—or women."

I reach for her hand across the table. "You can't think that way," I said. "It doesn't do any good and it makes you miserable."

"What if I can't help it?"

"You can." I had no idea if it were true, but I desperately wanted it to be. "Just don't dwell on things you can't change."

That was months ago, but the conversation replays in my brain as I read the email on my computer screen now.

Dear Donor 17677:
Thank you for your recent inquiry. We are unable to change your email address due to security protocol. As your contract stipulates, we will only change your personal information if you properly answer the security questions. After three wrong tries, the system locks down.

Huh? I hadn't tried to contact them, and I sure as hell hadn't tried to change my e-address. I continue reading:

Per the terms of your contract, we cannot comply with your request to inform you of the number of births that resulted from your donation. We do not disclose that information, nor do we facilitate contact between donors and donor recipients or donor-conceived children under the age of eighteen. These policies were established and are enforced in order to protect the privacy and well-being of all concerned.

If you have any further questions, please feel free to contact us at the above e-address or phone number.

Thank you,
Maria Martinez
Client liaison

CHAPTER FOUR

Jessica

I NEED TO seduce my husband, but I've forgotten how.

I drop a handful of vermicelli into the pan of boiling water on the stove and ponder it. I can't be obvious; if I greet him at the door naked or in sexy lingerie, it'll be too radical a departure from the way we've been with each other lately. I don't want to make Zack suspicious.

Suspicious. The word makes me feel guilty. Well, I *am* guilty; I've gone behind his back and done something that will make him furious if he finds out, and I feel terrible about it. I'm not sure how much, if anything, I'm ever going to confess; maybe I won't need to tell him anything.

All I know for sure is that I desperately need to reconnect with him, and sex is the fastest way to do that. Sex is the glue that holds a marriage together.

Sex, and children.

Unfortunately, those are two things our marriage lacks, and I'm at fault for both of them. I tell myself it's not anything I did or chose, so I can't really be blamed, but still, the fact remains: I'm the one who's defective.

And then there's the lack of sex. That's on me, too. The hormones I took for IVF made me feel half-crazy and bloated and depressed. There were hormones to stimulate my ovaries, then hormones to prepare my womb to nurture an embryo. None of them ever worked as intended. Although several embryos were produced and used in multiple IVF procedures—we used every single viable embryo—only one ever implanted. And that pregnancy, if you can even call it that, only lasted a week.

What it did, though, was give me hope—clinging, cloying, pathological hope, persisting even after the doctors said all hope was gone.

I'm accustomed to succeeding at whatever I put my mind to. I'm like NASA that way: failure is not an option. I've always been able to work harder, practice more, try a new method, or find a way around a problem. Why am I unable to succeed at something as basic as getting pregnant?

I stir the marinara sauce simmering on the stove. Infertility has been a heartbreaking journey. It's cost us a fortune, and now I'm afraid it's costing our marriage.

From what I've read, it's pretty normal for IVF to take a toll on a relationship. I felt awful because of the hormones, so I rejected all of Zack's advances and never made any of my own. Before we knew it, the sexiest things happening in our marriage involved third-party medical procedures and solo semen deposits into plastic cups.

I'm off the hormones now, but our default setting is "distant." We've stopped flirting, we've stopped cuddling, we've stopped really talking. The fact that Zack was a sperm donor only magnifies my sense of inadequacy. I feel like a failure as a woman.

Well, I need to close the emotional distance between us before I go to Seattle, especially in light of what I've done, so tonight I'm making an effort. I've put on a black lace thong and a matching bra under my favorite jeans and a red top he likes, and I'm wearing my hair down and loose because he likes that, too.

I'm cooking a homemade meal, as well. I don't really believe that the way to a man's heart is through his stomach, but hopefully it'll be a prelude.

I check the chicken cacciatore in the oven, then place a foil-wrapped loaf of garlic bread in beside it. The perfume I dabbed behind my ears mingles with the scent of garlic, making me feel a little sick—or maybe it's just guilt over what I did.

I hear the key turn in the door. My pulse races as I smooth my hair.

"Hey there," I call, trying to make my voice sound warm and upbeat.

"Hey," he responds, his head down as he steps in and closes the door behind him.

He's a great-looking guy—tall and fit, with thick brown hair, even features, and electric-blue eyes. The amazing thing is that he's just as nice as he is good-looking. If I'd made a list of everything I wanted in a spouse—and I did; I believe it's important to know what you want in life so you can go after it—I would have short-changed myself. Zack is everything I wanted and more. He has qualities I didn't even know were important, like being funny and thoughtful and generous.

I smile and move toward him around the gray granite island. We meet by the dining room table. Just as I lean in to give him a kiss, he turns and drapes his jacket over a chair. My lips land awkwardly on his cheek. I laugh and start to try the kiss again, but he deliberately shifts away. He straightens and looks at me, his gaze as stony as the countertop.

My stomach dips, as if I drove over a hill too fast. "What's wrong?" I ask.

He folds his arms across his chest. "I got an email from the New Orleans Cryobank today. Apparently someone signed into my account, inquired about the number of births from my donation, then tried to change the email address."

My mouth goes dry. I head to the stove and pretend an intense interest in the marinara sauce, my heart pattering hard.

"Would you happen to know anything about that?" he asks.

I react like the guilty party I am. I move to the oven and stall. "Why would you think that?"

A nerve jumps in his jaw. "Because I can't think of anyone else who would want that information."

I open the oven door as if the chicken urgently needs to be checked. "Maybe the cryobank confused you with another donor."

I'm peering into the oven so I don't see his face, but his voice is low and hard. "Is that really the way you want to play this?"

"I—I'm not playing anything."

"I spoke to a liaison at the cryobank, Jess. She confirmed that someone accessed my account, which means they knew the password. And you know the password I used to use for everything."

I'm tempted to put my head in the oven, but it's electric, not gas. I continue to stare at the chicken, the heat burning my cheeks. I feel sick and scared and so guilty I could die.

He's caught me. I close the oven door and lean against it. "Okay. Yes. I tried to find out if you have any children and, if so, how many."

"Why?"

"Because I thought we needed to know."

"Hell, Jess! Why would we need to know?"

How can I explain the way it's been gnawing away at me? There's no rational way to describe the aching emptiness I feel at the thought of another woman having his baby, when I'm unable to give him one myself. "I—I was curious," I say lamely.

"And that makes it okay to go behind my back?"

Of course it doesn't. I can't bring myself to look at his face. "No."

"How did you get the name of the cryobank and my donor number?"

My knees feel unsteady. I move back to the stove and turn the burner off under the pasta, then stir the marinara sauce again, hoping I look less rattled than I feel. "I—I ran across it in your desk drawer."

"You couldn't have 'run across it' without going through my private papers."

"I saw the envelope the last time you got out your passport."

"So you thought it was okay to just read my personal papers?" He's in full lawyer mode now. "I know where you keep your old journals. Does that give me permission to read them?"

Shame shrinks me. I feel small and petty and ugly. "You're right," I say, abandoning the spoon in the sauce. "I was wrong. I shouldn't have done it. I'm sorry."

"You know what's even worse than going through my private papers? You hacked into my email account, impersonated me, then tried to change the e-address so you could get information without my knowledge. On what planet is that an all right thing to do?"

"I'm sorry. It—it was a mistake." Although the word *hacked* isn't really accurate, when I know he used to use I8abagel as the password for all non-money-related accounts. "I just really wanted to know, because . . ." I run out of words. I can't come up with a single excuse that isn't covered with the ugly slime of jealousy, bitterness, resentment, or worse.

"Because what?"

"Well . . ." I turn off the burner under the sauce, move to the other side of the kitchen island, and perch on one of the barstools, hoping I can still turn his mood—and the evening—around. "Because I've changed my mind about using a donor egg."

This doesn't seem to strike him as good news. His brow pulls into a hard frown. "You've always hated the idea of a donor egg. Besides, we're moving so you can take on this big new job, and you agreed to take a break from all this starting-a-family stuff. It makes no sense."

"It makes lots of sense." I try to sound persuasive and enthusiastic. "I'd like to make a fresh start. One with better odds. You tried to persuade me to consider a donor egg."

His frown deepens. "That was a bunch of IVF procedures ago, and you were dead set against it. And anyway, I fail to see a connection. What the hell does a donor egg have to do with my account at the cryobank?"

Because if I use a donor egg, it'll be one more biological child you've created with a random woman's DNA, and I want to know how many of those are already walking around. But I can't say that, because it's wrong. It's small-minded and selfish and probably politically incorrect.

"What's really going on here, Jessica?" His blue eyes are troubled. I can tell he's trying to move beyond his anger, although I can see it hasn't entirely burned out yet. *He's such a good man.* The thought pierces me.

"Nothing." My eyes fill with tears. I look down and twist my wedding set on my finger.

He blows out a hard sigh and runs his hand down his face. "You need to level with me. If I can't trust you, what kind of marriage do we have?"

I wrap my arms around my stomach, which feels like a cannonball pressing against my spine. He's right. I'm destroying his trust in me. I feel like I can't even trust myself anymore. What kind of obsessed, desperate, crazy woman have I become? Tears drip off my chin, making splotches on my blouse.

He pulls a paper towel off the holder and hands it to me. This little kindness makes me feel worse.

"Come on, Jess," he says. "Tell me what's really going on."

I dab at my eyes. "I . . . I wanted to know if you had any children. It's been killing me."

"We've talked about this, Jess. I think you need to get professional help."

"A shrink won't change the situation."

"Well, neither will rooting around in my personal papers and trying to hack into my donor account."

"I have this need to find out, and it's gotten worse instead of better. I can't seem to let it go."

"We've discussed all this. I've explained over and over that the cryobank has rules and procedures in place to respect everyone's privacy."

"I know, I know. But a lot of time has gone by, and I thought that things might have changed. And . . ." The words pour out before I can stop them. "They have."

"What?"

"I—I found out something." I bury my face in the paper towel. Oh my God, what am I doing? *Shut up*, I tell myself. *Just shut up. Say no more.* But there's a part of me that can't keep quiet.

Zack blows out a long sigh. "I talked to a representative at the cryobank, and she told me they didn't release any information." He clearly thinks I'm still lying. "Truth and trust go together, Jessica. My father always said that trust is the most important thing in a relationship, and if you can't be honest with me, well . . ."

I interrupt, my voice muffled through the paper towel. "The cryobank isn't the only place that has information." I shouldn't be telling him this, I know I shouldn't, but I can't stand for him to think I'm dumb or lying.

"What?"

I lower the paper towel. "When I couldn't find out anything from the cryobank, I searched online." The words gush out, like water from a broken pipe. "There's an organization—the International Fertility Donor Registry. For a fee, you can post a donor number and the name of a cryobank on their website, and anyone else who has the same info—the donor, a child, siblings, or the donor recipient—can reach you." I venture a glimpse at his face. He's wearing his inscrutable lawyer expression. "Both parties have to sign up and be actively looking, so it's by mutual consent."

"Hell." He drags his fingers through his hair and draws in a long breath, then paces toward the window. "I suppose I shouldn't be surprised. Nothing's truly private anymore." He turns around, walks back, and folds his arms across his chest. His gaze is so pointed it practically pins me to the wall. "So what did you do?"

The paper towel crumples in my hand. "I, um, visited the site and registered as you."

"Jesus, Jess!"

"I-I'm sorry. I'm really, really sorry."

A muscle twitches in his jaw. His eyes make me feel like I'm under a laser telescope and he can see right through my skin, right into my black, guilty heart.

He takes a step forward, puts his hands on the granite island, and leans over it toward me. "What did you find out?"

I hesitate. "You said you didn't want to know."

"I didn't." His voice is hard. "I wanted to honor the contract I signed, but you've made that impossible."

"I—I don't . . ." I try to think of a way to make this better for him. He's acting like I've compromised his integrity. "I don't have to tell you."

His brows rise, then hunker low. His eyes are angry and incredulous. "You think this should be a *secret* between us?"

I crumple. It's impossible. I can't live with it. "No." My voice sounds as small as I feel.

"So tell me, Jess. What did you find out?"

A quote from Donald T. Regan runs through my mind: *When all else fails, tell the truth.* "I found out," I say, "that you have a child looking for you."

CHAPTER FIVE

Zack

THE NEWS HITS me like a blow to the solar plexus. I take several steps back, turn away, and then pivot again. Holy *hell.* "Did you contact him? Or is it a her?"

Jessica lifts her shoulders and shakes her head. "They just have little icons—one for a child, one for a mother, one for a donor. There's no information about gender or age. I would have needed to give your social security number to read the message or leave a message, but I felt like that would be crossing a line."

My face heats. "Oh. So that's where the line is, huh? No problem assuming my identity or trying to change the info on my cryobank account or lying to me about it."

"I'm so, so sorry, Zack."

A child is looking for me? Holy moly. My stomach feels like it's full of lead. I try to take it in, to wrap my mind around it, but I'm bristling with outrage. Jess had no right. She's opened a damned Pandora's box. I stride across the room, then back again. Silence, vast and distancing, stretches between us.

"Look, maybe I didn't handle this very well, but . . ." Her voice cracks.

"*Mayb*e you didn't handle this well?" I can't believe she'd go behind my back like this and then try to lie about it. I feel like I'm talking to a stranger.

She raises both of her hands. I'm not sure if it's a *stop* gesture or a sign of surrender. "I didn't. I know I didn't. I was wrong. I'm sorry."

"So am I, Jess. So am I." I pace to the window, then back. "What the hell was the point of this little snoop fest?"

"I don't know."

"What do you expect me to do with this information?"

"I—I don't know." Tears are forming in her eyes again. "I didn't mean to tell you yet. I thought if I were pregnant from a donor egg when you found out, it wouldn't be such a . . . wouldn't be so . . . we wouldn't feel so blindsided."

Whoa—she'd thought she'd go ahead and get pregnant with a donor egg without telling me I have a child looking for me? I'm too stunned to process the implications of that. "I feel pretty blindsided right now."

"You're upset."

"You think?" I hear the sarcasm in my voice and I know it's not kind. I always try to be kind to Jess—I learned that from my parents—but damn it, I feel absolutely gutted.

"I handled this horribly." Jess is shredding the damp paper towel. "I'm so, so sorry."

I don't know what to say, much less what to think or feel or do. That awful silence looms between us again.

"Look—you need some time to cool off," she says.

She's right; I like to have some space when I'm hot under the collar so I can avoid saying something I'll later regret.

"I'll just head to the airport early," she says. "You stay here and calm down, and we'll talk later."

I nod, not because I agree—I'm not wanting to agree with her about anything right now—but because it'll propel her out the door.

She gets a jacket from the closet, then picks up her purse and slings it over her shoulder. She walks to the entryway and pops up her suitcase handle. "Your dinner will be ready in ten minutes."

I know I should thank her for fixing dinner and reassure her that we'll work this out, but I can't force myself to say the words. I'm angry and stunned and . . . betrayed. Yes, that's the word for it. She went behind my back, violated my code of ethics, and then tried to keep me from finding out what she'd done. She wasn't even planning to tell me a child was looking for me until she was pregnant herself? *Christ.*

"W-we'll talk tomorrow." She hesitates and looks up at me, as if she expects me to open the door or kiss her or something.

I can't maintain eye contact. I want to storm away without saying another word, but hell—she's flying halfway across the country. What's the point of being a jerk? I step forward and open the door for her. "Say hello to your folks for me."

She nods, wipes a tear, and gives me a peck on the cheek. I don't respond. I hold the door as she wheels her suitcase into the hallway. Ordinarily I would walk her down to her car, but tonight I just don't have it in me.

"Good night," she calls.

"Yeah," I say. "Have a good trip."

I don't even wait for her to make it to the elevator. I step back inside and close the door, glad to put something solid in the aching emptiness between us.

I PACE AROUND the condo, then change clothes and go for a run. When I come back an hour later, the place is filled with smoke. I'd forgotten to take the damned chicken and garlic bread out of the oven.

I mutter some ugly curses, then turn the oven off. I pull out the blackened mess and toss it in the trash, dish and all, along with the smoking foil packet of bread. I open the windows and turn on the overhead fan, then take a quick shower. I'm still all pent up inside. I start to call my sister in Ohio, then remember that Thursdays are her date night with her husband, so I text my old buddy, Ben. Ben is always up for a drink. In fact, he's already at the long wooden bar at the District, a couple of drinks ahead of me, when I arrive.

"You look like hell, man," he says. Ben still looks—and lives—pretty much just as he did right out of law school. His dark hair is thinner and shorter, but he still chases ambulances and women.

"Yeah, well, I feel that way."

"What's going on?"

I tell him as he orders whiskey shots with beer chasers.

"So you were a sperm donor? Damn!" As usual, Ben seizes upon the tawdriest element of the story. "Did they put you in a little room with girlie mags or what?"

"Actually, they had videos."

"Was it embarrassing?"

I stare at the rough-hewn brick behind the bar. "A little, yeah."

"Were the nurses hot?"

I down my first shot, annoyed at his excessive interest in the prurient details. "I don't know. They were all older than me."

"How much older?"

"How the hell would I know? I was just nineteen years old. Everyone was older than me."

"Wow! If you were nineteen, your kid might be—what? Sixteen or seventeen years old now?"

My kid. Holy Moses. I run my hand down my face, then take a long pull of beer. "Yeah, I guess. Or younger. Could be a lot younger. They freeze the donations."

"Listen to you." Ben laughs, and hits me with his elbow. "Donations—like you're putting something in the Salvation Army kettle at Christmas."

I take another swig of beer. "I'm glad you're amused by all this."

"Sorry, man. It's just . . . you always seem to have it so together, and this is quite a situation." Ben tosses back his shot. "So what're you going to do?"

"I don't know."

"I'd make like the Invisible Man if I were in your shoes."

"Be serious."

"I am. When I was sixteen, my girlfriend thought she was pregnant. I figured I was going have to marry her, so I talked to my dad. Know what he said?"

I shake my head.

"'If I were you, I'd get in my car and drive as fast and as far as it would take me.'"

I tip back my beer. I can't imagine a father giving out that kind of advice. My own dad had been a straight arrow. "There's no price you can put on peace of mind, son," he used to say. "If you lose that, you'd give anything to get it back."

"Thank God it turned out to be a false alarm." Ben motions for the bartender to bring another round. "So this kid of yours—what do you think he or she wants?"

I lift my shoulders. "Probably just curious."

"What if he wants money for college? Jesus, man—you could be opening up a real can of worms. How many kids do you think you have?"

"Nothing like that Vince Vaughn movie," I say. "Most cryobank customers order a few vials because it can take several tries to get pregnant, and I think I donated less than ten times, so . . ."

"So chances are you only have two or three kids, tops."

Oh, man. I haven't adjusted to the idea of one out there who wants to contact me. I polish off my beer and reach for the fresh shot glass the bartender slides in front of me.

"Whatever you do for one, you'll have to do for the others, just to be fair."

I suppose that's true. I gulp the shot. The burn in the back of my throat moves to my chest and loosens the knot there. "The funny thing is, at the time, I wasn't thinking about kids at all. I was just thinking about making money." I shake my head. "How could I have been so shortsighted?"

"Don't beat yourself up," Ben says. "You were just a kid yourself, that's all. And look at it this way: you helped out some folks who really wanted to have a baby. The decision is all on them."

For about the millionth time since he died, I want to talk to my dad. So many times over the past few years I've wished I could take him out to a ball game or out to the lake to cast a line. We used to have the best talks when we were side by side, driving somewhere, doing something or watching a game.

I know what he'd say, though. *Do what you know is right. Do what you wouldn't be ashamed of anyone ever finding out.*

Fact is, I'm already ashamed of being a donor. If I could have a do-over, I'd undo that.

But wait. That would mean whatever kid is out there trying to contact me wouldn't exist. And that isn't right, either.

"So what're you going to do?" Ben asks.

"I don't know." I finish my beer. The booze is really hitting me. "I guess for right now, I'm going to call it a night."

I walk home, past a rowdy group of tourists wearing Mardi Gras beads. It's the classic mark of an out-of-towner; no native New Orleanian wears beads unless they've just caught them at a Mardi Gras parade. I've never understood why tourists buy them in souvenir shops and drape them around their necks.

But then, I've drunk a lot more than I usually do, especially after a hard run and no dinner, and right now I'm not too sure why anyone does anything. It's taking a long time to get home. Oh, hell—I've walked right past my building! I turn around and go back.

When I open the door to my condo, it still smells like burned Italian chicken. I turn up the air conditioner and flip on the ceiling fans, then go to my laptop and Google the words "fertility," "donor," "connect," and "international," because I can't remember the exact terms Jessica used.

There it is. *International Fertility Donor Registry—Connecting donor children, donor siblings, donor recipients, and donors.* The screen seems a little blurry, but I developed mad drunk-writing skills in college, and I call upon them now. I follow the prompts, enter my donor number, 17677—I'm proud I still remember it after all these years—and the name of the cryobank. My fingers feel fat and awkward, but I manage to put in my name, password, and email address.

Abracadabra! I've accessed the postings for my number.

Just as Jess said, the icon of a child pops up. It's just a big round head and a little body clad in short pants, nonspecific gender-wise, of the same ilk as the international male-female restroom symbols. A dotted line connects the kid icon to a male icon at the bottom of the page. The explanation at the top reads, *Icon in center of screen is seeking contact with icon at bottom.*

My heart stutters, then revs like a race car. Sure enough, there's a kid out there wanting to make contact with me!

I stare at the screen for a long moment, then go back to the prompts. It's a secure site. If I register with my social security number and pay additional money, I can read the message. I'll also be able to respond and post messages of my own. My fingers hover cautiously over the keyboard as if it's a swamp full of gators.

"What the hell," I mutter. I enter the information and pay the fee with my PayPal account.

Thank you for registering. Your application will be processed within forty-eight hours.

What? I have to *wait*?

Two minutes ago I didn't know I'd ever want to do this, and now I'm frustrated at the delay.

"You are one screwed-up dude," I mutter to myself. I turn off the computer and notice that the room seems to be tilting. It takes three tries before I can stand up. I stagger to the bedroom, collapse across the bed, and fall fast asleep.

CHAPTER SIX

Quinn

I'M THE FIRST to arrive for the May meeting of the single parent group on Thursday morning at seven thirty. We usually meet here at the Java Hut every first Saturday, but changed it to this morning at 7:30, before work because a couple of members have weekend conflicts. I get a chai latte and head to our usual table. This month, the painting on the wall is a sofa-sized acrylic of an empty armchair strapped into a roller coaster. According to the Post-it note stuck beneath it, a hopeful local artist wants to sell it for forty dollars.

I study it for a moment. It exactly captures the way I've been feeling for the last month; life has been a series of plunging lows, fast curves, and scary climbs, and I haven't felt securely strapped to anything.

Brooke was my human safety belt—the person who made me feel secure and grounded. She was the person I called first whenever anything happened, the person I could talk things through with, the person who would tell me, "You've got this," and make me believe it. She was smart and wise and kind, and I valued her insights and judgment. I really need her right now to help me sort through everything that's going on, but obviously, she's not around.

I take a sip of my steaming drink. I almost didn't come today because I knew her absence would be so pronounced. I started attending the meetings because Brooke encouraged me to accompany her to one when I first moved to New Orleans, and I kept coming back because it's such a great bunch of women. *Women, and one guy*, I mentally amend.

Brooke found the group listed in a free weekly newspaper shortly after she moved to New Orleans:

A support group for singles who are (1) interested in becoming parents without a partner through adoption, artificial insemination, surrogacy, or the old-fashioned way, or (2) choosing to raise a child without a partner.

Not having a parenting partner doesn't have to mean not having support!

Brooke discovered that the members were bright, funny, and warm, and they soon became close friends. I didn't fit the criteria, but they welcomed me with open arms anyway.

Everyone in the group is mourning Brooke. And while the thought of being around other sad people isn't exactly uplifting, I know it'll be good for us to get together. There's something healing about being with others who share your pain. Plus I have some personal news I can't wait to share.

The first member through the door is Annie, a human resources manager with an oil and gas company who suggested this meeting time. Annie has an eight-year-old son, Sean, who catches his school bus at seven. She'd been in a relationship with the child's father, but he took off before Sean was born. Pretty and tiny as a doll—she's a couple of inches shy of five feet—she has long brown hair and wears large black-rimmed glasses. She waves, then heads to the counter to order a coffee.

After she gets her drink, she makes her way toward me. We hug hello. "How are you doing?" she asks as she sits down.

"Fine."

She sees right through my automatic reply. Her dark eyes warm with empathy. "I know how close you and Brooke were. This must be a really hard time for you."

I nod, tears forming in my eyes. Tears are never very far away these days. "Brooke's grandmother said something a couple of years ago that kind of sums up how I feel," I say. "She'd just lost a dear friend to cancer, and Brooke asked how she was coping. Miss Margaret said, 'Well, back in the day, Johnny Carson did a recurring soap opera skit on *The Tonight Show*. The studio camera would focus on audience members, and Johnny would read ridiculous things about them. It was called 'The Edge of Wetness.'"

Annie laughed.

"Miss Margaret said, 'That's how I feel because I keep tearing up. I'm always on the Edge of Wetness."

Annie pats my hand, and then Sarah bustles through the coffee shop door. Her gray-streaked hair curls wildly around her head, and today she looks every one of her forty-four years. She waves, and stops at the counter to order coffee.

"Where are the twins?" I ask when she makes her way over, a large cappuccino in hand. Her nanny takes Thursday mornings off to take college classes.

"My mom's watching them," she says. "One hour is the most she can handle, so I can only stay for forty-five minutes."

It's no wonder her mother imposes a limit; the boys are human fidget spinners. The last time Sarah brought the two-year-olds to a meeting, they'd all left after fifteen minutes because the boys wouldn't stop tearing around the room and shrieking.

Sarah froze her eggs when she was thirty-five and without a partner. When she reached forty-one and was still single, she'd had them mixed with donor sperm and implanted.

I spot Lauren's dark ponytail next. She's about my age and attends the group as an inquirer—that's someone who's considering becoming a single parent. She's looking at both adoption and artificial insemination. She works as a nurse at Ochsner Hospital, and she's been coming to meetings for a couple of years.

Finally, in ambles Mac. He's a tall, shy man in his late forties or early fifties who works as an MRI technician. Mac seems to have trouble making eye contact and is a little socially awkward, but he has a heart of gold. He's raising his brother's teenage daughter, Kylie, because both his brother and sister-in-law were sent to prison for embezzlement. The girl, who is now fourteen, is a handful.

After everyone settles at the table with their beverage of choice, Sarah looks at her watch. She founded the group and works as a psychological counselor, so we happily let her run the meetings whenever she attends. "Well, it's five minutes after, so let's get started."

We all nod.

"I think we should start with a minute of silence for Brooke," Sarah says. "I'll set my timer in honor of her punctuality."

We all laugh, then hold hands. I close my eyes and say a silent prayer. The timer on Sarah's phone buzzes.

"We're all wondering about Lily," Sarah says. "So, Quinn, why don't you start?"

My pulse skitters. "I kind of wanted to be the last one to talk today—I have some personal news to share—but sure, I'll kick things off with a Lily update. As most of you know, Lily's living in Alexandria with Miss Margaret."

Annie's eyes are warm pools of concern. "How's that going?"

"Not particularly well." My heart feels like shattered glass, and a little sliver seems stuck in my throat. "Actually, it's not going well at all. Lily's regressed on her potty training, she complains of headaches, and she wakes up in the night."

"Poor little thing!" Lauren murmurs.

"I call her often, and I've been going to Alexandria every weekend to visit. Each time, Lily wants to know if her mommy came with me. I try to explain that she's dead . . ." Once again, tears well in my eyes. I hate how I'm a constant wet bucket of emotion, but I can't seem to help it. "But Lily doesn't seem to hear it. She changes the subject. Last Sunday at the end of my visit, she started talking about the things we would do together when she goes home and her mother is back. To tell the truth, it was kind of spooky."

"She's in denial. Young children can stay stuck there for a

while," Sarah says. Her expertise has been really helpful to the group. "When they lose someone, they pretend it hasn't happened."

I don't blame Lily. I'd like to pretend it hasn't happened, too. "When it was time for me to leave, Lily cried and clung to me and begged me to take her home to her mommy. I have to tell you . . . it completely broke my heart."

Annie puts her hand over mine. "That had to be so difficult."

I swallow hard, afraid the lump in my throat will make it impossible to talk. "Miss Margaret is the one who's really having a tough time. She's at her wit's end. She's following your advice, Sarah, and taking Lily to a child psychologist. The psychologist says Lily's behavior is pretty normal. Young children have trouble understanding death."

"Don't we all," murmurs Lauren.

"They're coming to New Orleans this evening so Miss Margaret can put Brooke's house on the market. I'm taking off work tomorrow to help, and I'll keep Lily for the three or four nights they're here. We'll take her to visit her old home if she wants, but Miss Margaret and the psychologist thought it would be confusing for her to stay there and then have to leave again."

"I wish Miss Margaret would just move to New Orleans," Annie says. "That way you and she could care for Lily together."

That's what I want, too. I've talked to Margaret about it until I'm blue in the face, but she won't even consider it.

"I can't just up and move!" Margaret had exclaimed when I'd broached the topic again this past weekend. Her brows had creased, and her fingers worried the pearls on her necklace. "This has been my home for forty-seven years. I can't handle another huge upheaval right now."

I'd bitten my tongue and reminded myself of a bit of wisdom from the reparenting book: *Let go of the things that are out of your control.*

"Miss Margaret is Lily's legal guardian, and Alexandria is her home," I say, sounding more stoic than I feel.

"How old is Miss Margaret?" Annie asks.

"Seventy-nine," I reply.

"Good lord!" Lauren's eyes widen. "She looks great for her age, but still . . . she's nearly eighty! How long is she going to be able to take care of a young child?"

The topic gives my stomach more twists than a balloon animal. I know that Brooke intended to change her will to make me the primary guardian when Lily turned four and Margaret turned eighty, but she hadn't lived that long, and Margaret is adamant that her guardianship is in Lily's best interests. The elderly woman loves the child, there's no question of that, and she's still physically capable of caring for her, so I don't feel like I have the right to legally challenge her. The only thing I can do is stay close to Lily and let her know that I'm there for her.

"She's providing Lily with a loving home, and that's what really matters." I look around the table, eager to get out of the hot seat. "So, Sarah—what's going on with you?"

She gives a gentle smile. She knows I'm deliberately changing the topic, and she's kind enough to go along with it. "Well, the twins are growing like crazy. In fact, 'crazy' seems to be the operative word in my life right now." She shakes her head. "Sometimes I wonder what I was thinking, having kids. There's no peace or quiet at my house. They need constant supervision from the moment they wake up until they fall asleep. There's no reasoning with two-year-olds! The sense of home being a place to relax and recharge is completely gone."

"It'll get easier," Annie says.

"Do you promise?" Sarah asks.

Annie nods. "But it might not settle down for another year or two."

"You all are scaring me." Lauren makes a terrified face.

"Oh, you'll be just fine." Sarah gives her a reassuring smile. "You're at least a decade younger than me, and you'll probably just have one child at a time."

"It's all totally worth it," says Annie.

"Absolutely." Sarah's head bobs. "I complain, but when I look at them sleeping, my heart feels so full I think it might burst."

Annie smiles, her eyes soft. "That never changes."

"Do you still watch your son sleep?" Lauren asks.

"Oh, yeah. And he still looks like an angel when he's sacked out," Annie says. "Really, motherhood is the most amazing adventure. It's incredible how fast they learn and how much enthusiasm they have about the world. I took Sean to the Audubon Butterfly Garden and Insectarium the other day, and it was like I was seeing bugs through entirely new eyes."

"You were." Lauren props her chin on her hands. "His."

Annie grins. "You're right. Whenever you introduce them to new things, it changes your outlook on them, too. Right now Sean and I are in a really good place."

"Oh, that's so great to hear!" Sarah says.

"Yeah. I'm trying to really enjoy it, because in another couple of years, here comes puberty."

"You'll be in for it then," Mac says.

Sarah turns to him. "So, Mac—what's going on with Kylie?"

He runs a hand through his short graying hair, which reminds me of the bristle on a schnauzer's head. "I wish I knew. She hardly talks to me, and she refuses to visit either of her parents. I make her write them once a week. Her last letters to each of them said, 'Uncle Mac says I have to write you, so I am.' That was the whole letter."

Sarah laughs. He shoots a worried look in her direction, as if he's afraid he's done something wrong.

"I think it's great you're making her send letters," Sarah reassures him. "I just had to laugh at what she wrote. It's such a classic teenage move."

"Yeah, I guess it's pretty funny." He gives a hesitant grin.

"Is she still seeing that therapist for kids with parents in prison?" Annie asks.

He nods. "She's even talking in the session now. The first three times she just sat there and refused to say a word."

"And you had to pay for that?" Lauren asks.

"Yeah." Mac chuckles. "Kylie thought I'd give up."

"Good for you for sticking with it," Sarah says. "Have you gotten any helpful insights?"

Mac nods. "The therapist says Kylie identifies with her parents, but she's ashamed of them. That means she feels a deep sense of shame about herself." He stares at his coffee cup for a long moment. "Sometimes I'm so angry at the two of them that I can hardly stand it."

"That's understandable." Sarah pats his hand, just as she had mine. Mac's neck and ears instantly flame—it's amazing how fast they redden—and his whole body stiffens.

Sarah pretends not to notice his discomfort. She casually pulls back her hand and turns to Lauren, who talks about the expense and difficulty of adopting a newborn.

Sarah glances at her watch. "I'm nearly out of time, and Quinn said she had something personal to share."

All eyes turn to me.

Lauren's are bright and expectant. "Did you meet someone?"

"Oh, right," Annie says. "At the last meeting, you said you were going on a blind date."

"It wasn't exactly blind." I'd decided to give internet dating yet another try, so I'd seen a photo of the guy beforehand. He wasn't smiling in his profile, which should have been a red flag, but as usual, I'd been overly optimistic.

It couldn't qualify as a blind date from the other potential meaning of the term, either; from the way he kept staring at my chest, he was anything but blind—although he might have been a little farsighted, because my shirt was cut no lower than my collarbone and my chest is in no way stare-worthy.

"I'm not even sure it was really a date." Does meeting for coffee in the middle of the afternoon qualify as a date?

But I know that Annie and Lauren mean well. The eager, expectant expressions on their faces are exactly the same look Ruffles gets when I hold a Beggin' Strips bag, and I want—I really *want*—to tell them what they hope to hear so that they can maintain some optimism about the dating pool.

"I went for coffee with a guy I met online, and it was a total bust," I say.

"A bust, how?" Annie asks.

"He didn't look anything like his profile picture, I had to pay for his coffee because he forgot his wallet, and he had absolutely nothing to say. It's like he'd undergone a personality extraction."

"Oh." A disappointed sigh collectively escapes from everyone at the table, like air from a deflating tire.

"So what's your news?" Annie asks.

Sarah leans forward. "Have you decided to freeze your eggs?"

"No." My heart hammers in my chest. The pressure that has been building in me, the pressure I've tamped down again and again, is expanding and swelling until it feels as though the words will burst out of my ears if I don't let them out of my mouth. "Actually, I'm already beyond that." My voice has a weird little wobble.

They all stare at me. Annie's brow pulls into a quizzical crease. Lauren looks baffled. Sarah's gaze is intense and focused. Even Mac is looking directly at me, something he rarely does with anyone.

I swallow hard. My tongue feels wrapped in cotton batting.

"What do you mean?" Sarah, always outspoken, voices the question I can read on everyone's faces.

Oh, my God. It's so inappropriate to feel this way with Brooke just gone, and yet, there it is—a shining bubble of pure, glowing joy.

I say the words that finally release my secret. "I'm pregnant."

CHAPTER SEVEN

Quinn

WHAT?"

"How?"

"Huh?"

"Whose?"

It would have been funny, the way everyone bombards me with questions all at once, if only I didn't feel like crying. This is a moment I should be sharing with Brooke. She and I celebrated and commiserated together over all of life's highs and lows. Right now I'm dealing with two major events that are literally life and death, the best and the worst I've ever experienced. Both are because of her, and she isn't here, and . . .

Oh, Lily was so, so right. It isn't fair.

"It's . . . it's . . ." I draw a breath and wipe my eyes. Annie reaches in her purse, then hands me a tissue. "I'm not sure where to begin."

"Who's the father?"

"When did you find out?"

"How did it happen?"

Everyone throws out questions at the same time.

Sarah holds up her hand and looks around. "There's a story here, and we need to let Quinn tell it at her own pace, in her own way. I'm texting my mom to tell her she'll just have to manage the twins for the rest of the morning." Her thumbs fly over her phone, then she puts it down, places her elbows on the table, and turns to me. "You have our full attention, honey. Take your time, and tell us all about it."

I wipe my nose and nod. Someone gets up, pours me a plastic cupful of water from the pitcher at the condiment bar, and places it in front of me. I take a sip. "It all started on my thirty-sixth birthday," I say.

February 25
7:00 p.m.

"Surprise!"

The unexpected chorus of voices on my thirty-sixth birthday makes me jump back as I open the front door of my home after work, nearly spilling the canvas tote of Whole Foods groceries in my arms. I stare at the beaming faces assembled in the living room of my uptown Victorian, most of them wearing cone-shaped birthday hats. There's the single parent group, and there's Terri, the fifty-and-fabulous blonde who helps me run Verve!—who left work an hour early today, allegedly to accompany her husband to an after-hours business event.

I also spot the couple who own the coffee shop where the single parents group meets, the Smiths from next door, an old friend from college and her husband, and, of course, Brooke. Jumping up and down beside her is Lily.

"What—what's going on?" I ask like an idiot. Surprises seem to drain my brain cells. My childhood was full of land mines: being awakened by slamming doors and loud, angry arguments; having no one show up for kindergarten parents' day; getting off the school bus in sixth grade to discover that Dad had moved out; learning that the dog wasn't around because Dad had run over him when backing out the car in a white-hot rage. It's probably understandable that I'm hardwired to be skittish of the unexpected.

"It's a surprise birthday party, Auntie Quinn!" Lily announces. She's wearing a pink princess gown—her favorite type of attire—

complete with a sparkling tiara, which gleams on her blond curls in front of her balloon-printed birthday hat. "Are you surprised?"

"Very much so." Smiling, I step into the room. Brooke takes the grocery bag from me so I can bend down and return Lily's embrace. I lift an eyebrow at Brooke as I straighten. "I thought I was having a low-key celebration this year."

Brooke is the self-appointed party planner for all the special people in her life, and I'd specifically told her that a thirty-sixth birthday didn't warrant a fuss. She'd acted as if she agreed. In fact, she'd invited me come over to her house, just two blocks away, for an after-dinner cupcake and glass of wine.

"I'm supposed to be at your place in an hour," I say.

"We just said that to trick you," Lily proclaims.

"Well, it certainly worked."

"That's 'cause I made a wish and used my magic wand."

I grin as Lily waves it. She thinks the fairies brought it to her, but in truth, I helped her mother make it from two pieces of sequined fabric, pillow stuffing, and a dowel rod.

I look around. Balloons float from the center of my midcentury coffee table. Boiled shrimp, a huge green salad, French bread, and jambalaya are laid out buffet-style on my Danish modern dining table, in front of a lovely bouquet of hydrangeas. Wineglasses and four decanted wine bottles cluster on the kitchen counter, and another chills in my cooler bucket. "You and your wand arranged all this?" I ask Lily.

"Well, Mommy and Miss Terri helped."

Everyone laughs.

"I'll bet they did." I hug Brooke. She's wearing jeans and a sleeveless black top, her golden hair curling loosely around her shoulders, and, as usual, she looks amazing. She's apparently changed clothes after work. She must have taken off half a day or more to organize this.

I hug Terri next. "So this is your husband's work event that made you leave early?"

"I believe my exact words were, 'There's an after-work social thing that Paul has to attend, and he really wants me to go,'" Terri corrects.

Laughing, I kiss Paul's aftershave-scented cheek.

"Don't feel bad," he says. "She pulls the wool over my eyes all the time."

"I don't need to know any of your kinky secrets," I say, waving my hands as if to erase the mental image. Laughter ripples through the room.

My college chum Lisette waddles up and embraces me, pressing her hugely pregnant belly against my side. It always surprises me, how firm a baby bump feels. "Happy birthday, Eskimo girl," she says.

My mother named me after a deceased family member, but friends always tease me about being named after the character in the Bob Dylan song.

"Thanks. And thanks for coming all the way from the North Shore. Aren't you due in just a couple of weeks?" I helped decorate her French country home in Mandeville, including the bedroom of her adorable six-year-old boy and the nursery for the new baby, so I'm well aware of her timeline.

She nods. "Sixteen days."

"Not that you're counting," I tease. Lisette and I lost touch after college, then reconnected when she'd read an article in *Northshore Living Magazine* about my design services and retail store.

"The promise of chocolate birthday cake lured her from nesting mode," her husband, Luke, says as he kisses my cheek. "She's forbidden me from keeping any chocolate in the house, but she constantly craves it."

"I have no willpower around chocolate," Lisette moans.

"Who does? And anyway, it looks to me like you have the perfect excuse to indulge."

"It's too hard to take off the weight afterward." She rubs her stomach in the way that all pregnant women do—as if they're unconsciously caressing their unborn babies. "I learned that with Ryan."

"Where is the little guy?" I ask.

"My parents are watching him," Lisette says. "They just moved to Mandeville to be closer to their grandkids and help us out."

I feel a pang. Not only is Lisette blessed with a loving husband, a beautiful child, and another one on the way, but she also has caring, involved parents.

Do you have to come from that kind of family to create one of your own? Oh, I hope not. My own mom never had many maternal instincts, and the few she had disintegrated after the divorce. At least she remembered my birthday today, although I suspect it was a last-minute reminder by Siri or Alexa. I'd received a gift card online this morning and a brief phone call this afternoon from Dubai, where she lives with her oil executive third husband.

My father, as usual, either completely forgot or ignored the occasion. It no longer hurts very much, now that I know not to expect anything from him. When I was younger, it used to cut me to the core.

But I'm over it. I have a full life with a thriving career and great friends. Brooke, Lily, and Miss Margaret are my adoptive family. When Brooke took me home with her that first Thanksgiving after we met, her grandmother welcomed me like long-lost kin, and I've spent every holiday with them ever since.

Last year, for my thirty-fifth birthday, Brooke arranged a lovely girls' night out, with cocktails at her house, dinner at Arnaud's, and a boisterous French Quarter pub crawl. It had been high-spirited and fun, and for the first time since my breakup with Tom, I'd felt full of optimism for the future.

Thirty-five seemed a celebration-worthy age; thirty-six feels like a whole different story. I'm on the dark side of the decade now, closer to forty than thirty, without a romantic partner in sight. I've spent nearly two years spelunking the endless dark caverns of internet dating. My dreams of love, marriage, and a family are dwindling as quickly as my egg supply.

To commemorate my thirty-sixth year on the planet, I'd sat down at my desk at Verve! that morning and actually crunched the numbers. It was an exercise in grim reckoning.

Even if I meet my ideal man tomorrow, we'll probably need to date for a year or two before we become engaged. An engagement will likely last six months to a year, and most men will want to be married for a year or more before trying to start a family. That will put me dangerously close to forty—an age when the likelihood of getting pregnant and having a healthy baby becomes terrifyingly small. Not for all women, of course—statistics are averages, meaning some women fare far better than others—but still, the odds are not good after forty. And since I haven't dated anyone in all my thirty-six years who actually turned out to be marriage material, the cold facts are icily glaring me in the eye: Prince Charming is unlikely to arrive in time to help me create the loving family I've always wanted.

I try to push this disheartening realization to the back of my mind as I greet my other guests, but I can't help but notice that almost everyone has a child or a husband or both. The uncharacteristic despondency that has dogged me all day now makes me want to run to my bedroom and bawl.

Instead, I drink wine, accept everyone's good wishes, eat jambalaya and salad, and blow out a birthday candle.

"Thanks for a great party," I tell Brooke when everyone has left, we've wrapped up the food, and we're carrying some of the plastic containers of leftovers to her house, just a couple of blocks away. This part of New Orleans is so quiet it's easy to forget you're in a city. Tree frogs chirp in the large live oaks and night jasmine scents the air. Neighbors sit on their gaslit front porches and wave to us as we pass by. "It was wonderful."

She shoots me a knowing look as she pulls out her keys while

Lily skips up the porch steps. "I wish I believed you meant that. What's wrong?"

Once we get inside and Lily heads to her playroom, I set the food containers on the kitchen counter and give Brooke the rundown on my come-to-Jesus about my prospects for marrying and having a baby. Her expression grows so somber that I find myself wanting to cheer her up.

"Hey, on the plus side, now that I'm thirty-six, I've known you for half of my life, so that's definitely worth celebrating," I say. "Half a lifetime officially makes us family."

"But we're already fam'ly," Lily declares, wandering back into the room with Sugar Bear dangling by a leg from her fist. "You're my aunt an' godmother."

They're both honorary designations, but I fully embrace them. I embrace Lily as well. "And you're my honey."

"And you're the sister I never had and always wanted." Brooke joins in to make it a group hug.

"I want a sister," Lily says as we break apart.

"One day you'll find a special friend like Aunt Quinn," Brooke says, picking up one of the plastic containers and opening the refrigerator.

"I mean a real sister, like Alicia has."

Brooke places the plastic bowl on a shelf in the fridge, then turns to take the next one as I hand it to her. "Sorry, sweetie, but I can't give you one of those. Remember how I explained to you that my baby-making parts are broken?"

Lily's head bobs. "That's why I have a donor instead of a live-in daddy."

"That's right." Brooke places another container in the fridge.

"Well, maybe Auntie Quinn can give me a real sister."

"Oh, honey—it doesn't work that way," I say.

"But you could have a baby." She turns her big blue eyes on me. "You could get a donor daddy like Mommy did."

"We just call him a donor, not a daddy, remember?" Brooke gently corrects.

"Grams says he's my daddy, too."

Brooke's face takes on a bit of an edge. "Well, things have changed since Grams's day." She points at the kitchen clock and gives an exaggerated gasp. "Oh, my, it's way past your bedtime! You need to run right upstairs and brush your teeth, sweetie."

I listen to Lily's footsteps thump up the staircase. "Is something up with Miss Margaret?"

Brooke sighs. "Just the usual. From time to time, we have the same old discussion." She holds her up hands and uses them like talking sock puppets. "She'll say, 'Lily's father should be a part of her life,' and I'll explain, 'He signed up for sperm donation, not fatherhood.' She'll say, 'He'd feel differently if he knew her,' and I'll say, 'The contract says he can meet Lily when she's eighteen if she's interested.' She'll say, 'You should try to contact him now,' and I'll say, 'That's not part of the arrangement.' Then I'll sidetrack her by telling her how grateful I am that he made Lily's life possible and how fortunate I feel to have such a wonderful daughter, and I'll mention some funny or amazing thing that Lily said or did, and the conversation will mercifully drift toward Lily's overall fabulosity."

I smile. "If I knew for sure I'd have a child as wonderful as Lily, I'd go for donor insemination, too."

"You can, you know."

"Consider insemination?"

"Have a child as wonderful as Lily." She places the last plastic container in the refrigerator. The door closes with a soft thud that echoes off the kitchen's hard surfaces. "A genetic sibling."

"Huh?" The air in the kitchen suddenly seems heavy, as if it's carrying the weight of something important. Goose bumps form on my arms, confirming the significance of the moment. What, exactly, is she saying?

Brooke picks up a blue dish towel, walks to the other side of the kitchen island, and starts wiping the granite. She avoids looking me in the eye. "I still have some frozen sperm at the cryobank."

"What?" Goose bumps spread up my neck, then down my legs.

Brooke looks over and meets my startled gaze, her blue eyes steady. "I have sperm left over from Lily's donor," she says. "If you're interested, you can have it."

CHAPTER EIGHT

Quinn

Friday, May 10

"JUST LOOK AT Brooke's linen closet," Miss Margaret says. "It's like a picture in a magazine."

I peer over the older woman's stooped shoulder at the neat stacks of sheets and pillowcases and towels and washcloths, all color-coordinated and precisely aligned, with the folded sides out. I can make a closet look like this once, but Brooke maintained this orderly perfection all the time. "She was the most organized person I've ever known," I say.

"Me, too, and I've got some years on you."

I'm helping Miss Margaret sort through Brooke's belongings and put stickers on things that are to be moved, stored, or donated. She and Lily arrived in New Orleans yesterday afternoon and will be here for a few days. We had dinner together at Joey K's Restaurant on Magazine Street, then Lily came home with me for the night. I invited Miss Margaret to stay with me, too, but she'd insisted on sleeping at Brooke's house.

"It'll help me say good-bye," she confided.

While waiting at one of the restaurant's outdoor tables for our order to arrive, Margaret asked Lily if she wanted to visit her old house.

"Is Mommy there?" Her little face peered up, her blue eyes heartbreakingly hopeful.

"No, honey," Miss Margaret replied. "She's dead, remember?"

Lily clutched Sugar Bear to her chest. The bedraggled stuffed animal is never far from her grasp these days. "I thought she mighta come back."

"She can't, sweetie," Margaret said. "That's what dead means."

Lily's bottom lip trembled. "I don' like dead."

"None of us do, honey." I put my hand on her back.

"Do you want to visit the house?" Margaret asked again. "I think it will make you sad, but we'll take you if you'd like."

Lily shook her head. "If Mommy's not there, I don' wanna be there, either." She stuck her thumb in her mouth—another bit of regression that had occurred in the last month.

It was late when Lily finally fell asleep in my guest room, but she'd slept soundly through the night. This morning she was upbeat and excited when I dropped her off at her friend Alicia's house before I came here to help Miss Margaret.

A moving company is scheduled to arrive in a few hours to start the actual packing. We're leaving the furniture and accessories in place while the house is on the market, but the movers will box and remove the contents of the cabinets, drawers, and closets.

Dismantling Brooke's home is a heartrending task, made worse by the fact that I remember the joy of helping her move in.

She'd been pregnant, and I'd flown in from Atlanta for a long weekend. I'd already made a few trips to New Orleans to help her with renovation and design decisions. As we unpacked, we played loud music, danced around, and talked a mile a minute. Everything was new and exciting. I set up the nursery while Brooke unpacked the kitchen, and I refused to let her see the baby's space until it was all finished.

When everything was in place, I led her to the closed door. "Ready?"

"More than ready."

"Welcome to your baby's nursery!"

She gasped when the door swung open, slapping her cheeks with her palms. I laughed, because I'd never seen someone actually do that in real life.

"Oh, Quinn—this is amazing!" Her eyes teared up as she walked around the room, taking it all in. "I can't believe how talented you are. This is just what I wanted and didn't know how to describe." She touched the canopy over the crib, then reached out and hugged me.

I hugged her back, thrilled that I'd made her so happy.

"You know what's even more amazing than this room?" she asked as we drew apart. "You. You're a wonderful, wonderful friend, Quinn. I feel so blessed to have you in my life."

My throat grows thick at the memory.

"I don't know how Brooke managed her job and a child and everything else she had going," Miss Margaret says now. "Why, when I was a newlywed, all I did was keep house, and I didn't do it nearly as well as Brooke."

We stand there and gaze at the closet for a reverent moment.

"It feels terrible, tearing apart her home." Miss Margaret's voice warbles a little. "I thought nothing would ever be as painful as going through my daughter's home after that accident, but this feels just as awful."

I don't know what to say, but I ache to console her. She looks frailer than she did just a few weeks ago. "Brooke would want us to move forward," I finally manage.

"Yes. Yes, you're right." She draws a deep breath and stands a little straighter. "Well, do you want to take any of these towels or sheets? I have more than enough linens."

"I'll take a few of the white towels."

"I suppose we should donate the rest," Margaret says.

I nod. "I know several places that can use them. I'll take care of that for you."

"Thank you, dear." She bends down to put a sticker on the bottom shelf, then loses her balance and topples to the floor.

"Miss Margaret!" I squat down beside her, alarmed. "Are you okay?"

"I'm fine." She sits up and straightens her pink button-up shirt. "Just fine. Nothing hurt but my pride."

"Well, let me help you back up." I reach out a hand.

"Thank you, but I can do it on my own."

It's an assertion of independence. She gets to her knees and places one black Easy Spirit lace-up on the floor, then staggers to her feet, puffing out hard little breaths.

The fault line in my heart widens a bit more. I hate that she's getting feeble, both for her sake and for Lily's. Regardless of whether or not she wants to acknowledge it, her age is catching up with her. It's important that I stay close to Lily, because the day will inevitably come when I'll need to take over guardianship.

I debate again whether or not I should tell Miss Margaret that I'm pregnant. If she knows I'm having Lily's half sister, maybe she'll be more inclined to let Lily come stay with me for extended visits.

On the other hand, it's very early days, and I want to wait until I'm safely through the first trimester before I announce my pregnancy to anyone outside of the single parent group. I'm especially concerned about Lily; the last thing I want is to get her hopes up and then dash them. And as for Miss Margaret . . . well, today seems laden with enough emotional baggage. It's probably best not to add a new complication.

A knock sounds at the door.

"Oh, my. Do you suppose that's the moving company already?" Miss Margaret asks.

"I'll go check," I say. I can tell that she's still out of breath from her fall.

"Thank you, dear. I'll finish placing stickers in this closet."

I head down the stairs into the foyer. Through the front door sidelight, I see a broad-shouldered, brown-haired man standing on the porch. He's just wearing a gray T-shirt and jeans, but he somehow looks too well dressed to be a mover. I glance at the driveway and street. I don't see a moving truck, but a BMW is parked in front of the house.

I open the door. The guy is tall—probably six foot one or two—and fit, like a runner. He's clean-shaven and good-looking. "Hello," I say.

"Hi. I'm Zack Bradley." His eyes are like little pieces of sky, and a dimple winks in his jaw as he smiles. The smile transforms him from attractive to devastating. "Are you Brooke Adams?"

Chill bumps chase up my arms, and it's not cold outside. He looks familiar, but his name doesn't ring any bells.

"Uh, no. She's not here right now." For some reason, I can't bring myself to say, *She's dead.*

His smile fades into disappointment. "Can you tell me when she'll be back?"

"Not, um, really. Is there something I can help you with?" I realize I sound like a clerk at a shoe store. I smile and stretch out my hand. "I'm her best friend, Quinn Langston."

"Nice to meet you." He takes my hand, and my palm is encased in warmth. More goose bumps instantly prickle up my neck. It's definitely a sign of something, but I don't know what.

"Her phone doesn't seem to be working," he says.

Miss Margaret has Brooke's cell phone. I'm not sure if she's already suspended service or just turned it off.

"The number I have is a landline," he continues, "and I thought maybe she doesn't use it anymore."

I nod. Like many New Orleans residents post–Hurricane Katrina, both Brooke and I keep landlines because they'll work in emergencies, but neither of us keeps the ringer on.

"Could you give me her cell number?"

The request makes me wary. If Brooke wanted this man to have her number, she would have given it to him herself. "I'm sorry. I, uh, don't feel at liberty to do that."

"Okay." He reaches into his pocket, pulls out a business card, and hands it to me. *Zack Bradley, Attorney at Law*, I read. The firm's address is downtown New Orleans.

"Would you please ask her to call me?" he asks.

I frown at the card. "Is Brooke involved in some kind of legal matter?"

"Not exactly."

I realize I'm coming off as nosy, but I can't seem to help it. "Are you trying to serve her with a summons or something? I mean, I don't want to pry, but it's weird that you came to her house, especially since you don't seem to know her."

He flashes that dimple again. "We connected online."

"On a dating site?" Brooke and I looked a lot alike, so it's not all that surprising that someone who'd only seen a photo of her might initially confuse us. What's surprising is that Brooke would trawl the online dating pool without telling me—especially after her last experience. In the middle of dinner at Brennan's, a couple had greeted her date and asked about his wife and children. Turned out the guy was married and looking for a little side action.

"Not a dating site." He shifts his weight from one Nike-clad foot to the other, as if uneasy. "It was a site about her child."

"Lily?"

"That's her name?" His gaze intensifies.

The goose bumps on my arms shimmy down my legs.

Something strange and portentous is going on here. It reminds me of a night in Atlanta, when I was walking back to my car on a nearly deserted street and I became aware of footsteps behind me. I glanced over my shoulder and saw a man about half a block away. He started walking faster, gaining on me, and I broke into a run. I ducked into a convenience store, where I spent twenty minutes pretending I couldn't decide which bottle of water to buy.

I feel the exact same sense of alarm now. I start to close the door. "Well, it was nice meeting you."

"Wait." He steps forward. He doesn't put his foot in the door or reach for it or anything, but I jump backward as if he had. "Maybe you can help me after all. The online site I mentioned—it's a donor registry."

Donor. The word pours over me like a cooler full of ice. I suddenly realize why he looks familiar. *His eyes are just like Lily's.* My heart batters wildly against my ribs.

"Lily tried to contact me," he says. "I—I thought it would be best to talk to her mother first, but I couldn't reach her by phone, so . . ." He holds out his arms, his palms up. "Here I am."

My brain tries to absorb this information. This is Lily's father. The father of . . . *Oh my God in heaven!* My hand reflexively covers my belly.

I know there are a million things I should be thinking about, but like a wet circuit board, my brain is shorting out. It takes all of my faculties to just address the actual words he said: *Lily tried to contact me.* "That's—that's impossible," I stutter.

"What do you mean?"

"Lily's three. She can't read yet."

He stares at me. "She's just *three*? Then how . . . who . . . ?"

"It was me," Miss Margaret says behind me. "I reached out to you on Lily's behalf."

CHAPTER NINE

Zack

HOLY CRAP—DOES everyone on that donor registry pretend to be someone else? First Jessica impersonates me, and now I discover that this elderly woman impersonated the child.

Not *the* child, I mentally correct—*my* child. My daughter. *I have a three-year-old daughter named Lily!* It's one thing to know, hypothetically, that a child with your DNA might be walking around out there somewhere; it's another thing altogether to learn the child's gender, age, name, and address.

The older woman steps forward. She reminds me of Dame Judi Dench.

"I'm Margaret Moore. I'm Lily's great-grandmother." She holds out her hand.

"Zack Bradley," I say as I shake it.

"I'm so pleased to meet you." Her voice is gracious and composed, as if she were expecting me for dinner, but I feel her hand tremble.

"Is Lily in the house?" Part of me is dying to meet her, and another part—the lawyer part—is clanging a loud warning. After all, the child is only three; legally—not to mention morally—I need clearance from her mother before we make contact.

"No. She's playing at a friend's home."

"Is she likely to come back before Brooke?"

"Um . . . no." She puts her hand on her chest and looks away. "Quinn will go pick her up in a couple of hours."

I look at the pretty blonde. She's been silent and rigid ever since I mentioned I was a donor.

"Please come in." Mrs. Moore sways a little bit. I notice that she's clutching the doorway as if she's holding it for support.

"All right," I say. "Thanks."

I follow the two women into a light-filled living room. Mrs. Moore motions me toward an armchair by the fireplace, then settles on the sofa. Quinn perches on the chair to my right, her face white, her mouth tight.

"How on earth did you find us?" Mrs. Moore asks. "As I recall, that registry only let me enter a phone number."

I nod. "I called, but I couldn't get an answer or leave a voice mail. Since it was a landline, it was easy to find out Brooke's name and address."

"Oh, mercy! I put down Brooke's old phone number? What was I thinking? I meant to write in mine." She makes a tsk-tsking sound and puts her hand on her chest again. "Well, there was so much going on at the time, it's not surprising I got confused."

Something is off about this whole situation. Why was she posting for Lily? "Is Brooke aware that you posted on the donor registry?"

"Um . . ." She glances quickly at Quinn, then looks at her lap. "Not exactly."

Oh, hell. Is the old gal here a little unhinged? My grandfather had had Alzheimer's, but you wouldn't have known it if you'd just met him. He might carry on a perfectly pleasant conversation about, say, the weather, then leave the room and return wearing nothing but his underwear.

"I really think I should talk to Brooke before this goes any further," I say.

"I'm afraid you can't do that." The older woman's face falls and sort of slumps in on itself. "Brooke is no longer with us."

I'm about to ask, *Where'd she go?* but then I glance at Quinn. She's looked stressed ever since I told her why I'm here, but now her eyes are radiating something else—something I recognize, but can't immediately place. I've seen it on my sister's face after my father . . .

It hits with sudden, surprising force: *grief.* These two women are in mourning.

"Good God. What happened?"

Mrs. Moore swallows and looks like she's about to cry.

"Brooke had a brain aneurysm." Quinn's voice quavers. "It happened about six weeks ago."

OF ALL THE situations I'd imagined walking into this morning, this wasn't one of them. And I'd imagined a variety of scenarios.

I'd awakened with a hellacious hangover, a rotten taste in my mouth, and the remnants of a dream about my late father flapping in my brain like a tattered flag. I dreamed I'd failed some kind of test and disappointed him, and it left me sick in the depths of my soul.

The rotten taste remained after I brushed my teeth, and I realized that it wasn't just too much booze on an empty stomach; it was the conversation with Jessica and the knowledge that I had a child out there looking for me.

I swallowed some ibuprofen and a tall glass of water. I'm sure I dreamed about my father because he's my moral arbiter. When I don't know what to do, I'll pretend my father is in the situation and imagine his reaction, because he was the most honest, upright man I've ever known. It's a less holy but more relatable version of WWJD. Whatever the problem, Dad believed in facing it head on and taking responsible action. "Just do what you know is right," he'd told me.

It was pretty clear to me what I needed to do in this situation, at least as far as the child was concerned. It wouldn't be right to ignore an outreach request. Maybe the kid needed a kidney or bone marrow transplant or something. As soon as I received the contact information for my child—*my child*; the solid reality of that still rattled me—I'd call. I wouldn't say who I was; I'd get his—or her—mother's phone number, then talk to the mom. Maybe she didn't know that the child—who's likely to be a teenager—was trying to find me. Maybe she won't want him or her making contact until age eighteen. Whatever the mother wanted, I'd follow her wishes.

I called in to my office that I'd be working remotely today—it's a common practice at our law firm—then took my laptop to an uptown coffee shop. That's where I'd been this morning when the donor registry emailed me the phone number. When I got no answer, a quick reverse search gave me Brooke's name and address. It was only a few blocks from the coffee shop, so I'd simply headed on over, hoping to meet Brooke or get her cell number from whoever answered the door. I never dreamed she'd be dead.

"I'm so sorry for your loss," I say now.

"Thank you." Mrs. Moore gives a small nod.

"So—is Lily living with her father?"

Mrs. Moore blinks. "*You're* the father."

I know this, but . . . *wow.* I sit there for a moment, wondering again about Mrs. Moore's mental status. "I meant Brooke's husband." The moment I say it, I realize there are other options. "Or ex-husband. Or—or partner. Or ex-partner."

"Oh, Brooke wasn't married or coupled up. She was a single mother by choice."

The hits just keep on coming. I don't know why this surprises me; my thinking is probably colored by all of the fertility treatments that Jess and I have been through and by my own two-parent upbringing.

I lean forward. "So who's Lily's guardian?"

"I am," Mrs. Moore says. "She lives with me in Alexandria now. It's lucky you came by this weekend. We're only in New Orleans for a few days."

Mrs. Moore strikes me as too old to care for a toddler. Wait—is a three-year-old still a toddler? There's so much I don't know about kids. "Do you have other family in Alexandria?"

"Other family?"

"A daughter or son or granddaughter or someone who can help you with Lily."

She shakes her head. "Lily and I are each other's only family."

"You have me." Quinn shifts toward the edge of her chair. "I'm like family."

"Yes, dear, but you aren't. Not real family. That's why I reached out to Lily's father."

Quinn's lips part. I'm sure my jaw drops as well. An awkward pause hulks over the room, punctuated by the ticking of the old clock on the mantel.

"Oh, my—I'm sorry, Quinn, dear. That didn't come out right at all," Margaret says. She touches her chest again. Her upper lip is perspiring. "I'm very fond of you, you know that. You've been nothing but splendid, and I know you adore Lily and Lily adores you. It's just that, well—blood is thicker than water, and since Lily still has a living parent, I thought it was important to get him in the picture."

Another round of uncomfortable silence hunches over us.

"Oh, goodness." Mrs. Moore struggles to her feet. I stand, too, ready to help her. "I'm forgetting all my manners. Let me get you some iced tea. Or would you prefer coffee?"

"I'm fine, thanks." Actually, I'm anything but fine. What does *in the picture* mean?

"Nonsense. Never in my life have I failed to offer hospitality. My mother used to say, 'It's rude not to offer, and rude to refuse.' So what would you like? Coffee, tea, or water?"

Apparently she's not going to take no for an answer. "Um . . . just water, please."

"I'll get it, Miss Margaret," Quinn says, rising from her armchair.

"Oh, no. No, no, no, no." She flaps her wrist. "This is my house now, and I insist on doing the honors. You stay here and keep Mr.—Bradford, was it?"

"Bradley," I supply.

"Mr. Bradley. Quinn, dear, you stay here and keep Mr. Bradley company. What can I bring you, dear?"

Quinn reluctantly sits back down. "Um . . . just water, too. Thank you."

"My pleasure."

I watch the older woman shuffle out of the room, then look at Quinn and sit back down. "I'm so sorry about Brooke."

"Thank you," she says stiffly.

"You and Lily are close, I take it?"

"Very. I'm her godmother and the backup guardian." She lowers her voice. "Brooke was going to change her will to make me guardian after Miss Margaret's next birthday, but she passed before . . ." Her voice breaks. She puts her hand over her mouth for a moment.

She has one of those expressive faces where every emotion shows. My heart goes out to her.

She swallows and takes her hand away. "Anyway, yes, I'm very close to Lily." She gives a wry smile. "And you might not know it from what she just said, but I'm close to Miss Margaret, too."

"She seems sort of frail."

Quinn's forehead creases. "She's not at her best today. She's in great shape for her age, but it's been really hard on her, losing Brooke. Being back in Brooke's home and going through all of her things to put the house on the market is taking a toll on her."

"She's selling this place?"

Quinn nods. "Movers are coming later today to pack up the contents of the closets and drawers. We've taken down all the photos to depersonalize the place so prospective buyers can envision . . ."

A thud sounds in the kitchen, followed by the tinkle of breaking glass. We both jump to our feet.

"Miss Margaret!" Quinn's eyes are wide and alarmed.

I race to the kitchen to find the elderly woman lying on the floor, facedown, one leg twisted at an unnatural angle. Shards of glass glisten near her right hand. A step stool stands in front of an open upper cabinet.

"Oh, my God!" Quinn gasps.

I kneel on the hardwood floor beside the too-still woman and check for a pulse. I can't find one. "We need to turn her over to see if she's breathing."

Quinn holds Miss Margaret's head as I carefully flip her over. Her face is white, her lips grayish blue. She looks completely lifeless.

"Call nine-one-one," I say. "I'll start CPR."

CHAPTER TEN

Jessica

THE DAY AFTER I jeopardize my marriage, I wake up in my childhood bedroom in a suburb of Seattle. What is it about being back in your parents' house that makes you feel like you're thirteen years old again? In my case, it might be because the room is a time capsule.

I turn my gaze from the frilly dotted swiss curtains to the faux French-provincial vanity. Jeez, the room could be rented out as a vintage movie set. Everything in it, from the floral border on the wall to the matching curtains and matching sheets, is dusky blue and dusty rose—color-challenged pastels that always look dirty, grayed over like a foggy day, or both. Not the best decor choice for a cloudy climate, but I suppose it was the very height of chic in the eighties.

It doesn't help that my mother has kept the room as a shrine to my school-age triumphs. There on the white dresser is the horseback-riding trophy I won when I was eight, as well as the trophies my piano teacher gave me for being her most prepared student. The spelling bee award I won in sixth grade hangs on the wall, next to honor roll certificates, National Honor Society plaques, and awards for junior and senior high math competitions. On the far wall are homecoming, prom, sorority, and graduation photos.

I sit up and push my hair from my eyes. My little sister, Erin, swears I deliberately tried to make her look bad by being the perfect daughter. I wasn't perfect, of course, but I sure tried my hardest to be. I still do. Back then, it seemed to be what my parents expected, and I never wanted to disappoint them. Now I don't want to disappoint myself. I've read this is a trait shared by many eldest children.

I've got another eldest-child trait that no one, my sister included, really knows about: no matter how well I do, I always secretly feel like I'm not good enough.

My gaze scans the framed photos on top of the dresser and zooms in on a shot of Zack and me at our wedding. Guilt grabs me like something from a nature documentary—hawk talons around a rabbit, maybe. I reach for my phone, hoping to see a message from Zack. Nothing.

Good morning from Seattle, I text. *I am so, so sorry about everything. I love you and want to talk.*

Zack is usually very prompt about replying when he's not tied up in meetings. I get up and take a quick shower in the Jack and Jill bathroom that adjoins my room with my sister's. By the time I've dried off, done my hair, and put on a little makeup, he's sent a text:

Glad you made it there safely. Not ready to talk yet. I'll call later.

Anxiety digs another claw into my stomach. It's not exactly the warm fuzzies I was hoping for, but at least he responded. Maybe he's not ready to talk because he's busy.

Or maybe he's still mad.

I throw on jeans, a long-sleeved T-shirt, a scarf, and a long sweater, then head downstairs in search of caffeine. My mom is in the kitchen, which is covered in fruit-themed wallpaper. My sister, Erin, is there, too. She and her husband live a few streets over with their two children, now aged eleven and fourteen.

"Good morning, Jessica," Mom says brightly. "My, don't you look lovely!"

I know I don't. Between the long late flight and the fight with Zack, I didn't sleep much last night. There's not enough under-eye cover cream in the whole state to hide my dark circles, but Mom will always find something nice to say.

"Thanks, Mom." I drop a kiss on her head as she hugs me.

My sister, Erin, harbors no such compunction. She also hugs me, then holds me at arm's length, and eyes me up and down. "Actually, you look like hell."

"Now be nice, Erin. She had a long flight and a horrible headache last night." That was the excuse I gave Mom and Dad to avoid having to act perky and make pleasant conversation when they picked me up at the airport. Mom's eyes are concerned. "How are you feeling today?"

"Better," I say.

"Well, good," Erin says, "because we're meeting Brett Ross at Starbucks in ten minutes."

"Who's Brett Ross?" Mom asks.

"The Realtor Erin lined me up with," I say. "I went to high school with him and now he's one of the biggest real estate agents in Seattle."

"Oh, I remember him," Mom says. "He played football and dated a cheerleader, didn't he?"

"Sue Anne Morrison," my sister chimes in. "They got married after college and he played pro ball."

"And now he's selling real estate?"

Erin lifts her shoulders. "He's got his own company and he's doing amazingly well."

"With the cost of real estate here, I'm sure it's lucrative." Trust Mom to home in on the money angle immediately. "Maybe that's something your brother can look into."

"I thought Doug was happy at the garage," I say.

"Oh, he is. Happy as a clam, actually. And if he had his way, he'd do nothing else for the rest of his life. But it wouldn't hurt for him to have a little bit more drive."

My brother had a tough time in school, largely, I believe, because of untreated ADHD. My mother refused to even consider it. "That's a phony diagnosis used to cover up a lack of self-discipline," she'd say if a teacher brought it up. I gave her articles about it, but Mom didn't want to hear it. My father was no help. As far as Dad was concerned, my mother's word was law. He never went against her.

"There's nothing wrong with working at a garage," I say.

"Of course not." Mom pours a cup of coffee and hands it to me. "If he'd apply himself, though, he could get a white-collar job."

My sister and I exchange a look. Mom hates the fact that my brother gets his clothes dirty. I understand where she gets it; her own father was a plumber, and she was teased as a child for having a father who worked on toilets.

"A lot of white-collar workers earn less than what he's probably making," Erin says.

"That's right," I say. "I read an article the other day about how there's a shortage of highly skilled technicians, and Doug is definitely highly skilled."

Mom sniffs. "Blue-collar jobs don't leave a lot of room for advancement."

Erin rolls her eyes. "Well, if he and Darla are happy, that's all that matters."

"That's all that's mattered until now, but . . ." Mom messes with the toaster.

"But what?"

"Nothing. I just wish he were more like you, Jessica."

Doesn't she realize how awful everyone feels when she holds me up as a gold standard against my siblings? "You were going to say something else. What's going on?" I press.

Mom hesitates.

"Darla's pregnant," Erin blurts.

A stab of pain shoots through me. I hate that I'm so small that my brother's good fortune bothers me. I fight to rise above it. "Oh! How . . . how wonderful."

"Yes. We're very excited," Mom says.

"Yeah, that's—that's great. When did Darla find out?"

"She's about four months along. But she only told us a few weeks ago."

Mom has known for a few weeks? That means she didn't tell me because she knew I'd find it painful. The kid-glove treatment makes it somehow harder to take.

"Well, I'm very happy for them," I make myself say. I feel as if a potato has suddenly lodged in my throat. "Do they know yet if it's a boy or girl?"

"They hope to find out at the next ultrasound."

"That's wonderful." I stretch my mouth into a smile. "I'll have to call and congratulate them."

"Actually, they're coming for dinner tomorrow night." Mom's eyes and mouth have that strained look she gets when she's worried.

Erin thrusts a steel coffee mug at me and nods toward the door. "We'd better get going or we'll be late."

"But you haven't had breakfast!" Mom says.

I pour my cup of coffee into the travel mug.

"We'll eat at Starbucks." Erin fills her own mug from the coffee-pot.

"You're taking coffee to Starbucks?" Mom asks.

"It's just enough to get us there," Erin says, heading out the kitchen door. I follow her out of the house and into her Honda.

"Mom is such a job snob," I remark.

"She was trying to be tactful," she says as she backs out of the driveway. "She thought she'd alleviate the sting of Darla's pregnancy by first pointing out how much better you're doing than Doug professionally."

"She didn't know how to tell me," I say. "Apparently you didn't, either."

"I still haven't gotten used to the idea of Doug as a father." She turns the car onto another street. "I mean, this is the guy who tried to tip a cow, but ended up with the cow falling on him and breaking his rib."

I smile.

"And then there was the time he tried to roof surf on his friend's car."

"How about when he thought he was smoking pot but it was just oregano?" I add.

Erin laughs. "And he was convinced he was high anyway!"

"Yeah, he did some really dumb stuff," I agree.

"It's a wonder he survived his teen years."

"And now he's going to be a dad." I try like hell to stop it, but my eyes fill with tears. I look out the window so Erin won't see. "How's Darla feeling?"

"Good. She's hardly had any morning sickness. She's excited."

"And Doug?"

"He's thrilled." She turns onto a side street. "And actually, despite what Mom says or thinks, he's making really good money."

"That's great." I try to wipe my eyes surreptitiously. "So—were you going to tell me if Mom hadn't brought it up?"

"Yeah. We're not actually meeting Brett at Starbucks—I'm dropping you at his office in an hour. I'm taking you to my place for breakfast first."

"I'm not all that fragile. I mean, I can be happy for Doug and Darla, even though I can't have . . . I haven't gotten . . . I can't get . . ." My eyes fill up again. "Ah, hell."

"It's okay, Jessie."

The use of the old childhood nickname makes the tears roll. She lets me sit in silence as she drives the two minutes it takes to get to her house.

"Hey—it's understandable that this is hard for you," she says as she parks in her driveway and hits the remote to open her garage door.

"It's more than not being able to get pregnant."

She frowns at me. "What's going on?"

"Let's go inside and I'll tell you," I say. "But you have to promise not to tell Mom."

"Since when do I tell her anything?" We climb out of the car and go through the garage into the mudroom. I follow her past a coatrack laden with windbreakers and sweaters into the kitchen, which smells of eggs and sausage.

I sink onto a barstool at her kitchen peninsula, moving aside a stack of school papers, mail, and a hair barrette. She puts two slices of bread in the toaster and looks at me with deep concern. "What's the matter?"

"It's Zack."

"Zack?" She widens her eyes and puts her hand to her chest, as if I'd said something was wrong with Santa Claus. "It's not another woman, is it?"

"No, nothing like that. But I just found out he has a child."

"What?"

I draw a deep breath. As she reheats the eggs she'd scrambled earlier for her family's breakfast, I spill the whole story.

"Jesus, Jess. I had no clue he'd been a sperm donor." She scoops some scrambled eggs on a plate and sets it in front of me, then adds a piece of toast. "Why didn't you tell me that?"

I lift my shoulders. "I was kind of ashamed."

"Why? Because it wasn't part of the perfect life you outlined for yourself?"

That's the problem with having a sister; she knows too damned much. I eat a forkful of eggs so I don't have to answer.

She sits beside me at the counter. "You've got to get over this always-wanting-everything-to-look-flawless thing, you know?"

"Yeah," I say. Hell, she's right. Maybe she'll lighten up if I admit it. "I'm working on it. But you can't tell Mom."

"I won't. That's not my place." She takes a bite of toast and chews thoughtfully. "But at some point, you're probably going to need to."

I blow out a sigh. "I don't want to disappoint her."

"If she doesn't like something, that's her problem. Don't make it yours." Erin's face is earnest. "Of course, that's easy for me to say, because I never had her approval."

"Oh, Erin, that's not true."

"It is, and you know it. I was Erin the Errant, the pregnant teen. You were Little Miss Perfect, who could do no wrong, and then there was poor Doug the Dummy."

I sigh. She's right—we all had our roles in the family. And, to some extent, we're all still playing them out.

"Well, I'm hardly perfect now." I tell her about the scene with Zack. She's shocked, but more empathetic than I had reason to hope for. I break down and cry again.

"This whole infertility thing has been rough for you," Erin murmurs.

"It's awful," I blubber. "It's like I'm starving and everyone else has lots of food, but I can't have any."

"Aw, sweetie—come here."

She hugs me and pats my back, as if I'm one of her children, until my tears stop.

"I'm sorry," I say.

"Sometimes it's good to get your feelings out," she says.

"What time do we need to leave?"

She glances at the clock on her stove. "In about five minutes. After I drop you, I have to pick up Jordan at school for an orthodontist appointment across town."

"Okay. Let me fix my face before we go."

She rolls her eyes. "Of course, Miss Flawless Perfection."

I should have known the remark wouldn't go over well with Erin, who rarely wears makeup, pulls her hair into a perpetual ponytail, and dresses like a Sasquatch hunter. "I'm not trying to be perfect," I snuffle. "I just don't want to show up looking like a mascara-streaked crazy person."

She steps back and scans me. "Yeah, you are kind of a mess." She grins, and waves me toward the powder room. "Okay. Not crazy is an acceptable goal. Go for it!"

THE BUILDING IS impressive—a three-story mirrored-glass office structure with a sign that reads *Ross Real Estate*. Just minutes after I speak to the receptionist in the modern entry, a familiar man emerges from a back hallway. "Hello. I'm Brett Ross."

"Yes, I know." I shake the hand he extends to me. He still looks like the high school heartthrob I remember—tall, dark, and handsome. His brown hair maybe isn't quite as thick as it was and his eyes are etched with fine lines, but in that unfair way of men, the years look good on him. "I used to watch you play football." *And fantasize you were kissing me when I kissed my own hand.*

"You did? I thought you were too much of a brainiac to bother with sports."

I lift my shoulders. "I made it to a few games."

"Well, it's great to see you. You look better than ever."

"Thanks."

"So you and your husband are moving to Seattle, huh?"

I hope so. When I checked my phone in the parking lot, I still hadn't heard from Zack. I hide any uncertainty behind a wide smile. "Yes," I say.

"Well, welcome back! I have a few appointments set up for you, so if you're ready . . ."

I nod and walk with him to the parking lot. He opens the passenger door of a shiny white Porsche SUV.

"Nice ride," I say.

He gives an apologetic smile. "I'm not normally into conspicuous consumption, but having a flashy car is part of the real estate game around here."

"It's lovely," I say. I notice a child's safety seat in the back as he rounds the car and gets in the driver's seat. "You have kids?"

He buckles his seat belt and starts the engine. "One. A boy. You?"

"No." I force a smile. "Not—not yet. So how's Sue Anne?"

"Okay, I think."

He glances over. My surprise must show on my face, because he smiles as he drives out of the parking lot. "We're divorced. It's been about a year and a half now."

"Oh, I'm sorry."

"Yeah, well, me too." He turns onto the street. "It's hard with a kid."

I don't know what to say. "You two always looked like the perfect couple."

He lifts his shoulders. "Things aren't always as they seem."

"Phaedrus," I say automatically.

"What?"

"The man who originally said that. He was a pal of Plato's, and the quote is commonly attributed to him."

"You are just too smart." He laughs and shakes his head. "How do you remember stuff like that?"

I learned at an early age that knowing the source of a quote is impressive, so I've memorized lots of them. It's only impressive if it seems effortless, though, so I never admit I work at it.

I shrug. "Useless trivia sticks in my brain."

"Not just useless trivia," he says. "You were valedictorian."

I nod, pleased he remembered.

The conversation drifts to other topics—what we did after high school, my job, my husband's job. I learn that Sue Anne works part-time as a speech therapist. We didn't really know each other in high school, but we have an easy rapport. It's like catching up with an old friend.

"What happened with you and Sue Anne?" I find myself asking. Too late, I realize I've overstepped the bounds of casual acquaintance. "I'm sorry. It's rude of me to ask."

"Oh, I don't mind. I've spent a lot of time trying to figure it out myself." He turns on the blinker for a right turn.

"What did you come up with?"

"I think our marriage died by degrees, you know? We took each other for granted and quit really being a couple. We focused on other things. And then . . . well, a guy she met through work started giving her a lot of attention, and it was a fast downward slide from there."

It's hard to imagine Brett Ross being thrown over for another man. "I'm sorry."

He lifts his shoulders. "The hardest part was Petey."

"How old is he?"

Brett turns onto a busy four-lane road. "Just turned six."

"How long were you married?"

"Eight years."

"That's all? But you dated in high school!"

"We broke up a few times before we got engaged. How about you?"

"Three years."

"Ah! You're still in the honeymoon phase."

I force a smile. "I don't think I'd call it that."

He keeps his eyes on the road. "Well, moving is a big stress factor."

"So is infertility."

He looks at me, his eyes sympathetic. "That's a rough one."

My face heats. "I don't know why I just blurted that out. I don't usually talk about it. Please—don't repeat it to anyone we went to school with."

"I wouldn't. But just for the record, I don't regularly hang out with anyone from school anymore." He looks at me again. "And you know what? I don't usually talk about what ended my marriage, either. I haven't even told my parents that Sue Anne cheated on me."

"Oh, God—parents are the worst, aren't they? I'd rather slit my wrists than tell mine something disappointing."

"Amen to that. Sue Anne and I had been separated three months and the divorce was filed and nearly over, and I hadn't even told them we'd split up. They thought I was staying in a house I was flipping because there was a problem with vandals. Then my brother saw Sue Anne at a restaurant with this other guy." He grins. "It's kind of comical, actually. My brother marched over to their table and confronted them. He was shocked when Sue Anne told him our divorce would be final in another couple of weeks." We drove in silence for a few moments. "My brother came to see me, mad as hell. 'What do you think family is for?' he said."

"That sounds like my sister this morning," I say. "I finally told her a little about a . . . a situation I'm having, and she was furious I hadn't confided in her earlier."

The conversation shifts to college and his football career, and before I know it, he turns the Porsche in to a driveway. I'm startled; I haven't been paying attention at all to where we were driving.

"Okay," he says. "Here's the first house. What do you think?"

It's a nondescript beige brick ranch. I make a face. "It looks like someone's grandmother lives here."

He laughs. "Yeah, it does. But by the time you get through renovating, it'll be fabulous."

"Whoa." I hold up my hands. "Renovating?"

"That's what you'll need to do to get what you want at what you want to pay. But don't worry—I have a building company that handles all that, and I'll get you the best prices in the area."

"So you're not just a Realtor—you're a contractor, too? You're like both Property Brothers rolled into one?"

"Yeah, sort of."

We look at three more houses, each uglier than the last. I'm enjoying Brett's company, but I can't visualize any of the houses he's showing me looking like places I'd want to live.

We stop for lunch at a little grill in Everett. The weather is perfect—spring-like but still cool, unlike the steamy May heat of New Orleans. I gaze out the window at fir trees blowing in the wind. I've really missed this view, I realize. In Louisiana, you only see firs on Christmas tree lots.

"You don't seem wowed by anything I've shown you," he says.

"I can't get over how much more homes cost here versus Louisiana."

"Yeah, well, that's the West Coast for you." He takes a sip of coffee. "Are you sure you want to move back?"

I nod. "Absolutely. I'm ready to get out of New Orleans."

"Why? It's a great city."

I sigh. "I miss my family. Plus I don't want to keep wondering if every child I see might be my husband's." The words pop out before I realize what I'm saying.

He grins at me. "I've heard a lot of reasons that people want to move, but I've got to say, that's a new one."

I give a nervous laugh, too embarrassed to look him in the eye. "I can't believe I just said that. That's the second time I've just blurted out stuff to you."

"That's not surprising. I'm known as the Blurtmaster." He leans forward, his expression comically intense, and looks from side to side, as if making sure no one can overhear him. "I really work for the CIA, interrogation department," he says in a loud whisper. "Real estate is just a cover."

I laugh. "I can almost believe it."

"Don't."

I laugh again.

He leans back and gives me a warm smile. "Seriously, if you want to talk, I'm a good listener. And anything you tell me is covered by Realtor-client privilege so I can't divulge it."

I laugh again. "Good to know." I take a sip of iced tea. "I think I've already told you way too much for someone I haven't seen in nineteen years, but I'll keep it in mind."

We talk about styles of houses and football teams and other people from high school as we finish lunch. We climb back into his SUV and tour three more houses, then he glances at his watch. "I have to pick up my son from school, but there are a couple of other places I want to show you. One of them is a condo; you're likely to need a place to lease for a month or two while you wait to close on a house and renovate. It's not far from Petey's school. Are you okay with picking him up and dropping him at my mom's before we go see it?"

I look at my phone. I've been checking it all day, but I still haven't heard from Zack. The knot in my stomach is growing bigger and tighter.

And the truth is, I'd far rather hang with Brett than go back to my parents' house. "Sure," I say. "I'd love to meet him."

BRETT'S SON IS adorable. He has dark hair, bright hazel eyes, and freckles sprinkled across his nose. He's wearing a blue-and-red-striped polo shirt and jeans, and he comes running up to the SUV as we move forward in the car line. "Hi, Dad!" he calls.

"Hey there, bud." Brett hits a switch and the back door opens. Pete starts to climb in, then freezes when he sees me.

"This is Mrs. Bradley," Brett says.

I turn around more fully and smile. "Hi, Pete."

His face falls. "Why'd you bring *her*?"

"Hey, that's no way to greet somebody," Brett chides.

"Nice to meet you," he mutters as he climbs into his booster seat.

I widen my smile. "Great to meet you, too."

Brett makes sure Pete's seat belt is fastened, then rebuckles his own and puts the car in drive. "Mrs. Bradley is moving here with her husband, and I'm helping her find a house."

"Oh." His eyes brighten considerably. "So you're not on a date with Dad?"

"No," I say with a smile.

"My mom is dating." His brow crumples in a dark frown. "She says she's going to marry Mr. James and have a baby with him, but I don't like him."

"He's a nice guy," Brett says.

This is very generous of him, to speak well of the man who, I assume, broke up his marriage. *He loves his son very much*, I think.

"He's a dork," Pete says. "Besides, I want you and Mom to get back together."

"I told you, sport. That's not going to happen."

"It could."

"Nope."

"Why not?"

"We've been over this a million times. The marriage is over."

"But it doesn't have to be," Petey insists.

"Yes, it does. Sometimes marriages are like Sammy. They get sick and die."

"Who was Sammy?" I ask.

"My goldfish," Petey says solemnly.

"Oh," I say. "Sorry for your loss."

Brett gives me a sidewise grin.

"You and Mom aren't even sick," Petey tells his father. "You could get back together if you wanted to."

"Marriage isn't just one person's decision."

"I'm working on Mom, too. If she gets rid of Mr. James, I know she'll love you again."

"Petey, married people need to have certain feelings for each other. If the feelings aren't there, the marriage can't work."

"Why not?"

"Because marriage is supposed to be a heart connection. If you don't have that, it's not really a marriage, and both people get more and more unhappy. It's bad for children to be raised in a miserable environment."

"I didn't think it was miserable."

"That's because we divorced before it got so bad that it affected you."

"But the *divorce* is affecting me!"

"I know, son." He glances at Petey's distraught little face in the rearview mirror. Brett's eyes are dark and somber. "And I'm sorry about that. But the divorce is a done deal and it's time to move on."

He steers the car into a neighborhood by the Puget Sound. "And speaking of moving on, I have your tablet and headset with me. Want to play a game?"

"Yes!" Pete exclaims. "But wait—will it count against my game time tonight?"

"No, bud. This'll be extra."

"All right!"

Brett reaches in the console, pulls out a digital tablet and headset, and hands them to Petey, all without taking his eyes from the road. He's had some practice at this, I think.

A moment later, Petey is happily occupied, the headset affixed to his ears.

"Whew." Brett cuts me a sideways glance. "Sorry you were a captive audience to that."

"No problem. You handled it really well."

"It didn't feel like it from where I'm sitting."

"Well, from the passenger seat, it was darn impressive."

He lifts his shoulders. "I do my best. Most days it feels like it's never enough." He flips on a turn signal. "I hate feeling like I've let Petey down."

I search my mind for something positive to say. "Hey, life and love are the biggest gifts of all, and you've given him both of those," I say. "You've got to look for the gifts, right? It's all a matter of perspective."

"Yeah." He glances over at me and shoots me a grin. "I guess the perspective is better in the passenger seat."

"It's always easier to be objective if you're just along for the ride," I say.

He stops at a stop sign and smiles at me. I feel a little flicker of attraction I haven't felt in a long time.

"I can slide over," I say. "There's room for two over here."

"Sounds great, but who would drive?"

"Maybe neither of us." I think about my infertility, about Zack's donor child, and about our argument. I feel a distance from my husband that's further than 1,500 physical miles. "Maybe we're all just passengers and we're fooling ourselves to think we're driving."

"Wow. That's deep, Jessica."

"Yeah." I grin. "Better put on your waders."

He pulls into a driveway. A fit woman in yoga pants with short gray-streaked hair is in the front yard, watering a rosebush. She smiles, waves, puts down the hose, and heads toward the car. Brett lowers his window.

Petey yanks off his headset and bounds out of the back seat, clutching his backpack. "Hey, Grandma!"

The woman hugs him. "Hey, sprout."

Brett gestures to me. "Mom, this is Jessica Bradley. She used to be Jessica Caldwell. She was valedictorian the year I graduated, remember?"

She leans in the car window. She has friendly brown eyes and an open smile. "Yes, I do! You gave a wonderful speech. And you're even prettier now than you were then."

I feel a rush of pleasure. Compliments always make me feel validated. "Thank you. It's nice to meet you."

"I'm showing her some houses," Brett says. "I'll be back in a couple of hours."

"Take your time. Petey and I will be just fine."

"Your mom is really nice, and Petey's adorable," I say after Brett closes the window and starts backing out of the drive.

He nods. "Mom is the best. And as for Petey . . ." He brakes, then shifts gears. "I didn't have a clue how much I could love someone until he came along."

Wistfulness fills my chest. "Everyone says that parenthood takes you to a whole other level of love."

"That's true, but it comes with a flip side." He turns beside a tall willow with branches that nearly sweep the ground. "Nothing hurts like having something hurt your child. And it especially sucks if that something is you."

"Like you told Petey, though—it's worse for a kid to be in the middle of a bad marriage," I say. "I think he's really lucky to have you as a dad. You seem great at it."

He looks at me, his eyes dark with appreciation. "I try."

I think about Brett's comment after he drops me off at my parents' house. *Nothing hurts like having something hurt your child.*

Is it true? I'm not a parent, so I can't really say. Right now, though, nothing hurts like not being able to have a child of my own, especially since learning that my husband has one with another woman.

I pull out my phone and call Zack again. He and I desperately need to talk.

CHAPTER ELEVEN

Quinn

TIME SEEMS TO go into an entangled dimension as soon as I see Miss Margaret on the kitchen floor. It slows down, it drags, it runs backward until it smacks right into *what the hell just happened?* I later learn it took less than five minutes for the ambulance to reach us, because one was parked just a few blocks away when I called.

As we're waiting, though, time is measured by Zack's compressions on Margaret's chest. An eternity seems to pass before the wail of a siren pierces the air.

I run to the door, jerk it open, and race to the street, waving my arm to flag the ambulance. Two blue-uniformed paramedics jump out.

"What's the emergency?" asks a woman with dark hair pulled into a ponytail.

My words jumble over one another as I try to get them out. "Seventy-nine-year-old woman. She fell off a step stool. No pulse, no breathing. Hip looks funny."

Both paramedics dash inside. I point to the kitchen, where Zack is working on Margaret. He doesn't stop until both paramedics kneel down and the woman says, "We'll take over now."

Zack straightens, stands, and steps out of their way.

"I've got a pulse," says the other paramedic, a fortyish muscular man with a buzz cut. He leans over Margaret as the female paramedic fits on a blood pressure cuff. "Ma'am, can you hear me?"

Margaret opens her eyes, then closes them again.

"Ma'am, are you in pain?"

She opens her mouth, but no words come out. The woman paramedic gently fits an oxygen mask on her. The man talks into a crackling radio. The woman runs back to the ambulance, opens the rear door, and wheels out a gurney, along with an assortment of traction devices. They put her neck in a brace, then attach a splint to her upper leg. Margaret groans.

"Do you know if she's on any medications?" the man asks me.

I nod. "For blood pressure and cholesterol, I think."

"Do you know which ones?"

"I'll get them from her room," I say.

"I'll drive you to the hospital," Zack tells me as they strap Margaret to the gurney. "Better bring her purse. You'll need her insurance information."

Good thinking, my mind registers as I race upstairs to her room.

"Grab a sweater, your phone, and whatever else you need," Zack says when I return. "You'll be there for a while. We'll follow the ambulance."

I reach into Brooke's coat closet, pull out a black cardigan, and carry it, along with my purse and Miss Margaret's, as we follow the paramedics pushing the gurney down the sidewalk. I hand her medicine bottles to the female paramedic, then I touch Margaret's gray hair as they open the back of the ambulance. "I'll see you at the hospital," I tell her. I don't know if she can hear me or not. Her eyes are closed, her lids blue-veined and thin as voile.

Across the street, Zack opens the passenger door of his BMW for me. As I climb in, I realize I'm shaking like poor Ruffles when she goes to the vet.

"You okay?" he asks.

"Yeah." I reach for the seat belt. "How—how did you know what to do?"

"I took a CPR course after my dad's heart attack."

I'd taken a CPR course for babysitters back when Lily was born, but I hadn't instantaneously gone into rescue mode like Zack. I'd stood there like a lump of lard, trying to comprehend what was going on, while Zack had quickly checked her pulse and respiration. "How many heart attacks did your father have?"

"One."

"Did he make it?"

I notice his hands clench the steering wheel. They're nice hands, large and strong and slightly tanned. "No."

The air leaves my chest in a sudden exhale. Zack pulls away from the curb, turns into a neighbor's driveway, backs up, and then steers his car directly behind the ambulance. As the ambulance moves away from the curb, Zack follows it.

"Dad might have survived," Zack says, "if someone with him had known how to do CPR."

"Were you there?"

"No. I was in New Orleans, and he was on a golf course in Ohio. But I wanted to learn what to do so I wouldn't ever be a helpless bystander like his golf buddy. Not knowing how to save my dad's life pretty much ruined the rest of his." He puts on his flashers and speeds up to close the distance behind the ambulance.

"How long ago did this happen?"

"Four years this June."

"I'm sorry."

He nods, wordlessly accepting my condolences.

I watch him turn the black leather steering wheel to follow the ambulance around a corner. The car lurches to the right, and my pounding heart lurches with it.

I suddenly notice something that I normally would have looked for right away, if I hadn't been thrown for such a loop when Zack first showed up at the door.

On the fourth finger of his left hand gleams a simple gold band.

Lily's father—who is also the father of the six-week-old embryo growing in my womb—is married.

CHAPTER TWELVE

Quinn

"FAMILY OF MARGARET Moore," calls a middle-aged man in blue scrubs and a surgical cap.

I put down my phone and jump to my feet, and Zack rises, too. We've been in the hospital's surgery waiting room for the last hour and a half, but it feels like twice as long.

I've spent most of that time avoiding him. I can barely mentally grasp the fact that he's Lily's bio dad, much less the father of my unborn baby. It just feels like too much, trying to deal with his unexpected appearance and Miss Margaret's health crisis all at the same time. Instead of trying to make conversation, I've paced the hallway and talked on the phone.

I called Alicia's mother, explained Margaret's emergency, and made arrangements for her to keep Lily until I can get free. I called the moving company and canceled the pack-up and moving appointment. I called Margaret's minister. I tried to call Annie and Sarah from my single parents group, but ended up leaving voice mails when neither picked up. I called the Realtor who was supposed to come by the house to sign a listing agreement with Margaret. Last of all, I called my assistant, Terri. I told her about Margaret, and then found myself spilling the whole story about Zack—including the fact that I'm pregnant with his child.

Terri is good in a crisis. After Hurricane Katrina hit New Orleans, she and her husband rescued people from attics and rooftops in their recreational motorboat. In one case, she'd coaxed an elderly woman into coming out her attic window and climbing into the boat. Hopefully she can talk me down, too.

"I can't even allow myself to really think about what his presence might mean to my life right now," I tell her.

"You'll figure all that out later," she says. "Right now you're doing what needs to be done."

I draw in a deep breath. Terri's advice is reassuringly similar to what I read in *Reparenting Your Inner Child* just that morning: *When you're overwhelmed, just do the next thing that must be done.* I take it as a sign I'm on the right track.

"What can I do to help?" Terri asks.

"You liked that last applicant for the part-time manager position, didn't you? I think her name is April."

"Yes," Terri says. "She seems perfect."

"Well, would you please call her, offer her the job, and see if she can come in Tuesday to man the store? I'll need you to take over my client appointments."

I make other calls—to check on an upholstery job, to discuss the widening of a doorway with a contractor, to make a bid on two chairs at an online auction.

I've just settled back into the chair beside Zack when I hear the call for Margaret's family. It takes me a moment to recognize the scrubs-clad man as Dr. McFadden, the cardiologist I'd met in the emergency room, because his graying hair is covered by a surgical cap. But then, everything happened so fast in the ER it's doubtful I would have recognized him anyway.

Zack had pulled his BMW right behind the ambulance to let me out before he went to park. I dashed over as the paramedics unloaded Margaret, then followed as they wheeled her through the automatic glass doors. Margaret's eyes had been closed, her face pale, and she'd been breathing through an oxygen mask.

Zack had joined me as the paramedics transferred her to a hospital gurney. "She coded again in the ambulance," the male medic said. He looked up at Zack. "You saved her life with that CPR."

The staff quickly determined that Margaret was suffering a major heart attack and needed immediate angioplasty and stent placement. They also diagnosed her hip as not only broken, but splintered; she needed immediate surgery for that, as well. They'd whisked her away and directed us to the surgery waiting room, where half a dozen other people awaited word about their loved ones.

Now I follow the lanky heart specialist into the hallway for a private conversation. Zack comes, too.

"How is she?" I ask.

"Well, three arteries were involved," Dr. McFadden says. "One was completely blocked. We put in two stents and did a balloon procedure, and we've restored adequate blood flow."

Relief rushes through me. "So she'll be okay?"

The doctor rubs his jaw and adjusts his wire-rimmed glasses. "We've fixed the blockage, but she suffered some heart damage. I'd estimate she's lost between twenty and thirty percent of her heart's function. Because she immediately received CPR, though, we hope to see minimal brain damage."

My stomach clenches. "Brain damage?"

His head dips in a curt nod. "Anytime the blood flow to the brain is blocked or compromised, you have the potential for damage. Because of her age and the hip fracture, we can't do a medically induced coma, which we might consider otherwise."

My thoughts tumble like socks in a clothes dryer.

"Her hip break is another story. She's in surgery now for that, and as you know, that requires total sedation."

I nod. An orthopedic surgeon had briefed me in the emergency room. As I understood it, the ragged edge of her splintered bone was in danger of puncturing an artery.

"The sedation alone is a risk at her age, and I don't like the added stress of a lengthy surgery right after the heart procedure, but we have no choice. The heart problem and the hip break complicate each other. Because of the complexity of the break, her movement will be severely limited for some time, which will put her more at a risk of heart failure."

"But you think she'll fully recover?" I press.

He hesitates, then speaks slowly, as if he's choosing his words with care. "If she does well through the hip surgery and stabilizes within the next twenty-four hours, I think she'll make it."

Make it. That means she'll stay alive. The fact that he's wording it this way indicates a distinct possibility she won't.

"As far as how full her recovery will be . . ." He takes off his glasses, rubs the bridge of his nose, and sighs. "I'm afraid this is a life-changing event."

"Life changing . . . what do you mean?"

"We'll have to wait and see, and of course we hope for the best possible outcome, but she's nearly eighty. She's in good shape for a woman her age, but it's likely she'll never have the same quality of life as before." The explanation sounds well practiced. I imagine it's one he has to repeat all too often. "She might achieve something close to it, but she'll need assistance and rehabilitative care for quite a long while."

"How long a while?"

"I honestly don't know. The orthopedic surgeon can give you some better answers, but it will depend on three factors. The first one is how well she comes through the hip surgery." He holds up a finger, then adds a finger with each point. "The second is how much, if any, brain damage she has from the heart attack; and thirdly, how well she's able to handle physical therapy."

My legs feel like they're about to fold beneath me.

"She's going to be hospitalized for a good while—a week or two. If things go well, she'll be transferred to our rehabilitation hospital or a skilled nursing facility for another few weeks. The staff here can help you sort out decisions about her long-term care as we get closer to discharge."

I bob my head, trying to process everything he's said. "Thank you, Doctor," I mumble.

Zack leans forward. "Will you continue treating her while she's in the hospital, or will another cardiologist take over?"

"I'll continue seeing her and monitoring her heart."

"What time do you make rounds?" Zack asked.

"Usually at six thirty in the morning. But she'll be in ICU for the next twenty-four to forty-eight hours." He turns to leave.

"One more question, Doctor. Do you know when the hip surgery is starting?" Zack asks. "I believe the orthopedic surgeon said it would take two to four hours."

The cardiologist nods. "He was scrubbing in as I left, so it should be getting under way now."

"Thank you," Zack says.

"My pleasure." Dr. McFadden shakes Zack's hand. "I wish you and your grandmother the best of luck." The doctor shakes my hand almost as an afterthought before he walks away.

"He thinks Margaret's your grandmother," I say, feeling a little slighted.

"Sorry." Zack's eyes—good grief, they look so much like Lily's—are apologetic. "I didn't mean to butt in, but those were the kinds of questions I wish I'd asked when my mom was in surgery."

It's hard to argue with that, even though a part of me would like to. Ever since I realized who he was, I've been filled with anxiety. What was Miss Margaret thinking, contacting a registry to find him? Brooke hadn't wanted the sperm donor to play any role in Lily's life.

And Lily's life isn't the only place he doesn't belong. He sure as hell doesn't belong in mine. My stomach pitches with nausea.

He gazes at me intently. His dark brows pull together. "Are you okay?"

Damn it, he doesn't seem to miss a thing—and I have one of those faces that shows everything I'm feeling. Morning sickness just started making an appearance this week, and it isn't limited to just mornings. The last thing I want to do is tell him I'm pregnant, though. I sink down on a bench in the hallway. "I think I need to eat something," I say. "I sometimes start feeling bad when my blood sugar gets low."

He sits down beside me. "Are you diabetic?"

"No, nothing like that." I dig a half-eaten energy bar out of my purse. "But stress and hunger are a bad combination for me."

"Well, let's go to the cafeteria," he says. "We have at least two hours before we can expect to hear anything."

I balk at spending more time with him. "Don't you have someplace you need to be?" As I say it, I hear how ungracious it sounds. "I mean, you don't have to stay here. I appreciate all you've done, but this really isn't your problem."

"It feels like it is," he says. "Maybe my showing up brought it on."

Part of me wants to agree. *I'd* nearly had a heart attack when I learned Lily's father was standing on the doorstep. But then, Margaret had initiated contact with him, so it couldn't have been a total surprise to her.

I take a bite of the energy bar. As much as I want to blame him, it's unfair to let him blame himself.

"Margaret was under the weather before you arrived," I say. "In fact, she lost her balance and fell earlier this morning."

"She did?"

I nod. "She didn't fall from a height and she landed on thick carpeting, so she wasn't hurt. But still, it was unlike her."

"What was she doing on that step stool in the kitchen?"

"She was getting down the good crystal for your water."

"Why?"

A wry grin pulls at my mouth. "You're not from the South, are you?"

He shakes his head. "Ohio."

"Well, down here, it's what ladies of her generation do for company."

"Oh, good grief! I thought she'd just bring me a plastic bottle."

The truth is, I'd thought that, too—which indicates I hadn't really given it any thought at all. If I had, I wouldn't have let her go into the kitchen alone, no matter how insistent she'd been.

But then, Margaret had already climbed on the stool and inventoried the contents of the upper cabinets last night or this morning before I arrived, because a sticker saying *Pack for Storage* was affixed to one of the glasses on the top shelf.

I tell him this. "You're not to blame, so please, don't feel like you have to stay here. Your wife must be wondering where you are." I'm ready for him to leave, because my queasiness is getting worse.

"She's, um, in Seattle."

"Oh, that's a beautiful city! What's she doing there?"

"Visiting her family and house hunting. We're moving there in a few weeks."

Moving? Relief floods me. If he moves to the West Coast, he won't be interfering in my life. I haven't had a chance to fully think through all the implications of having him show up, but I've thought through enough to be terrified.

"Anyway, if it's okay with you," he continues, "I'd like to hang around and find out how the surgery goes. I feel pretty invested in the outcome."

How can I say no? He saved Margaret's life. "Sure. No problem."

His disconcertingly blue eyes stay on me, and he pulls his brows together. "You don't look like you feel so good."

I don't. That bite of power bar isn't sitting well and the nausea is reaching a crisis point. "I—uh . . . Excuse me," I say. I rise from the hall bench and dash across the hall to the ladies' room.

I heave into the toilet. When I finish, I wash my face and rinse my mouth, then chew a couple of mints. I feel like a new person when I rejoin him in the hallway a few minutes later.

He gazes at me in that intense way again and I wonder if he can tell I just barfed. "Are you all right?"

I nod.

"Want to head to the cafeteria?" he asks.

"Okay." I try to make conversation in order to appear normal as we walk to the elevator. "This move to Seattle—is it to live closer to her family, or for work?"

"Both reasons." He tells me about his wife's career with an international hotel chain and her new regional position. "I've taken the Uniform Bar Exam so I can practice law in most states. I'm joining a new firm out there."

The elevator arrives, and we have it to ourselves. "What kind of law do you practice?"

"Corporate. I specialize in mergers, acquisitions, and mediation."

That sounds pretty specialized, all right. "When are you moving?" I ask.

"Well, Jessica has to be out there permanently at the beginning of June. I'll stay behind to finish up a couple of mergers, then I'll join her in mid-July, early August."

"Do you have children?" I ask as the elevator opens on the atrium level.

"No. Not yet."

So he wants them. I file that information away. "What does Jessica think about you seeking out Lily?"

He blinks, and his mouth briefly tightens. It's almost, but not quite, a flinch. "She doesn't know."

I raise my eyebrows in surprise.

He shrugs. "She's the one who found the donor registry site, uploaded my information, and told me a child was looking for me, so she must have figured I would."

"Your wife registered to find your child?"

"Yeah." The word comes out like a fastball—quick and hard, as if it's a topic he wants to blow right past.

"I don't really understand," I say. "You signed an agreement to remain anonymous. That was extremely important to Brooke."

He nods. "I get that, and I intended to honor that. But then Jessica found this site and told me a child was looking for me. I thought I was dealing with a teenager going through the 'who am I?' phase who'd registered on his or her own to find me, or maybe had a medical need. I had no way of knowing it was a young child—or the grandmother reaching out because the child's mother died."

"Great-grandmother," I say. "Margaret is Lily's great-grandmother."

"I stand corrected." The corners of his eyes crease as he smiles.

"What would you have done if your child had answered the door?"

"I wouldn't have said anything about who I was or why I was there, if that's what you're asking."

I nod. That's exactly what I wanted to know.

"I would have just asked for Brooke," he continues. "If she weren't at home or if we couldn't talk privately, I would have just left my business card." He opens the door to the cafeteria for me. "I don't want to cause any problems."

"That's good to hear," I say.

"So you'll take care of Lily while Margaret's in the hospital?"

"Yes—and probably from here on out. I'm her legal guardian if Miss Margaret is unable to care for her. It's in her mother's will."

"I see." His expression doesn't tell me what he thinks of the arrangement. He hands me a tray. "Who's watching her today?"

"She's playing with a friend who lives two doors down from her old house." I place the tray on the slide rail. I want him to know that I've already covered her care for the rest of the day. He needs to realize that I'm more than qualified to care for Lily. "I called the friend's mother and filled her in on what's happening. She said Lily's welcome to stay there as long as necessary so I can be here with Margaret." I move my tray forward. "I'll get her reenrolled in her old preschool on Monday morning. I know her schedule and her friends and their parents, so she'll be right at home back in New Orleans in no time."

"Sounds like she's lucky to have you," he says. "What's she like?"

"Oh, she's the sweetest, most adorable, smartest little girl in the world."

His dimple flashes as he smiles. "I'd love to meet her."

My stomach gnarls. Why, oh why had I made her sound so appealing? But then, how could I have done otherwise?

"I—I don't think that's wise right now," I manage. "She's just lost her mother, and now her Grams is seriously ill. I don't think she should have to deal with another big drama."

"She doesn't have to know that I'm her father. You could just introduce me as your friend."

Is he a friend, or is he a foe? My gut instinct is to keep him as far away from Lily as possible. "Let's see how things go with Margaret first."

"Sure. No hurry. Do you have a picture of her?"

My phone is full of Lily photos. I nod.

"I'd love to see them when we sit down."

I don't want to show them to him, but I can't find a reason to refuse. After all, Margaret reached out to him.

"Sure," I say. I take a turkey sandwich, but my appetite has deserted me.

CHAPTER THIRTEEN

Quinn

"WOW—SHE'S AMAZING!" Zack stares at a photo on my cell phone of Lily playing with Ruffles. We're seated at a table against the wall, our partially eaten food on trays in front of us. The hospital cafeteria is crowded and noisy, but Zack seems oblivious to everything but the image of Lily. "I can't get over the family resemblance. She looks like just like my sister!"

"You and your sister must look alike." I'm feeling better after forcing down a few bites of sandwich, but I'm too jangled by everything that's happened to want to eat.

"We do." He stares at the picture as if he's trying to memorize it. "Do you have any other photos of her?"

I give a wry grin. "As Miss Margaret would say, 'Does a sack of flour make a big biscuit?'"

He laughs. I take my phone and scroll to a photo of Lily, Brooke, and me at the Bacchus parade last Mardi Gras. Lily is wearing butterfly wings and antennae, Brooke is wearing matching antennae and a caterpillar cape, and I'm wearing a padded brown costume with a pointed brown cap. We're supposed to be the three stages of a butterfly's life cycle, but instead of looking like a chrysalis, I resemble a poop emoji.

I rapidly scroll to the next photo. Lily's arms are raised to catch an airborne string of beads while Brooke watches, her smile so fond and tender that my breath catches. I pass the phone to him again.

"That's Brooke?" Zack asks.

I nod.

"Tell me about her."

"Oh, I don't even know where to begin," I say.

"Well, how did you two meet?"

"In college." I tell him about sitting beside her in class.

"What was she like?"

"Supersmart and warmhearted and hardworking. She was one of those people who could do anything."

"I googled her while you were on the phone this morning," he says. "It seems like she had everything going for her."

I nod, my throat tight with emotion.

"So why did she go the donor route?" he asks. "Didn't she want to get married or have a partner?"

"Yes, but she hadn't met the right person, and she had severe endometriosis. She had surgery twice, but the doctors couldn't fix the problem. When she was thirty-three, a specialist told her, 'If you ever want to have children, you'd better do it soon.'"

My mind drifts back to the phone call when Brooke told me about it. I give Zack only a summary, but I can replay it in my brain practically word for word.

Five years earlier

IT WAS EARLY evening after work. I was heating up leftovers in my apartment in Atlanta when Brooke telephoned.

"I sat down today and made a list of the ways a woman can get pregnant," Brooke said. "I came up with four."

"Only four?" I opened the microwave and stirred yesterday's Chinese takeout. "Where's your imagination? The Kama Sutra lists more than sixty."

"Not positions, you perv. Situations."

I laughed. "And there are only four?"

"As far as I can tell."

"And you listed them." Of course she did; Brooke made lists for everything. "Did you make a spreadsheet of pros and cons?"

"No."

"Call me back when you've finished that," I teased. "I'll also want to see graphs, comparison charts, and illustrations."

"Very funny. Do you want to hear this or not?"

"Absolutely," I said. "I may even want to write it down myself."

"I definitely think you should."

I winced. At that point I'd been dating Tom for two years, and he still refused to discuss the future any further out than weekend plans. Brooke thought I should end it and move on, but I kept thinking—Brooke called it *fantasizing*—that he would change. "I'm all ears."

"All right." I heard clicking sounds, and pictured Brooke opening a file on her laptop. "Number one: a woman meets the love of her life and gets married."

"That's the dream."

"Yes, but neither of us has had any luck with that one so far."

"I'm still hoping," I said.

"Yeah, well, my doctor says I'm running out of time. And if you keep all your eggs in Tom's basket, you will be, too."

"Hey, thanks a lot!"

"I'm just being honest here." That was one thing about Brooke; you could always count on her to tell you exactly what she thought. "Number two: a woman has a relationship with a man, conceives a child, and may or may not get married."

"Wow. Very iffy and complicated. Also unethical if it's deliberate on the woman's part without the man's knowledge."

"I agree, so let's move on. Number three: a woman consumes massive amounts of tequila with a viable male stranger—preferably one she'll never see again, maybe in a foreign city or at an airport bar—and things just happen."

"That's absolutely terrifying!"

"I know, right?"

"So what's the last one?"

"Number four: a woman uses a sperm donor."

I gave a derisive snort. "Yeah, right."

"Hey—I'm completely serious about this." I could tell from the change in her tone that she was. "I haven't met anyone for the marriage route, so I'm going with number four."

"Did you talk to Miss Margaret about this?" I asked. "What did she say?"

"She's not a fan of the idea," Brooke admitted. "She said a child needs two parents. And I agree, that's the ideal scenario, but I'm in a less-than-ideal situation. I'd rather have a child on my own than never have one at all. If it's going to happen, I have to make it happen."

I'd been a little shocked. I'd never known anyone who just up and decided to have a baby on her own, but then, I'd never known anyone as self-directed as Brooke. With her typical hyperefficiency, Brooke set a plan into action.

Her doctor advised that she reduce the amount of stress in her life, so she left her high-pressured, near-constant-travel position in New York and took a less demanding job in New Orleans. She found a local organization of people who were contemplating single parenthood, were in the process of trying to conceive, or had already borne or adopted a child on their own. She attended a meeting, and was soon a regular at their monthly gatherings. The members gave her lots of advice, and she signed up with a highly recommended local cryobank. She pored over data about sperm donors and read reams of profiles.

"We went about dating in college all wrong. These men are fantastic!" she'd told me in another phone call. "We should have been hanging out at cryobanks instead of bars and sports events."

All of the men were tall—this cryobank didn't accept applicants under six feet, because, apparently, height was in demand—and they were all either college students or college graduates at the time of their donations. They were exceedingly healthy; they'd undergone blood, genetic, and personality testing. They'd written personal statements, submitted photos of themselves as children, and recorded audio interviews so we could hear their voices. There were no photos of the donors as adults in order to preserve their anonymity, but the cryobank staff had evaluated each one, compiled facial profiles, and given their overall impressions of each man. Brooke had insisted on seeing every donor, including those in the older "archived" files.

After weeks of study, Brooke had whittled down the field to one donor. "He's brilliant, good-looking, compassionate, kind, and he has a great sense of humor. But there's one thing that makes him absolutely irresistible."

"What's that?" I'd asked.

"He does yo-yo tricks!"

Wow, you think you know somebody. "You consider yo-yo tricks irresistible?" I'd asked incredulously.

"Absolutely," Brooke had replied. "My father did yo-yo tricks."

Brooke had adored her father, so that was that. She took fertility drugs, which, with her endometriosis, caused her excruciating pain—but the doctors were able to extract a few eggs. Only one was successfully fertilized, but one was all it took.

Nine months later, Lily was born—beautiful, wonderful Lily.

ZACK'S EYEBROWS RISE as I finish relating all this. "So Brooke picked me because I do yo-yo tricks?"

"That was a key factor, yeah." There were other things about him that played into her decision—not to mention mine. She'd shown me his profile when she first chose him, and then again when she'd offered me the remaining sperm.

Both of us had adored the essay Zack had written about his love of family and his desire to make the world a better place. We'd been impressed that he volunteered at Habitat for Humanity and wanted to do pro bono work when he got his law degree. The photo of him as an eight-year-old had shown off his dimple and his vivid blue eyes, and I think we'd both fallen a little in love with him when we heard the tape of his voice. He'd been answering the question, "Who is your role model?" and he'd been talking about his dad.

"That's crazy." Zack grins and shakes his head. "This whole situation is crazy."

Yeah, and you don't know the half of it.

A country song belts out of a cell phone at the next table, where two men in scrubs are eating. One of them picks up the phone and turns it off. "That's the ringtone for my ex-wife," he tells his companion. "'Crazy,' by Patsy Cline."

Zack glances over at the men, then looks back at me. "That's weird, isn't it? I just said the situation was crazy, and then that song played."

"That's the universe's way of confirming something." I smile as if I'm joking, but I mean it. I'm sure it's a sign, but I don't know if it's a good one or a warning. Given the events of the day, it's most likely a warning.

All of the warm feelings I had while thinking about Brooke suddenly freeze into worry. I worry how Margaret's doing in surgery and if she'll be okay. I worry how Lily will handle her great-grandmother's hospitalization. I worry about why Margaret contacted Zack, why he's here, and what that means to Lily. I worry what all this means to my baby.

I'm suddenly freaking out all over again about the fact that I'm carrying Zack's child. I just met this man, yet his child is growing inside me. How crazy is that?

"Are you okay?" he asks.

"Yeah," I say. "I'm just worried about Margaret."

And you, I think. *I'm very worried about you, and how you could affect the lives of those I love.*

CHAPTER FOURTEEN

Margaret

I'M SPINNING, SPINNING, spinning, like a soap bubble circling a drain. Only . . . the drain is upside down, and enormous. And instead of being full of water, it's full of light—warm, loving, beckoning light.

Light, and people. I squint against the glare, trying to see. I can only make out shadows, but they're familiar. I recognize the way they move. Is that my darling Henry? Oh, yes, that's him—I'm sure of it! I pirouette and jeté—I'm suddenly able to dance like the most talented ballerina, even though I've never had a lesson! Henry is dancing, too—dancing toward me. The images become clearer: there's my daughter, Julia, and—oh, just look!—there's Brooke. And my mother and father, and my grandparents, and my younger sister. They're all smiling and waving. I'm happy, so happy to see them. I've never experienced such intense peace, such profound joy.

I try to move toward them, to enter more fully into the embracing light surrounding them, but I can't break out of this circular current. I'm locked in a holding pattern, going around and around the entrance.

"Mrs. Moore?"

All of a sudden, the warm, loving light drains out, pulling my loved ones with it. I open my eyes and see a stranger's face looming over me, backlit by blinding fluorescent tubes on the ceiling. I close my eyes, wanting to go back to the other light, but I just see red through my lids.

"Can you hear me, Mrs. Moore?"

I try to talk, but my mouth is so dry I can't push words out of it. I make a noise that sounds like an animal's grunt.

"Mrs. Moore, you're in the hospital. I'm Melanie, your nurse. You had a heart attack and broke your hip."

I grunt again. Her words trigger no memories.

"You're in ICU," she says. "You just came out of surgery. Everything went very well and now you're recovering."

"Henry here?" My voice is a croak. "Julia?"

"Are those family members?"

"Yes." *They were with me a moment ago*, I try to say, but can't.

"There are two people waiting for you. Would you like to see them?"

"Yes."

"All right. Let me check a couple of things on you, and then I'll go get them."

Happiness bubbles inside me. Something squeezes on my arm—a blood pressure gauge, I think.

"Are you in pain?" the nurse asks.

"Throat. Hard to talk."

"That's from being intubated. It'll go away in a bit."

I close my eyes. The next thing I know, I hear a familiar voice. "Miss Margaret? How are you doing?"

I open my eyes and see a lovely, familiar-looking young woman leaning over me. She resembles my Brooke, but she isn't. I don't recognize the man beside her. "Where's Henry . . . Julia?" I rasp.

"They're not here," the young woman says.

I'm vaguely aware that disappointment and something else, something monstrous and dark and sinister, is in the room. The dark thing slithers around in a black corner. It's too terrifying to look at directly.

I open my eyes again and stare at my visitor. There seem to be several of her, and they're all fuzzy, like a TV screen that needs the antenna adjusted.

That's been a while, though. TVs don't have antennas anymore.

The concept of time as an ongoing, one-way street comes floating back; when I was in the other light, time didn't have any constraints. Here, under the greenish glare of fluorescent tubes, time confines me like a plaster cast, so prickly and painful it might be lined with cactus.

The beast in the dark corner rattles and snarls.

I didn't realize I'd closed my eyes until I force myself to open them again and try to focus on my visitor. "You—you look familiar."

"I'm Quinn. Remember? I'm Brooke's friend."

Brooke. Why isn't she here? Something flickers in my memory, and the monster growls.

"Are you in pain, Mrs. Moore?" the nurse asks.

Did I groan, or was it the creature? "I . . . yes." My hip and chest and head are throbbing, but I fear pain more than I feel it. I want to go back to the other light.

The nurse adjusts something by the bed. "I'm giving you some morphine. You should be more comfortable in a moment."

"Don't worry about anything, Miss Margaret. I'm taking care of Lily," my visitor says.

Lily! My memory flashes on the plump cheeks and blue eyes of an angelic child. My heart warms as I struggle to place her. She's Brooke's child, isn't she?

Brooke. Something happened to her—something monstrous. That's the dark thing lurking in the room, the thing I sense, but can't quite see.

It's suddenly beneath me, jaws open, swimming up like a shark, about to clamp razor-edged fangs around me. I try to get away; my heart rate rockets.

"V-tach!" someone calls. Immediately three people hover over me.

"I'm giving you something to lower your heart rate," the nurse says, messing with a tube in my arm.

The meds drag me under, and then, mercifully, everything goes black.

CHAPTER FIFTEEN

Zack

I DECIDE TO leave the hospital around five that evening, after making sure Margaret's heart has stabilized after that scary arrhythmia. A friend of Quinn's has shown up—a short young woman named Annie with big glasses. She eyes me curiously, but doesn't question who I am. I imagine Quinn told her on the phone.

"Can I give you a ride home?" I ask Quinn in the ICU waiting room.

"I want to stay for the next visitation time," she says.

"That's not for another three hours. You should at least let me take you to get your car."

"I'll take her," Annie says. "A friend who lives nearby has invited us over for dinner, so I'm planning on getting Quinn out of the hospital for a couple of hours anyway."

Quinn seems okay with that, so I say good-bye and head to my car. I know I need to call Jessica, but I put it off. I'm nearing my condo when my phone belts out "Endless Love"—the tune Jessica programmed it to play when she calls.

She phoned and texted several times earlier in the day and I just texted back, *Can't talk. Call you later.* She'd texted once to ask if I was still mad. *No*, I'd responded, although, hell, I probably am.

My shoulders tense as I answer the call on my car's Bluetooth. "Hi."

"Zack—I'm so, so sorry," she says in a rush. "I had no idea what a mess I was creating or how hard you'd take it when I went on that donor registry site."

I say nothing.

"I—I wasn't thinking. I apologize."

Again, I stay silent. I know it's hard for Jessica to make apologies. She hates to be wrong and it's hard for her to admit it when she is. Still, I just don't have anything to say.

"Are you there?"

"Yeah, I'm here."

"I've been thinking about you all day and wondering what you decided to do about the donor registry."

I blow out a sigh. "That's a long story."

"Well, it's two hours earlier here, so I have lots of time." Her voice has an artificially chipper tone to it. She's trying. Hell, I need to try, too.

I draw in a deep breath and launch into the whole tale. I explain how I'd gone on the site last night, how I'd received the phone number this morning, how I'd tried the number, how I'd gone to the address.

"You just went over there?" She sounds shocked. "That's kind of weird."

"It didn't seem it at the time."

"It's just not like you. It's sort of pushy and impolite."

So was impersonating me on a donor registry. "Hey, you're the one who set this whole thing in motion."

"I know, I know. And I'm so sorry. I-I'm sorry for everything." Her voice has the quaver she gets when she's about to cry. "I had no right to look through your papers or post your information on the donor site. I was completely out of line."

Damn straight, I think.

"Do you forgive me?" she asks.

"Yeah," I reply, although it doesn't quite feel like the truth. If I were being completely honest, I'd say something like, *I want to. I'm working on it.* But I don't think she can handle that, and I don't want to deal with a long-distance crying jag.

"So what happened when you went to the house?" she prompts.

I tell her the rest of it—about learning about Brooke's death, about Margaret's heart attack and broken hip, about Quinn being next in line as guardian, about Margaret's iffy condition.

"Oh, my God," she gasps. "My God!"

"And that's not all," I say. "I saw photos of her."

"Of Lily? What does she look like?"

I take a deep breath, then slowly exhale. "You know that big photo in my sister's house hanging over the piano, the one of her and me when we were preschoolers? The one I told you Mom used to keep in our living room?"

"The portrait where you and Charlotte look like twins?"

"Yeah, that's the one. Well, Lily looks like she belongs in that picture."

"Wow," Jess breathes. "So . . . what are you going to do?"

"About what?" I hedge.

"About Lily. I mean, where were things left as far as you're concerned?"

I blow out a sigh. "Nothing's settled. I need to talk to Margaret and find out why she wanted to contact me."

"Is she going to get better?"

"I think so, but she's unlikely to recover one hundred percent. In any case, she's in for a long haul of rehabilitation."

"So Lily will live with this friend? With this—this Quinn?"

"That seems to be the plan."

"I'll catch a flight back first thing tomorrow," she says. "We'll figure this out together."

"No. There's no need," I say quickly—maybe too quickly. I don't know why, but I'm not ready to see her. Maybe I'm still angry at her. Or maybe I want to figure out what *I* want to do before she tells me what *she* wants me to do.

That's probably the truth of it. I don't know my own mind on this yet, and I don't want to be influenced by her personal agenda. This strikes me as the wrong view to have in a marriage, but it's where I am at the moment. I decide to turn the conversation around. "So how are things out there? How's your family? How was the house hunting? Tell me about your day."

"My day pales in comparison to yours."

"Tell me about it anyway. You had an old high school chum show you some homes, right?"

"Brett went to my high school, but we moved in different circles. Anyway, he now owns a big real estate company, and he's a partner in a construction company that does renovations."

"Did you find a place you like?"

"There's one possibility. It needs some updating, but Brett says he could oversee the renovation, and the whole thing would come in under budget."

She launches into a detailed description, but I don't really follow what she's saying. My mind keeps rolling back to the photos of a little girl who clearly has my blood in her veins—a little girl who is technically an orphan.

CHAPTER SIXTEEN

Quinn

AFTER ZACK LEAVES the hospital, Annie drives me home. I feed Ruffles and call to check on Lily.

"She and Alicia are having a great time," Alicia's mother, Caroline, tells me. "She's welcome to spend the night."

I want Lily with me. I'm not sure how she'll react to learning that Margaret's in the hospital, and I want to be near to reassure her. Besides, Zack's unexpected appearance in our lives has made me feel oddly threatened. "If you don't mind keeping her awake until nine, I'll pick her up then," I say.

"No problem. It's the weekend, so we usually let Alicia stay up late anyway."

I drive to Sarah's house in Old Jefferson, a small neighborhood of raised cottages with large yards tucked between the hospital and the river levee. Sarah's home is nearly hidden from the street by oak trees and azalea bushes.

When I arrive, I realize she's invited the whole single parent group over for gumbo and salad. Mac is away at an equipment training seminar, but Lauren is there. She and Sarah greet me with hugs and a touching show of support. Annie has filled them in about Margaret's accident and Zack's unexpected appearance in my life.

By six fifteen, we're sitting on Sarah's back deck. Annie's eight-year-old son is pretending to be a robot as he chases Sarah's two-year-olds across the lawn, and the toddlers shriek with delight. I drink sparkling water while Annie, Sarah, and Lauren sip glasses of white wine.

"You won't believe how good-looking Lily's father is," Annie says. "Here—I pulled up his picture on Google." She passes her phone around.

Lauren's eyebrows rise as she looks at the photo, and she lets out a low whistle. "Oh, wow!"

"Lily looks just like him, doesn't she?" Annie continues. "You can see where she got those eyes. And that dimple!"

"He's amazing." Lauren smiles at me as she passes the phone to Sarah. "You're going to have a beautiful baby, Quinn."

I'd never thought otherwise. Lily is adorable, so I'd figured her sibling would be. I didn't really need to know that the bio dad is hot. In fact, it was simpler when he was nothing but a childhood photo, a bunch of data, and a donor vial. "Yeah," I mutter.

"And Zack is just as nice as he is handsome," Annie enthuses.

I didn't need or want to know that, either. I lift my shoulders. "I suppose."

"Wow, that's a less than ringing endorsement," Lauren says.

"Did I read things wrong?" Annie's brows crease.

"No, no, you're right," I say. "He's terrific. He saved Margaret's life, he drove me to the hospital, then he stayed all day to make sure she's okay."

"I sense a 'but' coming," Lauren says.

"Yeah," I say. "I have a big but."

"Not compared to me, you don't," Lauren says, sitting forward and slapping her curvy backside.

Everyone laughs.

"Sorry. I couldn't resist." Lauren grins. "You were saying, Quinn, that he's terrific, but . . ."

"He's supposed to be an *anonymous* donor—not a standing-on-the-doorstep, sitting-beside-me-at-the-hospital, asking-to-meet-Lily donor! Brooke didn't want him to play a role in Lily's life, and I don't want him in my baby's life, either. And quite frankly, I don't get why Margaret ever wanted to contact him."

"Brooke always said Margaret thought every child should have two parents," Sarah comments.

"Yes, and that worries me." I draw a breath and voice the fear that's made my blood run cold ever since I learned who he was. "I'm afraid Margaret wants him to be Lily's guardian instead of me."

"Oh, I can't imagine that!" Annie says. "She adores you, and so does Lily. And you've known Lily all her life. You were in the delivery room when she was born!"

"Yes, but Margaret totally believes that blood trumps friendship." I repeat what Margaret said that morning—that I wasn't really family because I wasn't a blood relative.

Lauren's eyes grew huge. "She said that?"

I nod. "She tried to soften the comment after she made it, but she also said that blood is thicker than water and she wanted to get Lily's father in the picture."

"'In the picture' could mean anything," Annie points out. "Didn't Brooke's parents die in an accident when she was young? And then Brooke's death was completely unexpected. Miss Margaret probably wants to line up another guardian for Lily in case, God forbid, something happens to you."

Lauren nods. "And you can't forget that when she said you weren't family, she was, what—a few minutes away from having a heart attack? She probably had reduced blood flow to her brain."

"I hope you're right," I say. "I'm afraid she thinks I won't be a good guardian to Lily because I don't come from a good family."

"Oh, Quinn—I'm sure that's not the case!" Annie exclaims.

I'm not sure of anything. Miss Margaret knows that my father left us and that my mother is a self-absorbed narcissist.

"All I know is that Zack's sudden appearance terrifies me," I say. "I don't want him meddling in Lily's life, and I don't want him thinking he has any claim on her or my baby."

"But how can he?" Lauren asks. "Didn't he sign away all his rights when he signed the donor agreement?"

"Yes, but then Margaret went on that registry looking for him," I say. "Who know what that does to the original agreement? Especially now that Brooke is dead."

"Miss Margaret doesn't know you're pregnant," Annie says. "If she did, she'd probably consider you a blood relative, too, because your child will be Lily's half sister."

"She's in no shape to comprehend that right now, so please don't tell her," I say. "I don't want her telling Zack he's the father of my baby, too." I fold my arms protectively over it. "I don't want to have to deal with custody arrangements and who gets who on holidays. I had so-called 'homes' with both parents"—I make air quotes around the word—"and it felt like I didn't have a real home anywhere."

Sarah has been quiet through the conversation. "That's because your parents mismanaged things," she now says softly. "Not every child in a shared custody situation has a bad experience. A lot of them thrive."

"But I don't *want* to share custody," I say. "I want Zack to stay out of my life."

"The original donor agreement will probably hold firm," Annie says.

"Zack and his wife don't have any children?" Lauren asks.

"I asked, and he said, 'not yet.'"

"So he wants them," Annie says.

"That's how I took it."

"What's the story on his wife?" Lauren asks.

"Her name is Jessica, she's a regional controller for a big hotel chain, and she just got a promotion to Seattle. I don't know much more than that."

Annie picks up her phone, punches a bunch of buttons, and scrolls the screen. "Found her!" She turns the screen toward us and flashes a photo of a beautiful brunette. Everyone leans in to look.

"Ooh, she's gorgeous," Lauren says. She takes the phone and scrolls down through her bio. "Apparently she's pretty brilliant, too."

"Sounds like Brooke," I say.

"And you," says Annie.

"This guy mates with very classy women," Lauren says.

Everyone laughs, but I squirm a little. "I didn't mate with him. Neither did Brooke!"

"One of your eggs sure did," Lauren says.

Annie turns to me. "If Zack is moving across the country in a few weeks, I don't think you have much to worry about. Distance will make it hard for him to interfere too much."

"He's already said he wants to meet Lily," I say.

"Uh-oh," Lauren mutters.

"Oh, wow," Annie murmurs.

"What did you tell him?" Sarah asks.

"That the last thing Lily needs right now is more confusion or drama."

Sarah leans forward. "How did he respond?"

"He said we don't need to tell her that he's her father. He just wants to meet her."

"That's kind of scary," Lauren said.

I nod. "I don't want him anywhere near her."

"On the other hand, you need to think about what's best for Lily in the long run," Sarah says. "She might resent it when she's a teenager if she learns you kept her from knowing her father."

My stomach tanks. "Oh, I hadn't thought of that!" There's so much about this parenting business that I don't know. I not only need to think about what's in Lily's best interests right now; I have to consider how every decision I make might impact her in the future. I've bought a bunch of parenting books since Brooke's death, but not every situation is covered.

"Maybe Zack can have some kind of limited role in her life," Sarah suggests. "He could be introduced as your friend and maybe become a distant uncle-like figure. That way Lily will grow up having a connection to him without it being anything official."

"What if he wants to make things official?" My fingers tighten around my glass of mineral water.

"Most things in life don't turn out to be as bad as we fear." Sarah's tone is calm, her eyes reassuring. "Maybe Lily can meet him, and the three of you can do a few things together before he moves to Seattle. Afterward, he could send birthday cards and Christmas cards to you and Lily—and include the baby, too, once it arrives. That wouldn't be so awful, right? Then, when Lily and your baby are older, you can tell them the truth—that their father has cared about them from the moment he first learned of their existence, but stayed in the background to honor the terms of the contract."

"That doesn't sound too bad," says Lauren.

Annie nods. "Actually, it sounds like a really good plan."

It does, if it's not too good to be true. In my experience, plans involving men tend to go south. I look at Sarah. "What would you do if the twins' father showed up on your doorstep?"

She lifts her hands, palms out. "Oh, I don't have a clue! A lot would depend on my gut instinct, I guess." She smiles. "Just because I'm a counselor doesn't mean I have all the answers. I pose questions to help people find their own solutions."

"But you seem to think Zack should meet Lily."

She lifts her shoulders. "In my experience, it's an asset for kids to have a variety of adults in their lives who love them and give them positive attention."

"That's a good thought," Annie says.

Lauren murmurs accord.

"Yeah, it is." I look at the caring faces of my friends and feel the tightness in my chest soften. "That's why I love you guys so much. I know you'll do that for Lily and my baby."

Annie nods. "Well, you give us and our kids lots of love and positive attention."

My eyes tear up. "I feel a lot better about things than I did when I got here."

We smile sappy smiles at each other. Annie pats my arm. "What time do you need to be back at the hospital?"

I glance at my watch. "In an hour. Evening ICU visitation is from eight to eight thirty."

Sarah stands up and gestures to the kitchen. "Well, then, ladies—I say it's time we eat!"

CHAPTER SEVENTEEN

Quinn

IT'S NEARLY NINE that evening when I arrive to pick up Lily at her friend Alicia's house. A piece of notebook paper is taped to the front door: *Please don't ring doorbell. Baby sleeping.*

I softly knock. Through the sidelight, I see Lily and Alicia race to the foyer. Caroline, a freckled, sweet-faced woman about my age, is right behind them.

"Auntie Quinn!" Lily exclaims in a whisper. She bounces up and down on her toes as Caroline opens the door, then hurls herself into my arms.

I crouch down and hug her. "Good to see you, sweetie! Did you have a nice day?"

"Yes! We played dress-up an' went to the snowball stand an' I rode Alicia's tricycle an' we watch'd-ed *Pinocchio*."

"For about the five hundredth time," Caroline says dryly. "Then I chased them outside."

"An' we looked for crickets an' had hot dogs for dinner," Lily reports.

"Soy dogs," Caroline corrects. "With carrots and peas."

"Where were you? I thought you an' me an' Grams were gettin' pizza tonight."

I shift from a crouch to a kneel. I put my hands on the backs of Lily's arms and look into her blue, blue eyes. "Well, that was the plan. But your grams got sick and had a bad fall, so she had to go to the hospital."

Lily's mouth opens. Her bottom lip quivers. "Is she dead?"

My heart aches that she immediately goes to the worst-case scenario. "No, honey. But she had to have an operation, so she has to stay there for a little while."

"Hospitals are where people go to die." Her eyes fill with tears, and she sticks her thumb in her mouth.

"Hospitals help people get well, honey."

"But Mommy died goin' to one."

My throat swells. "Your mom had an unusual health problem that happened very fast, and she died before she could get to a hospital. But Grams got to the hospital in time and the doctors treated her."

"So she'll get better?"

How am I supposed to answer that? I don't dare promise she will, but I don't want to upset Lily any more than necessary. "The doctors think so. They're doing everything they can to give her the best chance of recovery."

"What's a 'chance of 'covery'?"

Oh, the things that a three-year-old has yet to learn! I hate that these lessons have come so early in Lily's life. "It means she'll probably get well, but it's not definite."

"What's 'def'nite'?"

Nothing but death and taxes. Jeez, what's wrong with my brain? It's been a long, long day. "'Definite' means something we know for sure. Like how I love you and always will."

"Will you take care of me now?"

Tears gather in my eyes. "Yes, sweetie. I'll do my very best to take very, very good care of you."

Her eyes brighten. "So I get to live with you?"

"Yes, honey."

"Forever an' always?"

"Well, we'll have to wait and see how thing go with Miss Margaret, but you'll be with me at least through the summer."

"Yay!" Alicia cheers. Lily cheers with her.

"We don't want to wake the baby," Caroline says, putting her finger to her mouth. "Lily, you'd better go gather up your things to go home. Alicia, please help her."

I stand up as they scamper off.

"Kids this age are totally focused on the moment," Caroline says apologetically. "Please don't think they don't care about Margaret."

"I don't. Lily was relieved her Grams isn't dead, and relief translates into happy."

"That's it, exactly," Caroline says.

I only wish my reactions were as simple. I'm exhausted and overwhelmed by everything I'm thinking and feeling. How can so many emotions—sadness about Margaret's health, joy about my baby, grief about Brooke, delight to have custody of Lily, and terror about Zack's sudden presence in my life—coexist in one person at the same time?

THIRTY MINUTES LATER, I've tucked Lily into bed in my guest bedroom and fallen into a restless doze in my own. I don't think I fully sleep; my dreams are a weird mishmash of memories that slide back and forth in time and keep me tossing and turning. I dream of Brooke. I dream of my brother, who is ten years older than me and as distant as a total stranger. I dream of my father's second wife and my mother's third husband. I dream of my childhood home in the Lakeside area of New Orleans.

I dream of my eighth birthday—or do I just remember it? It's as if the years roll back and I'm living it again.

I'm waiting in the front yard early on a Saturday afternoon, because Daddy said we'd go to the zoo when he gets home. There's a chocolate cake in the kitchen from Schwegmann's grocery for later. Mommy didn't bake it; she says baking's a waste of time and that store-bought birthday cakes are better, anyway. I wanted to have a party, but Mommy says a roomful of children would work on her nerves and make a big mess, and wouldn't it be better to spend the afternoon at the zoo with her and Daddy?

I'm really excited. I can't remember the last time we all went someplace together, and I love the zoo. I wait and I wait, and the sun sinks lower in the sky. I go inside and ask Mommy why Daddy's taking so long. Mommy's opened a bottle of wine, and she's drinking it from a big plastic cup as she talks on the phone. I can tell she's talking to her friend Michelle because she's using her loud laugh and bad language. She puts her hand over the receiver and arches an annoyed eyebrow at me. She says Daddy probably went to the racetrack to spend all our money and get drunk. I hear the faint braying of Michelle's laugh through the receiver.

It doesn't sound to me like Mommy's joking, but Michelle's laughter makes me hope she is. I go back outside and wait some more. It's starting to get dark and cold, and Daddy still hasn't come. My chest feels all hollow. I go back inside the house.

Mommy's still on the phone. She says Daddy's not going to show up and that I'm creating a spectacle for the neighbors, mooning around on the porch all woebegone. She says Daddy's unreliable and that I should know better than to count on him. She says I should put a frozen dinner in the microwave if I'm hungry.

I don't have any appetite. When Mommy gets off the phone, she goes in her bathroom and puts on lots of makeup, like she does when she's getting ready to go out to clubs with her lady friends. She sometimes goes out and doesn't come home until really late. The next morning she reeks of wine and cigarette smoke, and her eyes are all rimmed with mascara because she didn't wash it off before she went to bed.

Mommy comes out of her bedroom smelling of perfume and wearing a dress that Daddy said is too low-cut. She looks really pretty, but I beg her not to go out tonight, because it's my birthday.

"Oh, that's right!" she says. She opens drawers, looking for candles, and only finds two. "These are special candles," she says, holding them up. They look like the same candles she used on my cake last year. "They're each worth four years. Since you're eight, we only need two." She sticks them in the cake, lights them, and sings me the birthday song.

I make a wish—I wish that Daddy and Mommy won't fight and that we'll go to the zoo tomorrow—and I blow out the candles. She cuts me a piece of cake, then gives me three gift-wrapped boxes. I open the pink one first and find new pajamas, almost exactly like the ones I already have. The yellow box holds underwear and socks. I smile, because I can tell Mommy wants me to be pleased, but pajamas, underwear, and socks are not what my eight-year-old heart desires. I want a Polly Pocket Cozy Cottage play set. I don't need a dozen sets like most of my friends have, but I only have the Pony Stable play set, and I want my doll to have a home.

The turquoise package holds a Polly Pocket play set, all right—but it's the Shetland Pony Stables, exactly the same as the one I already have.

"Do you like your toy?" Mom's mouth stretches over her big teeth into the smile she gets when she's pleased with herself. "It's really cute, isn't it?"

I try really hard not to cry.

Mother's forehead gets that ugly frown that makes my stomach feel like someone's pulling a belt too tight around my insides. "What's the matter?" she demands.

I don't dare tell her. She'll call me an ingrate and get mad like she did at Christmas. I'm not crying because I didn't get the right Polly Pocket; I'm crying because my mommy doesn't know which one I already have, even though I play with it all the time. There must be something with wrong with me, because my mother doesn't pay attention to me the way my friends' mothers do. She's always telling me I'm a big bother.

But I can't tell her that's the reason I'm fighting back tears. "I don't want you to go out and leave me by myself," I say.

"You won't be," she says. "Jade's coming over to babysit you."

I don't like Jade. She's the thirteen-year-old daughter of Mom's friend and she never wants to play. She just watches grown-up TV shows and talks on the phone, and if I say something to her, she tells me to shut up and leave her alone.

"Don't leave me on my birthday," I beg Mommy.

She takes a big slurp of wine. She tells me I'm selfish and childish, and I have no idea what she's going through. She's the one who gave birth to me, so she should be the one to get presents on my birthday, anyway. I should feel bad for being such an ungrateful daughter.

And I do. I feel so, so bad that I cry. She gets even madder at me for crying, so I go back outside and wait for Daddy. He doesn't come. Instead, Michelle drives up, drops off Jade, and . . .

"Auntie Quinn?"

I open my eyes. Lily is standing by my bed, sobbing. Her thumb is in her mouth, and Sugar Bear is clasped in her other hand.

I abruptly sit up. "What's the matter, sweetheart?"

"I had a bad dream."

It seems to be a night for those. But I wasn't really dreaming, was I? It doesn't count as a dream if it really happened.

"I'm so sorry, honey." I swing my feet to the floor and hold out my arms, and Lily climbs into my lap, dragging Sugar Bear with her. I feel her tears on my shoulder as she snuggles her head there. I pat her back, between her slight shoulder blades. "It's okay. Dreams aren't real."

"It felt real."

"Sometimes they do." My fingers sift through her hair. "Do you want to talk about it?"

She nods. "I was lost-ed in a big crowd of peoples. I kept lookin' an' lookin' for Mommy, but I couldn' find her. An' then I looked for Grams or you or someone I knew, but no one had the right face." She wraps her arms around my neck.

I put my chin on top of her hair and pull her close. "Oh, sweetie—that was a bad dream, for sure. But it wasn't real."

"But what if it 'comes real? What if everyone I love dies an' goes 'way?"

"That won't happen, Lily."

"But Mommy died, an' Grams is in the hospital."

"I know, sweetie, but I'm taking care of you. I love you and I'll always be here for you."

"But what if *you* die? If Mommy could die, you could, too."

Poor honey. And oh, dear God—I can't deny that she has a point. "That's very, very unlikely to happen. And anyway, you have other people who will always love and take care of you. There's Alicia's mother, and Miss Terri, and Miss Sarah, and Miss Annie, and . . ." I run out of names. In truth, I'm naming people who might babysit, not people who are lined up to actually take her if I can't. I need to figure that out—both for Lily and for the baby I'm carrying. I push the troubling thought aside to deal with later. "You'll never be alone, sweetheart. I promise. You just had a really bad dream."

"It made me feel 'fraid and terr'ble."

"Bad dreams can make us feel that way."

"But this feeling is the 'wake kind, too."

Inadequacy rolls over me like a street paver. I pray for the right thing to say, then pull out a Sarah-esque question. "What are you thinking about now?"

Her voice is small and muffled against my neck. "I'm afraid I made Grams sick."

I hold her close and pat her back. "Oh, honey—you didn't. I promise."

"But I wanted to move back here and live with you, and I wished I could. I didn' mean to wish her sick."

"Of course you didn't, sweetheart."

"But what if I did?" She pulls back and looks at me. Fresh tears flow down her face.

"It doesn't work like that. You can't just wish for things and make them happen."

"But Mommy said I could do anythin' I set my mind to."

"She didn't mean just by wishing, honey. People make dreams come true by taking action like going to school and studying and practicing and working really hard. None of us has the power to just wish for something and make it happen."

"That's the way how it worked in *Pinocchio*."

"Sweetheart, you know the difference between pretend and real life, right?"

"Yes."

"Well, *Pinocchio* is pretend."

"Are you sure?"

"Very sure."

"But the Pinocchio story is old!"

"Make-believe stories can be old. Besides, if wishes came true, your mom would still be here, right? Because that's what you really wish."

Her head is warm against my shoulder. "Yeah. I wished an' wished for that, an' even used-ed my magic wand over an' over an' over. An' I prayed to God."

I stroke her silky hair, lifting a strand and letting it filter through my fingers. My chest aches like a cracked tooth.

"Why did Mommy have to die?"

"I don't know, sweetie."

"Does God know?"

"Yes. He knows everything." Unlike me. Right now, I feel like I know nothing—least of all how to comfort this grieving child.

"Can he see Mommy?"

"Yes, sweetie."

"I want to see her, too. I want us to be together."

I say a silent prayer and take my best shot. "You're still together in your heart." Even to my ears, it sounds like a useless platitude.

"I don' jus' want her in my heart! I want Mommy *here*, with arms an' a face an' a *lap*!"

My eyes fill. "I know, sweetie. I know." I feel entirely inadequate. I don't know what else to say. I rock her until Ruffles jumps on the bed and uses her paws to try to wedge between us.

Mercifully, this makes Lily giggle.

"Ruffles wants a hug, too," I say. The little dog licks Lily's cheek.

Lily smiles and embraces the long-haired moppet. "Can I sleep with you and Ruffles?"

"Sure," I say, then remember the potty training slips Miss Margaret mentioned. "But first, I think we should both use the bathroom."

"Okay."

Afterward, Lily, Sugar Bear, Ruffles, and I pile back into my bed. I read a story about a puppy, a kitten, and a rabbit until Lily falls asleep.

I turn out the lamp, then snuggle next to her, listening to her soft, rhythmic breathing. The room is dark, and so are my thoughts.

Another memory floats through my mind. I'd just come into the house from school, and my mother was on the telephone. I heard my name and froze.

"Quinn was a mistake," I heard her say. "I never intended to have another baby after Will. I was already four months gone when I found out I was pregnant, so there was nothing to be done but have her. I cried for a full week."

I stood there in the hallway, my eleven-year-old body quivering. I was too young to fully understand, but I understood enough: I wasn't wanted.

A mistake. What child deserves to be labeled that? I feel a flash of anger now as I think about it. How that word colored me—as if the word *mistake* had been scribbled on my forehead in permanent marker. How I tried to prove to my mother that I wasn't.

But it seemed like Mom never really saw me, never fully acknowledged my existence. I always felt like I was just background noise or a bit player to the center-stage drama of her own life.

How am I supposed to be a good mom with a mother like that as my example? I'm reading how-to-be-a-parent books and studying one that's supposed to help me reparent myself, but it seems like putting a thin patch on a bad tire. Why, oh why had Brooke thought I was capable of caring for Lily? What was I thinking, getting pregnant on my own? Why did I ever believe I could raise a baby by myself?

But then—I never really did, did I? I always thought Brooke would be here. I'd thought she and I would raise our children together. I certainly hadn't thought I'd be raising Lily *and* a baby all alone.

I put my hand over my mouth to stifle a sob. *Damn it, Brooke! How could you just go off and leave us? How am I supposed to answer all of Lily's questions? What should I do about Zack? What if Miss Margaret doesn't get better? What if she does, and wants to take Lily back to Alexandria, where another health crisis could happen at any time?*

I realize it's not just Brooke I'm angry at. *Oh, dear God—I'm angry at* you*! How could you let this happen? You're supposed to be good! What the hell am I supposed to do?*

There are no answers—just Lily's steady breathing in the dark. I close my eyes and inhale the sweet scent of her hair, and eventually match my breathing to hers. And then, in the silence, I hear Brooke's voice echo through my mind: *You can do this.*

How many times did she tell me that over the years? Too many to count. Sometimes she'd say, "Remember our favorite quote?" and one of us would recite Maya Angelou: *Do the best you can until you know better. When you know better, do better.*

A surge of my old optimism starts to pulse through me. I know a lot more than my mother knew. I know that children need to feel loved and wanted and secure. I know they need to feel heard and supported and encouraged, that they need to feel cared for and special and cherished.

I can give Lily everything I needed and didn't get, everything I've gleaned from books and friends and friends' families and kind teachers. I have a heart full of love to give and a deep desire to give it. "I'll do my best," I softly vow into Lily's hair. "My very, very best."

I hope that will be enough. I pray it will be enough.

As sleep finally starts to claim me, I swear I hear Brooke whisper, *You've got this.*

CHAPTER EIGHTEEN

Zack

I SPEND THE evening on the internet, searching for information about my daughter's mother and guardians.

It's relatively easy to flesh out Brooke's professional profile. She spoke at a lot of conferences and was quoted in *Logistics Management* magazine—apparently she was a well-respected expert. I learn that she left a high-powered executive position that required worldwide travel to move to New Orleans and focus on her family nearly five years ago.

Finding any more personal information than that is difficult. From an online bio, I learn that she was from Alexandria, graduated magna cum laude from LSU, and held a master's degree. She was pretty circumspect on personal sites. She had an Instagram account and Facebook page, but both reveal disappointingly little to people she hadn't befriended. Her obituary mentions that she belonged to a couple of professional organizations, served on a committee for United Way, volunteered with a few other charities, and was a member of a local church. Her survivors are listed as Lily and Margaret.

As for Quinn, her Instagram and Facebook pages are also only visible to friends. She has a professional-looking website, though, for her decorating store, Verve!, and her design business. I stop first at the bio page. There's a photo of Quinn, seated at a glass desk, smiling up at the camera. She's absolutely stunning. The copy says she's a New Orleans native, holds a degree in design from LSU, and specializes in eclectic, personalized designs. I learn that she worked at a major design firm in Atlanta before moving back to New Orleans a couple of years ago. A quick check of the Georgia firm reveals that it's one of the top three design companies in that city.

Back on Quinn's website, I browse through a collection of photos showing living rooms, kitchens, bedrooms, bathrooms, and foyers. I don't know much about design, but these photos look like something from a magazine. It looks like she's really good at what she does.

When I search for Margaret Moore on Facebook, I hit the jackpot. Her page is wide open to the public, and there are tons of pictures. Holy profile—Margaret must have uploaded every image that crossed her phone in the last few years.

"Hot damn," I mutter as I scroll through about a bazillion photos of Lily. Here she is as a newborn; she's wrapped like a burrito in a pink blanket, her face puffy, her eyes little slits, and she's wearing a pink knit hat. It does something spongy to my insides to see Lily as a brand-new earthling. In most of the photos, she's cradled by Brooke, who's wearing a jubilant smile of pure delight, her face radiant, her eyes smitten.

A few photos feature a glowing Margaret holding the newborn, and one picture shows Quinn smiling down at the infant in her arms with rapt tenderness. I stare at this photo for a long time.

Here's a picture of all three women and the newborn baby together on a sofa in what looks like Brooke's living room. Lily is without the cap, and her hair is a little dandelion puff of blond fuzz.

I scroll through the photos and watch Lily grow. She's an older baby on a blanket, laughing at the camera. Now she's in her mother's arms clad in a christening gown, a long lacy affair that looks like an heirloom. Quinn, Margaret, and a black-robed minister pose beside them, smiling at the camera.

Here's Lily in a high chair, with something orange smeared all over her face. Here's a photo of her wearing a reindeer-motif bib that reads *Baby's First Christmas*. Here she is in a fancy dress with an Easter basket.

I study these photos, mesmerized at the way the pink burrito matures into a toddler. There she is, standing upright, holding on to the sofa. Now she's taking a step, holding on to Margaret's finger. She's sitting in a high chair in Brooke's kitchen with a cake with one candle. Brooke, Quinn, and Margaret are gathered around her, and a crowd of other people are in the background.

This photo shows all three women and the baby at Thanksgiving—I can tell the holiday from the horn of plenty centerpiece and the turkey on the table.

Here's Lily at another birthday party with two candles—and yet another one at age three. This was less than a year ago, I realize—yet look how much she's changed!

I scroll back further and realize that Margaret was chronicling Brooke's life before Lily was in the picture, almost as if Brooke were her child—her only child. There are graduation photos, Christmas photos, Mardi Gras photos, prom photos, and vacation pictures. Since I can't picture Margaret actually attending some of the events—days at the beach, for example, with a bunch of other young people—I surmise that Brooke sent these photos to her.

Many of these photos include men. I'd begun to wonder if Brooke and Quinn were a couple, but, no—here are photos of Brooke kissing a man. Here's another one with Quinn on a boat, sitting close to a man who has his arm looped around her.

The thing that seems to be missing in all of the photos—even the holiday photos, and there are a lot of those, spanning different years and hairstyles—is anyone who looks like a parent to either woman.

One photo in particular grabs my attention. Quinn and Brooke are ice-skating at Rockefeller Center in New York, each with a man on her arm. The two women are looking at each other and laughing uproariously. I lean closer to the screen to study the picture. They look a lot alike, and it's not just because they're both blondes in black jackets. There's a joie de vivre about them, a sense of delight in each other's company. They're attuned to each other and caught up in the moment. They're having freewheeling, uninhibited *fun*.

I feel weirdly jealous. Have I ever had that good a time with anyone in my life? I don't think I've ever laughed like that with Jessica.

The thought makes me sit back in my chair and run my hand down my face. I don't want to think like this. I love my wife. That's the kind of man I am—the kind who loves the woman I married, not the kind who looks at other women and feels like I'm missing out on something.

Not that I'm looking at Brooke or Quinn and lusting after them. They're attractive, yeah, but I'm not thinking about sex—well, no more than any guy does when he looks at pretty, fully clothed women. I haven't thought very much about Jess in terms of sex in a long while, either, though. It's as if someone hit the pause button on my libido.

The thing that strikes me in this photo of Quinn and Brooke is their sense of connection—the way they seem to be sharing a vibrant bond that transcends their surroundings or the other people around them. I haven't felt really close to anyone, including Jessica, in a while. In fact, I've felt kind of lonely for most of my marriage.

The thought makes me push back my chair. Maybe I'm still angry, even though I don't want to be. I want to forgive and move on. I need to; I know I do. Learning about Lily was hard on Jessica. She was already having a difficult time accepting her infertility; it must be killing her to know that the whole time she and I were struggling to conceive, this little girl was growing from a baby into a child.

Oh, God—Jessica will be back in a few days, and I'll have to share all of this with her. The thought makes my stomach drop and my skin feel clammy. I don't like this sensation. I don't like it at all.

I close my computer, stand, and run my hand down my face. I'm tired; that's all it is. It's been a long, stressful day. I'll go to bed and get some sleep, and when I get up in the morning, hopefully I'll be able to think more clearly.

But a question haunts me: *What's wrong with me, dreading the return of my own wife?*

CHAPTER NINETEEN

Quinn

Saturday, May 11

MORNING VISITING HOURS for ICU are from eight thirty to nine. I arrive on the sixth floor at eight twenty-five, feeling harried and hurried and badly dressed because all my favorite jeans seem to have shrunk overnight.

I thought I'd allowed myself plenty of time, but I'd forgotten how long it takes to get a small child out the door in the morning. There's breakfast to dawdle over, toothpaste to over-squirt, funny faces to make in the mirror, and hairstyle choices to consider.

Lily is very particular about her hair. Today she wanted a French braid, then cried because I couldn't fix it exactly the way her mommy did. I realized that her tears were more about the loss of her mother than about my sadly lacking hairstyling skills, but still, I felt painfully inept. This, I think, is how grief ekes out—unexpected and raw, in small, inconvenient moments.

I held her and comforted her, and Ruffles worked her magic again. A little dog who wants to get in on all cuddle action is turning out to be a godsend. Lily finally settled for a side part and a barrette, then moved on to wardrobe selection.

Margaret hadn't packed very many of Lily's clothes—she thought she and Lily would be in New Orleans for only three or four nights—so mercifully the choices were limited, but the time she took deciding made me understand why Brooke used to ask Lily to select her next day's outfit before she went to bed. The memory brought Brooke to mind so fully that I had to sneak off to another room and wipe away grief tears of my own. *It's no wonder I'm nearly late*, I think, as I round the corner to the ICU waiting room.

It's full of solemn, fatigued-looking people, but my gaze immediately flies to a handsome broad-shouldered man in a blue shirt, sitting in a chair against the wall. *Zack.* My heart rate jackrabbits. What the heck is he doing here again?

He stands and walks toward me, his mouth curved in a smile. "Good morning. How're you doing today?"

I'm fighting morning sickness, having a bad hair day—I spent too much time coiffing Lily to do more than run a brush through my own tangled tresses—and now I'm feeling ambushed. He probably came here in hopes of meeting Lily.

"Fine. I dropped off Lily with a friend," I say, my tone a little too sharp. Several faces in the waiting room—a woman with pointed features, a man with eyes like a forlorn beagle, a gray-haired matron who looks like she hasn't slept in days—turn toward us, their expressions curious. I step back into the hall so we can talk without being overheard.

He follows me. "How did she take the news about Margaret?"

"She was upset. She thinks people go to hospitals to die."

"Oh, wow." His blue eyes are troubled. "Is that what happened to Brooke?"

I shake my head. "She was already dead when . . ." My eyes unexpectedly fill. Pregnancy hormones, grief, and Lily's meltdown have made me hyperemotional. "When the ambulance arrived."

"Hey. Oh, hey . . ." He reaches out and touches my arm. I feel a little electric shock and must have flinched, because he drops his hand. "I'm sorry. I didn't mean to upset you." His eyes are so sincere and kind that I feel ridiculous for behaving so defensively.

I blink a little and fight to get my emotions under control. "I'm sorry. I had a bit of a rough night. Lily woke up crying from a bad dream."

He looks so concerned that I feel the need to clarify, so he won't think I just abandoned a sobbing child. "She's fine this morning. She was excited to see my friend Sarah and her two boys."

"So someone different is caring for her today?"

I nod. "Sarah's a psychologist, so I thought it might be helpful for Lily to spend part of the day with her. That way I can get some professional feedback on how she's doing."

"Good idea."

I toy with the shoulder strap on my handbag and try to think of a diplomatic way of asking, *What the hell are you doing here again?* "I'm surprised to see you here this morning."

"I wanted to see how Margaret's faring." He steps closer to the wall to let an aide wheel an empty gurney down the hall. "I hope you don't mind, but I came by at six thirty to catch the doctor."

"What?" I do mind. I mind very much. Zack is not the person who should be talking to Margaret's doctor!

He lifts his shoulders. "I thought it was a way I could help."

"You should have called me." Zack and I had exchanged phone numbers yesterday.

"I'm sorry. You're right." He runs a hand through his hair, his gaze apologetic. "But I knew you were taking care of Lily and probably wouldn't be able to get here that early. When my mom was in the hospital, I learned that catching the doctor on morning rounds is often the only way to get any information."

I don't really want to be appeased, but I sort of am. This is the second time he's mentioned his mom in a hospital setting. I make a mental note to ask him about it later. "Did you see Dr. McFadden? What did he say about Margaret?"

"He's encouraged. He said it's too soon to tell for sure, but so far she isn't showing signs of major cognitive impairment."

"That's great!"

He nods. "He said she's responsive and conscious. She's got some confusion and forgetfulness, but he said a certain amount of that is normal, and hopefully it'll get better with time. She's having a little arrhythmia, so he's prescribed a drug to control that. If she continues to improve, he'll move her to a post-ICU room tomorrow."

"That's fantastic!" I immediately feel lighter. I didn't realize how worried I was that she wouldn't make it.

"Yeah."

The door opens. A nurse stands in the doorway. "Immediate family may come in. No more than two visitors per patient, please. We ask you to keep your voices low. The maximum amount of time you can stay is thirty minutes, but we prefer that you limit your visit to fifteen minutes so as not to tire out the patient. Please use the hand sanitizer on the way in and out. Thank you."

"I'll wait here," he says.

I'm glad he's not going to be pushy about this. I get in line with the other visitors and we file into the large room. Medical equipment beeps and swooshes beside every bed. Most of the patients in them look unconscious—or worse.

Margaret's bed is on the left. Her eyes are closed. I touch her hand—the one that doesn't have an IV in it. "Margaret—it's Quinn."

She opens her eyes and looks at me. I can't tell if she recognizes me or not. "Hello, dear." Her voice is weak. "How are you?"

"Fine. I'm fine." I give her an encouraging smile. "You seem much better this morning. How do you feel?"

"Like someone worked me over with a bully stick."

I grin. "You took quite a tumble."

"What happened to me?"

"You had a heart attack, then fell off a stepladder at Brooke's house."

"Brooke!" Her eyes brighten and seem to focus. "Where is she, dear?"

My heart catches. "She's gone, Miss Margaret. Remember?"

She closes her eyes and turns her face away for a moment. My heart aches as a tear trickles down her cheek. I find a tissue on the tray beside her and press it into her hand.

"I knew something awful had happened, but I forgot what." She dabs her eyes. "Something with her head, right?"

I nod. "She had an aneurysm. A little over a month ago."

"And her little girl?"

"I'm taking care of Lily. She's at a friend's house this morning."

"Lily," she murmurs. She wipes her eyes. "Did I dream it, or did Lily's dad show up?"

My chest squeezes. Why does she remember *that*? "Yes."

"I want—I want Lily to know him. There's no substitute for family. There needs to be a line of blood."

It sounds like something from a gothic novel. The nurse who escorted us in from the waiting room approaches to check one of Margaret's IVs. "All—all right," I manage.

"Is he here?" Margaret asks.

I nod, a little unnerved by the question.

"I want to see him. Can you bring him in?"

"Well, um . . ." Everything within me counsels against it.

"Do you want me to go get the gentleman?" the nurse asks.

"Yes," Margaret answers before I can get out a word.

I can't argue that he's not immediate family, because I'm not, either.

"I'll be right back," the nurse says. "But you need to stay still and calm, Mrs. Moore. Your heart rate is going up."

"Tell me about Lily," Margaret urges.

I babble a bit. I'm describing what she ate for breakfast when Zack walks up to her bed. "Hello, Mrs. Moore."

Margaret's face lights up. "You were here earlier."

"That's right. I'm Zack Bradley."

"Zack," she murmurs, as if she's trying to commit this to memory. "Have you met Lily?"

"Not yet, but I want to. Quinn showed me pictures." His dimple flashes. "She's a beautiful little girl."

"Yes, she is. And so bright!"

"Are you all right, Mrs. Moore?" the nurse asks.

"Yes, yes." Margaret dismissively flaps her wrist at the nurse, then gestures toward Zack. "I want you to meet her."

"I'd love to," Zack says.

She turns her head toward me. "You, dear—will you please arrange it?" I think she's forgotten my name.

"Mrs. Moore, you need to lie back and rest," the nurse says. "Your heart rate is too fast." She adjusts a bag attached to Margaret's IVs, watches the monitor, and then turns to us. "I'm sorry, but you'd better leave. We need to keep her heart rate stabilized."

My own heart is tripping all over itself. "We didn't mean to upset her."

"Oh, I don't think you did." She gives me a kind smile. "For some older patients, though, any emotion—even happiness—is just too much stimulation for their fragile condition."

I reach out and touch Margaret's arm. "We'll see you later, Miss Margaret."

"All right, dear," she says weakly. "Give my love to Lily."

"WELL," ZACK SAYS, once we're again out in the waiting room.

Well, indeed, I think, walking into the corridor. Morning sickness is putting in another unwanted appearance. "I'll be right back," I say, and head down the hall to the ladies' room. I use hand sanitizer, pull a cracker out of my purse, and force myself to eat it. I phone Sarah. After giving her a quick update about Margaret, I get to the point of the call.

"Margaret wants Lily to meet Zack," I tell her. "What's the best way for me to arrange it without telling Lily that he's her dad?"

"I'd suggest meeting in public and keeping things light," Sarah says. "Maybe you can run into him while you and Lily are out shopping or getting ice cream or something. That'll be easier than a big, heavy, 'there's someone I'd like you to meet' kind of thing."

I like the sound of that. "What if Lily asks how I know him?"

"Just say he's a friend. Don't lie, but don't give unnecessary information. Children don't usually press for specifics."

"Thanks, Sarah," I say.

I draw myself up, pull in a deep breath, and remember something I read that morning in the reparenting book: *Address troublesome issues head on. The sooner you act, the less time you'll spend worrying.*

My upper lip is perspiring. I splash some water on my face, then head back into the corridor.

"There's a coffee shop in the atrium," Zack says. "Want to go there and talk?"

"Sure," I say.

It's a PJ's, my favorite New Orleans coffee franchise. I order an iced tea and a carrot muffin. He gets a black coffee. We settle at a table near the front.

"Margaret was a lot more coherent this morning," Zack says.

I nod. "The heart thing was scary."

"Not as bad as yesterday, though. The nurse stayed calm, and that's always a good sign."

He talks like a man who's had a lot of experience with ICUs. "You mentioned that your mother was in the hospital," I say. "What happened to her?"

He blows out a long sigh. "About six years ago, she was jogging in the neighborhood. A car came around the corner too fast, and the driver didn't see her."

"Oh, how awful!"

"Yeah, it was." He gazes at his coffee for a moment. "She ended up partially paralyzed."

"Is she okay now?"

He shakes his head. "No. After thirteen months, three additional surgeries, and a bunch of complications, she died."

"I'm so sorry!"

He nods, acknowledging my condolences. "It was rough, especially on my dad. He had a heart attack less than a year after she passed away." He takes a sip of coffee. "I think he died of a broken heart."

My chest feels hot and tight. "So your parents had a good marriage."

"Oh, yeah. Mom once said that home is a person, not a place. They adored each other." He's silent for a beat, his mouth curved in a soft smile. "They were married forty years, and they still held hands. I used to catch them dancing together in the kitchen with no music."

"Oh, how wonderful!"

"Yeah." He takes a sip of coffee. "They adored my sister and me, too. We were a really close family."

"You were lucky."

"Yeah." He looks at me, and I get the feeling he's seeing far too much. I'm afraid he's picking up on my badly parented inner damage and is going to ask about my family, so I change the subject.

"The kind of law you practice—it sounds really . . ." I search for a word.

"Boring?" His lips quirk up.

I smile. I'd looked up his firm on the internet. "I was thinking 'dry,' but I was going to say 'complicated.'"

He grins. "Very diplomatic of you. You might have a future in corporate law."

"No, thanks."

The prototype of Lily's dimple flashes when he smiles. "Actually, my work's a lot more interesting than it sounds. I mainly figure out compromises. I try to find win-win solutions."

My eyebrows rise. "For both parties, or just your clients?"

"Ouch." He puts a hand on his chest as if I'd just wounded him. "Sounds like you don't have a very good opinion of attorneys."

I don't, but it's an opinion I formed when my parents divorced. My mother complained long and loud about the incompetence of her attorney, the viciousness of my father's lawyer, and how they both were only interested in making money. I lift my shoulders.

Zack leans forward. "Here's the way it works: it's my job to help my clients get what they want, but in order to do that, I have to convince them to make concessions, too. That's really the hardest part of my job. Our firm has a reputation for settling things quickly, but that won't happen if deals aren't equitable."

I raise my eyebrows. "So you're an attorney who believes in fairness?"

"Yeah, I do. That's the whole concept of justice." He says this with an utter lack of guile."I know it goes against the stereotype."

"How did you end up practicing this particular type of law?"

"My dad's grocery store went through a hard time when I was in college. A big-box store tried to buy him out for a ridiculously low amount—they wanted to tear down his store and expand their parking lot. Dad refused. They told him he couldn't compete and they'd run him out of business, so he'd better fall in line. He still refused."

He takes a sip of coffee. "The new store went up, and things got nasty. They lowballed him on everything. He started selling specialties they didn't offer—organic foods, local bakery items, special cut meats—but every time, they'd add something similar. And with their advertising budget, they'd outpromote him."

"That's terrible!"

"Yeah. The big corporation must have spent a fortune, trying to run him out of business. Dad finally hit on something they couldn't duplicate: he started barbecuing meat. He put a smoker right outside his store. The scent wafted over the parking lot and attracted shoppers in droves."

I smile. "What a great idea!"

He nods. "They tried to sell their own barbecue, but Dad had won the barbecue competition at the state fair and was well-known around town for bringing his smoker to charitable benefits. He had a local reputation and a secret recipe, and they wouldn't compete. When people came in to buy Dad's take-home barbecue, they'd find all kinds of other locally made specialty products and buy those, too." He grins. "Within a year, Dad's business was flourishing again."

"That's a great story."

Zack leans back in his chair. "Dad said that if they'd made him a decent offer at the beginning, he would have taken it. It was the bullying that made him fight. So that made me realize this is an area of law practice where there was a lot of room for improvement."

It occurs to me that Zack is his father's son. If I try to keep him from seeing Lily—especially now that he knows Margaret wants him to—he's going to persist.

Besides, I've been weighing Sarah's comments about Lily resenting it when she's older if I keep her from knowing her father.

I set down my cup. "I've been thinking about you meeting Lily."

He leans forward. "And?"

"I'm okay with it, but now is not the time to tell her you're her father."

"I'm fine with that."

I tell him about Sarah's suggestion for a casual encounter. He grins, showing his dimple. "Where and when would you like to run into me, old friend?"

"How about the Creole Creamery on Prytania Street at three o'clock tomorrow?"

His eyes, so much like Lily's, light up. It's hard to ignore how attractive he is, and noticing it disconcerts me.

"Sounds great," he says. "I'll see you there."

CHAPTER TWENTY

Zack

Sunday, May 12

I ARRIVE AT the ice cream shop early, park at the curb about halfway down the block, and wait in my car. I see Quinn drive by in a white Equinox and then parallel park down the street. I get out of my vehicle, pretending to be engrossed in my phone, as Quinn climbs out and opens the back door. She's wearing jeans and a white shirt, nothing fancy, and her hair is pulled back in a simple ponytail, but I'm sure my friend Ben would give himself whiplash doing a double take. As I watch, she helps a little girl scramble out of a safety seat and onto the sidewalk.

I suddenly feel as if my airways are being throttled—it's that hard to breathe. Nothing prepared me for the emotional punch of seeing Lily in person. My brain kind of shorts out. *That's my child!* I think. *My actual flesh and blood! A real live person I helped create!* My heart skips. My palms sweat. I try not gawk, but it's hard.

Lily looks a lot like she did in the Mardi Gras photos, but I think I would have recognized her even if I hadn't seen them. She's a doppelgänger of my sister at that age. Hell, if you take away the long hair, she looks just like *me.*

I watch as she grabs Quinn's hand and bounces on her tiptoes as she walks. I can tell she's talking a blue streak; Quinn is smiling, her head inclined toward her. If I didn't know otherwise, I'd think they were mother and daughter.

I stroll toward the ice cream shop, pretending to be absorbed in my phone, and we arrive at the door at the same time.

I feign delighted surprise. Well, the surprise part is feigned; the delight is one hundred percent genuine. "Quinn! It's great to see you."

She does a slightly better acting job. "Zack! Long time, no see!"

I give her a hug, the way I'd hug a friend I haven't seen in a while. I can't help but notice that she smells wonderful—like herbs and flowers and sunshine. Not that I've ever noticed that sunshine has a scent, but if it did, it would smell like Quinn.

"What are you doing here?" I ask.

"I'm bringing my goddaughter for some ice cream," she says.

I pull back and smile down at the little girl beside her. She's wearing strawberry-printed shorts with a strawberry-themed shirt and holding Quinn's hand. Her skin is smooth as cream, and her blue eyes have the longest lashes I've ever seen. Her blond curls are parted on the side and held with a large red bow. My heart dissolves in a warm puddle.

"This is Lily Adams," Quinn says.

I bend down and hold out my hand. "Hello, there. I'm Zack."

Lily puts her hand in mine and gives it a big up-and-down pump. "It's very nice to meet you," she says solemnly.

My heart melts a little more. "Wow, you have lovely manners."

"Thank you. Mommy says manners are important."

"She's right. They are."

"We're about to go inside," Quinn says. "Want to join us?"

"I'd love to." I hold the door, and Quinn and Lily walk in. "How old are you, Lily?"

"Nearly four," she says. Her voice is sweet and high-pitched.

"Wow. Nearly four is a great age."

"Yes."

The customer in front of us finishes paying and moves down the counter. A white-haired woman comes into the shop and stands in line behind us.

"May I help you?" the teenage girl taking orders asks. She's wearing a blue-and-white-striped apron, has dark hair pulled back in a thin ponytail, and is chewing gum.

I look at the board. It has a bewildering number of flavors. I wonder if we need to read all of them aloud to Lily. I look down at her. "Do you know what kind of ice cream you want?"

Lily nods. "Cookie dough with colored sprinkles."

"Sounds delicious."

"Cookie dough is my mommy's favorite."

I'm a little confused by her use of the present tense when talking about her mother, but then, I don't really know how well three-year-olds talk. "Is that right?"

She nods. "Mommy is dead."

"Oh. I'm very sorry."

"Do you think she has ice cream in heaven?"

I have no idea if people eat in heaven or not. I realize Lily's looking at Quinn. I'm relieved that the theological question isn't aimed at me.

"I'm sure they do. She can probably have as much ice cream as she wants, whenever she wants it," Quinn says.

Lily smiles.

"One child-sized cone with cookie dough and colored sprinkles," Quinn tells the girl behind the counter.

"We can't put sprinkles on cones," the teenager says, chomping her gum.

"That's okay. Put the sprinkles in the bottom of a cup, scoop in the ice cream, then place the cone upside down on top, like a clown hat," Quinn says.

I can tell she's done this before. It occurs to me that caring for a child requires more skills than I realized. Even ordering an ice cream cone requires some know-how.

Quinn orders a small cup of chocolate almond ice cream for herself. I order a cappuccino chocolate chunk cone, then pull out my wallet and pay.

"Are you datin' Quinn?" Lily asks.

The question makes me freeze, my wallet halfway back in my pocket. "No. We're just friends. I'm, uh, married."

"Oh." She sounds somewhat disappointed. "So where's your wife?"

"She's on a trip to Seattle."

"What's she doin' there?"

"She's visiting her parents and doing work stuff."

Lily seems to find the answer acceptable. "Do you have chil'ren?"

I hesitate. This is a tricky one. I don't want to say anything that might later seem like I'm not claiming her. "My wife and I want them, but we haven't had any yet."

"How long have you been married?"

"Three years in June."

"It doesn't take that long to make a baby. You must be doing somethin' wrong."

The woman behind us in line chortles. Quinn's face grows pink.

"My friend Alicia jus' got a little sister," Lily continues, "an' her mother said it took nine months for the baby to grow in her stomach. An' there are twelve months in a year, so you should have one by now."

"Well, aren't you smart!" I say.

"My goodness, yes!" says the woman behind us. She's wearing a colorful flowered dress and has glasses hanging on a chain around her neck. She leans down to address Lily. "How old are you, honey?"

"Three. Nearly four."

"Goodness gracious! I'm amazed you can remember numbers, much less figure out months and years at your age."

"I can count all the way to a hun'red," Lily volunteers.

The woman straightens and smiles at Quinn and me. "That's a very bright little girl you've got there."

My heart swells with an intense sense of pride. I'm about to say, "Thank you," then catch myself.

"Yes, she is," Quinn says, patting Lily's back. "We're all very proud of her."

We move down the counter to wait for our ice cream.

Lily looks at me. "Are your baby-making parts broken? That happened to my mommy. Her baby-making parts were about to break. That's why I have a donor instead of a daddy."

So she knows about the donor situation. "It's, umm, something like that," I say. "My wife . . ." Hell. I don't want to throw Jessica under the bus in front of Quinn. I start again. "My wife and I are seeing doctors to try to help us."

Thankfully, our ice cream arrives. Quinn gathers up napkins and a spoon, and we head toward an empty bistro table by the window.

Lily's feet dangle from the chair as she sits down. "Could you please fix my cone?" she asks Quinn.

Quinn presses the cone into the scoop of ice cream. "Presto change-o." She covers the ice cream and cone with a napkin, then flips it over. "Ta-da! Your magic cone, my princess."

Lily laughs. "That's not really magic."

"How do you know it's not?" I ask.

"Because I know how she did it." She watches Quinn use the plastic spoon to scoop the remnant sprinkles from the bottom of the cup onto the top of the ice cream. Quinn hands it to her, and she takes an eager bite.

"How is it?" I ask.

"Yummy! My mommy would love this."

Quinn nods. Her eyes are sad.

Lily licks some sprinkles off the top. Her eyelashes brush her eyebrows as she peers up at me. "Did you know my mommy?"

"No. I've heard about her, but I never got to meet her."

"She was beautiful. Like Auntie Quinn." Lily's tongue flicks around the edges of her ice cream.

"Why, thank you, Lily." Quinn smiles.

"Welcome." She nibbles at the edge of the cone. "People think they're sisters."

"We were as close as sisters," Quinn says.

Lily nods. "My grams is in the hospital, so I live with Quinn now. Did you know I have my own room at her house?"

"No, I didn't."

"Well, I do. We're gonna dec'rate it to make it more kid-like. But it's already my room, because it's got lots of pitchers of lilies an' roses on the wall, an' my name is Lily Rose."

"That's a beautiful name."

"Yes." She takes a mouthful of ice cream, managing to get some on her chin. "Rose is Auntie Quinn's middle name, too."

"I didn't know that." I look at her.

"My mommy an' she were best-est friends an' I got middle-named after her."

"That's really special, being named after someone," I say. "It's a good thing Quinn's middle name wasn't Stinky."

Lily bursts out in a loud laugh, resulting in ice cream spillage. Quinn laughs, too, then takes a napkin and wipes Lily's jaw as naturally as if she were wiping her own.

"That would be a terr'ble middle name!" Lily says.

"Yeah, it would," Quinn agrees.

"I'd be Lily Stinky, an' you'd be Quinnlyn Stinky!"

Grinning, Quinn nods. "I like Rose so much better, don't you?"

"Yes. Roses smell nice." Lily looks at me. "You're funny!"

I grin. "I try."

We eat our ice cream in silence for a moment. I realize I don't have a lot of experience initiating conversation with kids. "So, Lily—what kind of things do you like to do?" I ask.

"What do you mean?"

"Well, do you like to paint, or swim, or play board games or computer games, or play on swing sets or what?"

"Yes."

"Yes, which ones?"

"All of them! I love to do all kinds of things." She points out the window. "Oh, look! That dog's wearin' a little dress! She looks like Ruffles with all-white fur!"

Quinn gazes out the plate glass and smiles. "Yes, a bit."

I turn and see a woman on the sidewalk, walking a small dog in a yellow froufrou outfit past the ice cream shop. "Is Ruffles your dog?" I ask Lily.

"She's Auntie Quinn's, but she loves me, too."

"Are dogs your favorite animal?"

"Yes! Although I love koalas and giraffes and all kinds of baby animals. Especially the baby 'rangi-tangs at the zoo."

"You like to go to the zoo?"

She nods vigorously, her curls bobbing.

"I do, too," I say. "Maybe we can all go to the zoo some afternoon this week. Maybe tomorrow." I look at Quinn. "Your store is closed on Mondays, right?"

Lily bounces up and down in her chair. "Yay!"

The moment the words leave my mouth, I know I've said the wrong thing, because Quinn's face freezes over. Too late, I realize I should have asked before I mentioned it to Lily. "If that's okay with Quinn, that is."

Her face looks kind of tight. "We'll have to see how Miss Margaret is doing. And I want to get Lily reenrolled in preschool." She puts her plastic spoon in her ice cream, then looks up. "Besides, what about your wife?"

"Oh . . . Jessica will still be on the West Coast. She's visiting some hotels in her new region, so she'll be going to Portland and San Francisco. She won't be back until next weekend."

"Wow, she goes a lot of places," Lily says.

"Right now, she does," I agree. "She works for a hotel chain."

"I didn't realize she'd already started the new job," Quinn says.

"She hasn't—at least not officially. But corporate wants her to visit some of the larger properties before she starts the regional position, and the hotel here can't very well tell the corporate office no."

"Does she live in a hotel like Eloise?" Lily asks.

I smile at her. "No. She's staying with her parents right now, but she's looking for a house. We'll be moving out there in a month or so."

Lily takes a big bite of ice cream. "Do you have any pets?"

"No. I love dogs, but we both work too many hours to care for one."

"Quinn has a doggy door," Lily says. "That way Ruffles can go outside whenever she needs to."

"That's a good solution," I say.

"It won' work for a baby, though," Lily says.

Quinn laughs and I smile, but the comment hits more nerve than funny bone. Jessica mentioned a donor egg again when I talked to her last night.

"So can we go to the zoo tomorrow?" Lily asks.

Quinn gives me a quizzical look. "How did you know my shop's closed on Mondays?"

"I saw it online."

"Can we go?" Lily turns pleading eyes on Quinn. "Can we?"

"I don't know yet, sweetie," Quinn says. "As I said, I have to check on Miss Margaret and get you enrolled in school, and I need to touch base with Miss Terri about client appointments."

I pull out my phone and scroll through my schedule. "I can move things around for any afternoon this week."

"Put it on your calendar," Lily tells Quinn in an officious tone.

Quinn's eyebrows rise.

"Put it on your calendar to check with Miss Terri an' give him a call. If you schedule it, you won' forget."

I laugh at her precocious efficiency, but Quinn's eyes fill with tears.

"Hey, Lily," I say, "would you go get me another napkin from the counter, please?"

"Sure!" She hops up and heads to the front of the shop.

I lean over the table toward Quinn. "What's wrong?"

She wipes away a tear with her napkin. "What she just said—she sounded just like her mother. Brooke scheduled everything." Quinn dabs her face again. "Can you watch her for a moment while I run to the ladies' room and pull myself together?"

"Sure."

As I watch Quinn leave the table and Lily come back, I think about the movie *Sliding Doors* and the concept of parallel universes. How could I have lived on earth for the last few years and not known that I had a daughter? I think about the photos of Lily on Margaret's Facebook page, about how much she's already grown and changed in her short lifetime, and I have the strangest feeling that a large chunk of my life has somehow gone by without me.

CHAPTER TWENTY-ONE

Quinn

Monday, May 13

SO HERE I am once more, with plans to go to the zoo with a father, only this one isn't mine, and this time—just my luck—he's going to show up. Zack just texted me that he's on the way.

I stash a tube of sunblock and a package of hand wipes in my purse as Lily skips into the kitchen, her friend Alicia behind her. "Auntie Quinn, can Ruffles come with us?"

"No, sweetie," I say. "Pets aren't allowed at the zoo."

"Aww!"

"She'll take a nap while we're gone, then be ready to play when we get back home. Zack is on his way, so please go put on your shoes."

"Yay!" Both girls run away shrieking. I smile as I watch them race to the back door and pull on their sandals. Alicia is accompanying us. She only goes to preschool on Tuesdays and Thursdays, and I owe her mother some payback. She watched Lily again this morning while I went to the hospital to visit Margaret and handled Lily's preschool reregistration, and she's agreed to do so once more this evening. There's another reason, too: I hope that having another child along will dilute some of the tension I feel around Zack.

I'm don't like secrets, and I'm really uncomfortable with the secret connections between the three of us. Lily doesn't know Zack is her dad, and Zack doesn't know I'm carrying his unborn child. It's still early days and I'm not yet showing, but I'm feeling so unlike myself that it's hard to believe the world can't tell I'm pregnant. My tummy is bloated, my breasts are tender, and my stomach is alternately—and sometimes simultaneously—nauseous and ravenous.

Zack's presence in my life has other complicating factors, as well. It's raising eyebrows with those who don't know the full story. Alicia's mother looked at me questioningly when I'd said a male friend was going to the zoo with us when I picked up Alicia.

"Is this someone you're dating?" Caroline asked.

"No, nothing like that. He's just a friend. Actually, he's a friend of Miss Margaret's."

"Is this the same guy you and Lily had ice cream with?"

So Lily has been talking. "Yes."

"Lily said he looks like a prince. I asked if he was a friend of Brooke's, and she said no." She paused and looked at me expectantly, obviously waiting for me to contribute information.

I just smiled and nodded.

"Does he live in the same town as Margaret?"

"No, he lives here. But he and his wife are about to move to Seattle."

Her eyebrows arched upward. "He's married?"

"Yes."

"And you're going with him to the zoo." Her voice held a question, although it wasn't asked as one.

I lifted my shoulders. "You know Lily—she enchanted him. When he heard about Margaret being in the hospital and Lily losing her mother, he wanted to do something to cheer her up." The more I talked, the odder the whole thing seemed. My face grew hot.

"Well, that's really nice of him." Caroline's expression said she found this all very peculiar.

Did she think I was getting involved with a married man? *Open, earth, and swallow me now.* "Yeah," I muttered. "He's a nice guy."

Maybe too nice. He'd dropped by the hospital again this morning to meet with Dr. McFadden. I appreciate hearing what Margaret's physician has to say, but I find Zack's involvement disconcerting. I'd hustled Alicia out her front door and back to my place before Caroline could pose any more awkward questions.

The two girls are playing zoo with Lily's stuffed animals in the living room when Zack rings the doorbell ten minutes later. Ruffles barks and races to the front foyer. The two girls charge after her. I try not to notice how good Zack looks in jeans and a Tulane T-shirt when I open the door. He's changed clothes; he was in a suit and tie at the hospital.

He flashes his dimple as he says hello. "Great house," he comments as he steps inside.

"Thanks." I catch myself folding my hands over his baby in my belly—*his baby!* Why does my brain insist on thinking in those terms?—and force my arms to my side.

Lily jumps up and down. "We're ready!"

"Awesome," Zack responds.

"This is Ruffles," Lily says. "And this is my friend Alicia."

Alicia shyly hangs back. Zack squats down to her height and holds out his hand. "Nice to meet you, Ruffles."

She giggles. "I'm Alicia!"

"Oh! I got confused."

Both girls laugh.

Lily cocks her head at him. "Did you really?"

"Why, yes," Zack says.

"He's teasing," I clarify.

"Alicia, he has his hand out so you can shake it. Like this," Lily says. She grabs Zack's fingers and gives a vigorous demonstration.

To my surprise, Alicia steps up and pumps his hand up and down. She's usually very reticent around strangers.

"Does Ruffles know how to shake?" Zack says.

"No, but she can high-five," Lily says. She sticks out her hand, and Ruffles taps her palm with a paw.

"Wow. That's awesome! Did you teach her that trick?"

"No. Auntie Quinn did. She teached Ruffles to sit an' speak an' lie down an' stay an' go in an' out the doggy door an' to fetch her ball. Wanna see?"

"Sure!"

The girls race off to get the dog's ball, and Zack straightens.

"You did an impressive job getting Alicia to warm up to you," I say.

He lifts his shoulders. "I've had a little practice with my sister's kids and my wife's sister's kids. I only see them once or twice a year, so they always start out acting shy."

The girls bound back into the entryway. "Fetch, Ruffles!" Lily says.

She tosses the ball into the living room, and Ruffles gamely retrieves it. The girls take turns demonstrating the floppy-haired dog's fetching prowess. Zack watches, appearing suitably impressed.

After about the seventh or eighth round, I decide to call a halt. "Who wants to go to the zoo?"

"I do! I do!" Both girls raise their hands and jump up and down.

"Okay, then. Does anyone need to use the potty before we go?" I ask. Brooke taught me the importance of asking that question. Both girls shake their heads no.

"We'd better take my car," I tell Zack. "It has two safety seats in the back."

We all traipse out to the driveway. Lily and Alicia pile into the back and climb into their seats. I fasten Alicia's five-point harness while Zack fastens Lily's.

I check Lily's seat belt when I go around the car. "It's not that I don't think you did it correctly," I say apologetically as I climb into the driver's seat. "It's just that Brooke told me I always needed to check, so—"

He lifts his hands. "Hey, I'm happy to be with someone who knows what they're doing."

I'm a little nervous backing out of the driveway. Zack is watching me, and being watched makes me feel like I'm being judged.

It's a holdover from my childhood, when being noticed meant being criticized. I peer in the rearview mirror and turn my attention to the girls.

"What's the first animal you want to see at the zoo?" I ask.

"The ele-funks!" Alicia says. "They're my favorites."

"Then the monkeys," Lily says. "I love monkeys!

"What's your favorite an'mal, Mr. Zack?" Lily asks.

"Hmm. It's probably a tie between gorillas and bears," he says.

"I know Auntie Quinn's, 'cause it's the same as my mommy's. Giraffes!"

"That's true," I say.

"It's 'cause they have long eyelashes like mine. Right?"

"Yes, baby girl," I tell her. I smile at her friend in the rearview mirror, not wanting Alicia to feel left out. "And Alicia has beautiful giraffe eyes, too."

The conversation is child-driven and animal-centric all the way up Magazine Street. Alicia is nearly as talkative as Lily by the time I pull into the parking lot. We all pile out.

"Please hold an adult's hand until we get inside," I tell them. Alicia grabs mine, and Lily takes Zack's. I'm surprised by how easily she goes with him.

He pays for everyone's tickets at the gate. The woman in the ticket booth smiles at him. "You have a beautiful family."

"We're not a family," Alicia informs her.

"We could be," Lily says. "We're friends, an' my mommy says friends are the family you choose."

"Friends aren't family," Alicia insists.

"They can be." Lily turns to me. "Right, Auntie Quinn?"

"There are different kinds of families," I say, not wanting to have this particular conversation in front of Zack. "Who knows the way to the elephants?"

"I do! I do!" Lily and Alicia bounce up and down, then charge toward the entrance.

"Don't run, and stay within eyesight," I call.

They slow down, but it's surprising how fast their little legs can move. Zack and I have to hustle to keep up.

At the elephant exhibit, they move to the front, joining a cluster of other children. Zack and I stand back and watch them.

"Lily's amazing," Zack says. "So smart and polite and enthusiastic!"

I feel a little burst of pride, although I don't know why—I certainly can't take any credit for her. "She's a great kid. Brooke was a terrific mother."

He folds his arms as he watches her. His forearms are muscular and dusted with light brown hair. "I can't get over how young she is. I was just nineteen when I donated, so when I learned I had a child, I thought he or she would be older."

"I didn't know you'd been that young." I stop myself from putting my hand over my stomach. *Don't think about being pregnant when you're around him*, I tell myself. *And for the sake of everything holy, don't think about how attractive he is!* "What does your wife think about you meeting Lily?"

He shoves his hands in his pockets. "It's a little complicated."

He's trying to sidestep the question. I don't want to let him; I have deep stepmother issues, so if there's a problem with his wife, I want to know about it. "You said she signed you up on the donor registry site," I push.

"Yeah." He rubs his jaw, glances at me, and then blows out a sigh. "The truth is, Jessica's having a hard time with it." He fixes his gaze on the elephants. "We've been going through fertility treatments for the last two years. As the treatments failed, she became kind of obsessed with whether or not I have any donor children."

My stomach tightens. This can't be good.

"She's started wondering if every child she sees in New Orleans is mine. That's one of the reasons this move to Seattle seems like a good idea."

The shriek of Lily's laughter carries over the noise of the crowd.

She twists toward us. "Auntie Quinn! Mr. Zack! The ele-funk's takin' a shower!"

I look over, and sure enough, one of the elephants has lifted her trunk over her head to spray her broad gray back with water.

"Come up here an' watch with us!" Lily calls.

"We're being summoned," I say to Zack.

"So it appears." He grins, then gestures for me to precede him through the crowd. As he follows me to the front of the exhibit, I tell myself two things. One: the only reason my heart skips when he smiles is because his dimple is a dead ringer for Lily's; and two: he's absolutely right about his move to Seattle being a good idea.

CHAPTER TWENTY-TWO

Jessica

"HOW WAS THE ZOO?" I ask when Zack answers his phone.

"Oh, man, it was awesome!" His voice is more upbeat and exuberant than he's sounded in weeks. Maybe months. Possibly even years.

"That's terrific." I try my best to sound cheerful. I excused myself from looking at a house with Brett and went outside to place this call. The truth is, I'm almost sick with jealousy that he spent the day with Lily and Quinn, but I'm relieved that Zack no longer sounds tense or angry.

"Lily is just amazing," Zack says.

"Yeah?"

"She's a bundle of pure, unfiltered joy. She and her friend literally jumped up and down when they were happy or excited. I always thought 'jumping for joy' was a figure of speech."

"Kids are fun," I say.

"They are," he agrees. "One of the elephants gave himself a bath, and you would have thought it was the funniest, most exciting thing that had happened in world history. And then there was a little orangutan who cracked us all up, and Lily wanted to know if he was being funny on purpose. We went to the petting zoo, and her little friend Alicia was afraid of the goats, but Lily just went right up to them—she was fearless, but extremely gentle. Really, Jessica—she's just amazing! At the giraffe exhibit she started crying because giraffes were her mother's favorite animal, and she misses her mom."

"Oh, how heartbreaking!"

"Yeah. It was tough to take." I can tell that he was really moved.

"But Quinn is fantastic with her. She got Lily to talk about the fun times she'd had with her mom and told her that she's probably riding giraffes in heaven, and before I knew it, Lily was back to smiling and chattering."

"That's great." A bitter taste fills the back of my throat.

"Kids are really resilient, you know? I don't think a three-year-old totally understands the concept of death, but it's probably for the best. Anyway, by the end of the day, it was as if Lily had known me her whole life. I carried her for a while because her shoe started to hurt and we had to find a Band-Aid. She calls me Mr. Zack."

"I can't wait to meet her," I tell him. "In fact, I'm thinking about coming home early."

A long, awkward silence follows. I'm beginning to think the connection has dropped. "Oh, you don't need to do that," Zack finally says. Is there something a bit off in his voice, or am I just paranoid?

"I know I don't need to, but I want to. I miss you."

He hesitates again. It's a really short pause—no more than a heartbeat, really. "I miss you, too."

I don't know if it's that tiny hesitation or if something in his voice sounds forced, but the words somehow don't ring true. I feel as if all my blood has drained away.

"How about you? How was your day?" he asks.

"It's two hours earlier here, so it's still in progress. After a long morning meeting and lunch with the regional staff, I met up with Brett to tour a house that just came on the market. We're at the property now."

"Well, I won't keep you." Am I imagining it, or does he sound eager to end the call?

"How is Margaret?" I ask.

"She's holding her own. She'll probably be released from the ICU to a private room tomorrow or the next day."

"That's good."

"Absolutely," he says. "Look, I know you're busy, so I'll let you go."

He's definitely wanting to end the call. "All right. I love you!" I say.

"Back at you." This is our standard sign-off, but under the circumstances, I don't feel good about it. I don't feel good at all.

I hang up and wander back into the house. Brett looks at me. "Bad news?"

"Yeah, sort of." I muster a smile. "It's that obvious?"

"I make a living reading clients' facial expressions and body language, because they're often too polite to say what they really think. So either you just had an upsetting phone call or you hate the house."

"It's not the house."

"Well, then, let's get out of here and go for a drink. I don't want the bad mojo to bleed onto the place, because I think you could really like it."

"I could use a drink." My parents are having my brother and pregnant sister-in-law over for dinner this evening, and I'm not looking forward to it.

We settle at a bar named the Tiki. Through a large tinted plate-glass window, I watch waves bob on the Puget Sound, one after another, white-capped and foamy. I know that the water's cold, despite the bar's tropical decor. I feel cold, too, despite the unusually warm weather. I order a glass of wine. "This is one of the perks of not trying to get pregnant," I say. "I can drink."

"Sue Anne hated everything about being pregnant. She complained the whole time."

"Really? And here I'd give anything to have a baby."

"My mom said she felt the same way."

I look at him, not getting it.

"My mom couldn't have children," he explains. "My brother and I are adopted."

This shocks me. "But you look so much like her!"

"Everyone says that. Know what I think?"

"What?"

"People see what they expect to see." He gives a slight grin. "I think that's one of the great unspoken truths of life."

"Maybe so. Did you ever look for your birth mother?"

"No. There was a nanosecond when I was fifteen and rebellious, and I told my parents I wanted to find her and go live with her. My dad said, 'Okay. I'll help.'" Brett smiles. "That was the end of it. I never had any real desire to follow through. No one could have made me feel more loved than my folks did."

The waitress brings our drinks. Brett hoists his beer. "Here's to finding you a home in Seattle."

I clink my wineglass to his stein. "To a home in Seattle."

We both take a drink, and he studies me over the edge of his mug. "I know it's none of my business, and if you don't want to, I totally get it. But if you want to talk about that phone call, well, I'm a good listener."

I sip my wine for a moment. "I screwed something up."

"Hey, that's called being human."

"No, I mean I *really* screwed up. I did something seriously wrong—a breach-of-trust kind of thing with Zack."

His expression stays the same, but his neck kind of stiffens. "Another guy?"

"No, not that. But I went behind Zack's back to find out some personal stuff from his past, and, well, now it's backfiring."

He leans forward. "I gotta say, you've got me intrigued."

Before I know it, I'm spilling out the whole story.

"Wow," Brett says.

I take a sip of wine. "I told you I screwed up."

"It's not irreversible. I mean, no one's dead. But I do have a question."

"Shoot."

"Did you really think you'd feel better once you found out he had a child?"

Both Zack and my sister had asked the same question. Apparently it's something I should have considered more carefully. I blow out a long breath. "It's hard to imagine now, but yeah—I guess I did. I thought knowing would be better than wondering. It's part of my personality, you know? I don't like uncertainty. Maybe that's why I'm into numbers and accounting. I like to know what I'm dealing with."

"What kind of reaction did you think Zack would have?"

"Well, that's the thing: I wasn't going to tell him because he didn't seem to want to know. But then, when I found out a child was looking for him, I knew I needed to tell him. But I thought I'd wait until I got pregnant before I broke the news."

"Wait." He furrows his brow. "I thought you couldn't get pregnant."

"I can't—not with my eggs. But finding out Zack already has a child made me decide to use an egg donor. He'd encouraged me to use a donor after the first two IVF transfers failed, but I refused, because I wanted the baby to be genetically my own."

The waitress sets down a fresh glass of wine. I take a big swallow. "Anyway, when the cryobank alerted him that someone tried to change the email address on his account, he knew it had to be me. I didn't intend to tell him anything yet, but I felt so guilty it just kind of spilled out."

"Wow." Brett takes a drink, the whole time eyeing me over the rim.

I sigh. "I told you I screwed up."

"Yeah, but you came clean with him. That shows an honorable intention."

"Zack doesn't see it that way. I thought he'd be glad I'd finally decided to use an egg donor, but he doesn't even care about that. All he cares about is this donor child." I give him a rundown of my latest phone conversation with Zack, and pull up a photo of Lily on my phone. "He's completely head over heels."

"Holy moly," Brett says. "She's adorable."

"Yeah. I opened a real Pandora's box."

"I guess you have."

My eyes fill with tears.

"But, hey—if you two love each other, you can work this out." He lifts his beer. "And maybe it'll all turn out for the best."

I take a long gulp. "Yeah, right."

"I mean it." He leans forward. "You said the child's mother died, that the great-grandmother is elderly and in the hospital, and that there's no other family. That means your husband is the only blood relative. Maybe you two can get custody of the little girl."

I shake my head. "The child's godmother is designated as guardian in the mother's will if the great-grandmother can't take care of her. She has a really close relationship with the child." I outline the therapist's plan for Zack to be a distant family friend.

"Yes, but you said your husband's an attorney. I'm sure there're ways to override the will. Usually a natural parent is favored by the courts. Maybe your husband could be named guardian, and the child can come out here to live with you."

The idea doesn't appeal to me at first. I want a baby, one that grows under my own heart. My hesitation must have shown on my face.

"I'm thinking like a father here," he says. "Three is still really young. Lily's unlikely to remember much, if anything, of her life before you. She needs a mother and a father. You and your husband could be that for her."

The concept starts to gain some luster. I don't really think it would work, but maybe making the offer—letting Zack know I'm willing to take in his child—would go a long way toward healing our marriage.

Brett's gaze is warm. "I can tell you from my own experience, both as a father and as an adopted child—what matters to a kid is the day-in, day-out love and attention. My parents and I were a lot closer than most of my friends who lived with their biological moms and dads. There's more than one way to build a family."

We finish our drinks, and he drives me to my parents' home. The more I think about what he said, the more appealing the concept grows. I pause after he pulls into the drive and puts the vehicle in park. "Thanks for the house tours—and the drinks, and the advice."

He smiles at me. "No problem."

"What are you doing this evening?"

"Little league practice. Want to come?"

"Sounds like fun." I smile, my hand on the door handle. "I wish I could, but Mom's planning a family dinner."

"Maybe another time."

"I'd like that." I open the door, but stay seated. "I'll think about the houses we've seen. That last one might be a possibility, but I can't really picture the renovations you suggested."

"I'll work up some graphics and send them to you."

"That would be great." I smile. "Hey—I've enjoyed getting to know you."

"Back at you." He has no way of knowing that's what Zack and I say to each other in response to *I love you*. My face heats all the same.

"So you're flying to Portland tomorrow?" he says.

"I'm supposed to. But right now, I'm thinking I might cancel the rest of my business trip and go back to New Orleans."

"I think that's a good idea," he says. "For what it's worth, I think you should meet this little girl, her guardian, and her great-grandmother."

"That's what I'm thinking."

He nods. "Keep me posted."

"I will."

He smiles and I linger in the car, just smiling back. I hate to leave. There's something effervescent and kind of exciting between us.

"Well, I'd better go," I say.

"Take care." He pats my shoulder as I climb out.

My shoulder tingles as I hoist my purse on it. I'm still smiling as I let myself into the house through the kitchen door, just as I did when I was a teenager and someone dropped me off.

There's a major difference, though: when I was a teenager, I never dared to dream I'd actually be driven home by Brett Ross.

CHAPTER TWENTY-THREE

Zack

Wednesday, May 15

I'M IN MY office, working on one of the biggest mergers of my career. It involves hundreds of health care facilities in two dozen states, and it has about a million moving parts. I need to make sure that we're meeting the legal requirements of every state and city, not to mention that the selling party is meeting all the standards set by the purchasing party.

I'm behind schedule, so I've turned off my phone, skipped lunch, and asked my assistant not to disturb me unless it's an emergency. My office has a glass wall, and I've put my laptop on the credenza behind my desk so I'm facing away from the entrance and am less likely to be distracted.

I hear the door to my office open and the click of heels on the floor. I figure it's Maggie, the paralegal, bringing me the additional research I requested.

"Just leave the papers on my desk," I say without turning around. "Thanks."

"You're welcome, but I didn't bring any papers."

It's not Maggie's voice—it's my wife's. I jerk up my head and swivel around in my chair. "Jess! What happened to all your meetings on the West Coast?"

"I missed you," she says.

I know that's not enough of a reason for her to cancel a series of meetings, but I decide to go along for the moment. She's wearing a tailored navy dress and her hair is down. She looks polished and professional and gorgeous, and most importantly, she's smiling.

I stand up and she crosses over to me, stepping behind my chair. Her perfume, Beautiful, wafts around me. I kiss her, and she gives me a hug. Through the door, my assistant, Gwen, is watching, her expression anxious. I'm sure she's wondering if she did the right thing, letting Jess interrupt me.

I give Gwen a thumbs-up. Her face creases into a relieved smile and she turns back to her computer.

"How did you get past Guard Gwen?" I ask.

Jessica glances at the woman with closely cropped gray hair who runs the office at optimum efficiency. "I told her I wanted to surprise you. She's really a romantic at heart."

I raise a skeptical eyebrow.

Jessica laughs. "Okay, okay. I told her I'm hoping to drag you to lunch. She said you've been eating at your desk or skipping lunch entirely."

"That's more like the Gwen I know." She's a pro at guarding me from unwelcome clients and other distractions, but she's all about three squares a day. I glance back at my computer. "Sorry, Jessica, but I'm really behind with this project."

"Hey, I got up at three this morning and flew cross-country to see you," she replies.

"Yeah, but . . ."

"You took off Monday afternoon to go to the zoo," she reminds me. "Surely you can spare the time for a quick bite with your wife."

I don't like the reprimand in her voice about taking some time off Monday, but it's not worth arguing about. "Okay, okay. But it'll have to be quick."

"No problem. I understand deadlines and work pressures."

"I know you do." That's one thing we have in common. At the moment, I'm feeling kind of hard-pressed to think of anything else. I grab my phone off my desk and my jacket off the back of the chair. "Let's go."

We head to the Store on Gravier Street—a deceptively plain-looking little diner that serves fabulous New Orleans food. I order the shrimp 'n slaw po'boy, and she orders the house salad with blackened shrimp.

"Why did you really bail on your meetings?" I ask, after we've settled at a table by the window.

She unfolds a napkin. "I hated the way we left things. I feel awful about what I did, and I want to make it up to you."

I squeeze a lemon wedge into my iced tea, putting my hand over it to contain the spray of juice. I want to say something like, *You can't put toothpaste back in the tube*, but opt to keep my mouth shut.

"You sounded so excited on the phone when you talked about Lily."

"Yeah, well, she's really something." I can't help but smile at the thought of her.

"So maybe you can forgive me a little?"

"I do." I say. What I don't say is, *But I'm not sure I entirely trust you*. "She's a terrific kid."

"I'd love to meet her."

I kind of freeze. Jess said this on the phone yesterday, but I can't help remembering all the times she launched into a crying jag at the possibility of me having a child. "Don't you think that'll be hard on you?"

"No, no—I'll be fine. I've done a lot of soul searching over the last few days, and I've really had a change of perspective."

She would have needed to have a complete change of personality. My expression must give away my thoughts, because she leans over the table.

"I mean it," she says. "I used to think it would be the worst thing in the world if another woman had your child when I can't give you one, but now, well . . ." She takes a sip of iced tea. When she puts down the glass, I notice her hand quivers a little. "Our argument made me realize that the worst thing in the world would be losing you."

It's the sort of comment that should move me, but it doesn't. I wonder if she's trying to play me somehow, and then I'm ashamed of the thought. *She's your wife*, I think. *Just tell her what she wants to hear.* "You don't have to worry about that. We're married, for better or for worse."

"I hope it's for better." Her smile seems a little forced. "Oh, I have some family news! My brother's wife is pregnant. We had a family dinner last night to celebrate."

"Oh, yeah?" She's always been distraught whenever anyone close to her becomes pregnant. *It's like they stuck a knife in a bleeding wound*, she once told me. *As if they're saying, "Na na na na boo boo, I can do what you can't do."*

"That must have been difficult for you," I say.

"It was when I first heard about it, but then Brett—he's my Realtor—said pregnancy isn't a competitive sport. And you know what? He's right. He also pointed out that my brother's baby has absolutely nothing to do with me, aside from being my new little niece or nephew. So I changed the way I think about it, and I'm happy for them."

I don't believe it; it's too pat and simplistic. I suspect my wife is feeding me a line of bull. This disturbs me a lot; whether she actually is or whether I just think she is, it doesn't speak well for the state of our marriage. "I wish I'd thought of that 'competitive sport' comment a couple of years ago and saved us both a world of pain," I say drily.

She gives a little laugh. "Yeah. I think my hormones must finally be balancing out or something."

"Well, great. That's great." I'm still not buying it. This is a pretty drastic transformation in three days' time.

"Have you told Lily yet that you're her father?" she asks.

"No."

"Don't you think you ought to?"

I'm more than a little confused by this. "I would have thought that's the last thing you'd want."

She tucks a strand of hair behind her ear. "Well, I imagine you're going to want to continue seeing her, so it seems like a natural next step."

Who are you, and what have you done with my wife? "Legally, I'm a donor, not a father," I say. "Besides, this is a bad time to pile on any more family confusion. And there's another issue at stake here: I want to honor the wishes of her late mother. Brooke intended to adhere to the terms of the donor contract, which means Lily's not supposed to find out the identity of her father until she's eighteen."

"Who said that? Quinn or Margaret?"

"Well, Quinn."

"But Margaret's still the legal guardian, right?"

I don't like the tone of these questions. "I haven't seen the will, but from what I understand, Quinn is primary guardian if Margaret is incapacitated. And Margaret is definitely incapacitated."

"Don't you think you ought to look at the will?"

I've thought of this, but I'm startled that Jess is bringing it up. "Why?"

She lifts her shoulders. "Just to know what it says about guardianship. You're the child's father, after all."

"Legally, I'm the anonymous donor. Where are you going with this?"

Jessica folds her hands on the table. "You're the next of kin. Maybe you could get guardianship, then I could adopt her and we could raise her in Seattle."

I stare at Jessica. "You've been freaked out about me having a child ever since you started trying to get pregnant."

"Zack, I've been thinking about it, and this might be the ideal solution for us. We'll get Lily, and then we'll have a child with a donor egg, and that child will be Lily's half sister. We'll be a complete family!"

Has she come *unhinged*? I raise my hands. "Whoa. This whole issue—it's not about *us*. This is about *Lily*."

"Well, sure, but it could work out in everyone's best interests."

"Not everyone's. I don't think it's in Lily's best interests, and it's sure not in Quinn's or Margaret's."

"Well, Quinn's not a blood relation, and it sounds like Margaret's too old and frail to care for her." She reaches across the table and puts both of her hands on top of mine. "This could be perfect for us. A whole new beginning—new jobs and a new home in a new state with a new family!"

I straighten my spine and pull my hands into my lap. "Jessica, you can't blithely dismiss the two people who're the center of Lily's world." My tone is terser than I intend, but I can't believe how self-absorbed she sounds. "Lily loves them. They're her family."

"She'll learn to love us. Sounds like she's already halfway in love with you."

I've already thought about trying to get guardianship of Lily. How could it not have entered my mind? For half a minute, I even allowed myself to fantasize about it, so I know how appealing the concept is. I also know it's wrong.

I shake my head. "I signed a contract stating I had no parental rights. Her mother made plans for Lily's care in the event she died, and I need to honor those plans. Besides, Lily loves Quinn, and Quinn is wonderful with her. I can't see putting Lily through any more upheaval."

"She's going through upheaval anyway. Why let her adjust to living with a stranger when she could be adjusting to living with her biological father?"

"Quinn's not a stranger. She's Lily's godmother, and she's known her all of her life. Quinn is already a mother figure to Lily."

"I could be just as good a mother."

I'm beginning to think that Jess has had some kind of breakdown or something. "Jess, you're not looking at this from the child's perspective."

She bulldozes on, as if I hadn't spoken. "Brett says that courts usually favor blood relatives."

"Brett seems to have a lot to say."

"Is he right?" Jessica presses.

"In a regular guardianship case, if all other things are equal," I concede, "but not in an anonymous donor situation. The chances of the donor contract being overruled are minute."

"You could try."

What part of this isn't she getting? "It isn't right, Jess—and not just because of the contract. The court always tries to do what's in the child's best interests, and in this case, that's Lily staying with Quinn. That was the mother's wish, and Quinn is the person Lily is most attached to."

"Yes, but Margaret reached out to find you while she was the primary guardian."

"Which I never would have known about if you hadn't gone through my papers."

Her mouth flattens. "That's water under the bridge."

To you, maybe. I don't want to hold a grudge, but damn it, I don't feel the same about Jessica. The whole incident has opened my eyes to some things I've avoided looking at. I blow out a hard sigh. Hell. I need to get over it.

"Margaret obviously wants you in Lily's life," Jessica says.

"Yes, and now I am."

"What if Margaret wants you to have custody?"

Jess has always been persistent—it's a quality I admire about her—but right now, it's getting under my skin. "Even if that were the case, Lily belongs with Quinn. The mother's wishes should take precedent."

She opens her mouth as if she's about to argue with me further, then closes it without saying a word. She toys with the paper napkin under her glass of iced tea. "I wonder if the will says who's supposed to be Lily's guardian if something happens to Quinn?"

"I don't know."

"You should find out, just so you know where things stand. Don't wills get filed somewhere after they go through probate?"

"In Louisiana, it's called succession instead of probate, but yeah, most wills are filed at the parish courthouse."

"So you could easily take a look at it."

"Yeah, if it's been filed." I tap my fingers on the table. It wouldn't hurt to know exactly what Brooke specified.

The waitress brings our food, and the conversation drifts to Jessica's family, but there's a stilted, phony feeling between us. I'm acting like an attentive husband instead of really being one. I feel like Jess is pretending, too. Her voice sounds a little too peppy and she keeps giving me her selfie smile.

"Is something wrong with your po'boy?" the waitress asks as she passes our table.

"Nah. I just don't have much appetite," I say.

"What time will you be home tonight?" Jessica asks after the waitress whisks our half-full plates away.

"I'm supposed to meet Richard for a drink after work," I tell her, naming a mutual friend who works at another firm. "He's giving me some help on my pro bono case."

"Can you cancel?"

I hesitate. "Why don't I see if Karen can join him, and we'll make it a double date for dinner?"

"Sure!" Jess agrees. "I haven't seen Karen in ages."

I'm relieved at the thought of not being alone with Jessica for the whole evening, then I feel bad about feeling relieved.

"It'll give me a chance to tell her good-bye before we move," Jessica says.

I don't want to move. The thought jars me. I've never been as enthused about the idea of moving to Seattle as Jessica, but I've never outright admitted that I don't want to leave New Orleans. *You agreed to it*, I remind myself. *A good man keeps his word*. It was something my father used to say, along with *your word is who you are.* Keeping my commitments is a cornerstone of my life.

And yet, everything is different now. When I agreed to move to Seattle, I didn't know I had a young daughter in New Orleans.

And I didn't know I had a wife who would betray my principles to get her own way.

CHAPTER TWENTY-FOUR

Margaret

"MA'AM? WE'RE GOING to move you to your room now."

My eyelids feel as heavy as boardinghouse biscuits. It's an enormous effort to open them just a sliver. When I do, I see a man in a short-sleeved aqua shirt beside me. My Henry had a shirt that color when Julia was a child, back in the sixties. He wore it to a crawfish boil we hosted on Mardi Gras; it was the month after Jackie Kennedy's televised White House tour, because I remember talking to a friend about how elegant her taste was, and how . . .

"We're going to lift you and put you on a gurney."

I will my eyes to open again. This young man isn't Henry, and his shirt doesn't have buttons down the front. It's some kind of medical attire.

"Am I in the hospital?" I croak.

"Yes. We just took you for an X-ray."

"Am I in ICU?"

"You were, but you're better now. You're going to a post-ICU room."

Better? I must have been really sick if this is better. I ache all over, and my hip feels even worse than it did after childbirth, when I tore a muscle while I was under the influence of "twilight sleep." The nurse told me I'd writhed around and refused to cooperate when they were putting my legs into slings, but I don't remember any of it. I just remember waking up and my hip hurting like the dickens, and . . .

"One, two, three."

The man in the blue-green shirt and someone on the other side hoist me up, and the next thing I know, I'm being I'm shifted onto a gurney. I'm vaguely aware of being wheeled down a long hall and around several corners. I may or may not have had a little ride in an elevator. After more wheeling, I'm lifted and shifted again, this time onto a bed. I'm turned on my side, and the sheet beneath me is pulled away. My hip throbs.

"Mrs. Moore?" I open my eyes and see a middle-aged woman with glasses smiling at me. "My name is Wanda. I'm the charge nurse, and I'm going to be taking care of you this evening."

My brain feels like a shaken snow globe—as if it's filled with thick liquid, and all of my thoughts and memories are little pieces just drifting around. My eyelids close as she arranges the covers over me and a memory floats by.

I'm five or six years old, lying in my old iron bed in the Lafayette house, covered with outdoor-scented sheets and a quilt my grandmother made. My skin is itchy and spotted and I feel sick, so very, very sick. I'm freezing; I never knew a person could feel so cold. A doctor hovers over me, his stethoscope like ice on my chest. After a moment, he removes it and talks. His words are mostly a murmur, but I clearly hear the word measles. *Mama walks him to the door, then comes back.*

"I'm so c-c-cold." My teeth are chattering. I'm afraid my upper and bottom teeth—I have some brand-new ones that feel too big for my mouth—will break against each other.

"Poor darling. You're burning up with fever." My mother pulls down the bedcovers, gently lifts my pajama top, and swabs a cold washcloth over my chest. "We have to cool you down so you won't feel so chilled."

I believe her, even though the cool cloth makes me flinch and shiver harder, and I don't understand how getting cooler will make me warmer. But I know she loves me, and I trust that she knows things I don't.

A woman's voice interrupts my thoughts. "Are you in pain?"

I can't keep my eyes open for more than a second. It's a nurse. "My hip hurts. Did I just have a baby?"

She gives a soft laugh. "No, ma'am. You had a heart attack, then fell and broke your hip."

"Oh." I don't remember anything about that, but I remember something else, something about another hospital a long time ago.

I'm nine years old, and my mother is in the hospital. I don't know what's wrong and children aren't allowed in patients' rooms. All I know is that Mama hasn't been herself lately—she lies down a lot and hasn't played with me in a while—and Papa's eyes are sad. Papa's sister, Aunt Kathy, and her husband, Uncle Floyd, have come to help Papa take care of me and my little sister. They all whisper whenever they talk about Mama.

Everyone but Uncle Floyd. He has a loud voice, and I hear him say exploratory surgery *while he's talking on the telephone. I wander into the hallway where he's sitting on the gossip bench, but he doesn't notice me. "The doctors cut her open and took a look," he says to whoever's on the other end of the line, "then they just closed her up again."*

A panicky feeling jumps in my stomach, like channel mullet in Lake Pontchartrain. I tug on his jacket. "Are you talking about Mama?"

He looks at me, surprised. Aunt Kathy comes in the hall and whacks him on the shoulder. "I told you not to talk about certain subjects in front of certain little somebodies."

He holds his hand over the telephone mouthpiece. "I didn't know she was there!"

"Miss Margaret?" A familiar voice jerks me back to the present. I find myself gazing into a young woman's concerned hazel eyes. "It's Quinn."

"Yes, I know, dear," I say, although I couldn't have come up with her name for love or money.

"Are you feeling better?"

"They say I am, but everything's fuzzy." My mind feels like a ball of yarn, and thinking is like trying to knit a sweater. Only thing is, I never learned to knit.

"That's the pain meds," the nurse says. She looks down at me from the other side of the bed. "You were given an extra-large dose before they took you to X-ray to check your lungs."

"Are they worried about pneumonia?" Quinn asks.

"That, and congestive heart failure," the nurse says.

I know about pneumonia—my aunt Kathy died of that. And heart failure . . . well, my father passed of a heart attack. "Am I dying?" I ask.

"No. You're getting better," the nurse says.

They won't tell you truth. The worse off you are, the more likely it is they'll lie about it. There are matters I need to settle. Now, if I can just remember what they are . . .

I pull my brows together and try to focus. Quinn is Brooke's friend. Brooke is gone. "You're caring for Lily," I say, remembering. "And I found her father, right?"

"That's right."

"Has Lily met him?"

"Yes. We went for ice cream and then to the zoo together."

"Good, good. How did Lily react to meeting him?"

"She—uh, I didn't tell her he's her father. She thinks he's just a friend of mine."

I frown.

Quinn continues on in a rush. "My friend Sarah is a psychologist—you met Sarah after Brooke died, remember? She was a close friend of Brooke's, as well. Anyway, I talked to Sarah about this, and she thinks we should wait."

The memory of seeing all my deceased family members fills my mind. "But she needs to know she has a blood relative. I may not have much time."

"Oh, don't say that!" Quinn's voice is full of distress.

"I'm old, dear." I pause. I'm trying to remember a conversation I had with a man in a white coat—my doctor. Was it just this morning? I believe it was. A sense of urgency rises inside me. I need to tell her this. "I asked my doctor when I would be well enough to care for Lily, and he said . . ." My throat grows thick, and it's hard to force the next words out. I make myself do it. "He said I'll probably never be strong enough for that. He said I should make alter . . . alternate plans."

Quinn's eyes are suddenly full of tears. She squeezes my hand. "I love Lily. I'll care for her as if she were my very own."

"I know, dear, but things can happen. I know all too well how . . ." The past is a swamp, and I feel like I'm sinking in it. "Lily needs to know her father."

My thoughts are as muddy as marsh water. I need to be clear-headed to have this talk. I see the nurse writing something on the whiteboard across from my bed. "How long until this medicine wears off?" I call to her.

She turns to me. "The extra dose should clear in three or four more hours, but you'll be on morphine for the next few days. We need to stay ahead of the pain, because the doctor thinks that's what made your heart race in the ICU."

"Oh, fiddle!"

"We'll talk about everything later." Quinn's voice is gentle, and so is her touch on my hand. "I have a meeting scheduled with your doctor to discuss your treatment plan. For now, just rest and get better. Lily is fine."

My sense of urgency battles with debilitating fatigue. Fatigue is winning. "All right," I say, "but Lily needs to know." My eyes are already closing, and I'm sinking into blissful oblivion.

CHAPTER TWENTY-FIVE

Jessica

THE WINDOW DISPLAY of the decor shop, Verve!, looks like the exquisite Parisian apartment of someone with beaucoup more style than moi. I admire designs that combine unexpected elements with panache, but it's not something I could ever pull together myself, so I'm intimidated as I open the door and step off the Magazine Street sidewalk.

The first thing I notice inside the shop is the scent. It's exotic and earthy, like amber and black cardamom, and it strikes a note of wistfulness in my chest like a haunting piano chord. If I were to give it a name, I'd call it "Longing." The place smells of beautiful things I don't have, can't fully understand, and will never be. It's the kind of place that rattles every insecure bone in my body.

I know that on the outside, I appear to have it all together. I've worked hard to curate my image, but inside, it's a different story. I've always wanted to be the best at everything, and, of course, that's just not possible. I'm constantly judging myself against others. *How am I doing? How do I compare? Do I measure up?* I'm particularly uncomfortable when I feel like I'm competing in an arena that's not one of my strengths. Like this.

The shop is unattended, so I walk around. The merchandise is a mix of new, vintage, and antique furnishings. Overhead, light fixtures twinkle—classic crystal chandeliers, Sputnik-shaped pendants, shaded ceiling lamps—and throughout the space, artwork and accessories highlight distinctive furniture groupings. The items are all striking and tasteful and arranged in beautiful vignettes. I appreciate and admire this complicated aesthetic, but I could never personally orchestrate it. Consequently, my decorating style defaults toward modern furnishings that are clearly designed to go together.

I'm practical when it comes to interior decor; why can't I apply that same approach to other areas of my life, such as wanting to have a child? Probably because of the universal truth that Emily Dickinson so eloquently penned: "The Heart wants what it wants—or else it does not care."

I cross the room and examine a midcentury lamp. I think it would go well with our living room furnishings, but I'm pretty sure Zack would be upset to learn I've been in Quinn's shop. From the way he avoided my question about when I'll meet Lily, I'm afraid he doesn't want me involved in his child's life—or, by extension, in Quinn's life, or Miss Margaret's.

I'm even more afraid of something else: that I've irrevocably broken our marriage.

Thinking about it makes me feel as if air is in short supply. I inhale deeply and search my mind for a more optimistic way to look at things. I'm usually able to spin things to a more positive perspective.

Up until now, Zack and I have always worked things out. A little time would go by, and whatever disagreement we had would fade into the background. We'd reconnect and move on.

But this situation is different. I feel it in my gut, in the place where hard truths live. We were already unraveling before we had that argument. Instead of reconnecting with me, Zack is connecting with his newly discovered daughter.

His daughter, not *our* daughter. That little possessive adjective looms large. He's forming a relationship with Lily, and that relationship has nothing to do with me.

I couldn't believe how hard and how fast he shot down my idea of us trying to get custody of her. I'd thought that was the answer—for me to embrace her, for us to become a family, for all of us to move to Seattle and leave these outsiders behind. I'm shocked by how badly I miscalculated his reaction. I'm starting to feel like I'm married to a stranger.

I pick up an antique perfume atomizer from a mirrored boudoir tray and lift it to my nose, hoping to get a hint of what it used to hold. It smells vaguely sweet and distant. If I were naming it, I'd call it "Memories of My Marriage."

Well, I intend to revitalize our relationship. I've read that the easiest way to feel closer to your spouse is to share a great experience together. I need to give the whole seducing-my-husband concept another try tonight. That's the real reason I flew home. There are some things you just have to handle in person.

We need to reestablish our marital bond. I'm not liking how much time and emotional energy he's spending with Quinn and Lily.

Especially Quinn. She's pretty, accomplished, and the guardian of his child, and . . .

"May I help you?"

An attractive blond woman in her late forties or early fifties steps from a back room. She's wearing a cream-colored shift with a Ferragamo scarf and Tabitha Simmons sling-backs, and she looks as well put together as the store displays.

I put the perfume bottle back on the tray. "Oh, I'm just looking."

"Of course. Take your time."

Maybe she's the one who arranged all the merchandise. "It's a beautiful shop," I say.

"Yes, isn't it? The owner, Quinn Langston, is very talented."

So much for my hopes.

"I'd love to meet her," I say. "Is she here?"

"Not at the moment. She left to pick up her godchild from preschool, but she should be back in a few minutes."

So maybe Lily will be with her? My heart pounds hard. I don't know what Quinn has or hasn't shared with her employees about Zack's appearance in her life, so I don't ask.

"Are you wanting to schedule a consultation?" the woman asks.

"She doesn't have any openings right now, but I'm her assistant, and I'm available." She gives a diffident smile.

"Actually, I'd just like to browse."

"Of course. Make yourself at home." She retreats to the back of the store.

I amble through the displays until I hear a door open in the back. "Hello there, Lily," the older woman says.

"Hi, Miss Terri!" exclaims a high, childlike voice.

Loud smooching sounds follow. I hear another woman talking with Terri, and then Quinn walks into the front room. I recognize her from her photos, but she's taller and prettier in person. I feel a stab of jealousy. She's wearing jeans, a black shirt, and a thin gray sweater. Her hair is pulled back in a ponytail, and what looks like an antique turquoise necklace hangs around her throat.

She gives me a friendly smile. "Hello. Is there something I can help you with?"

"I'm just enjoying your lovely store."

"Thank you. Is there anything in particular you're looking for?"

I lift my shoulders. "I'm going to be moving soon, so I'm collecting ideas. I hope you don't mind."

"Oh, no, that's exactly what this place is all about."

"Is the bunny chair still here?" The child's voice floats from the side room.

"The what?" I recognize Terri's voice.

"You had a chair with bunnies on it the last time I was here."

"Oh, right—the Easter display. The chair's still here, but I'm afraid the bunnies are all gone."

"Oh."

The little girl steps into my view. She's wearing capris printed with lollipops, a T-shirt with a ruffled neckline, and a pink tutu. Her hair is light blond and wavy, pulled away from her face with an enormous pink bow. And her eyes . . . my breath hitches in my throat. Her eyes are exactly like Zack's.

"How 'bout the Sunshine King's chair?"

Quinn puts her hand on the child's head. "Clever girl—you remembered that Louis the Fourteenth was called the Sun King."

She nods.

"That chair sold," Terri says.

"Aww!" Lily exclaims.

"But we have a new one that's painted like the Cat in the Hat."

"Ooh! Ooh! I want to see!" She yo-yos up and down on her toes, then spots me and ducks behind Quinn. "Who's that lady?" she whispers very loudly.

"She's a customer," Quinn whispers back.

"Oh. She's really pretty."

Quinn looks at me and smiles, apparently knowing how the child's voice carries. "She is, isn't she?"

"Thanks," I say to Lily. "You're very pretty, too."

Lily steps out from behind Quinn. "Thank you." She smiles, and my heart swoons. She's got Zack's dimple!

She tilts her head as she looks at me. "You kinda look like the mommy of one of my friends. Are you a mommy?"

"I don't have any children," I say, "but I'd like to."

"Well, you'd better hurry up."

"Lily!" Quinn scolds. She gives me an apologetic smile.

"My mommy says ladies shouldn' wait too late to have chil'ren," Lily says.

"Oh," I say, a little flabbergasted. Lily—or maybe her mother—seems eerily psychic.

"My mommy died," Lily announces.

"Oh!" I know this, of course, but I'm jarred to hear her say it. "I'm—I'm very sorry."

Lily nods somberly. "She's in heaven. An' my grams is in the hospital, but she might not die because she got to have an op'ration. I was livin' with her, but now I live with Auntie Quinn."

"Oh. Well. How . . . nice," I say, at a loss for words.

Quinn puts her hand on Lily's head and gives me an apologetic smile. "I'm sure that's more information than you bargained for."

"Mommy says it's always good to have lots of information," Lily pipes up.

"She sounds like a very smart lady," I say.

"She is."

"I can tell you take after her." I smile at Lily, then turn to Quinn. "Well, I'd better be going. Thank you for letting me look around."

"Come back anytime." Quinn walks me to the door and picks up a business card from a silver bowl. "If we can help with any of your design needs, let us know."

"I'm afraid I'm about to move out of state," I say.

"Not a problem. We do video phone consultations with long-distance clients all the time."

"Terrific." I take the card. "Thanks." I wave at Lily, who is climbing on a rocking horse at the side of the room. "Good-bye."

She waves back. "Bye."

The bell above the door tinkles as I hurry outside. About half a block away, I toss the card into a trash can, wishing I could rid my life of this whole complication as easily.

CHAPTER TWENTY-SIX

Quinn

I GET GOOSE bumps when I first see the beautiful brunette in my store. She looks familiar, but I'm not entirely certain who she is until I pull out my cell phone and re-google Zack's wife.

"Sure enough," I murmur.

"What's going on?" Terri asks.

I put my finger to my lips and eye Lily, who's climbed off the rocking horse and is now playing tea party with a vintage Raggedy Ann doll. I hand Terri my phone. She studies the photo, but still looks confused.

"Lily," I call, "Terri and I need to look at the window display from the street. We'll be right outside on the sidewalk. You can see us through the window, and we can see you."

We hustle out the front door.

"That's the woman who was just here, all right," Terri says, pointing at the photo on my cell phone screen. "Who is she?"

"Jessica Bradley. Zack's wife."

"Oh!" Terri's eyes widen. "Why didn't she just say so?"

"I imagine she wanted to quietly scope out the situation."

"Why?"

I blow out a long breath. "I hope she's just curious, but I'm afraid that Zack wants guardianship of Lily."

"Oh, no!" Terri's brows pull together over worried eyes. "Quinn, you need to talk to your lawyer."

I nod, my stomach tight. "You're right."

"Why on earth did Margaret stir all this up?"

I lift my shoulders. "I think she was going to tell me yesterday, but she was too groggy."

"How's she doing? You had a meeting with her doctor today, didn't you?"

I nod. As the legal guardian of her great-grandchild, I qualify as her next of kin. "I met with the hospitalist overseeing her care to discuss her treatment plan. Tomorrow or the next day, they hope to move her to a regular patient room on a floor where she'll get more extensive physical and occupational therapy. She'll be there a week or two, then she'll go to an inpatient rehabilitation facility for a few weeks."

"Here in New Orleans?"

"Yes. There's no one in Alexandria to care for her. Her friends are all her age or older."

"So you're Lily's permanent guardian?"

I nod. That's the one good thing that's come out of all this. "Seems like it. I need to talk to my attorney, but Margaret seems accepting of the fact that she won't be able to care for Lily. My fear is that she'll want to get Zack named guardian instead of me."

"She can't do that, can she? She's not even mentally stable."

"She's less out of it than she was right after the surgery, but she's not completely clearheaded. She had some heart damage and she's intermittently on oxygen. The doctors aren't sure if it's fluctuating oxygen levels or if she has a little brain damage or if she's just confused from the anesthesia and all the pain meds."

"Oh, dear."

"Yeah," I say. "And her birthday is Friday."

"She turns eighty?"

I nod. "I want to hold a little party for her in the hospital. I thought I'd get a cake and invite the single parent group. And you, of course!"

"Oh, that sounds lovely!"

"I'm hoping it will perk her up."

"Count me in! You know I'll do whatever I can to help out in any way."

"You've been an amazing help," I say. "You've taken the burden of running the shop and the business off my shoulders and you've been a wonderful friend."

She shrugs. "I always dreamed of having a shop like this, so getting to run it is a dream come true."

My heart swells with fondness. "Thanks, Terri."

"Don't mention it." She looks at her watch. "You need to call your attorney before his office closes. I'll go back inside and check on Lily."

"I don't know how I'd manage without you."

"Well, hopefully you'll won't get a chance to find out." She points to the phone in my hand. "Use that thing and call!"

CHAPTER TWENTY-SEVEN

Zack

Thursday, May 16

I'VE ALMOST MADE it out of the bedroom without waking Jess, but then my keys jangle against the stainless steel tray on my bureau when I pick them up.

"Are you going for a run?" Jess asks in a sleep-muzzy voice.

"Sorry—I didn't mean to wake you." The keys rattle a little more as I put them in my pocket.

"What time is it?"

"Early."

She reaches for her phone on the nightstand and brings it in front of her face. "It's just five forty-five." She raises up on an elbow and squints at me in the semidarkness. "And you're already dressed for work?"

"Yeah. I'm going by the hospital to talk to Margaret's cardiologist. He makes rounds early."

She sits up, flips on the bedside lamp, and scowls. "Why would you do *that*?"

Her tone needles me. "Quinn can't do it because she has Lily, and children her age aren't allowed in the post-ICU rooms. It's a way I can help out."

She pushes her hair out of her face, settles back against the headboard, and folds her arms. "You're more involved with Quinn than you are with me."

I draw a deep breath. *Love is patient, love is kind*, I remind myself. "Look—Lily and Quinn and Margaret are in a difficult situation right now. I can help out, so that's what I'm going to do."

"But, Zack, going to the hospital at this hour and talking to her doctor—it's too much. It's overinvolvement. It's—it's inappropriate."

I feel my face turn to granite. My sister used to call me Stoneface Zackson, because my face gets kind of hard and unmoving when I'm upset. My voice gets hard, too. "I'm sorry you feel that way."

"So you're just going to ignore my feelings and do it anyway?"

"I care what you think and feel, Jess, but I can't let your insecurities run my life."

"My insecurities?" Her eyes go wide and hurt.

I sigh. I know better than to speak so bluntly, but it's hard to constantly tiptoe around her. "Sorry. I should have worded that more sensitively." I grab my phone and my watch and start toward the door.

"Wait—you're right, Zack. I do feel insecure. Truth be told, I feel threatened as hell."

It's a new move for her, admitting she's vulnerable. I turn back and circle the bed to kiss her good-bye. "You have nothing to feel threatened about."

"I know I don't. I'm being ridiculous." She clasps her arms around my neck. "I enjoyed last night."

"I did, too." We'd made love for the first time in a long, long time. Having dinner with friends had been good for us—we'd laughed and talked and had a few of drinks, and things had loosened up between us. And then, as soon as we stepped through the door of the condo, Jess had pressed herself against me and unfastened my belt.

"I want you," she'd whispered, her mouth against my lips, her fingers moving on to my zipper. "Right here. Right now."

We'd stripped off each other's clothes in the living room, then I'd carried her to the bedroom. It wasn't tender makeup sex; it was hard and fast and primal, more about physical release than emotional connection. When it was over, I'd held her close and listened to her talk about houses in Seattle. She always likes to talk after sex, but all I really wanted to do last night was sleep.

"I'll see you this evening," I tell her now.

"What time?"

"I don't know. I'll call you."

"I'm looking forward to it." She playfully twirls my tie. "But instead of waiting all day, you could just take off that suit and come back to bed right now."

I grin and back away. "Sorry, but I can't."

"I'll make it worth your while."

"I'm sure you would, but I have to go."

She huffs out a displeased sigh. "You don't *have* to. You *want* to."

"Come on, Jess, It's the right thing to do."

"And it's not right to care about your wife's feelings?"

"Don't turn this into something it's not." Damn it, I hate it when she tries to manipulate me. I head to the door. "Talk to you later."

I take the stairs down to the parking garage. It's probably not fair to Jessica, but ever since the donor site debacle, I've found myself critical of her behavior. I keep thinking, *Who is this?* She wasn't like this when I married her—was she?

Maybe she was and I just couldn't see it. We became involved just a few months after my father died, when I was in a pretty dark place. I'd lost my mother the year before, and when Dad passed so suddenly and unexpectedly, I'd felt completely unmoored. I missed having a sense of family.

I met Jessica at the wedding of a law school classmate at the Columns Hotel on St. Charles Avenue. I was a groomsman, and she was a work friend of the bride. The couple had tried to set us up earlier, but I'd declined; I hated fix-ups.

The bride's sister sailed over to my table at the reception. "I was told that one of my duties as matron of honor was to introduce you to Jessica and make sure you danced with her."

"Okay," I said. I followed her across the room, and she introduced me to a knockout brunette in a burgundy dress.

Jessica bowled me over with her looks and her smarts. That dance had led to brunch the next day. She made it clear early on that she wanted marriage and children, and that she'd always dreamed of a summer wedding. Six months later, I proposed to her under the branches of a sprawling oak at New Orleans City Park during the annual Christmastime Celebration in the Oaks. Everyone said, "Wow, this is all happening really fast," but I figured, what's the point of waiting?

She planned an elaborate wedding in Seattle for the following summer. As the event drew closer, dread loomed over me like a storm-threatening cloud. I didn't want to admit it even to myself, but I was having second thoughts. I lost sleep, I lost weight, and I lost my ability to concentrate.

An older attorney at the firm took me for a drink three weeks before the ceremony. "You look like hell, son. What's wrong?"

I spilled my worries about my upcoming marriage. "I don't know if she's the right woman, or if she just came along at the right time."

"There's not a lot of difference," he said. "You could build a good marriage with any number of women. It's a matter of making a commitment and sticking to it."

The words sounded practical.

"You made a commitment to marry her when you proposed, so you're in pretty deep already," he added.

"Yeah." I've always been big believer in honoring commitments—my dad was a stickler about keeping your word—which was why I was so freaked out to be having second thoughts. "But what if proposing was a mistake?" I asked. "I'm not sure I feel as strongly about her as I should."

"It's normal to have doubts before making a major life step." He swirled his tumbler of scotch."The question is, are you unsure enough to break her heart, embarrass her and her family, and cost her parents all the wedding expenses that can't be recouped?"

In the end, I wasn't sure I was *that* unsure. I couldn't even articulate my reasons for having cold feet, so I kept my mouth shut, chalked it up to pre-wedding jitters, and married Jessica as planned.

As far as I'm concerned, marriage is for life; I said those words at the altar, so I intend to stick by them. *I need to have more compassion*, I think now as I cross through the parking garage. Jessica's been through a lot; she sees her infertility as a personal failure, and the miscarriage and unsuccessful treatments have really taken a toll on her. They've taken a toll on me, too, but mostly they've taken a toll on our marriage.

Going through a hard time can put lot of pressure on a relationship. Sometimes it pushes a couple together; I think about my parents, working so hard to reimagine and rebuild my father's business when the big-box store moved next door. Other times it pulls them apart; I think about my buddy Austin, whose marriage broke up after he lost his job and he couldn't find a comparable one.

I feel for Jess, I really do. I know that suddenly having Lily in my life is tough on her, but she's the one who couldn't leave well enough alone, who insisted on finding out if I had a child. Despite my empathy for her, I can't seem to let go of the fact that this is all her doing.

That's one of my character flaws; I have trouble letting things go. *I need to work on that*, I think as I climb into my car and start the engine. *Love* is an action word; it's something you do, not just something you feel. I need to try harder, to put in more effort, to be more understanding.

The sun is rising over the bend in the levee as I pull out from the parking garage, and I squint in the glare. I always heard that marriage is a lot of work, but my parents never seemed to struggle at it.

Another, more unsettling thought hits me as I look both ways before turning onto Tchoupitoulas: at some point, isn't marriage supposed to be a two-way street?

CHAPTER TWENTY-EIGHT

Quinn

"THANK YOU FOR working me into your schedule, especially on such short notice," I say to my attorney as his assistant escorts me into his office at ten Thursday morning.

The nameplate on his desk says, *Martin Stephen Schiller, Esq.*, but everyone calls him Marty. He has a slight paunch, a nearly bald hairline, and bushy gray eyebrows that look like caterpillars, but the brown eyes under them are warm and intelligent, and he has a fatherly way about him that puts me at ease. He has photos of his wife and two grown daughters on his desk. Every time I come to his office, I wonder if they realize how lucky they are to have such a great guy as their dad.

I first met Marty, as I met practically everyone else I now know in New Orleans, through Brooke. He handled her will and other legal affairs. When I first became interested in moving to Louisiana, she referred me to him, and he helped me set up my business.

Margaret and I went to his office together shortly after Brooke's death, and he gently guided us through her will. Brooke had considerable assets from her late parents' estate and life insurance benefits, and she carried a large life insurance policy herself. She left Lily well provided for. Among other arrangements, she set up a trust to pay Lily's guardian a generous monthly stipend for her care.

Marty rises from behind his desk and walks around in front of it as his assistant leaves the office and closes the door. "It's always a pleasure to see you, Quinn." He shakes my hand in both of his and we exchange pleasantries. "I was so sorry to hear about Margaret's health problems," he says. "How's she doing?"

I'd explained the situation to his receptionist when I made the appointment. "She's better, but she's in for a long rehabilitation, and she's had some permanent damage to her heart. The doctor calls this a 'life-changing event.'"

"I'm so sorry to hear that," Marty says. "I assume that means it's a life-changing event for you and Lily, as well."

I nod. "It looks like it. I have a few questions about Brooke's will."

"Of course, of course." He gestures for me to sit down across from his desk in a navy armchair printed with tiny fleurs-de-lis, and he seats himself next to me in an identical one, eschewing his desk chair. "This seems to be a day for that."

I lift my eyebrows. "What?"

"Well, I wouldn't say anything if it were the other way around, but you're my client." He puts his left ankle over his right knee, revealing navy-and-white-polka-dot socks. "An intern from another law firm came by asking for a copy of Brooke's will this morning."

Goose bumps rise on my arms. "What law firm?" I ask, but I'm afraid I already know.

"Schoen, Roberts, Moreau, and Associates. I was in court when he dropped by, so he talked to my assistant. He said a member of his firm had asked him to get a copy of the will from the courthouse. It isn't yet on file there—I'm afraid my office is a little behind on paperwork. My assistant knew it would soon be public record, though, so she gave him a copy."

I suddenly feel ill. I move my hands from my lap to my stomach.

"Are you all right?" he asks. "You look upset."

I draw a deep breath and tell him about Zack entering the picture.

"I see." His forehead creases like corrugated cardboard. He steeples his fingers together.

"There's more." I clasp, then unclasp my hands in my lap. "I'm pregnant."

His eyes go wide. "Well, congratulations."

"Thank you. The baby . . ." My mouth is suddenly dry. "The baby—well, I wanted to use a donor, like Brooke, and Brooke had some extra, um . . ." I hate to use the word *sperm*; I don't know why I'm so prissy about it. "Donor material frozen at the cryobank." I draw a deep breath. "So the fact is, I'm pregnant with Lily's half sibling. It—it's also Zack's child. Zack Bradley—that's the name of the father. He's an attorney with the law firm you mentioned. So I want to make sure . . ." I stop and swallow. "I'm afraid, especially after what you just told me about someone from his firm getting a copy of Brooke's will, that Zack might try to get custody of Lily." My heart patters hard. "And—and of my baby, once he finds out about it."

"Oh, my. Yes, I can see how that's concerning."

"I brought a copy of the donor contract he signed. The cryobank said that the same terms would apply to me as applied to Brooke if I were inseminated at a physician's office. I was, of course." I reach into my leather tote by the chair, pull out a file folder, and hand it to him. "I also brought a copy of my medical records."

He takes the papers from me and looks at them. "This is the same donor agreement that's in Brooke's files, I assume?"

"Yes."

"I looked at that again when I pulled out her will." He leans back and taps his fingers on the arm of his chair. "Has Mr. Bradley said anything about wanting guardianship?"

"No, but why else would he want a copy of the will? I happen to know that he and his wife are having fertility issues, and I don't want him to think he can swoop in and grab up a ready-made family. And Margaret—well, I don't know her reasoning in contacting him right after Brooke's death. She may *want* him to have custody." I tell him about her odd comments about the importance of family and her desire for me to tell Lily that Zack is her father.

"I see. I see." He frowns and sits forward. "Well, I'll have to research this, but my understanding is that donor contracts are almost always upheld, although, of course, he can challenge it. If he decides to mount a legal challenge, your biggest problem will be that he's an attorney."

My brow knits. "But he specializes in corporate mergers."

"Yes, but regardless of his specialty, he can stretch things out and file suit after suit until you're financially exhausted."

My stomach knots. "I don't think he's that type, but . . ."

"I hope you're right. Custody situations tend to bring out the worst in people."

My spirits start to sink.

"He may not want guardianship at all; he might just want to see what the arrangements are for the child's care and to make sure that the mother's wishes are being followed. Or perhaps he's looking for some kind of visitation."

"Can he do that?"

"Anyone can sue anybody for anything. It doesn't mean he'll get it. But considering that he's an attorney—and it looks like a good one; he's with a very well-respected firm—my advice would be to work out some kind of friendly arrangement, if that's what he's after." His gaze is direct and somber. "The donor contract should be binding, but you don't want to get into a legal showdown. And the children might resent it if down the road they learn you kept them from knowing their father."

That's what Sarah had said. I fight back a rising wave of despair. "So what's my status right now? Am I the legal guardian of Lily, or can Margaret overrule me?"

"According to the terms of the will, you are now Lily's guardian, because Margaret is incapacitated." He pulls a notebook from his jacket pocket and jots something down. "I'll handle the paperwork to get the trust payments for Lily's care sent to you."

"Is there any way Margaret can cause problems if she recovers enough to think she can care for Lily?"

He taps his fingers together. "I don't think that'll be an issue. There's a note in Brooke's papers that she wanted you named primary guardian when Margaret turned eighty, and that ought to hold up in court. If you can get a statement from her doctor that her health is precarious and that, in his opinion, she's permanently unfit to care for a young child, well, that would be helpful, too."

I'm pretty certain the hospitalist I met with will write a statement to that effect. "All right."

"Is there anything else I can help you with?"

"I'm going to need to update my own will."

"Oh, yes! Yes, you certainly will. I'll send you home with some papers. You can email them to me, then we'll set up an appointment for you to come back when you're ready." He stands, signaling the meeting is over. "Try not to worry, Quinn. Hopefully Mr. Bradley is just trying to ensure that Lily's interests are protected."

"I hope that's all it is," I say, but not worrying is easier said than done.

CHAPTER TWENTY-NINE

Jessica

IT FEELS WEIRD to be at home during a workday, but since I skipped the meetings in California because I said I had a family emergency, it would be even weirder to go into my office at the New Orleans hotel. I decide to get a head start on packing up the condo for the move.

I'm sorting through some items in the back of the clothes closet when my phone dings, indicating I've received a text. I pick it up and see that it's from Brett: *Hey, how are things in the Big Easy?*

My mood immediately lightens. *Great*, I text. *How are things there?*

Good. Is now an ok time to call?

Sure.

A few seconds later, my phone rings. "Hi, Brett," I say. My voice sounds slightly breathless.

"Hi. Did I catch you in the middle of something?"

"Not really. I'm home playing hooky." I walk into the living room and plop down on the sofa. "How was Petey's softball game?"

"Great! He hit two base runs and caught an outfield fly ball. I'm especially proud of that catch. Kids his age hardly ever do that."

"He must have gotten his father's athletic prowess."

"His father has prowess, huh? That sounds kinda sexy."

"Well, it kinda is." I feel my face heat. OMG, am I *flirting*? "But that wasn't the point I was trying to make; I was saying your son is a chip off the old block."

He laughs. "I knew what you meant. I was just joking around."

"I figured."

"I, uh, I probably shouldn't have said that. Sometimes I don't think things through before I say them. I didn't mean to be sexist or offensive or—or make you uncomfortable."

"You weren't. And you didn't."

"Good."

I smile at how relieved he sounds. He's a lot more sensitive than I figured an ex-jock would be.

"Listen, I'm calling because I've drawn up some graphics showing how we could remodel that last house. They're preliminary, of course—just a starting point. But it'll give you some idea of the possibilities for that place, as well as the cost estimates."

"This really is like *Property Brothers*."

"I don't have a twin, but I do the best I can."

I laugh. "You're as good as two people."

"Do you want me to text or email them?"

"Email, please."

"Will do. I didn't put the timeline on there, but the whole project would probably take about eight weeks."

"That's not bad." I turn and pace back to the kitchen. "Especially if we can lease the condo you showed me for the eight weeks."

"Absolutely."

"Sounds great. I'll look forward to seeing the graphics. And I'll be back out there next week."

"Good." His voice is warm. "How is everything else going?"

"With Zack? It's kind of a mixed bag." I stare out the window. "He seemed less than thrilled at my unexpected return, but I interrupted his workday and he's under a lot of pressure. We had a great evening, though. But then, this morning, he left before six to go to the hospital." Before I know it, I've told him practically everything—including how Zack didn't seem interested in getting full guardianship, how I went by Quinn's store undercover, and how seeing Quinn and Lily had affected me.

"Lily looks so much like Zack that it shocked me. It was like a punch in the gut or an out-of-body experience or being punched in the gut while having an out-of-body experience. But that's a non sequitur, because if I were out of my body, I'd have no gut to punch."

"Yes, that's a consideration." I could hear a smile in his voice. "I get what you mean, though." There's silence over the phone, but it isn't uncomfortable. "I think you were wise to go home and be with your husband."

"I do, too, but it feels like *he's* not really here with *me*."

"Hoo boy." He sighs. "I know that feeling."

"Any suggestions about what to do?"

"I'm the wrong person to ask." His voice has a rueful tone. "Your situation is different from mine, though. Off the top of my head, I'd say you need to hang in there and get to know the key players."

"That's what I think, too."

"But, Jess—you have to be up front about it. You can't give your husband any more reasons not to trust you."

I feel a little stab of guilt about going by Quinn's shop the way I did. "Yeah. You're right."

We share another second of silence. "Well, I'd better let you go." He sounds a little reluctant to hang up, and I'm not eager to get off the line, either. But it's time.

"Okay. I'll look forward to seeing the house plans."

"Good. I'm eager to know what you and your husband think. And, Jess?"

"Yes?"

"You can text or call me anytime." He pauses a moment. "About anything."

I feel a rush of gratitude. "Okay," I say. "Thanks. That means a lot."

A lot more than it probably should, I think as I hang up my phone. I can talk to him more easily than I can talk with anyone else in my life right now, even my sister. Certainly more easily than I can talk with Zack. I have a clean slate with Brett. He seems to accept and like me just as I am.

He seems to feel about me, I realize, the way I always wanted to feel about myself.

CHAPTER THIRTY

Quinn

"YOU DON'T NEED to undress for your ultrasound," the nurse says, after she takes my blood pressure and temperature in the small examination room. Sarah is with me. "You'll just need to lie back on the exam table and loosen your pants. Is your bladder full?"

"Yes," I say. I'd been given instructions to arrive that way, and as usual, I'd overdone it. I feel in danger of peeing my pants.

"Good. That should help us see the baby." The nurse, a petite woman with shoulder-length dark hair, smiles. "Normally Dr. Mercer would use the transvaginal ultrasound this early, but that machine is out of our office this week. This new abdominal one is really sensitive, though, so hopefully we'll still get a relatively clear image. If not, you can come back next week."

I nod. An assistant called this morning to tell me this and to see if I wanted to postpone my appointment, but I'm too eager to see the baby. I'd rather try and fail than wait another week.

"I'm so glad you could come with me," I tell Sarah as soon as the nurse leaves the room.

"I'm thrilled you asked me. I was so excited when I had my first ultrasound. The excitement turned to shock when I learned I was having twins."

"I can't even imagine!" I say. "I don't know what I'll do if I have multiples. I'm worried about being able to take care of Lily and a baby all at the same time."

"Do twins run in your family?" Sarah asks.

"Not that I know of."

"You weren't taking fertility drugs and you had insemination instead of IVF, so your chances are low. And as for taking care of Lily and a baby, you'll be a wonderful mother."

"When I decided to get pregnant, I thought I'd have Brooke by my side." A wave of grief washes over me. Will I ever be able to think of Brooke without feeling sad about her death? "I was with her at the ultrasound where she found out she was having a girl."

"I know you miss her," Sarah says.

"I do." Especially at moments like this. I blink back the tears gathering in my eyes.

"Have you thought about who you want as your labor coach?"

I'd been unable to go to classes with Brooke because I lived in Atlanta, but I'd read several books, and I'd taken a leave of absence so I could be with her for the delivery.

"I figure I'll use the doula that Brooke used. She was terrific."

"Don't you want a friend or family member with you, too?"

"I don't really have any family I'm close to," I confess.

"What about your mother? I know she's in Dubai, but surely she'll want to come."

I haven't really discussed my mother with Sarah. "We're not close. We talk every couple weeks or so, but . . ." I stop. I don't think I can get into it without crying, and now is not the time.

Sarah's eyes are warm and sympathetic. "If you decide you'd like me to be there, I'd be honored to help you."

Tears fill my eyes. "Oh, Sarah—that's so very, very kind!"

"Don't answer now," she said. "I don't want you to feel pressured. Take your time and think about it, because everyone in the single parents group would love to do it—we've all talked about it."

Before I can answer, Dr. Mercer comes in. She's a middle-aged woman with a dark pixie haircut and friendly brown eyes. She asks for Sarah's business card when I tell her that Sarah's a psychologist. "I have some patients who could use your services," Dr. Mercer says.

She turns to me and rubs her hands together. "Ready to see if we can view this baby?"

"Absolutely."

It was the same thing I said when I came here to be artificially inseminated.

"Are you completely sure you want to do this?" Dr. Mercer asked me.

"Absolutely," I replied.

"Okay. Here's the specimen I'm going to use." She handed me a medical vial. "Check and make sure it's the right donor number."

I compared the number on the vial with the number Brooke had copied for me. "That's it," I confirmed.

"All right, then. Lie back and put your feet in the stirrups."

"Can you sing a few bars of 'I Will Always Love You' while you do this?" I joked.

Dr. Mercer laughed. "Sorry, but that's beyond my skill set."

I lie back on the exam table now, Sarah on one side of me, Dr. Mercer on the other. I pull up my black-and-white top and tug down my black pants to expose my stomach. She tucks a paper medical cloth into my pants' waistband. "I'm going to apply some ultrasound gel, and I don't want to get it on your clothes."

"I appreciate that," I say. I raise my eyebrows as she squirts the gel over my belly. "Oh, it's warm!"

"We do everything we can to make our mothers comfortable." She turns on the ultrasound machine, and the screen lights up. Then she picks up an object that looks like a computer mouse. "This is the transducer." She puts it on my belly and slides it around. "Let's see if we can find this little one. At nine weeks, your baby is basically the size of a grape."

"Nine weeks?" I lift my head from the table. "I was inseminated just seven weeks ago!"

"Yes, but pregnancies are dated from the mother's last period."

"Even when you know the exact date of conception?"

She nods. "Even then." She runs the transducer over my belly. "Let's see if this new machine lives up to its hype."

My heart feels as if it's about to beat out of my chest. Sarah stands beside me and holds my hand.

"Ah—there it is! Hear that? That's the heart." She turns up the volume, and I hear a loud, fast swooshing sound. "That's your baby's heartbeat!"

"Oh, wow. *Wow!*" I listen in amazement, my throat growing thick. "Is it supposed to be that fast?"

"Yes," Dr. Mercer says. "At this age, it's supposed to be between about one hundred and fifty and one-seventy beats per minute, and this is showing one hundred and sixty-five. That's perfect. As your baby gets older, it'll slow down a little bit, but it'll stay really fast."

"That's incredible."

"Everything looks wonderful," Dr. Mercer says. I stare at the screen, tears pooling in my eyes. I can only make out black and gray shapes. Nothing looks like a baby.

She adjusts a knob on the machine, zooming in on part of the image. "That's the head."

I squint. "It looks enormous!"

Dr. Mercer laughs. "Don't worry. The rest of the body will catch up. All of your baby's organs are starting to grow. The heart already has all four chambers."

I peer at the screen. "That's what we're hearing?"

"Yes."

"The chambers of my baby's heart," I murmur. Goose bumps run up and down my arms. "I'm listening to chamber music."

"Yes." The doctor smiles. "Yes, you are."

My heart feels so full I think it might burst. This is really happening. Thanks to Brooke, Lily's half sibling is growing inside me. "Sarah, would you please grab my phone out of my purse? I want to record this."

"I'll make a DVD you can take with you," the doctor says.

"Oh, that's great! But I still want it on my phone so I can listen to it anytime I want."

Sarah pulls out my phone and hands it to me. I put it on Voice Memos, aim it at the screen, and hit record.

"I'm going to measure the baby." The doctor puts some dots on the screen, and during the silence I record the lovely *swoosh* of my baby's heartbeat.

"It's perfect," Dr. Mercer says. "Just where it should be."

She turns off the machine. "The next time we do an ultrasound, you'll be able to see a lot more. The face, the arms, the feet—even whether it's a boy or girl."

For now, I think, it's enough to know that he or she has a beating heart, a heart that is rhythmically beating right beneath my own.

Chamber music, I think. *Chamber music of the heart.*

CHAPTER THIRTY-ONE

Margaret

Friday, May 17

I AWAKEN FROM an afternoon nap, and it takes me a moment to reorient myself. I'm in the hospital, but I'm in a different room. Oh, right—they moved me yesterday after lunch. How long have I been in this place? Before I can figure it out, the door to my room starts to open.

"Jessica!" I hear a man's voice from the hallway say. "What are you doing here?"

"I came to see Miss Margaret," replies a woman. I don't recognize the voice, but "Miss Margaret" is what my granddaughter's friends call me. A female hand curls around the door, holding it ajar. It's a lovely hand, with silver bangles on the wrist, shiny nails, and youthful skin.

I don't remember any of Brooke's friends named Jessica. The male voice sounds like the man who was here this morning—what's his name? Oh, shoot! He has some connection to Brooke. My memory these days is as full of holes as a fishing net.

"You don't even know her," I hear the man say.

"I want to meet her. She's become a big part of your life, so I naturally want to include her in mine. Besides, you said that today is her birthday, so I wanted to bring her a little gift."

The doctor and nurses wished me happy birthday this morning, and an aide told me that some friends are bringing me a party. Apparently I'm eighty years old today. Eighty! How on earth can that be? "I can hear you talking about me out there," I call. "You might as well come on in."

A beautiful young woman pushes open the door. She has long dark hair, brown eyes, and a big smile, and she's carrying a large bouquet. It looks like sunflowers, oleander, roses, and tulips. "Hello, Mrs. Moore," she says.

"Hello," I say.

"I'm Jessica Bradley—Zack's wife."

Zack—that's his name! He follows her through the doorway, looking a tad apologetic. "Hello, Miss Margaret."

"Oh! I didn't know you were married, dear," I say. From the expression on the young woman's face, this appears to be exactly the wrong thing to say.

"We've been married nearly three years," she says.

"I'm sure he told me, and I just forgot," I say, although I'm sure of no such thing. "My memory is like a colander lately." Zack's relationship to Brooke suddenly pops into my head: he's Lily's father. And he's married? Oh, dear. I'm sure I was never told that!

"I'm so sorry about your heart attack and fall," Jessica says.

"Thank you. I don't remember anything about it, but apparently Zack saved my life."

"He's handy to have around," she says.

"Handy as a paddle in a pirogue," I agree.

She laughs. "How are you feeling?"

"Getting better every day." I was taught that when someone inquires about your health, a lady always gives a positive response. I'm not at all sure my health is improving, but at least I still have good manners.

"That's wonderful to hear."

"Thank you, dear." I smile at her. "Forgive me if I'm being rude, but have we met before?"

"No. I was in Seattle when you fell."

"Seattle!"

"Yes. I was house hunting. Zack and I are moving there in a month or so."

"You're moving to Seattle?" I look at Zack. "I don't remember you telling me that, either."

"I'm, uh, staying in New Orleans for a while longer."

"Oh?"

"Just for a few weeks," Jessica adds, giving him the kind of disapproving look married people sometimes use on each other. Thank heavens Henry never tried that with me.

"While he finishes up a couple of cases at his law firm," she adds.

"I see." I hadn't considered the possibility of Zack moving so far away, just as I hadn't considered that he might be married. That makes this woman Lily's stepmother. My stomach drops, but I keep my polite face on. My experience with stepmothers is not good—not good at all.

I look from her to Zack and continue smiling. He's the child's father, I remind myself—her blood relative. "Lily's coming to the hospital today. Quinn has arranged a little birthday party for me." I'm pleased I remember this. A nurse's aide told me just before I dozed off for that little nap. "They should be here any minute. You're welcome to stay and meet them."

"Oh, that's very kind of you, but I don't want to crash your party," Jessica says.

"You won't be crashing, dear. I'd love to have you." It will give me more time to assess her and see what she's like.

"Well, then—I'd be delighted." She steps forward and lifts up the vase of flowers. "I brought you these."

"How thoughtful! They're gorgeous."

"I'll put fresh water in them, then set them down." She moves to the sink in the bathroom. I hear the faucet turn on, then the door connecting the room to the hallway bursts open again.

"Grams—look what I brought you!" Lily skips into the room, holding a big bouquet of shiny balloons anchored onto a weight.

She's wearing a pink-and-white dress. Her hair is pulled back from her face and fastened on top with an enormous pink bow.

My heart leaps at the sight of her. "How wonderful to see you, sweetie! Oh, I've missed you!"

"I missed you, too, Grams. I was very, very worried that you'd die 'cause you're in a hospital."

"Oh, sweetheart!" I say.

Quinn is right behind her. She's wearing a blue dress and sandals, and she's carrying two large gift-wrapped packages. "I'm so glad they moved you to a room where Lily can visit."

"Me, too," I say.

Lily studies me. "Do you hurt?"

"No," I lie.

"Can I give you a hug?"

"Of course."

Zack takes the balloons from Lily, and Quinn picks her up.

"Be very gentle," Quinn tells Lily as she carries her to my bedside. "Don't hit her hip or squish her oxygen tube."

Lily puts her arms around my neck and gives me a wet smooch on the cheek. My eyes grow full.

"Grams! You're crying!"

"It's because I'm so glad to see you." I kiss her back, and Quinn lowers her to the floor.

"I love you, Grams," Lily declares.

"Oh, I love you too, honey."

Lily turns to Zack. "Hello, Mr. Zack."

Zack squats down. "Hi there, peanut." He, too, gets a big hug from Lily.

As he releases her, Lily spots the brunette standing in the bathroom doorway, the vase of flowers in her hands. Quinn notices her, too.

"This is Zack's wife, Jessica," I say. I'm pleased that I remember her name.

"You're the pretty lady from Auntie Quinn's shop!" Lily exclaims.

Zack's eyebrows rise in surprise. He looks at Jessica. "You were in Quinn's shop?"

"I went by a couple of days ago." The color in her cheeks rises. "We met, but we didn't introduce ourselves." Jessica crosses the room, puts the flowers on the window ledge, then holds out her hand to Quinn. "Nice to officially meet you. I'd heard a lot about you and I was in the area so I thought I'd run in, but then it just seemed awkward to explain the connection, so . . ."

"No problem," Quinn says, smiling and shaking her hand. "It's nice to meet you, too."

Jessica bends down and extends her hand to Lily. "Hello again, Lily."

Lily shakes it. "Hello, ma'am."

"Birthday party coming through!" calls a voice from the hallway door. I look up to see some of Brooke's and Quinn's friends entering the room.

Lily jumps up and down like a frog on a pogo stick. "Miss Sarah brought cake!"

Sure enough, the salt-and-pepper-haired lady I remember from Brooke's funeral is carrying a bakery box. Behind her is the sweet, petite young woman with big glasses who's always been so kind to me. She's carrying a present and a bag of what looks like paper plates and forks. Another woman I've met before, older than the others, trails in behind them.

"Sarah, Annie, Terri—some of you have already met Zack. For those who haven't, this is Zack—and this is his wife, Jessica."

Hellos are said all around.

Another woman I remember as being a part of that group comes in, carrying a small green plant. She's dressed as a nurse. Quinn touches her arm. "Lauren, this is Zack and his wife, Jessica. Lauren works in the pediatric oncology department here."

They all say hello. "I'm on my break, so I can only stay a minute, but I wanted to pop in and wish Miss Margaret a happy birthday." Lauren comes to my bedside, bends down, and gives me a kiss. "You're looking so much better than you did when you first got here."

I didn't remember seeing her, but then, I don't remember anything about the accident or much about the first few days after it.

"Thank you, dear."

She lifts the plant. "I brought a bit of greenery to cheer up your room, but it's mighty cheerful already. Look at all these flowers and balloons!"

"That was very thoughtful of you," I say.

A man with short, bristly gray hair hesitantly enters the room.

"Mac!" Quinn exclaims. "So great to see you!"

"Welcome back!" Sarah says.

"I got the email about the birthday party and came straight here from the airport," Mac says. He holds himself very stiffly and looks in my direction, but not quite at me. He doesn't smile, but he dips his head in a "hello" bow. "Happy birthday, Miss Margaret."

"Thank you." I vaguely remember him as the sole male member of the single parent group. "Where have you been?"

"In New Jersey, then in Illinois. I had two back-to-back training seminars on new equipment," he says.

Now I remember what it is about him. Quinn had explained that he has trouble making eye contact and he's awkward around people. I think his shyness is endearing.

Quinn steps forward to play hostess again. "Mac, this is Zack and his wife, Jessica."

Mac shakes his hand, but he looks puzzled, as if he's trying to place him.

"Zack saved my life when I had a heart attack," I say.

"Oh, yes." He pumps Zack's hand harder. "You're Lily's dad—and the father of Quinn's baby!"

Silence falls over the room.

Lily's sweet voice cuts through the sudden, unsettling quiet.

"Did that man jus' say Mr. Zack's my daddy?" She peers up hopefully at Quinn.

Quinn's face is the shade of a bleached sheet. Her eyes, frightened as a startled bunny, cut toward me. "Uh . . ."

There was something else the man said, something that pulls on my thoughts, but right now, Lily's question is at the forefront of my mind. Why keep such a wonderful thing a secret? "Yes, Lily, he is," I say.

The child's face—well, it reminds me of the way my daughter looked when she was three, and Henry turned on the Christmas tree lights for the first time. It was as if her face were wired to the electrical cord and it, too, suddenly lit up. "Really?" Lily whips toward Zack and bounces on her toes. "You're my donor daddy?" You can practically hear her hold her breath.

"Yes, honey, I am."

"Oh! Oh, I'm so glad!" Lily throws herself at him. He bends down and hugs her back. Everyone chuckles and murmurs. A couple of people clap.

I put my hand on my heart, which overflows with joy. "You got a gift on my birthday," I tell Lily.

"The bestest gift ever!" Lily says. "I got my daddy!"

Zack picks her up and holds her, beaming. It's one of those rare, shining moments in life, where everything seems bathed in light.

"Wait," Jessica says. She touches the older man's arm. "What did you say about Quinn's baby?"

She's ruining the moment, and it irritates me. "Quinn doesn't have a baby," I say.

"She's going to," Mac says. "She used the same donor as Brooke."

All of the hubbub in the room hushes in a heartbeat.

Jessica looks as if she witnessed a shooting. Zack seems stunned. Everyone else is frozen into place or guiltily exchanging glances, as if they'd conspired to keep a cat in the bag, and it's just sprung out.

"Uh-oh." Mac's brows pull together. "Did I say something I wasn't supposed to?"

CHAPTER THIRTY-TWO

Quinn

OH MY GOD—I want to melt into the floor. There's no point in denying it—my baby's heartbeat is recorded on my phone, so there's solid proof this is really happening—but I don't know what to say.

Zack is still holding Lily, but he's turned into a statue.

"You're pregnant?" Jessica sounds horrified. "With Zack's baby?" She turns stunned eyes to Zack, then back to me. "How the hell did this happen?"

Zack's face is ashen. His eyes are astonished and locked on me. I see his Adam's apple bob.

I turn back to Margaret. Her mouth is agape, her eyes wide.

"I, uh, was waiting until I got through the first trimester to say anything outside the single parent group," I tell her.

"What's goin' on, Donor Daddy?" Lily pats Zack's face. "I don' understand."

"I don't, either," Jessica says.

Annie steps forward and holds out her arms to Lily. "This is a grown-up conversation, Lily. Why don't you come with me?"

"But I jus' learned he's my donor daddy, an' we haven' even had cake!"

"We need to go find some ice cream to go with it," Annie says.

"That's right, Lily," I manage.

Lily looks at Zack. "Will you go with me?"

"He needs to be here for the grown-up talk," Annie says.

Zack gently places Lily on the floor. "Go with her, Lily-kins. I'll be here when you come back."

"An' you'll still be my daddy?"

"Yes."

"Crotch your heart?"

Her mangled phrasing used to make Brooke and me collapse with laughter. Brooke had declared it too adorable to correct.

Zack gives Lily a little smile. "Yeah."

"You have to say it."

"I cross my heart." He makes an X on his chest.

"Okay." Lily takes Annie's extended hand.

"Thank you," I whisper as Annie leads Lily from the room.

The door closes with a soft click behind them. There's a moment of breath-holding silence.

"So what's going on?" Jessica asks. She gives a tremulous smile, as if she's trying to keep it together, but there's a razor-like edge to her voice. She looks at Zack.

"I—I honestly don't know," he says.

He and everyone else are staring at me. "You're pregnant?" Margaret asks.

I sink down on the chair beside her bed. It's easier to talk to her than to Zack or his tightly wound wife. Besides, Margaret has more of a right to know; she didn't sign any papers with a fertility center surrendering all claim to any donation-created children.

"Yes, I'm pregnant. It's very early, though."

"Did—did Brooke know?" Margaret asks.

I nod. "It was kind of her idea." I pluck at Margaret's blanket, because it's easier than looking at anyone's face. "I told Brooke that I'd consider being a single parent myself if I knew I'd have a child as wonderful as Lily, and she said, 'You can. I bought the entire supply from Lily's donor, and the cryobank is keeping it frozen for me for another five years. I'll give it to you.'"

I draw in a deep breath. Margaret's gaze is riveted on me. Her mouth is no longer hanging open, but her face is pale and her eyes are enormous. I figure the best thing to do is to keep talking. "Brooke checked it out with the cryobank and verified that the contract allowed for a transfer. The only requirement was that reporting procedures had to be followed. I needed to be artificially inseminated at a doctor's office, and the doctor needed to comply with the reporting requirements. So Brooke signed over the remaining donation, and I arranged for it to be sent to my ob-gyn. I was inseminated a couple of days before Brooke died."

I pause. "I didn't find out I was pregnant until after she was gone. I shared the news with my single parent group, but I didn't tell you, Miss Margaret, because I wanted to wait until I was safely through the first trimester. My obstetrician said up to twenty-five percent of pregnancies don't make it past the first twelve weeks, and I didn't want you or Lily to have to deal with another loss."

"You didn't know?" Jessica is looking at Zack.

"This is the first I'm hearing of it," he says.

"I didn't know I wasn't supposed to mention it," Mac says. He looks utterly miserable. "I'm so sorry. I feel terrible."

"Don't feel bad, Mac," I tell him. "You had no way of knowing. You were out of town when I told the others I wanted to wait before I told Miss Margaret or Lily." I swallow. "Besides, the news was going to come out eventually."

"I hope I didn't spoil Miss Margaret's birthday celebration," Mac says.

"You didn't spoil it." I try to smile at Margaret, but my lips don't quite comply. "It's happy news, isn't it?"

Margaret blinks several times. "Your child will be Lily's half brother or sister?"

"Yes."

"A sibling. A blood relative." She lies back against her pillow, her expression thoughtful.

I hold my breath.

A large smile blooms on Margaret's face. "Why, I think that'll be very good for Lily. Wonderful, in fact."

"It *is* wonderful," Lauren says, clapping her hands.

"It's fabulous," Sarah states with conviction.

"We need cake to celebrate!" Teri exclaims.

Mac, Teri, Lauren, and Sarah swarm around, pat my back, and give me hugs.

I avoid looking at Zack or Jessica. I can't bring myself to face them.

CHAPTER THIRTY-THREE

Jessica

I FEEL LIKE I'm about to be sick. I look at Zack. He's staring at Quinn as if she's just levitated off the floor or done something equally miraculous.

"Quinn, can I tell them about your visit to the doctor yesterday?" the woman with silver-streaked hair asks.

Good Lord—there's more? I brace my hand against the wall. *Please don't let it be twins!*

Quinn nods.

"I went with Quinn to the obstetrician's office for her first ultrasound and we heard the heartbeat."

A knife blade of jealousy twists in my gut.

"Oh, how wonderful!" all the women murmur. Everyone, that is, except me.

Even Zack mutters an awestruck *wow*—which makes my blood boil. I want to slap him. I want to cry. Instead I pinch myself, partly on the off chance I'm having a bad dream and I'll wake up, and partly because pinch pain is a hurt I can control.

"So you're going to be a father for the second time," Margaret says.

"I—I guess that's what this means," he says.

I'm angered by his response, although I dimly realize there's not a single thing he could say or do that would seem right at this moment. I'm so upset, I'm shaking.

"Let's go," I murmur to him.

"I can't. Lily's coming back," he says. "I promised her I'd be here."

"Yeah, well, you made some promises to me, as well," I whisper fiercely.

Zack takes my elbow. "Excuse us for a moment," he says to the group.

I let him steer me across the room because I can't see through the wet haze of tears clouding my eyes. Zack opens the door and I dash through it, then pause in the hallway and turn my back to him.

He closes the door and puts his hand on my shoulder. "Jessica."

I whip around to face him. "How the hell could you let this happen?" I demand.

"Jessica—be reasonable. You knew when you married me that I'd been a donor. I had no way of knowing about any of this."

"You should have thought things through before you jacked off into a jar." Something caustic is boiling inside me. "Or maybe I should have thought things through before I married you."

"Maybe so," he says.

What? He's agreeing I should have had second thoughts about marrying him?

He sighs. "Look, I know how hard this must be for you."

"Do you? Do you really?" I jerk away from his touch. I point a shaking finger at the door we just exited. "That woman in there has your baby growing inside of her. The very thing I've tried and tried to do, the thing that I have the sole *right* to do, she's doing without my knowledge or consent."

"I know it's not fair, but . . ."

"But what? What are you going to do about it?"

He looks at me as if I'm out of my mind, and maybe I am. No, I definitely am. I'm on the verge of hysteria, asking an unanswerable question.

Because there's nothing he can do about it. He can't shoot Quinn or demand she get an abortion. And there's nothing I can do about it, either. Not a damn thing.

I heave out a hard breath. "I'm freaking out. I know I'm not being reasonable. I'm—I'm just . . . I'm devastated."

"Jess . . ." He puts his hands on my shoulders again.

Once more, I step back. I can't stand to have him touch me right now. "I'm having a hard time with this." I rub my forehead, where a headache is building. "I'm going home."

"I'll be along in a bit."

"Yeah, right—take care of your priorities first," I say. *Be there for the daughter you had by another woman and the woman you knocked up before you take care your wife.* I manage to keep the words inside, but I'm sure the ugliness of my thoughts shows on my face.

I hate the way I'm feeling, hate the way I'm thinking, hate the person I am right now.

I start down the hallway, wanting to make it out of the building without seeing Lily again.

"Are you okay to drive?" Zack calls. "Maybe you should call an Uber."

"Maybe you should keep your dick in your pants," I say, although it makes no sense. I know he didn't cheat on me, but it feels like he did.

I keep walking until I hit the stairwell. I duck in, race down four flights of stairs, and then go through the lobby to the parking garage. It takes me a moment to find my car. It seems like I parked it two days ago, so much has changed. I locate it on the second level and climb inside, then sit there, my heart hammering.

I need to talk. I pull out my phone, then face the dilemma of who I can call. I don't have any girlfriends I've stayed close to since I married Zack; I've been completely caught up in the in vitro hell of trying to make a baby. There's no way I can talk to my mother. I think about calling my sister, but she'll flip out and go on a rant that will wend its way back to *I can't believe you didn't tell me Zack was a sperm donor.* I don't need to be scolded about keeping private things private.

I call Brett.

"Hey there, Jess," he says. He sounds glad to hear from me. "How are things going?"

"You won't believe it when I tell you."

"Try me."

"Can you talk?"

"Yeah. I'm alone in the car, and I've got the phone on Bluetooth. What's going on?"

"The woman who has custody of Zack's kid—she's pregnant." I pause. "With Zack's baby."

"What?"

I relate what just happened in the hospital room.

"Jesus, Jess. That's insane!"

"Good word for it. I feel completely certifiable," I agree.

He laughs. "I can't believe you're joking about this."

"Oh, I'm not. I feel like I'm about to explode or go postal or something. I wasn't very nice to Zack before I left. In fact, when we went out in the hall to talk, I was a total bitch."

"Well, no one can blame you."

"Oh, I think they can." I tell him what I said.

Brett chortles. "That's not so bad. Hell, Jess—you're human, and this is a huge shock. It's normal to be emotional."

The kind words make tears run down my face. "Thanks for being so nice," I say. I watch a woman with a young child and a baby in a stroller cross the parking garage, and feel a familiar jab of pain. Other women's babies are everywhere.

"You have every right to be upset," Brett says. "Where are you right now?"

"In my car at the hospital. I wanted to calm down before I drove. I thought that talking might help, but I didn't know who to call." I reach in the console, grab a tissue, and wipe my tears.

"I'm glad you called me," he says.

"Yeah. Me, too."

"It's a lot to process."

"It is," I agree. "Do you think my life is completely screwed?"

"I think you have an amazing life ahead of you. I have no doubt that you'll handle this."

"Well, then, you believe in me more right now than I believe in myself."

"That's because you're in the middle of the situation and you're overwhelmed. You'll figure this out."

"Thanks, Brett." We're silent for a moment. I hear a siren wail loudly through the phone, and I welcome the distraction. "Where are you going?"

"To look at a house in Issaquah."

I like picturing him in his Porsche, going to a destination I know. It's way better than reliving the hell that just happened in that hospital room. "Is it a house I'd like?"

"Nah. It's too traditional for you. It's also a couple million over your price range."

"Send me a photo when you get there."

"Why?"

"To remind me that life is happening elsewhere."

He laughs. "Okay."

"What are you doing this evening?" I ask.

"Well, Sue Anne has Petey, so I'm going to the gym."

"The gym, huh?" I turn the rearview mirror, look into it, and blot my face.

"Yeah. Gotta stay lean and mean."

"I don't think you have a mean bone in your body."

"That's because I take out all my aggressions on weight machines."

"Maybe I should do that," I say.

"Can't hurt. Might help."

I smile. "I like that. When in doubt, go with the 'can't hurt, might help' option."

"I recommend it."

"Well, then, maybe I'll go home and hit the gym. There's one in our building."

"Sounds like a plan. You're always at your best when you're following a plan."

"You're right." I straighten the mirror and buckle my seat belt. "How did you know that about me?"

"You told me the other day."

"And you listened. I'm impressed."

"Are you okay to drive now?"

"Yeah. I feel a lot calmer."

"Good. Go slow—with the driving, and with everything else. And call me later and let me know how you're doing, okay?"

"All right."

"And, Jess? You'll get to the other side of this, and things will be great."

I don't know that I believe him, but I believe that he believes that about me. I hang up and start my car, comforted to have a plan for the immediate future—but even more comforted to have someone in my corner who makes me feel supported.

CHAPTER THIRTY-FOUR

Zack

I STEP BACK into the hospital room, feeling conspicuous without Jessica. Everyone looks at me, then glances away, as if trying to help me save face.

"My wife was a little thrown by the news," I say, shoving my hands in my pockets.

"I imagine so," says the woman with a little gray in her dark hair—Sarah, I think.

I glance at Quinn. Her face is flushed. She looks embarrassed.

I pull my hands out of my pockets and rub my chin. "It's a lot to take in."

Sarah pulls a card out of her purse and crosses the room to hand it to me. "I can recommend some really fine counselors if you and your wife want some help working through this."

I look at the card. *Sarah Merckel, Psychologist, Individual/Family Counseling.* "Thanks." It would be great if Jessica would agree to talk to a professional, but I don't hold out much hope. I stick the card in my pocket all the same.

Lily bursts through the door like a little cannonball. Annie is right behind her, carrying a bulging white paper bag.

"Daddy!" she exclaims, hurling herself at me. I pick her up again. "Can I call you that, or do I need to call you Donor? Mommy tol' me I had to say 'donor,' not 'daddy,' but now you're here, so you're a daddy, right?"

"You can call me whatever you like," I say. My heart seems to have migrated to my throat, where it sits in a lump.

"Good." She hugs my neck as if she's known me forever.

Annie opens the bag and pulls out single-serve vanilla ice cream cups like I used to get in grade school. "We couldn't find any ice cream in the cafeteria, but a nurse helped us raid the patient freezer."

"Well, let's get this party started!" Lauren says.

The women bustle around, cutting the cake and putting pieces on little pink plastic plates. It's red velvet cake with vanilla icing.

"Lily, would you like to pass out the party gear?" Quinn asks. Lily scrambles out of my arms, takes a plastic bag marked *Party City* from Quinn, and hands out pointed hats and noisemakers as if it's extremely important business.

"Lily, what's the rule on birthday hats?" Quinn prompts.

"Everyone has to wear one," Lily announces.

All of the women smile and gamely don little dunce hats printed with cakes and candles. I do, too, and so does Mac. "Is it just me, or do we all look like we just increased our intelligence?" I joke.

Everyone laughs.

"I have a princess crown for Grams," Lily announces. Quinn pulls a rhinestone tiara from her purse and carefully places it on Miss Margaret's head.

"We can't have candles because of the oxygen, but we can sing 'Happy Birthday,'" Quinn says. She hands Lily a plastic plate with a piece of cake and an ice cream cup on it, and whispers something in her ear.

Lily carefully carries it over to the bed and holds it up toward Miss Margaret. "Happy birthday to you . . ." she sings in an angelic little voice. Everyone joins in, and the song ends in a boisterous finale.

"Oh, how nice. How very, very nice!" Margaret says, accepting the cake from Lily. "This looks delicious."

Cake and ice cream are handed out all around, along with paper cups of sparkling water. I stand against the wall and eat cake with a white plastic fork.

My eyes keep going to Quinn. *She's carrying my baby.* It's an unnerving, jarringly intimate thing to contemplate.

No wonder Jessica is upset. I toss my plate in the trash, wondering what on earth I can say or do to help her cope with the situation.

A woman in pink scrubs walks in. Her badge identifies her as a nurse's aide. "It's almost time for physical therapy, Mrs. Moore."

"Oh, no!" Margaret says. "Can we do it later? I've got guests."

"I'm sorry, but the therapist is nearly ready, and you're her last patient of the day."

"We promised we'd only be here an hour," Quinn says. "I think we've overstayed our welcome."

"But you haven't opened your presents!" exclaims Lily.

"I can do that later, dear," Miss Margaret says. "It'll extend the pleasure of the celebration."

"I'll be back with the therapist in a moment." The aide leaves the room.

"Well, we'd better say our good-byes," Quinn says.

Annie gathers up everyone's plates and cups, then puts them in the trash. Mac picks up the hats, Sarah collects the extra supplies, and everyone files by Miss Margaret to kiss her cheek and tell her good-bye.

"Let's leave the extra cake and hats at the nurses' station," Quinn suggests.

"Good idea," Lauren says.

"Thank you—all of you. This has been wonderful," Miss Margaret says. "And, Quinn, dear—congratulations! When is your wedding?"

Quinn's eyebrows rise. "Oh, I'm not getting married!"

"No?" Miss Margaret frowns.

The room goes silent. Everyone looks so frozen and surprised, it could have been a bad Botox party.

"No. I'm having the baby as a single mother, like Brooke. Zack already has a wife."

"Oh, yes. Yes, of course." She smooths the covers of her bedding, as if trying to smooth over the gaffe. "Silly me—she was here earlier. My mind just doesn't work right yet. You're having Lily's brother or sister, right? And it's wonderful—just wonderful."

Lily looks at Quinn. "You're having a baby?" she asks.

Apparently she'd been too caught up in discovering that I was her father for the news about the baby to register.

Quinn looks frazzled. "Yes, sweetie, if everything goes right."

"Whaddya mean?"

Quinn brushes a strand of hair out of Lily's eyes. "Well, remember when you and your mommy planted those bean seeds? Some of them sprouted and grew into healthy plants and some didn't. It's sort of like that right now with the baby. It's too early to know for sure whether or not it will keep growing."

"But if it does, I'll be a big sister?"

"Yes."

"Yippee!" Lily jumps up and down like a wild thing, hopping across the room.

The aide returns with a wheelchair. A woman wearing a lanyard printed with *Occupational Therapist* is right behind her.

"I'm gonna be a big sister!" Lily announces, hopping from leg to leg. She points at me. "An' I just found out he's my daddy!"

I muster a tense smile for the stunned-faced therapist, then turn to Margaret. "Happy birthday. It was nice seeing you again."

"The pleasure was all mine," she says.

"Say good-bye to Grams," Quinn tells Lily.

"Bye, Grams. I'm gonna be a big sister!"

"Yes, dear. That's what I hear," Miss Margaret says.

I hold the door. Lily stops and turns to me.

"Are you coming home with us?"

"What?" I ask.

"Well, now that you're my daddy, won't you live with us?"

I'm keenly aware of the occupational therapist and the aide standing in the room, unabashedly listening to every word. I wish

Lily would just go out the door, but she's blocking the opening, waiting for an answer.

"No, Lily," Quinn says. "Zack's married to Miss Jessica."

"The pretty lady who got sad?" Lily asks, turning to me.

The aide and the therapist's eyes get even larger and rounder.

"Um, yes," I say.

"Why was she sad?" Lily asks.

"Good Lord—sounds like an episode of *Maury Povich* just happened in here," the aide whispers to the therapist.

I urge Lily through the door and quickly follow her out.

"Why was she sad?" Lily repeats in the hallway.

I'm relieved to hear the door close behind me.

"It's all grown-up stuff," Quinn says.

Lily wrinkles her nose. "Grown-up stuff seems awful."

Yeah, kiddo—a lot of it is.

Quinn pauses to leave the rest of the cake at the nurses' station and to thank them for their care of Margaret. We head to the elevator, and ride down to the lobby with Sarah, Annie, and two strangers.

We manage to make it down to the lobby before Lily speaks again. "Maybe Daddy an' the sad lady can both move in with us."

"Honey, they have their own home," Quinn says as we walk into the atrium, "and they're moving far away in a few weeks."

"What?" Lily sounds stricken. "Daddy's moving away?"

Quinn gestures to a grouping of chairs. "Maybe we should sit for a minute so we're not blocking people."

I nod. We sit down in side-by-side chairs, and Quinn gathers Lily on her lap. Sarah and Annie move to the other side of the lobby, but don't leave.

"How far away is he moving?" Lily asks.

"A long, long way," Quinn answers.

"As far as Grams's house?"

"A whole lot further."

Lily turns to me, her eyes distressed. "Why do you have to move? I want you to be like Alicia's daddy."

"Honey, Zack was a donor." Quinn rubs Lily's arm. "He was never supposed to be a real father. Your mommy explained it to you, remember? Your donor is a nice man who made it possible for you to be born, but he's not a part of your life like a real father."

"But why not? He's here, an' he likes me, an' he says I can call him Daddy."

"That's just a name; it isn't what he'll really be, not in the day-to-day sense."

Quinn gives me a look. If expressions could talk—and hers most certainly does—this one is saying, *Listen up, buddy, and listen good.*

"If Zack wants to, he can write you letters and you can draw him pictures and send them to him," Quinn says. "But he'll have his own life, and his own family."

Lily twists toward me. "Why can't I be your family, too?"

I want to tell her that she is. Quinn must sense it, because she puts a staying hand on my arm and shoots me a warning glare.

"Because your mommy never met him, and he signed a contract saying he was just a donor." Quinn's voice is firm, her tone final. "You weren't supposed to meet him or even know his name until you're all grown up. The fact that you've met him now is lagniappe."

"What's lagniappe?"

"It's a bonus—something extra that you didn't expect to happen."

"Like when Mommy died?"

The color leaves Quinn's face. She blinks fast. "No, honey. That was a tragedy. A tragedy is when something terrible happens."

"I really miss Mommy." Lily's blue eyes fill with tears. "An' I hoped I had a real daddy."

"I know, Lily." Quinn uses her thumb to wipe away a tear on Lily's cheek. "But Zack is a really nice donor."

"It's not the same." Big tears drop from both of her eyes.

"No, honey." Quinn looks at me over the top of Lily's head. This look begs, *Please don't confuse the issue for her*. "It's not."

"But I'm still gonna be a big sister?" Lily says hopefully.

"Yes, you are—if the baby continues to grow."

"Yay!" She smiles, her face still wet with tears.

Sarah has been lurking at the edges of the waiting area. "Hey, Lily," she calls. "Will you help me look in my purse? I think I have a package of Bubble Yum, but I can't seem to find it."

Lily bounds across the room.

Quinn looks at me. It's a leveling gaze; she's just told me the lay of the land.

WE SIT IN silence for a moment, watching Lily paw through Sarah's large bag. "This news comes as quite a shock," I say.

"I didn't intend for you to find out like that."

"Did you intend for me to find out at all?"

She looks away. "Like Brooke, I thought I was getting an anonymous donor."

Of course she did. That's what I agreed to on the contract. I blow out a sigh. "You and I need to talk."

"Yeah. But not here, and not now."

I run my hand down my face and nod. I'm emotionally fried. I need to get my thoughts together, and I still have to deal with Jessica. "Tomorrow afternoon, maybe?"

She nods. "I'll make arrangements for someone to watch Lily."

I'd never really thought before about how a parent or guardian has to make arrangements in order to do anything without the child. I mean, I'd known a child ties you down, but I hadn't really thought about what that meant on a day-to-day basis. I'd thought in terms of babies, and they seem pretty portable. Quinn's world must have been turned upside down by getting guardianship of Lily. "Where and when do you want to meet?"

"How about five thirty at my shop? I don't usually work on Saturdays, but I need to go in for a few hours."

"Great. I'll see you then."

She stands. "Tell your wife it was nice to meet her."

Jessica. The thought of her makes a knot of dread spin in my chest.

I head over to Lily, who has successfully extracted a pack of sugarless gum from Sarah's purse and is now chomping on a big pink wad. I squat down to her level. "See you later, princess."

"Okay." She flings herself into my arms. "I love you, Daddy."

"Back at you, Lily." I kiss the top of her head. She smells like baby shampoo and bubblegum. I breathe it in and smile. The scent and the smile stay with me as I push through the exit into the heat of the parking garage, but I lose them both when I open my car door and inhale a trace of Jessica's perfume from the night before.

JESSICA'S CAR IS in her parking spot in the garage, but our condo is empty when I walk through the door. I'm relieved to have some time to myself. I pull an Abita out of the fridge and head out to the terrace. It's only May, but in New Orleans, that can mean eighty-plus degrees. The worst of the day's heat is over, though. The terrace is in the shade, and a breeze from the river is cooling things off.

I pop the top on my beer and gaze out at the rooftops. Man, I wish I could talk to my dad! Why can't we have visiting hours with folks in heaven, like they have in the ICU?

I decide to call my sister. I've been in touch with her since I discovered Lily, and I texted her photos after our day at the zoo.

"How's that adorable little girl?" she asks after we exchange initial greetings.

"She's amazing. Can you talk?"

"Sure, if you don't mind the clatter of pots and pans. I'm fixing dinner."

I tell her the day's events.

"A baby?" Her voice is incredulous. "You're going to have another donor child?"

"Looks like it."

"Oh my gosh! And Lily knows you're her father?"

I can't help but humble-brag a little. "She calls me Daddy."

"Oh, Zack! How's this going to work?"

"I don't know. I'm meeting with Quinn tomorrow to talk about things." I sigh. "I don't want to show up and then disappear, like some kind of deadbeat dad. Yet I'm technically just a sperm donor."

"But you want to be more than that, right?"

"Absolutely."

"I can't even imagine meeting one of my kids for the first time at the age of three." I hear pots clang on her end of the phone. "From the way you talked about Lily before, I could tell that she really affected you."

"Yeah. And now to learn that there's another baby on the way . . ."

"It's mind-boggling!"

"Exactly."

"How did Jessica take it?"

"Not well." I describe what happened.

"Poor thing!" I hear more dishes rattling around. "After all her efforts to get pregnant!"

I hear the key in the door. My stomach feels like I ate a bunch of rocks. "She's home," I say. "I'd better go."

"All right, Zack-man." I smile at the childhood nickname. "Good luck with everything."

"Thanks. Talk to you later." I hang up, take a long pull of beer, and then walk back into the living room.

Jessica is wearing workout clothes. "I thought hitting the machines might help with the stress."

"Good idea." I'm relieved to see that she's calmer than she was at the hospital.

She perches on a barstool at the kitchen island and tilts her water bottle to her mouth. I sit down beside her.

"What happened after I left?" she asks.

"Lily came back with ice cream, and we had ice cream and cake."

She gives me an exasperated look. "Seriously."

"I'm completely serious," I say with a cajoling smile. "It was red velvet cake. We all put on hats and sang 'Happy Birthday.' Except Margaret—she wore a tiara."

Anger flares in her eyes. "I can't believe you're jerking me around right now."

"I'm not jerking you around," I say. "I'm telling you exactly what happened, and hoping to lighten things up a little." I used to be able to do that.

"I'm not in the mood for trivia or levity. What happened with Lily?"

I blow out a sigh. "She got all excited when she realized she was going to be a big sister. She'd been too distracted by the news that I was her father to grasp that Quinn is having a baby."

"Does she know it's your baby?" Her eyes fill with tears.

"I'm not sure."

"She must, if she's excited about being a sister."

I lift my shoulders. "Quinn is her mother figure, so maybe that's the reason."

Jess rises and gets a paper towel. She dabs at her face. "I can't believe this is happening. You had no clue Quinn was pregnant?"

I shake my head. "No. Looking back, there were a few things I maybe should have picked up on. She got nauseated a couple of times and treated it by eating something, but she said it was low blood sugar."

"You didn't tell me that."

"Yeah, well, there was a lot going on."

"How do you feel about it?" Jessica asks.

"I'm in shock."

"That's all you have to say?" She looks at me with affronted eyes, as if I'm offering her a piece of celery while I'm wolfing down a cheeseburger.

I struggle to come up with something she wants to hear. "I—I wish it were you."

This earns me a tremulous smile. "Me, too. This is probably the most awful thing that's ever happened to me."

"I don't think you should look at a child coming into the world as an awful thing," I say.

Her eyes flash. "I'm feeling what I'm feeling. Sorry if it's not PC enough for you."

A muscle jerks in my jaw. I tip back my beer and swallow about a half dozen biting retorts.

"Did you talk to Quinn?" she asks. "Do you have any idea what kind of role she wants you to have with Lily and the baby?"

"We talked a little. She made a point of mentioning that the donor agreement is in effect with the baby."

"What else did she say?"

"That's about it. We're going to talk more tomorrow when Lily's not around."

"I thought about this while I was on the treadmill. I realize it's unlikely a judge is going to take a baby away from its mother, but we could still try to get guardianship of Lily."

I can't believe she's bringing this up again. "Jess, that's not going to happen. It's not right, and it's not in Lily's best interests. Quinn's baby doesn't change that. The baby will be Lily's sibling, and they belong together."

"Half sibling," Jessica corrects. "If we have a child, he or she will be Lily's half sibling, too."

"That's not part of this equation."

"Not yet. But hopefully it will be."

I don't want to even open that discussion. "Let's stick with what's on the table right now."

"I can be just as good a mother to Lily as Quinn."

"Like your Realtor friend said about getting pregnant—it's not a competition, Jessica. I don't want to go against the birth mother's wishes, I don't want to drag Lily away from the only family she knows, and I don't want to violate the terms of a contract I signed. Plus it's such a legal long shot it's ludicrous to even discuss it."

She looks like she might cry. "Did you get a copy of the will?"

"Yeah."

"And?"

"It's pretty much what we thought."

She stares at her water bottle for a moment. "Well, if you're so keen not to violate the terms of your donor contract, you should just stay out of their lives until they're eighteen, like you agreed."

"But Lily knows I'm her father, and I assume the baby will, too. Do you want them to grow up thinking I don't care about them?"

"But you weren't *supposed* to be a part of their lives. You were supposed to be an anonymous donor."

You should have thought about that before you impersonated me on that website. I sigh. "But I'm not anonymous anymore, am I? You can't unring the bell."

"David Foster Wallace."

"What?"

"He's widely considered the source of that quote because it appears in his fiction, but it was used in a trial in Oregon before he was born."

"Your memory is amazing," I say. *If somewhat irrelevant,* I think.

She gives a stiff smile.

"There's another possibility." I shift on the barstool to more fully face her. "We could eliminate the distance."

"What?"

"We stay here. I'm sure the New Orleans hotel would be delighted to have you stay on. And I'm up for partner at my old law firm."

She puts a hand on her chest. Her expression reminds me of the time we were walking in the park and she realized she'd stepped in dog poop. "But . . . we decided! You agreed to move, and I'm looking at houses."

I raise both hands, trying to placate her. "Please—just think about it. The situation is different now. Two children are involved, and we didn't know that when we made the decision about Seattle. Staying here might be best for everyone."

"You think it would be best for me to turn down a promotion and give up living near my family so I can watch another woman have your baby and raise your children?"

She's looking at it all wrong. "If we're here, we could help raise them, too."

"No." The barstool squeaks on the floor as she rises from it. "No freaking way. Not just no, but *hell, no!* I didn't sign up to be a stepmother to your children!"

"Jessica . . ."

She throws out her arms in a large gesture. "I don't want to live here and play second fiddle to another woman. No! That sounds like my worst nightmare."

I know it isn't how she imagined things, but her stance strikes me as completely self-centered. Before I know it, the words I managed to squelch earlier are flying out of my mouth. "You should have thought about that before you impersonated me on that donor website."

"Oh, wow." She plops back on the barstool and holds the paper towel to her face for several seconds, as if I'd struck her.

I blow out a long sigh. "I'm sorry, Jess. That was an unkind thing to say."

She lowers the paper towel. "You have no idea how much I regret that."

"I think I do."

Her expression is more resentment than remorse. "Speaking of things we shouldn't have done, why the *hell* did you look up

Brooke's phone number and go to her house? Why didn't you talk to me first?"

"Oh, like you talked to me before you went on the registry?" I feel my pulse throbbing in my temple.

She pulls in a sharp breath. Her cheeks puff out as she exhales. "You're right." Her voice sounds completely deflated. "I started all this. It's my fault, and I know it."

"I don't want to cast blame," I say. "I just want to do the right thing now."

"For whom?"

"For Lily. For the baby. For you."

"You just named me last. I see where I fall on your list of priorities." Her voice has a bitter, acidic tone.

"Damn it, Jessica. You're just looking for things to be mad about."

"I don't have to look very far, do I? What about the baby we planned to have together?"

Not again. "Jessica, we've tried and tried."

"We haven't tried with a donor egg. I told you I'm willing to do that now."

"Well, I'm not. We've got enough on our plates without getting into that."

"It's the only thing I want on my plate."

You only considered it after you learned I have a donor child. I refrain from saying it aloud. "I don't want to talk about it." I stand up. "I'm going for a run."

"You don't want to talk about having a baby with your wife, even though a stranger is carrying your child? Nice, Zack. Very nice." She swings herself off the barstool. "I'm going to see if I can catch the flight to Seattle."

I stand perfectly still. "You're leaving tonight?"

She lifts her shoulders. "There's no point in waiting until tomorrow. We're both too upset to have a civil conversation or get any sleep together."

She's right, but it doesn't make me feel any better. I run a hand down my face. "I'm sorry, Jessica."

"Yeah, well, me, too."

"Will you do me a favor and at least think about not moving?"

"How can you even ask that?" She throws out her arms, palms up. "There's nothing to think about. The answer is no. I'm all in at the new job. And I thought you were all in, too." She takes out her phone and pulls up the airline website.

We've always dealt with anger and disagreements in the past by giving each other space to cool down so we don't say things we'll regret. Right now, though, it feels as if there's already too much space between us.

I go into the bedroom and change into my running gear. By the time I return to the kitchen to fill my water bottle, she's hauling two suitcases out of the hallway closet. "I'm booked on the eight thirty flight," she says. "I'm going to shower and get to the airport."

I nod. "We'll talk tomorrow."

"Sure. Have a good run." She gives me a quick peck—you couldn't really call it a kiss.

My stomach sinks as I watch her disappear into the bedroom. I consider trying to talk to her some more, but I know it's futile in her current mood. To be truthful, mine isn't much better.

I put on my headset, turn on Springsteen's "Born to Run," and head out the door. I can run off some stress, but I can't outrun the feeling that our marriage is in serious trouble.

CHAPTER THIRTY-FIVE

Quinn

Saturday, May 18

SINCE EVERYONE ON the planet now seems to know I'm pregnant, I figure I might as well tell my mom. I decide to call her around nine Saturday morning—it's five in the evening in Dubai then—while Lily is upstairs playing with Alicia.

But first, I have to overcome my dread of the conversation, so I put in my EarPods, reach for my phone, and listen to the recording of my baby's heartbeat. The fast *whoosh whoosh whoosh* always makes me smile. According to the baby books, he or she should be the size of a strawberry by the end of the week; by the end of the week after, the size of a fig. The thought buoys me enough to punch my mother's number.

"Hi, Mom," I say when she answers. "Can you talk?"

"For just a few minutes. We're meeting some people for drinks in half an hour."

I used to think you couldn't drink in Dubai, but I've learned that's not true. Knowing my mother's affinity for booze, I'm sure it's something she checked out before she agreed to move there.

"How's Larry?"

"Fine. Busy. Busy with business, I mean. Not busy like your father was." She gives an overly bright little laugh. I hear a tinkling sound that I recognize as ice in a glass. My mother is already drinking. Possibly wine; she used to think that if she put ice in wine, it negated the alcohol content. "Larry adores me."

"That's great, Mom."

"He's gotten a promotion, did I tell you? He's a vice president now."

"Yes, you told me." Over and over. Mom is all caught up in the pecking order of oil company execs, and she's thrilled that she caught a big fish who moved higher up the food chain. Larry even looks a big fish; he's got big fleshy lips and eyes set so far apart he resembles a flounder. "Congratulations to him."

I hear the ice clink against the glass again. "Oh, I have some news. The expat group here is putting on a play—*Barefoot in the Park*. And I'm playing Corie!"

"That's wonderful." She's told me this, too, the last three times we talked.

"Rehearsals are going really well."

"That's great. I'm sure you'll do a wonderful job."

I can practically hear her preen. "You know, a producer I met before I married your father told me I could have had a career in Hollywood."

I've heard this a million times, too. "I'm sure you could have."

"Larry and I are going to Singapore in a couple of weeks. I just love the shopping there."

"Terrific. Any plans to come to the States?"

"Not anytime soon. You know we hate that long flight."

"Yes, well, I have some news that might encourage you to visit a little more often."

"Oh?"

"Yes," I say. "I'm pregnant."

Nothing. The silence stretches until I wonder if she didn't hear me.

"I'm going to have a baby," I say.

"I know what 'pregnant' means." Mom's voice is curt. "By whom? I didn't know you were even seeing anybody."

"I'm not."

"Quinnlyn Rose, is this some kind of joke? Because if it is, I don't find it amusing."

Hoo boy. I brace myself. "I'm going to be a single mother. The father is a donor. In fact, it's the same donor Brooke used. It's Lily's father."

"Good God! What in the world were you *thinking*?"

I knew I was likely to get a negative reaction from her—that's just Mother's way. All the same, I find myself swallowing my disappointment as I explain it to her.

"Good Lord, Quinn!" I hear a brief splash. She's probably refilling her glass. "Please tell me Margaret is going to take Lily back."

My whole body stiffens. "Lily isn't a piece of merchandise I want to return." *Unlike how you felt about me*, I think hotly. "Lily is a child I *love*."

"Oh, don't go getting all high horsey on me. I'm just asking if Margaret will get well enough to raise her."

"Margaret's slowly making progress, but I'm going to be Lily's permanent guardian."

"And you'll have a baby to take care of, too? Oh, Quinn!" Her tone is full of melodrama and disapproval.

I've heard that soul-crushing *Oh, Quinn!* my whole life—when I got my clothes dirty playing outside; when I didn't get a part in the junior high play (which I'd only tried out for to please her); and—in what is probably the most telling incident—when I refused to dye my hair red at age fifteen to help Mom look "like a natural redhead."

She has a way of saying my name that proclaims my complete failure as a human being. *Oh, Quinn!* used to make me cry myself to sleep, because more than anything, I wanted my mother's approval. It wasn't until I was grown that I realized I was never going to get it.

Judging from the way my stomach tightens now, I'm still not immune to longing for it.

"I'm very excited and happy," I tell Mom now. "And Lily's thrilled to have a new little brother or sister on the way."

"Of course she is. She's three. She'd be equally excited about a puppy."

Wow. Mom may have hit a new low. "Well, I know you're busy, so I won't keep you. I just thought you'd want to know you're going to be a grandmother."

"Oh, Lordy! I'm way too young for that."

Trust Mom to make this all about herself. I hear a jingle and a clink. I can picture her bracelets hitting her drink glass as she raises it to her lips. "Quinn, you'll be so tied down! And it'll be next to impossible to find a man who'll want to take on two kids."

"I'm not looking for a man. I plan to be a single mother."

"Yes, but you didn't know you'd be raising Lily, too. How far along are you?"

"It's early days. But I heard the heartbeat, Mom. It's recorded, and it's amazing."

She sighs. "I suppose it's too late to change your mind."

My muscles knot. "That's not something I'd ever consider."

"No need to get all snippy. I'm just interested in your welfare."

Is that why you haven't asked how I'm doing? "I'm feeling fine, thanks," I say.

She totally misses the sarcasm. "Well, that's good. I was constantly nauseated with you."

"I'm having a little morning sickness, but it goes away if I eat something."

"I'm glad it's manageable. Just be careful not to gain too much weight. You had that little chubby spell in junior high, remember?"

I sigh. Some things never change.

THE CONVERSATION WITH my mother casts a pall over my mood. I take Lily and Alicia to a playground, then drop Alicia at her home for lunch. Lily and I eat chicken sandwiches, play Candyland, and take naps. Around three, I take Lily to Sarah's house and head to my shop.

I'm worried about the meeting with Zack. Now that Lily knows he's her father, I'm sure he's going to want to be more involved in her life. The fact that he sent a minion to the attorney's office to get a copy of Brooke's will doesn't bode well, either. And then there's the baby to consider; whatever level of interaction he has with Lily will no doubt be what he expects with the baby.

THE WORRY MUST show on my face, because Terri looks at me with concern. "Are you feeling okay? Do you need to lie down or eat something?'

"I'm fine," I tell her.

We rearrange some items at the store, go over the books, and discuss upcoming client appointments. At five o'clock, I turn the Open sign on the door of the shop to Closed.

"Do you want me to stay so you'll have someone in your corner?" Terri's face is earnest, her eyes warm with concern.

I smile. "You're a sweetie, Terri, but really, there's no need."

"Well, feel free to call me if you want to talk afterward."

She leaves, and I putter around the store, looking through the day's sales receipts and seeing to odds and ends. About fifteen minutes before Zack is due to arrive, I call Sarah. "I'm nervous about talking to Zack. What do you advise?"

"Be cordial but direct," Sarah says. "You need to know what you're dealing with. You need to know his thoughts and how his wife feels about things."

"I'm really worried about her."

"I know you are. Maybe you and Lily should try setting up an outing with both of them so you can see how things go."

"Not a bad idea," I say. "Thanks, Sarah."

Zack arrives five minutes early, which is fine with me, since I'm working myself into an increasingly high state of anxiety. I spot him through the window as he approaches. My heart knocks against my ribs as his knuckles rap against the door.

I answer it, and my skin gets the premonition prickles. Every time I see him, I'm shocked all over again by how his eyes mirror Lily's.

"Hi," he says.

"Hi." I'm usually a hugger, but with him, I hesitate. Maybe it's knowing I'm carrying his child; maybe it's the fact that he's married and so darned good-looking.

I hug him anyway, and it's every bit as unnerving as I feared. My goose bumps get goose bumps.

"Come in, come in," I say, stepping back from the door.

He glances at my belly. It's funny how people do that as soon as they find out I'm pregnant, even though it's too early for me to be showing.

He steps across the threshold and gazes around the shop. "Wow—what a great place!" He heads toward an old secretaire from an estate in Scotland and bends to look at the brass handles. "Does this fold down into a desk?"

"Yes." I turn the skeleton key in the keyhole, and the cabinet drops to reveal a leather-lined writing table.

"Oh, that's beautiful." He runs his hand over the table. "My great-grandmother had a piece like this. Not as fancy, but the same general concept. I always thought it was so cool."

"What happened to it?"

"My sister has it." He opens a little drawer at the back of the desk.

"You like antiques?"

"Oh, yeah, I love them. Especially things that are handmade."

"I'm surprised. I had you pegged as the contemporary type."

"I guess I am now." He closes the drawer. "Jessica's taste runs to modern things."

"I could tell when she was in the shop."

"I didn't know she was going to come by here," he says. "Or crash Margaret's party. I apologize on her behalf."

"She was curious, that's all." I close the leaf of the secretaire and turn the skeleton key. "I probably would have done the same thing if I were in her shoes." I wouldn't have, but I'd googled her, hadn't I? "Let's go into my office to talk." I gesture toward the back of the store. "Would you like something to drink?"

"No, thanks."

"You sure? I promise not to have a heart attack or fall off any stepstools getting it for you."

He laughs. "Thanks, but I'm good."

He follows me through the store. "Where's Lily?"

"At Sarah's house."

"You're fortunate to have a friend like that."

I nod. "She's been a great resource for Lily since Brooke's death—not to mention a big help to me." We walk into my office, which suddenly feels too dark and intimate. I usually sit side by side with my clients in one of the two chairs opposite my desk, but this time I circle it, keeping the desk between us. I turn on the lamp on my desk. "How's your wife handling things?"

"Okay, I guess." He rubs his leg.

There are varying degrees of okay. From his tone, I surmise Jessica's is on the low end of the scale. "It must be difficult for her."

"Yeah." He looks like he's about to say something more and then changes his mind.

"This is difficult for all of us," I say.

He nods. "That's why it's important we talk. Do you want to go first?"

"Okay." I sit there in silence for a moment, the light from the fringed lampshade on my desk throwing shadows on the framed photo of Lily. "There's something I need to ask you about." My lungs seem to tremble as I inhale. "Brooke and I used the same attorney, and I went to see him Thursday. He told me that you sent someone by to get a copy of Brooke's will."

"Yeah—an intern. I didn't exactly send him, though." He crosses his right foot over his left thigh. My office, which I've always thought of as spacious, suddenly feels a lot smaller. "I asked him to get a copy of the will from the courthouse, assuming it had already been filed. It hadn't been. He's something of a go-getter, so he took it upon himself to look up the obituary. He contacted the funeral home, and they gave him the name of the attorney handling the estate—apparently the estate paid for the funeral services. I had no idea he was going to the attorney's office. I apologize if it seems intrusive."

"'Intrusive' is one word for it," I say. "'Weird' is another. So is 'worrisome.'" So is *getting all up in my business*, but that's more than a single word. I look straight into his blue, blue eyes. "Why did you want to see the will?"

"To read the wording about Lily's guardianship."

"Why?"

"Because I'm an attorney, and that's what we do. If an issue has a legal document attached, I want to read it." He grins. "But I also wanted to know if there was a third party named in addition to you and Miss Margaret."

"There's not."

"I saw that." He uncrosses his leg and leans forward. "I was wondering who you're going to list as the guardian on yours."

My fingers tighten on the arm of the chair. "I haven't made any decisions about that yet. This all happened really suddenly. I'll want it to be someone Lily and the baby know really well, like Sarah or Annie or Terri."

His gaze is steady and direct, and so is his voice. "I'd like to be someone they know really well."

My mouth goes dry. "But you're moving to Seattle."

"Yeah, that's the plan. But I have a month or more to get to know Lily before I move. And I could come back here two or three times a year to see her and the baby. We can write and call and video message. And maybe you can bring them both out for a visit once a year or so when they get older."

"I doubt your wife will welcome us with open arms."

"She'll be fine once she gets used to the idea."

Is he trying to convince me or himself? I decide to take another tack.

"Look, Zack—you signed a contract agreeing to be an anonymous donor and to stay out of the children's lives until they're eighteen. Neither Brooke nor I intended for the biological father to play a role in their lives."

"Yes, but I'm not anonymous anymore. Lily knows I'm her father."

There it is—the thing that can't be undone. The thing that kept me awake much of the night before.

"Lily knows you're her *donor*," I say. "She's always known she didn't have a co-parenting daddy."

"I don't think she's making that distinction now," he says.

No. I don't think she is, either.

"She knows I'm her father," Zack says. "The question is, what kind of father am I going to be?"

I close my eyes for a moment, draw a deep breath, and ask the question that feels like an elephant kneeling on my chest. "I need to know your intentions."

"I don't want to take Lily or the baby away from you, if that's what you're worried about. Lily obviously adores you, and I think you're doing a great job."

I don't realize I'm holding my breath until I exhale. My hands have been clenched so tightly my fingers throb. "Are you going to try to get joint custody or visitation? Because I have to tell you, I hated splitting my time between my parents when they divorced."

He shakes his head. "I'm not looking to complicate your lives. I just want Lily to know that I'm there for her. And I want to be there for your new baby, too. I want to keep this easy and flexible. I want to be a positive in your lives, not a negative."

It's better than anything I could have hoped for, short of him going away until Lily is eighteen. And as Sarah pointed out, that might not be best for Lily or the baby, anyway. "Your wife agrees to this?"

"She will, once she gets used to the idea."

This is the second time he's used that phrase—which means she isn't okay with it at all. She sure didn't look okay when she learned I was pregnant. "Look—I don't want Lily or the baby exposed to a reluctant stepmother. I lived through that scenario, and it was miserable. It's awful for a child to feel like an unwanted third wheel."

"I won't let that happen. Jessica loves children. She'll come around."

"But what if she can't?"

"Then I'll see them without her."

It's the answer I wanted to hear, but I don't know if it's a feasible plan for the long haul. I draw a deep breath. "Maybe you, Jessica, and I can do something together with Lily next weekend and see how it goes."

"I'd like that," he says. "But Jessica's back in Seattle, and she's likely to stay there through the weekend."

"Oh. Well, then, maybe the weekend after?"

"Sure, if she's in town. Absolutely."

It seems weird to me that he doesn't know for sure whether or not his wife will be back in two weeks, but I nod.

Silence stretches between us. "I'm starving," he says at length. "Do you want to get something to eat? Maybe we can pick up Lily and take her with us."

"Lily's eating with Sarah and her kids."

"Well, what about you? Do you have any plans for dinner?"

"No, but . . ." I don't know how to finish that sentence. *No, but you're married?* He isn't asking me on a date, for heaven's sake. We still have a lot of things to iron out about Lily and the baby.

Communication is the foundation of every type of relationship. I'd just read that in the reparenting book; there's a whole chapter on the subject. The better I know Zack, the easier it'll be to work things out between us.

"No, I don't have plans," I say.

"Well then, let me buy you dinner."

"Okay," I say. "Sure. I need to lock up here, then I'll be ready to go."

CHAPTER THIRTY-SIX

Zack

WE DRIVE OUR separate cars to Jacques-Imo's on Oak Street. I called ahead, and it's early enough that they can seat us. I park behind Quinn's Equinox around the corner.

"This is one of my favorite restaurants," Quinn says as we step into the dim bar. The walls and ceiling are completely covered with framed paintings. "I love the decor."

"Oh, yeah?" I brought Jessica here when we were dating, but she didn't care for it. She thought it was unrefined.

Quinn nods. "It's quirky and colorful and over-the-top. It makes coming here a real New Orleans experience."

"I thought the food did that."

"That, too." She laughs.

We're seated in the back corner of the dining room and presented with menus. I order the blackened redfish with crab-chili hollandaise, and Quinn decides on the shrimp étouffée. They bring their signature cornbread with garlic butter. Quinn takes a bite, then looks heavenward and gives a little moan. "Oh, this is so delicious!"

I like the way she enjoys food. Jessica avoids carbs and is very particular about what she eats. Quinn has a refreshing way of . . .

But I shouldn't be comparing the two women.

"Why did you decide to use a donor?" I ask, determined to straighten out my thinking. "I mean, you're the kind of woman any guy . . ." I stop. I sense I'm stepping over some kind of line. I'm a married man; I probably shouldn't be telling another woman she's desirable.

Oh, jeez. She's blushing.

I shouldn't be asking such a personal question, either. I stumble on, trying to fix things. "What I mean is, why didn't you go about creating a family the usual way, when . . ." Oh, hell—I'm only making things worse! I inwardly wince. "I'm sorry. It's none of my business." I grab my water and take a gulp.

"It's okay." She smiles and takes another nibble of the cornbread. "I knew I wanted a child, even if marriage wasn't in the cards for me."

I'm still not understanding. "Why would marriage not be in the cards for you?"

"I haven't had a lot of luck finding the right kind of guy. Brooke said I pick emotionally unavailable men." She thanks the waiter as he sets down her iced tea, then looks back at me. "I think she's right. I've been in a couple of long-term relationships, and in both cases, I was way more invested than the guy was. Brooke said I projected my hopes and dreams onto them instead of seeing them as they really were." She takes a sip of tea, then give a rueful smile. "I broke up with the last guy, Tom, right before I moved to New Orleans, and I haven't met anyone since. The biological clock was ticking, and well . . ." She lifts her shoulders and looks away. "Single motherhood had worked out well for Brooke and I just adored Lily, so when Brooke offered to give me the rest of her donor's, um . . . *donation*, I went for it." She looks back up. "How did you and Jessica meet?"

"At a friend's wedding."

"Oh, that's so romantic! How long have you been married?"

"Nearly three years."

"How long have you . . ." She stops and looks sheepish. "This time *I* was about to ask an inappropriate question."

"When did we start trying for a family?" I guess.

She gives an embarrassed smile and nods.

"Pretty much right away. Jessica was worried about the biological clock, too. When nothing happened after six months, she went to a doctor and learned her ovarian reserves were low. We started IVF and went through five rounds."

"That's a lot."

"Yeah. Two or three too many, really."

The waiter brings our salads. I want to steer the conversation back to her. I picked up from her earlier remarks that her parents were divorced. "You haven't told me much about your family. What were your parents like?"

Quinn sighs. "What do you want to know?"

"Everything."

"Well, Mom is on her third marriage, and she lives in Dubai with her oil executive husband. We talk every couple of weeks and see each other maybe once a year."

"What's she like?"

Quinn gives a dry smile. "How much time do you have?"

"As long as it takes."

"Well, Mom was Miss Strawberry Festival and Miss Southeast Louisiana, and I think that was the highlight of her life. She was an only child and the apple of her parents' eye, and she was brought up to think the world revolved around her. She still kind of thinks that way."

"Uh-oh."

"Yeah." Quinn grins. "She wanted to be an actress—a movie star, actually—but she got pregnant with my brother and married my father. She said that's what you had to do in those days. Neither of them were eager to be parents."

Wow. Not exactly Mother of the Year material. "Are you and your brother close?"

She shakes her head and spears a piece of lettuce. "He's ten years older than me. By the time I was eight, he was away at college. I grew up feeling more like he was an uncle than a sibling. Now he lives in Indianapolis and works in IT."

"Do you stay in touch?"

She lifts her shoulders. "We email on holidays, but that's about it. I've tried, but he has no interest in connecting more."

"What about your dad?"

"He was a technical sales manager with an oil service company, and he traveled quite a bit. He wasn't around a lot even when he was in town, though. When I was twelve, he left us for the other woman. She was a divorcée with two small children, so he moved on to a whole new family. I think that lasted for about four years, then he left her for someone in Texas. Mom heard he abandoned that woman, too, and now . . . I really don't know where he is." She lifts her iced tea.

"That has to be tough."

"It's okay now, but the divorce was awful. My mother was angry and vindictive. And I . . . well, I was stuck in the middle. I had to go stay with Dad every other weekend and for half of the summer. After I visited, Mom would pump me for details. Sometimes she'd drink too much, call Dad, and twist around everything I'd said."

That explains her aversion to a split guardianship arrangement.

"Deborah thought I was a troublemaker and a liar. It was clear she didn't want me there, although she didn't mind using me as an unpaid babysitter for her kids. And Dad . . . well, he was just as much of a missing person in that marriage as he'd been with Mom."

What a horrible situation for a child to be in.

"My escape from it all was school. I studied hard, and I was a good student. When it was time for high school, I said I wanted to go to the Louisiana School for Math, Science, and the Arts in Natchitoches—it's a state boarding school for gifted students. I acted like I was passionate about getting a really good education, but mostly I just wanted to get away."

She gives an embarrassed smile. "I'm sure that's way more information than you bargained for."

"No. I'm glad you told me."

She fixes me with an earnest gaze. "I didn't have a great childhood, but that doesn't mean I can't be a good parent."

"I don't think that. I think you're wonderful with Lily."

"I see my upbringing as a cautionary tale. It made me keenly aware of how sensitive kids are. I know how important it is that they feel wanted and valued and listened to."

I nod. "I can understand that."

We eat our salads in silence for a moment.

"Do you have grandparents or any other family?" I ask.

She shakes her head. "Both sets of grandparents were already dead when I was born, but I had some supportive adults when I was growing up. I had some really encouraging teachers, and the mother of a friend in elementary school kind of took me under her wing. And then there was a neighbor across the street—an elderly woman, Mrs. Robichaux—who moved in when I was nine. She was a real character." Quinn smiles.

"Oh, yeah?"

Quinn nods. "Mom said she was crazy and Dad thought she was superstitious, but she was really kind to me, and my folks didn't mind me being over there all the time. I quickly learned it was best not to repeat everything she said, though." Her eyes go soft and fond. "Mrs. Robichaux said that coincidences are miracles where God chooses to remain anonymous, and that heaven gives us little signs to guide us. She said that if you get goose bumps and a strong feeling, that's your angel whispering in your ear."

"And you believed it?"

"I still do." She grins. "When you think about it, it's not as crazy as it sounds. There are lots of things we can't see—things like air and sound waves and gravity. So why is it so far-fetched to believe that we might get a little divine nudge through a song, or an overheard snippet of a stranger's conversation, or even our hair follicles every now and then?"

I smile. "I don't think it's all that far-fetched." I like the fact that she believes in a spiritual dimension. Jessica thinks it's all baloney. "So how did you end up in interior design?"

"I had embarrassingly simplistic motives." She grins. "I loved the idea of creating happy homes—places that are warm and welcoming and beautiful, where families want to spend time together and gather with friends."

There's an honesty about her that touches me. It's easy to see how her childhood shaped her adult life.

The waiter brings our entrées, and she starts quizzing me about my family and growing up in Ohio. I end up talking far more than I intend to.

The waiter is clearing our dishes when Quinn's cell phone vibrates. She checks it.

"It's Sarah. She's watching Lily, so I need to take this."

"Sure," I say. "Go right ahead."

I watch her brows furrow after she answers. "Does she have a fever?" she asks.

Uh-oh. I signal for the waiter to bring the check. He hustles over.

"I'll be right there," Quinn says, then ends the call.

"What's going on?" I pull out my credit card and hand it to the waiter.

"Lily's sick." She gathers up her purse. "I need to go."

"Hang on a moment, and I'll follow you over there."

"You don't need to," she says.

"I want to. Maybe I can help."

QUINN DRIVES LIKE Dale Earnhardt Jr. after six double espressos. I have trouble keeping her in sight; I'm beginning to wish I'd asked for the address when I see her turn into the drive of a little house near River Road that's nearly hidden from the street by trees and shrubbery. She's out of her car and inside before I even make it up the porch steps.

Sarah smiles and opens the door wider. "Hi, Zack. Come on in."

Two toddler boys in shorts and striped T-shirts are jumping up and down in the hallway. I find Lily lying on a brown sofa in the living room, looking limp and pale.

Quinn leans over her. "Hey, Lily."

"Oh, Auntie Quinn—I'm so, so glad you're here." Lily's voice sounds as wan as she looks.

"Poor baby girl." Quinn perches on the edge of the sofa and strokes Lily's cheek. "I hate it that you don't feel well."

"I hate it, too."

Quinn lays a palm on her forehead. My heart gives a strange lurch at the familiar motherly gesture. Lily closes her eyes for a moment, then abruptly opens them. Her face has a weird expression.

"Uh-oh," Sarah says. She surges forward, grabs a plastic bucket off the floor, and thrusts it under Lily's chin, just in time.

"Good save," I say as Sarah pulls back the bucket and takes it in the other room.

"Urpity urp!" says one toddler, peering over the back of the sofa.

"Big barf!" says the other. They collapse on the floor, laughing, then stand up and run around the sofa.

"Boys, leave Lily alone," Sarah calls. She returns in a moment with a wet washcloth. She hands it to Quinn, who gently wipes Lily's face.

Lily looks up, obviously feeling better, and notices me for the first time. Her face brightens. "Daddy!"

Delight pulses through me at the effusive greeting. "Hi, Lily."

"I'm sick."

"I see. I'm so very sorry."

Quinn finishes wiping Lily's face and folds the washcloth. "When did it start?" she asks Sarah.

"Lily didn't want any dinner," Sarah replies. "She said she didn't feel well, so I put her on the sofa and fetched the sick bucket. I barely made it to her in time. I called you right after that."

"Poor darling." Quinn strokes Lily's hair. "Does your tummy hurt?"

"It did, but I throwed up and it's better."

"Can I touch it?"

Lily nods and lies back. Quinn gently presses her abdomen. "Does this hurt?" she asks. Lily shakes her head. Quinn repeats the press-and-question sequence several times, without discovering any tender spots.

"It's probably a stomach bug," Sarah says. "It's been going around."

"I hope your twins don't get it."

"Oh, Lily probably got it from them," Sarah says ruefully. "They were sick last week. If it's the same thing, it lasts about twenty-four hours."

"Do we need to take her to an emergency room or a doc-in-the-box?" I ask.

"I think we just need to take her home," Quinn says.

"I'll give you some Pedialyte and Children's Tylenol," Sarah said. "That's what the twins' doctor said to give them."

"And I can call her pediatrician if she gets worse," Quinn says. "I have the number." She turns back to Lily. "Let's get you home, sweetie. Can you stand up?"

Lily sits up, slowly stands, and then sinks back on the sofa. "The room feels all wobbly."

"Do you want me to carry you to the car?" I ask.

"Yes, please," Lily says. She holds up her arms, her eyes so trusting that my heart melts. I pick her up. She seems to weigh practically nothing.

Sarah bustles to the kitchen, the twins following her like loud, raucous ducklings. Quinn goes with her and washes her hands.

"Here's the Tylenol and Pedialyte," Sarah says, placing the bottles in a grocery tote. "I'm putting in some paper towels and a plastic bag in case she gets sick in the car. Better safe than sorry."

"Good thinking," Quinn says as she dries her hands. "Thanks."

"And here's her book bag. And Sugar Bear."

Quinn takes the bags and the stuffed animal, and heads for the front door. "Thank you, Sarah. I really owe you."

"Just take care of Lily, yourself, and that baby." Sarah gives her a hug. "You don't need to get run-down and sick yourself."

"Will do," says Quinn.

I carry Lily down the porch steps to Quinn's car. Quinn opens the back door. I gently settle Lily in the safety seat and fasten her seat belt.

Quinn pauses by the driver's door and looks at me. "Thanks for everything," she says, as if this were good night.

"I'll follow you home," I say.

She hesitates. I'm afraid she's about to tell me, *No, thanks. I've got this*. "You might need help getting her into the house," I say. "And I can run to the store to stock you up on extra Pedialyte or anything else you might need."

I can see her weighing things. "Okay," she says, her eyes grateful. "Thank you."

CHAPTER THIRTY-SEVEN

Quinn

LILY IS FINE during the drive home, but she gets sick again as I unfasten her seat belt. I silently bless Sarah for sending the plastic baggie.

Zack comes around and lifts Lily out. We walk to the front door and I unlock it, gingerly holding the barf bag. Ruffles barks.

"Ruffles, this is my daddy," Lily says from her perch in Zack's arms.

"Where should I put her?" Zack asks me.

"On the sofa," Lily replies. Amazing, how emptying her stomach immediately perks her up. I head to the kitchen, throw the sick bag in the trash, wash my hands, and then grab a big plastic bowl and place it on the floor beside Lily.

"What can I do?" Zack asks.

"Why don't you bring a couple of warm, damp washcloths? There are some clean ones in the bathroom cabinet."

He returns in a moment. I wipe Lily's face with one and her hands with the other, then notice her shirt has not come through her sick spells unscathed.

"Let's get you into your jammies," I say.

"Okay," she agrees.

Zack fetches another couple of warm washcloths as well as Lily's pajamas from her room, then feeds Ruffles while I clean and change Lily. He's at ease in my house, helping out as if it's no big deal. *I could get used to this,* I think. I immediately censor the thought. *He's married. He's moving to Seattle. Stop that right now!*

I turn on a Disney movie and give Lily some Pedialyte, but she can't keep it down. I decide to call her pediatrician. I get the answering service, then wait for the doctor to call back.

"It sounds like a virus," Dr. Zegetti says when she returns my call. "Let her stomach settle for thirty minutes to an hour, then give her a few sips of Pedialyte. If she keeps it down, slowly rehydrate her. If she gets tired of Pedialyte, ginger ale or Popsicles will work. If she's no better in the morning, bring her in."

Zack runs to the store and brings back everything Dr. Zegetti suggested. We both sit on the sofa with Lily, her feet on his lap and her head on mine, and watch Disney princess movies.

It's a long night of bodily functions gone awry. Through it all, Zack is patient, gentle, and easygoing. Lily dozes off sometime around one in the morning, reclining against him.

"I think you missed your calling as a health care professional," I tell him.

He shrugs his shoulders. "Life put me through basic training."

"With your mom?"

He nods. "She had a lot of internal injuries. I took a six-month leave of absence from work and went home to help Dad care for her."

I raise my eyebrows. "Wow. Didn't that throw a wrench in your career?"

He nods. "One of the firm's partners warned me it would probably set me back a couple of years."

"And you did it anyway?"

"Sure. Family comes first."

I don't know many men who'd deliberately take time out from a promising career to go home and help care for a sick mother. Correction: I don't know any. I don't know if it's pregnancy hormones, worry about Lily, or fatigue that makes me emotional, but my eyes grow teary. "That was noble."

He gives a little laugh and looks embarrassed. "It's what families do. My sister tried to help out, but she had two toddlers and lived two hours away. Anyway, I think Dad was in worse shape than Mom. She was his whole world."

"Your family sounds wonderful."

"Yeah." He looks down at Lily, then back up at me. "You know, watching you with Lily tonight reminded me of Mom. The way you put your palm on her forehead and smoothed back her hair and cleaned her face—it was just like she used to do when my sister and I were little."

I realize he's paying me the highest of compliments. "Thanks," I say. My throat feels strangely thick. "I only did what I always wished my mother would do for me."

"And she didn't?"

I shrug. "There were little stretches of time when she would, but it always seemed like she was performing in a production called *The Really Good Mom*, starring Deirdre Langston. After half an hour or so, she'd get tired of the part."

And if she didn't have an audience, all bets were off. I decide that's TMI.

He blows out a soft whistle.

"She wasn't all that bad," I backtrack. "She just wasn't cut out to be a parent. Maybe that's the difference between having a child you want and a child you don't."

"Love isn't always something you know you want in advance," Zack says. He looks down at Lily, his eyes soft. "Sometimes it's what you choose to open your heart to."

His words seem to echo around the room. They bounce off the walls and ceiling, and ricochet dangerously in my mind. Goose bumps rise on my arms.

We sit there in silence for a moment. On the TV screen, Aladdin kisses Jasmine. *It's a sign!* I think.

No, I immediately reprimand myself. *It's not a sign; it's a Disney movie. And Zack is not a guy you can open your heart to. He's married.*

"You need to take care of that baby you're carrying," he says. "I'll stay here with Lily. Go get some sleep."

I don't argue; I'm too fatigued to even pretend I'm not. Fatigue must be the reason I'm having these unnerving thoughts about

Zack, because I have no interest—*none at all*—in harboring even the slightest romantic feelings for a married man. I head to my bedroom, pull off my clothes, put on a T-shirt and yoga pants, and fall into bed.

I AWAKEN TO the smell of coffee. When I roll over and look at my bedside clock, it's five minutes after eight.

I wash my face, brush my teeth, and peek into the living room. Lily is still sacked out on the sofa. I head into the kitchen and find a shirtless Zack on a barstool at the island, looking at his phone.

I stop and gawk. My pre-coffee brain can't process the sight of this half-naked man in my kitchen. He's fit, with defined biceps, taut abs, and muscled pecs. He has just the right amount of chest hair that narrows to a happy trail that disappears into his jeans. My mouth goes dry.

He notices me staring and self-consciously runs a hand over his chest. "I, uh, wasn't fast enough with the sick bowl around two this morning," he says apologetically. "I threw my shirt in the washer. It's in the dryer now."

"Oh, good. Great. I'm glad." I realize I'm not making a lot of sense. "I—I don't mean I'm glad you took a hurl hit. I mean I'm glad you helped yourself. To using the washer. And the dryer. And that you found the detergent." Jeez, why can't I stop babbling? "How was Lily the rest of the night?"

"She drank some Pedialyte, kept it down, and conked out. She's been asleep ever since."

"Oh, thank heavens! The active-volcano stage is over." I pour half a cup of coffee. My ob-gyn okayed a little caffeine, and I really need some this morning. Zack seems to have made himself right at home, I note, finding the filters and brewing a pot in my ancient drip coffee maker. I don't mind at all. In fact, it's really nice. "And thank *you*. You were a godsend last night."

"Glad I could help out. I hated seeing her so sick."

"Me, too. It was scary."

"Yeah."

But something else scares me even more: how easily Lily took to him. She relied on him and trusted him as if he really were her father—a father she'd known all her life.

Just as scary is something I don't want to admit, much less really look at: how very much I relied on him, too. And how easily he seems to be fitting into my life.

CHAPTER THIRTY-EIGHT

Jessica

"BUT, JESSICA, I don't understand."

"What don't you get, Mom?" I'm sitting in my hotel room in Seattle on Saturday morning, my cell phone set on speaker. My sister sits across from me on the bed, giving me an encouraging look. She insisted that I needed to tell Mom what's going on in New Orleans, and I know she's right. I can't keep Zack's child and baby a secret from my family forever.

"How could Zack have been a sperm donor? Wasn't he thinking about the future?"

"No, Mom, he wasn't. He was nineteen years old. All he was thinking was that his father's business was in trouble and he wanted to pay his own way through college, which is completely commendable."

"But you said you knew this when you married him. Why didn't you tell me?"

"Because I knew you'd be upset, and I wanted to marry him anyway."

"But I'm your mother. You should have told me."

My sister rolls her eyes.

I cross mine back at her. "Sorry, Mom. I guess I didn't want to disappoint you."

Erin whispers, "Welcome to my world."

"There's something else I don't understand," my mother continues. "Why on earth did you stir up this whole hornet's nest now?"

I blow out a sigh. I thought I'd already adequately explained how I screwed things up, but apparently I need to admit my failure yet again. "I didn't mean to, Mom. Things spiraled out of control. It was a mistake."

"Oh, Jessica." The disappointment in her voice makes my stomach squeeze. "I could expect something like this from your sister or brother, but you, Jess . . ."

My sister stabs her index finger at me. "See?" she hisses.

"I messed up," I say. "I'm furious at myself, and I've got to figure out what to do. I just called to explain the situation and to let you know I'm back in town."

"Yes, well, I appreciate that. Oh, honey." Her voice is so sympathetic that tears well up in my eyes. "This is so unlike you. I hate that you're going through this."

"Thanks, Mom."

"Don't you want to come home instead of staying in that cold hotel?"

"No, this is a lot more convenient. I have several early and late meetings this week, and I don't want to fight the traffic."

"Plus there's room service and a Starbucks in the lobby," my sister says.

"What?" Mom says.

I shoot my sister an evil glare. "That was the TV in the background."

"Well, do you have any time to see your family in that busy schedule of yours?"

"I'm free tomorrow night."

"Can you come for dinner?"

"I'd love to," I say.

"I assume your sister knows all this?"

"Yes. But I only told her a couple of weeks ago."

"Still, that's two weeks sooner than you told me."

I blow out a sigh. "I don't worry as much about Erin's opinion of me."

"Oh, honey! I just want the best for you."

"I know, Mom." I want that, too. No, the truth is, I want to *be* the best. I want my parents and the rest of the world to say, *I'm so proud of you*, and *atta girl!* and, *Jessica, you're so wonderful and smart and amazing!*

Most of all, I want to feel that way about myself. "I have to go, Mom."

"Wait—who picked you up at the airport?"

"Huh? Oh. I, um, got a ride from the hotel. Gotta run now. I'll talk to you later, Mom. Love you! Bye." I click off quickly.

"'I'd expect something like this from your sister or brother,'" my sister says, her voice high and Mom-like. She shakes her head. "I told you she thinks you're the perfect one."

"Not anymore." I want to say, *Do you realize what a burden it is, always trying to live up to that level of expectation?* But I know that Erin will just say something like, *So stop trying to be the golden child.*

"I told you she's always asking me, 'Why can't you be more like your sister?'" Erin says.

"Yeah, well, next time you can reply, 'At least I didn't marry a sperm donor who turned out to have a three-year-old orphaned child and another on the way.'"

"Can I use that?" Erin asks. "Because I think it might be effective."

Now that the worst is over, I think about the reactions I'm likely to get from my other family members. "What about Dad? How do you think he'll take it?"

"He'll look up from his desk for a couple of moments, ask if you're okay, then tell Mom not to worry."

Our father, an aeronautics engineer with Boeing, is brilliant, but he's a man of few words and even fewer expressions of emotion. Erin is probably right.

"What about your kids?" I ask. "How will you explain that Zack has a daughter we just discovered and a bun in another woman's oven? They're old enough to understand that this is really messed up."

She shrugs. "They're also young enough to be okay with just about anything."

"Yeah." My thoughts turn to my brother. "I'm not too worried about Doug."

"Nah. He won't care at all." Erin narrows her eyes. "But who gave you a ride from the airport?"

"What?" I stand, walk to the dresser, and pick up my hairbrush.

"You heard me. Mom asked, and you totally lied."

I should have known she'd pick up on that. A sister can always sense your weak spots. I consider saying Uber, but she'll know it's not the truth. "Brett gave me a lift."

"Oh, really?" Her eyebrows rise.

I ignore the innuendo in her voice, look in the mirror, and run the brush through my hair. "He sent me computerized renovations of a house we looked at, and when I texted back that I was coming in on a late flight, he offered to pick me up."

"Wow. That's what I call service!"

"Yeah, well, I'll be a double client if I buy a home and have him do the renovation."

"I doubt that's why you're getting the red carpet treatment." She crosses to the dresser, picks up my expensive face cream, and opens it. "Not that you ever get anything less."

"Would you stop it, already?" The words come out a little harsher than I'd intended.

"Whoa!"

"Sorry. I didn't mean to bark at you."

Our eyes meet in the mirror. Hers are full of sympathy. "This is really hard on you, isn't it?"

"Yeah. And there's something more." I blow out a hard breath. I need to talk to someone about this, and Erin is my only option. "Zack wants to stay in New Orleans."

"What?"

"He asked me to think about staying there, so we'd be closer to his children."

"Jiminy, Jess!" Her brows furrow. "What did you say?"

"Hell to the no."

"Good for you!" She dabs some of my face cream under her eyes and looks at me in the mirror. "How serious was he?"

"I think he was just testing out the concept." I hope. I hope to high heavens.

She turns around to face me directly. "So . . . Zack will still move here, right?"

"Yeah, I think so."

"You *think*? Give me a percentage."

I've dealt in percentages since junior high. "Seventy percent. No, maybe sixty-five."

"Jesus, Jess! Those aren't the greatest odds."

"Well, he's big on keeping his word, and he accepted the job out here."

"So why only sixty-five percent?"

I put down my brush, lean forward into the mirror, and smooth an eyebrow. "He said he didn't know about Lily when he agreed to the move, and that having a child changes things. And that worries me."

"It worries me, too."

"Lily was bad enough, but the baby . . . Well, it feels like everything's been turned upside down."

"It kind of has." She gives me a direct, sisterly, no-BS kind of look. "If he insists on staying in New Orleans, would you reconsider staying there, too?"

I shake my head. "I don't want to watch him play Daddy to another woman's baby. It makes me sick to even think about it." My phone dings. I pick it up and read the text. "Brett's downstairs."

"Wait a moment, Jessie," Erin says. "So . . . would you divorce Zack?"

The thought of divorce makes me sick, too. "I might threaten to, just to get him to move." I pull my purse onto my shoulder and head for the door. "Will I see you tomorrow night at Mom's?"

"Of course. We'll all be there." She puts the lid back on my face cream, heads back to the bed, and flops on it. "Would you mind if I stay here in your room for a while and just enjoy the peace and quiet, without being reminded of the laundry I need to do?"

"Knock your bad self out."

She picks up the TV remote and gives a blissful sigh. "Love you, sis."

I OPEN THE passenger door of Brett's SUV and lean in. "I feel like I've taken up too much of your time," I tell him. "And the way things are with Zack and me right now, I'm not sure we're ready to put in an offer on a house."

"I'm going to see this new property anyway," he says. "And I'd enjoy your company."

I smile and climb in. We'd talked last night when he picked me up at the airport, so he knows the whole story about Zack. I think he's just being polite, but I'm glad to have an excuse to be out of the hotel. My meetings don't start until Monday.

As he drives, I ask Brett about his work. He tells me about a renovation he's working on, and then the conversation wends its way back to personal topics.

"I'm starting to feel like a third party in my own marriage," I tell him.

"I totally get that," he says.

"You do, don't you?" His ex-wife and child are living with another man—a man she plans to marry and have another child with. "It's good to have someone who understands."

"I'm pretty much over it now," he says, "but at first it seemed like James had replaced me in my own life."

"That's exactly how I feel about this—this Quinn person." I have trouble even saying her name. I look at him. "You don't feel that way now?"

"No. At first all I could feel was loss and hurt and anger. But the truth was, I hadn't felt all that connected to Sue Anne in a long time."

"Things haven't been very close between Zack and me for a while now," I admit.

"Marriages can go through rough spots and still make it." He brakes for a light and looks over at me. "It all kind of comes down to why you got married in the first place, and if those reasons still hold. Why did you marry him?"

"Because I loved him, of course."

"What did you love about him?"

"He's smart and successful and good-looking. He's just a really great guy. He hit every item on my husband criteria list."

Brett shoots me an amused look. "You had a list?"

"Of course. I have criteria lined out for my whole life, with goals and deadlines." I sat down when I was eighteen and wrote out a list of objectives I wanted to achieve by certain ages. So far I've hit every one of them, except for having a baby.

"That figures." He laughs. "You said your husband is a really good guy. Is he the kind of guy who would want to do right by his children?"

"Yes." I blow out a sigh. "I see your point."

He flips on the turn signal. "Well, then, I think you're going to have to compromise. If you want the marriage to work, you'll have to love his children, too."

"I can do that," I say. "I'd love to adopt Lily, but Zack won't even considering trying for guardianship."

"The baby changes the whole equation." Brett makes a right turn, then glances at me. "So does the fact that Lily is nearly four. At first I was picturing her like a toddler, but by the end of that third year, they're solid little people with solid attachments."

"So what are you saying?"

He looks over. "I was wrong to suggest that you try for custody. Both kids belong with Quinn."

I feel as if the air has been punched out of me. I fold my arms across my stomach. "Well, I don't want to be a stepmother. I never did. Before I married Zack, I considered men with children undatable."

"Ouch," Brett says, clasping his chest as if I'd shot him. "That hits close to home."

Too late, I realize he fits in that category. I feel a little flustered. Was that an exploratory remark, or just an observation? "This was back then," I say quickly.

"You could be a stepmother *and* a biological mother," he says. "One doesn't exclude the other."

I shake my head. "Zack won't even talk about any more IVF."

"Well, maybe that can be *his* compromise. Maybe he'll agree to try for a child with an egg donor if you agree to stay in New Orleans to be near his children."

My muscles tense. "But I don't *want* to stay in New Orleans! I've taken this new job, and I want to live here. Most of all, I want to get away from Quinn and her kids and this spell they've cast over Zack. I don't want to have another woman in the picture."

He looks me full in the eye. "If you really value your marriage, you probably need to reconsider that."

In my gut, I have an awful feeling he's right. But the whole thing completely goes against my grain. I shake my head. "I don't want to watch him co-parent another woman's children."

He slows as the road turns. "Here's the bottom line, Jess—and I know how you like bottom lines: Zack is now a father. And as a father, I'll be honest: I couldn't move away and leave Petey behind."

My heart cracks a little. "But you're his *real* father. I mean, you were there when he was born and you've always been in his life. Zack is just a donor. He wasn't supposed to be involved at all."

"Yes, but now he is."

Now he is. There's the rub.

Brett looks at me again. "If he's the kind of guy who wants to be a good dad, well, that's your new reality."

His words have a stomach-churning ring of truth. "Great, just great."

"You act like it's a tragedy." Brett changes lanes. "Don't you think Lily and the baby will benefit from having Zack in their lives?"

"Well . . . yeah. I suppose."

"So maybe it's meant to be."

"Oh, Christ." I roll my eyes. I really hate this kind of nonsense. "Are you talking about some sort of woo-woo everything-happens-for-a-reason thing?"

He laughs. "I wouldn't put it that way, but yeah, I guess I am."

"I don't believe in that."

"It doesn't really matter. Facts are facts, and the facts are, most children benefit from having a father in their lives. So instead of fighting it, maybe you should just embrace it."

"But I don't *want* to embrace it." I stare out the window. "They're not really his children. They're his sperm donations."

"They were. They aren't anymore." He glances over at me. "You said Lily calls him Daddy."

"Hell," I mutter.

"Think it all the way through," Brett urges. "If you insist that Zack moves here, he'll go back to see the kids as often as he can. That's going to leave you out of the loop, unless you go with him every single time. You said you two are pretty distant right now. That distance will just grow further and further if you don't embrace this new part of his life." He brakes to let a car merge in front of him.

"Wow. You could have sugarcoated that a little."

He laughs. "I'm not good at sugarcoating. Sue Anne used to say I'm 'harshly direct.'"

"You are." I stare out the windshield. "Emphasis on 'harsh.'"

"I just call 'em as I see 'em." His eyes turn serious. "I had my future all lined out once, too, you know. I was going to be a big shot NFL player. Then I busted my knee, which completely busted my plans. I thought my life was over." His jaw tightens. "In fact, I was ready to end it."

I stare at him. "Really?"

He gives a curt nod. "Fortunately, a former teammate hauled me to a support group. They taught me how to recognize what's really important. That's the stuff you hold on to. The other stuff—well, sometimes you just have to jettison it. Let go of how you think things should be and accept what is. When you do that, you can start finding a way to be happy, no matter what your circumstances are."

I blow out a sigh. "You're saying I need to stay in New Orleans."

"I'm saying you need to seriously consider what you want. Do you want to be with Zack? If so, that means you're going to have to adapt to his new situation. Can you love and accept his kids? Can you support his involvement in their lives? If not, you need to level with him and tell him the truth."

"And what's that? That I want a divorce?"

He lifts his shoulders. "All I know is that marriage has to be all in. You can't accept one part of a person and reject another part." He brakes at a stoplight and looks at me. "I think marriage should be about two people wanting what's best for the other. Couples should help each other achieve their dreams, live according to their values, and become the best versions of themselves. They should make each other feel accepted and supported and cherished and trusted, and help one another contribute their gifts to the world. If you reach a place where you can't do that—where your values don't line up anymore or you don't accept or trust or support each other—well, then, maybe it's not a marriage any longer."

Or maybe it never was. The thought knocks the breath out of me.

I've always been focused on attaining my goals. I thought a successful life was all about hitting certain markers—get good grades, get a scholarship, get a degree, get a job, move up the ladder; look a certain way, meet a man who checks all the boxes, get engaged, plan the perfect wedding, buy a house, and have a child. My life has always been about achievements and kudos and following the script I'd created.

Hell. My life—and my marriage—has always been about me.

I never gave any real thought to helping Zack live according to his values or become the best version of himself or contribute his gifts to the world.

I lean back against the headrest. Oh, God! Everything Brett just said rings true, and none of it is what I want to hear. My whole world has just tilted on its axis.

"Are you okay?" he asks.

"Yeah."

"I talk too much. I probably should have kept my mouth shut."

"No. You've given me a lot to think about." I stare out the window as he brakes at a yellow caution light. If I were driving, I would have blown right through.

"And what are you thinking?"

"I just never imagined my life would look like this."

"Me, neither." His mouth curves up in a wry grin. "But then, whose life does?"

CHAPTER THIRTY-NINE

Zack

Sunday, May 19

A LITTLE BEFORE eight in the evening, I knock on Quinn's front door. I hear Ruffles bark, and I have a moment of anxiety, wondering if I should have called first.

Well, duh, of course I should have called first; it's what civilized people do. Jessica would have a cow if someone just dropped in unannounced. But if I'd called, I would have gotten the update about Lily over the phone, and I would have lost my excuse to stop by.

I'm relieved that Quinn is smiling as she opens the door. She's wearing shorts, flip-flops, and a pink T-shirt, and she looks more like a college student than a thirty-six-year-old business owner. Her hair is pulled back in a ponytail, but little wisps have escaped around her face. *Pretty*, I think. I squelch the inappropriate thought.

"I'm making rounds," I say. "I just saw Margaret, so I thought I'd check on our littlest patient."

"How's Margaret doing?"

"She's better. The physical therapist got her up today. She's exhausted and sore, but being able to get around will be a game changer for her."

"That's great."

"How's Lily?"

Quinn opens the door wider. "Come in and see for yourself. The way she's bouncing around, you'd never know she'd been sick."

I step into the foyer and bend down to pet Ruffles, but before I can even touch the dog's fur, a yellow-nightgown-clad Lily barrels toward me, her arms flung wide. I hunker down as she throws herself at me. Her face is alight. "Daddy! I'm so, so glad to see you!" She hugs me as if I'm an adored family member she hasn't seen in months instead of just since this morning.

I hug her back, my chest tight. When I move to Seattle, months *will* pass between the times I see her. I inhale the sweet baby shampoo scent of her damp hair, then look at her as we draw apart. "You look like you feel much better."

"I do. I just had a bubble bath an' it feels so won'erful not to be sick anymore!" She grabs my hand. "Come see the pitchers I drawed for you an' Auntie Quinn an' Grams!"

I raise my eyebrows and look at Quinn. "Is it okay?"

Her mouth curves in a wry grin. "As if I could say no after the hazard duty you pulled last night."

I let Lily pull me into the kitchen, Ruffles cavorting beside us. Lily leads me past the island to the refrigerator, where Quinn has posted the latest round of artwork. Lily points a chubby finger to a crayon picture of stick figures with big heads and hands. "That's you an' me an' Auntie Quinn on the sofa when I was sick," she says. "An' that's Auntie Quinn an' you with the sick bucket takin' care of me. An' this one is when I got sick on your shirt."

"Hey, Quinn wasn't standing there smiling!"

"No, but she was in the house, an' she woulda laughed if she hadda been. An' this one is when you carried me in, an' this is when you came back with groc'ries."

I can't help but be struck that all three of us are in every drawing. "Nice, Lily."

She points to the urp picture and the carrying-in picture. "These two are for you, an' the others are for Grams an' Auntie Quinn."

"Thank you very much, Lily."

"You're welcome."

"I was just about to put Lily to bed," Quinn says.

"Can Daddy help tuck me in?" Lily whips around to face me. "Can you read me a story? Pleeease?"

Quinn smiles. "It's okay with me, if he can spare the time."

Lily fixes me with a pleading gaze. Like the Grinch—I remember reading that book aloud to my niece and nephew a few Christmases ago—I feel like my heart grows three sizes. "Sure."

Lily jumps up and down. Ruffles jumps, too. "I'm gonna pick out some books!" She runs upstairs to her room.

"How many do we read?" I ask Quinn as I follow her up the stairs.

"The rule her mother set was three, but Lily always talks me into more."

Her mother. It's easy to forget that Lily recently lost her mom. They seem like such a tight little family unit that I think of Quinn as her mom. "What's the limit?"

"Depends how long the books are. I'd say we read to her for about twenty minutes, tops, because it's getting late and she's recovering from being ill."

I follow Quinn into a room with a queen-sized bed covered in a fluffy white coverlet. Prints of lilies and roses hang on the walls. A comforter printed with pink lilies is folded at the bottom of the bed.

It's a grown-up bedroom, but Quinn has added a lot of childlike touches. Lily's stuffed animals are in a large basket on the floor, and the bottom two rows of a bookshelf hold children's books.

Lily climbs into the bed with a stack of books and her raggedy teddy bear. "You get on this side, Daddy, 'cause Auntie Quinn gets on the other." Lily points to the left of the bed, then pats the right side for Quinn.

Ruffles hops up and makes herself at home on Lily's lap. Lily grins hugely, making me marvel at her perfect little baby teeth.

She hands me *Curious George Goes Camping.* "I want you to

read this one first, an' then Auntie Quinn can read this." She hands her *The Runaway Bunny*, then puts her head on my shoulder.

My heart feels like a soft, ripe peach. The sweetness of the moment triggers a memory, and my mind flies back to my boyhood.

Every summer, my family visited my mother's parents on their sorghum farm in rural Georgia. My sister and I loved to go with Granddad into town whenever he ran an errand, because he'd always stop at a roadside stand and buy some locally grown peaches. We'd sit on the tailgate of his rusty Ford pickup and bite into them, the juice running down our chins, all over our hands, and onto our clothes. The taste was bright as sunshine.

Every time we'd leave the house, Gramma would warn, "Now, Harold, don't let them get all messy."

And Granddad would reply, "Some things are worth the cleanup, because they last longer than the moment."

This is one of those longer-than-the-moment occasions. It's a summer-peach moment, sweet and pure and juicy with life, and I know I'll remember it long after tonight. I wonder if Lily will remember it, too. If I move to Seattle, cuddling up to read bedtime stories will be a rare occurrence.

My chest aches like an extracted wisdom tooth. I open the book and begin to read.

THIRTY MINUTES LATER, Quinn looks at her watch. I decide to step up and be the bad guy. "Lily, it's way past bedtime."

"Just one more?"

"You've just-one-mored your way through about four extra books. It's nighty-night time."

"Okay," she says.

Quinn gets up to put the books away, and Lily scoots off the bed. I'm not sure what's going on until Lily kneels beside the mattress. "Thank you for the day, dear God. Please bless Auntie Quinn an' Daddy an' Grams. Get Grams well real quick, an' give Mommy a big hug an' kiss in heaven. Oh—an' bless Ruffles an' my sister in Quinn's belly. I hope she's a sister, but I'll be okay with a brudder. Amen."

"Amen," Quinn repeats.

"Amen," I add.

Lily crawls back into bed, and Quinn folds down the sheet, tucks the covers around her and her stuffed teddy bear, and kisses her forehead. "Sweet dreams, Lily. I love you."

"Love you too, Auntie Quinn!"

I lean down and kiss her cheek. "Sleep tight," I say.

"Okay. I love you, Daddy."

"I love you, too," I say, with no hesitation.

And I do, one hundred percent. It took me forever to say those words to a woman, but with Lily, they just fly out.

"She's amazing," I tell Quinn as we go downstairs and head into the kitchen.

"That she is."

"She's so resilient and upbeat and energetic," I say.

"She's all that and a bag of chips." Quinn smiles. "Speaking of chips, would you like something to eat?"

"No, thanks."

"Well, how about a beer? I have a couple in the fridge that will just be sitting there for seven more months or so." She puts her hand on her belly, over the baby she's carrying.

"Okay—sure."

She hands me a beer and takes a sparkling water for herself.

"So the baby's a couple of months along?"

She nods. "The doctor says nine weeks, although I was inseminated seven weeks ago."

"Sarah said you had an ultrasound."

Her eyes grow bright. "Yeah."

I remember my sister getting copies of her ultrasounds. "Do you have a DVD of that?"

"I do. Would you like to see it?"

"I'd love to."

"There's not a lot to see, but you can hear the heartbeat."

I follow her into the living room, adrenaline pumping.

"Have a seat." She gestures to the sofa, then slides a DVD into the player connected to the TV. She joins me on the sofa, tucks her feet under her, and reaches for the remote.

The screen lights up, but it's hard to make out what I'm seeing. Everything is gray and black, and the camera seems to be moving. "The doctor was rubbing the transducer across my belly to find the baby," Quinn says.

The movement settles. I see a little mass of something gray at the bottom in what looks like a cave. I hear a *whoosh whoosh whoosh.* My heart feels like a fish jumping out of the water.

"That's the baby's heartbeat?"

"Yeah."

"Wow. It's so fast!"

She nods. "The doctor said it's supposed to be."

She gets up, goes to the screen, and points at a little mass. "The doctor said this is the head."

It takes me a moment, but I think I see it. "Wow!"

"The baby is about the size of a grape. All of the organs are forming, and the heart already has all four chambers." She smiles as she comes back the sofa. "I call the heartbeat 'Chamber Music.'"

"That's perfect." I stare, transfixed.

"I have it on my phone. I listen to it every night before I go to sleep. And sometimes during the day when I'm alone and I want to get some perspective on what really matters, I play it."

"That's a great idea. Do you mind if I record it?"

"No. Go ahead."

I pull out my phone.

"I'll turn up the volume, but only a little," she says. "I don't want Lily to hear it yet. I think it might make it harder on her if something were to happen." Her hand protectively covers her stomach. "The doctor warned me there's a high chance of miscarriage in the first trimester."

I nod. "Jessica had one."

"Oh, no." She sits very still. Her brow creases. "I'm so, so sorry."

"It was the second IVF try. We'd only known she was pregnant for six days."

Her eyes are full, as if she's about to cry. "That must have been devastating."

"That's the word for it. I was so excited, I bought a fetal Doppler so we could listen to the heartbeat, but . . . well, we never got that far. I never even told Jessica I'd bought it. I buried it in the back of the closet."

"I'm so sorry." A tear tracks down her cheek. She quickly brushes it away.

I'm moved by her empathy. I think you can tell a lot about a person by what makes them cry.

Quinn turns up the volume. I aim my phone at the screen and press record. We sit in silence for a full two minutes, watching the blurry image on the screen and listening to our baby's heart.

Our baby. My emotions and thoughts are skipping all over the place. I feel a tenderness and a connection to Quinn that I have no business feeling.

I think about the sweet child upstairs, and the way Quinn has unhesitatingly embraced her as her own. I think about how Quinn has rearranged her life to care for Margaret. I wonder if our paths ever crossed during all the years we were both in New Orleans. Surely I would have noticed such a beautiful, warm, generous-hearted woman. I wonder what would have happened if I'd met her before I met Jessica. I can't help but wonder if . . .

No. I refuse to let my thoughts go there. I'm a married man.

The thought of Jessica leaves me feeling vaguely ashamed and guilty. This is all so unfair to her; I hate how this hurts her. And yet . . .

I click off my phone's camera, check that the video and sound have recorded, and then stand and put my phone in my pocket. "Well, I guess I'd better go."

"Thanks for coming by. And thanks for checking in on Margaret." Quinn unfolds her legs and walks me to the door. She smiles as she opens it. There's a moment when I could have hugged her good-bye, but the moment passes, and the whole concept of physical contact seems too fraught with peril anyway.

I inhale Quinn's soft scent as I step past her on my way out the door. The night air is thick and warm and humid, and I feel oddly like I'm swimming through it.

This evening was one of the most moving, magical nights of my life. I tucked my sweet daughter into bed, heard her prayers, and told her that I loved her. I heard—and saw—the heartbeat of my baby. Tonight was miraculous and loving and right.

And yet, it's not something I can tell my wife without wounding her.

So what am I supposed to do—basically ignore the two lives I helped create, the lives that are a part of me? Can I really just go off to Seattle, send a few cards and letters, occasionally video chat with them, and maybe see them a few times a year?

I climb into my car and try to picture what my father would do. He would never have given his children anything less than one hundred percent. On the other hand, he would never have hurt my mother.

I sit in silence, trying to imagine how my father would have handled this situation. I can't. My father never would have gotten himself into such a dilemma.

What's the right thing to do here? I blow out a sigh and hit the ignition.

A thought fires along with the engine: I need to have a serious talk with Jessica.

CHAPTER FORTY

Jessica

I'VE BEEN GRILLED more than the salmon Dad smoked outside, so I'm relieved when this excruciating family dinner nears its end. My mother is pale and her eyes are red. My father is quiet and stalwart, but Erin's kids and my brother have peppered me with questions throughout the meal.

"So, Aunt Jess, I still don't get it," my fourteen-year-old niece says as she spoons the last of the chocolate chip ice cream into her mouth. "Why, exactly, did you go on that donor site?"

I must have already explained this a dozen times. Isn't it punishment enough that my husband's donor spawn are ruining my life? Do I really need to admit, over and over and over again, to a colossal act of foolishness driven by jealousy and insecurity? "I was curious. It was a bad mistake." I rise from my chair and start clearing the plates. My phone blares out the sixties tune "My Guy." "It's Zack," I say.

"I hope he isn't calling to tell you he's discovered another kid," my brother says.

My niece and nephew laugh, and my sister's husband snorts.

"Doug!" My mother shoots him a scolding look as if he's twelve.

"Doug!" his wife simultaneously exclaims, elbowing him.

"Sorry. Just trying for a little comic relief," he mumbles.

My sister frowns at her chortling husband.

"Excuse me," I say, grabbing my phone and heading out of the room.

"How are things going?" Zack asks when I answer it.

"Well, I'm at my parents' house." I head up the stairs toward my old bedroom. "I just faced the family for the first time since telling them about your kids."

"Oh, yeah? How did they take it?"

"They're upset." I step into my bedroom and close the door. "Mom looks like someone's died. It's a complete shock."

He's silent for a moment. "They didn't know I was a donor?"

"No." I wonder if he's going to ask why I didn't tell them before we married. I feel defensive about that.

"So the news hit them out of the clear blue," Zack says.

"Yeah." I hear traffic noises in the background of his phone. "It sounds like you're driving. Where are you headed?"

"Home."

I glance at my watch. It's nearly eight here, which means it's nearly ten in Louisiana. "From where?"

He pauses, and I get a sinking feeling before he even says it. "I went by Quinn's."

The mattress dips as I sit on it. So does my stomach. "Why?"

"Lily was sick last night, and I wanted to see how she was."

"Did you see her last night, too?"

"Yeah."

"Jesus, Zack. Are you seeing them every freakin' *day*?"

He blows out a breath. "I'm trying to sort things out. I talked with Quinn yesterday, and then she got a call that Lily was sick just as we were finishing dinner, and . . ."

"You had dinner with her?"

"Yeah."

"Where?"

He sighs. My I-can-read-Zack-like-a-book radar tells me he's about to name a place I won't like. "Jacques-Imo's."

"Jesus!"

"I wish you'd stop saying that."

"I wish you'd stop giving me reason to." The thought of my husband at a trendy restaurant with an attractive woman—the woman who's carrying his baby!—makes my throat constrict with jealousy. I try to hide the ugly emotion. "Is Lily okay?"

"Yeah. It was just a stomach bug." I hear his turn signal click on. "So how is everything out there?"

"Well, the weather is fantastic," I say. I decide to lay it on thick so he'll be less likely to suggest I give up my promotion. "I love being back in Seattle and near my family. I haven't found the perfect house yet, but Brett has a condo we can lease and move into right away."

He's quiet for so long I wonder if the call has dropped. "Jessica, we need to talk."

That has to rank as one of the most terrifying phrases in the English language. "So talk," I say, sounding far braver than I feel.

"I mean in person. When are you coming home?"

He wants to discuss staying in New Orleans again. My blood turns to ice water. I think of what Brett said—that I need to consider it.

But how can I? How can I live with a man who's spending all his emotional energy and every available moment with another woman and the family he has with her? "Maybe you should come here."

"I can't get away. I have client meetings all this week, and maybe the week after."

"Yeah, well, I'm busy, too."

"This is important, Jess." He sounds as if he's running out of patience. "You're still officially working at the New Orleans hotel, so I know you'll be back. Will you please just tell me when?"

I sigh. "I have a meeting there a week from Monday, then there's a going-away party for me the following Tuesday afternoon."

"So you'll be home weekend after next?"

"Yeah. I'll probably fly in that Sunday," I hedge.

"Come earlier. I'd like for you to spend some time with Quinn and Lily, and maybe we could see a counselor. We need to figure out what to do."

I have no intention of spending any time with your other little family. I can barely stop myself from saying it aloud. "The only thing we need to figure out is whether I should arrange to have my car driven to Seattle, or if I should just sell it there and buy a new one here."

"Jess, you're not making this easy."

And why should I? I think hotly. I pause and draw in a breath. Brett's words float to the forefront of my mind: *Married couples should help each other achieve their dreams, live according to their values, and become the best versions of themselves. They should make each other feel cherished and supported and trusted.*

I haven't done a good job at any of that, have I? A sense of shame suffuses me. Hell; I hate failing. Not only have I not been a good partner, I haven't even been a very good person. I've been trying to cross items off my success list without giving much thought to why—without really considering what I had to contribute or how I could make the world a better place. And I sure haven't given much thought to helping Zack do that.

I try to swallow, but it feels as if a Ping-Pong ball is wedged in my throat. "I'm sorry," I make myself say. "I'll—I'll see if can make the Friday flight the weekend after next." I hesitate, then force myself to take it further. "I'm okay with spending time with Lily and Quinn, but, Zack—don't set up any counseling sessions."

"Okay," he says.

"Okay," I echo. "Well, I should get back to my folks. I'll talk to you tomorrow."

"All right. Bye."

"Back at you," I say.

For the first time since we started saying *I love you*, we end a conversation without either one of us uttering the words. I stand there for a moment, the dead phone in my hand. It's funny how something unsaid can be so loud.

I just said *back at you* to *good-bye.*

CHAPTER FORTY-ONE

Quinn

Saturday, May 25

MAYBE I SHOULDN'T have taken Zack up on his offer to accompany me to an estate sale, I think on Saturday morning. Lily and I are seeing way too much of him, and I don't want Lily to become too accustomed to having him around. I hadn't arranged care for Lily, though, because Terri was supposed to go with me. I figured, between the two of us, we could manage to keep an eye on a three-year-old and still find merchandise for the store.

What I hadn't figured was that our new assistant manager would get sick on Friday afternoon, which meant that Terri would need to man the shop today. So when Zack called to see what Lily and I were doing that weekend, I told him about the estate sale dilemma.

"I'd love to go," he said. "You can shop, and I'll keep Lily away from breakable objects, sharp knives, and loaded guns."

Lily, of course, is thrilled. She jumps up and down when Zack shows up bright and early, with a Starbucks tea for me in one hand and a cooled-down hot chocolate for her in the other.

"Thanks," I tell him, opening the door and taking the tea. I tamp down my own delight at seeing him. *He's married, and he's moving*, I remind myself as I try not to notice how nice he looks in jeans and a black T-shirt.

Lily bounces around and shows Zack her latest artwork while I gather up my tape measure, a stack of sticky notes with the word *Sold* written on them, a packet of crackers for dealing with sudden-onset morning sickness, snacks for Lily, and water bottles. I also stuff a small magnetic puzzle and a travel doodler in my bag to keep her occupied.

We pile into my car and head out. Lily jabbers about her preschool class during the short drive, then quizzically scrunches up her face when I pull into a residential area. "Where's the store?" she asks. "These are all houses."

"Estate sales are held when someone wants to sell their furniture and belongings," I tell her. "A lot of the merchandise in my shop comes from sales like this."

"The stuff in your store used to be in people's houses?"

"A lot of it. You can find all kinds of cool things at estate sales. I like to think of them as treasure hunts."

"Ooh, I love huntin' treasure!" Lily says. "What kinda treasure?"

"You don't really know until you get there and look around. Today I'm mainly looking for furniture that my clients will like."

"Furniture's not treasure," Lily says.

"It can be," I tell her. "Treasure is anything that someone thinks is beautiful and precious."

Zack turns around and smiles at her. "Do you know my favorite treasure?"

In the rearview mirror, I see Lily shake her head.

"You!" he says.

She giggles. "You're silly! I'll show you what treasure looks like. Can I have the travel doodler?"

"It's the thing in my bag that looks like an Etch A Sketch with a magnetic pen," I tell him. He digs it out and passes it to Lily, and she settles down to draw.

Zack looks over at me. "How do you know which one of these to go to? There must be dozens every month."

"I'm on the contact list of the major companies that run them," I explain. "They send me emails and photos of some of the items going up for sale. This one looks really promising."

"Do they let you call dibs on things?"

I shake my head. "Everything's on a first-come, first-served basis. That's why we have to get there early."

The next few moments pass with Lily showing Zack a picture she's drawn of treasure chests and pirates. I slow as I get close to our destination and search for a parking place. I find one a block away. I kill the engine, grab my tote bag, and open the door. Zack gets out, too, and unbuckles Lily from the back seat. She bounds down, holding Sugar Bear by a paw.

People are milling around the front lawn of the large two-story galleried home on Perrier Street as we walk up. I recognize the owner of the antique store on Royal Street, the buyer for an eclectic lighting store in midtown, and a woman who runs a vintage clothing store in the French Quarter.

"I need to go get a number from the man on the porch and say hello to a few people," I say.

"We'll wait for you back here," Zack says.

I return ten minutes later to find Zack playing "Which hand has the penny?" with Lily. I can't help but smile at Lily's exuberant delight. Something warm and tender starts flowing through me. I try to shut it off, but Zack grins at me as I approach. My emotional faucet seems to be broken where he's concerned, I think with chagrin.

"All set?" he asks.

I nod. "We're number thirteen, which is really lucky. They're only allowing fifteen people in at a time, and I wanted to be in the first group."

"Wow, this is serious business."

"I'll say," chimes in an older man waiting behind us. He's wearing a newsboy cap and a Hawaiian shirt, and he's standing with a gray-haired woman in a floral dress. "My wife got me up at the crack of dawn."

I nod. "It's kind of a race to see who gets the best stuff first."

"I love to race," Lily says.

"When the doors open, I'll want to head upstairs to the bedrooms," I tell Zack. "I'm specifically looking for dressers and bureaus."

"Okay. Where's the best place for Lily and me to go?"

"I asked the man at the front door if there were any toys for sale. He said there are some in the breakfast room." I grin at Lily. "There's also some costume jewelry in the downstairs bathroom."

"Oh boy!"

"Those are our two treasure-hunting spots, then," Zack says.

"Why are the people who live here sellin' their things?" Lily asks.

"They're probably moving," I reply.

"Why don' they take their stuff with them?"

"Well, sometimes people move to smaller places."

"Or die," says the elderly man who'd spoken before.

His wife hits his arm. "George!" she scolds.

But the damage is done. Lily's face crumples. "Did Mommy's stuff sell at a 'state sale?"

The fault lines in my heart crack a little more. "No, sweetie." *Not yet, anyway.*

"So everythin' inside my house looks jus' like it did?"

I search for a way to be gentle but truthful. "The furniture is there. Some photos and other personal things were moved, but Miss Margaret is keeping them for you for when you're older."

"What 'bout Mommy's clothes an' stuff?"

"Well, your grams saved some of her things, but most of them were given away."

Her eyes fill with tears. "What if she needs them? At Christmas, I'm gonna ask Santa Claus to let her come back."

I kneel down to Lily's level. "Sweetheart, she died. Santa can't fix that."

"Why not? How do ya know for sure?"

I meet Zack's gaze over her head. He squats down beside me.

"That's just the way it is, Lily," he says softly. "When someone dies, they're gone and they can't come back. No one likes it, but that's just how it is. It's a fact of life."

She wipes her eyes with her fists. Her eyelashes stick together in wet clumps. "I don' like fac's of life."

Zack nods somberly. "Some of them are hard to take."

"Yeah." She sniffs.

"But others are wonderful," he says.

"Whaddya mean?"

"Well, it's a fact that your auntie Quinn is going to have a baby, and that means you'll have a new little brother or sister."

"Sister." She wipes her eyes again. "It's gonna be a sister, like Alicia has."

"It might be," he says.

"It will. An' I'm gonna be the big sister." Her tears have stopped, and her voice is gaining strength.

"I bet you'll be the best big sister ever."

"Yeah." Her face brightens. "I'm gonna help pick out her clothes and toys, and I'll sing her songs. An' when I learn to read, I'll read her books."

"What books do you think she'll like?"

"*Curious George*. An' *Goodnight Moon*. I have that one prac'ly mem'rized, so I can sorta read it already."

It's like a thunderstorm has passed, and the sun is shining again. I breathe a sigh of relief and smile at Zack. He grins back, and another flood of warm emotion pours through me.

A whistle pierces the air. I look up and see the man at the front porch with two fingers in his mouth. The crowd quiets as he opens the door. "Numbers one through fifteen can enter," he calls. "The payment desk is by the exit to the back porch."

"That's our cue," I say.

"Ready to hunt for treasure?" Zack asks Lily.

"Yes!" She takes his hand, then grabs mine, her teddy bear's paw clasped between our palms. The three of us surge forward together, looking like a close-knit nuclear family.

But we're not. Zack is married. It's one of those immutable hard facts.

And here's another, I think with a wistful ache. *Sometimes life can be like an estate sale: by the time you find exactly what you want, it's already been claimed by someone else.*

CHAPTER FORTY-TWO

Zack

THE ESTATE SALE was a study in frenzied shopping, but Quinn and Lily made out like bandits. Quinn scored three dressers, a sideboard, a large starburst mirror, an enormous brass tray, a coffee table, and a pair of lamps; Lily left with a long rope of faux pearls, a hat that looks like a UFO with a black veil, and enormous screw-on earrings the size of chandeliers, all of which she insisted on wearing.

After Quinn made arrangements for her contracted movers to pick up the furniture, she suggested we go by the Walnut Street Playground at the front of Audubon Park to let Lily burn off some energy before lunch. Lily is enthusiastic about the plan, but once we get to the playground, she balks at removing her "treasure joolry." She agrees to take it off when Quinn promises she can put it back on when she finishes playing.

"You have to keep it safe," Lily tells us as she takes off the bounty and hands it over. "Pirates might be after it."

"I promise to guard it with my life." I hold up my hand in a three-finger Boy Scout salute. Quinn laughs, and the two of us sit down on a bench under a live oak. Lily runs toward three children playing on a piece of climbing equipment.

"Does she know those kids?" I ask.

"No, but Lily makes friends easily." Quinn smiles. "She gets that from Brooke."

I glance over at her. "I've noticed some things she gets from you."

"Oh, yeah? What?"

"When you're trying to decide about something, you'll put your finger on your chin. Lily does that, too." I scroll through my phone and pull up a photo. "Here."

I lean in and show her a picture of Lily in the pose at the estate sale. "That's when she was trying to decide between the pearls and a rope of purple Mardi Gras beads. She did it with the hats, too. And you do the same thing when you're studying a menu."

Quinn stares at the photo, amazed. "I never realized she does that." She looks up at me. "I never really realized I do it, either, but now that you say it, I guess I do."

"There are other little things you two do alike. You both tilt your heads when you're listening."

"Brooke did that! Maybe I got it from her."

I lift my shoulders. "Or she got it from you."

"No, I probably got it from her. She had a big influence on people."

"You do, too," I tell her.

She looks perplexed. "What do you mean?"

"People start smiling and just generally perk up in your presence."

Her face turns pink. "They do not."

"Yeah, they do. You just can't see it."

Something like shy pleasure flickers across her face. She turns her head and watches the children on the playground. "What else do Lily and I do the same?"

"When you eat something sweet, you both close your eyes after the first bite. It's like you're savoring it or trying to commit it to memory."

She laughs.

"And you both dab your napkins at your mouth in the same dainty way."

She laughs again. "We probably got that from Miss Margaret. I don't remember, but I bet Brooke did the same thing. It sounds very Southern and ladylike." She smiles at me. "You notice way too much. I'm going to be too self-conscious to ever eat in front of you again."

"Oh, I hope not. It's all adorable."

Her eyes go soft. I look into them longer than I should, then my gaze travels to her lips. In another lifetime, I would have leaned in and . . .

"I lost-ed my mos' special treasure of all!" Lily runs toward us, sobbing.

Quinn holds out her arms, and Lily races right into them.

"I lost-ed Sugar Bear! I left-ed him at the 'state sale!"

Good gravy. I'd just thought about kissing Quinn! I didn't act on it—I *wouldn't* have acted on it; the thought was framed in terms of "before I was married"—but still, it was wrong. I shouldn't be having thoughts like that—period, no excuses.

"We'll go back and get him," Quinn says.

"What if someone else took-ed him?" Lily's eyes are large and fearful. "What if they thought he was their treasure an' bought him?"

I think of the love-worn brown bear, flattened from hugs and missing a tiny piece of his ear. It's more likely Sugar Bear ended up in the trash.

"I have a feeling he's just fine," Quinn says. She gives me a small smile over Lily's head.

"Is it one of your knowin' feelin'?" Lily persists.

"What's that?" I ask.

"Mommy used to say Auntie Quinn sometimes knows things through her feelin's."

I wonder if Quinn knows what I was thinking. I'm afraid she does, because a moment ago, I could have sworn the light in her eyes said we were on the same page.

"I'm not certain, but I'm pretty sure," Quinn says to Lily. "Where do you think you left him?"

"I don' know." Tears run down Lily's cheeks.

"We looked at the toys and then at the women's accessories," Zack says. "He'll be at one of those two places."

"Let's hurry up an' go get him!" Lily takes both our hands and pulls us toward the car.

"Do you want me to drive so you can call the people running the sale?" I ask.

"That would be great." Quinn hands me the keys to the car. I unlock it, lift Lily into her safety seat, and buckle her in.

Quinn and I get settled in the front seat.

"Hurry!" Lily urges. "We need to rescue Sugar Bear!"

The reality, I think as I start the engine, *is that Sugar Bear rescued me.*

CHAPTER FORTY-THREE

Margaret

Monday, May 27

"LOOK AT YOU, out of bed and sitting in a chair!" Quinn smiles as she comes into my hospital room, and it feels like the overhead lights increased their wattage. She leans down and kisses my cheek, then sits in a chair beside me. "How are you feeling?"

I pat her hand. "Well. Very well." Although I'm not. I'm sitting in a chair, all right, but I needed help to get in it, and I couldn't stand on my own to save my life. A walker is right there beside me, but I can't use it without assistance; I'm not supposed to put much weight on my broken hip. The truth is, I'm weak as dishwater and I wear out faster than dime-store socks. The worst part, though, is my mind; my attention wanders, and I'm having trouble remembering recent events. I know that Lilly was ill recently and I think she got better, but I don't remember what was wrong with her or how much time has passed. "How's Lily?"

"She's great." Quinn sets her purse on the floor. "She's at a friend's birthday party this afternoon."

"How nice," I say. It's amazing how many parties and events that child has been invited to since I've been in the hospital. I never managed to find her any friends or connect with any mothers of three-year-olds in Alexandria. It's yet another reason Quinn is better suited to be Lily's guardian than I am.

"I'm sorry I didn't bring her," Quinn says. "I had an appointment in this part of town and thought I'd go ahead and come on by."

"I'm glad you did, dear. There's something I need to talk to you about."

"Oh?" She smiles again and regards me expectantly.

My mind goes blank. I pull a little notebook from the pocket of my sweater. The occupational therapist gave it to me, and I've started making notes in it. I thumb through it and peer at my wobbly handwriting. Oh, yes. Now I remember. "I had a visitor this morning. Brooke's attorney."

Quinn's brows rise in surprise. "Marty?"

I nod. "He was visiting a friend in the hospital and thought he'd drop in to see me while he was here."

"How nice."

I look at my notes again. "He said you're already Lily's primary guardian because I'm disabled. He wants me to sign some papers making the change permanent and transferring Lily's monthly trust payments to you."

"What did you say?"

"That I wanted to talk to you, dear. I wanted to make sure you're willing to take it on."

"Oh, yes! Of course!" She reaches over and takes my hand, her eyes full of emotion. "I love Lily as if she were my very own."

I already knew this; seeing them together here in New Orleans has confirmed the depth of Quinn's attachment to the child, and Lily's attachment to her. Besides, Marty said he'd already discussed it with Quinn. All the same, it touches my heart to hear her say it. "I'm so glad, dear. I know that she'll be in good hands with you—as good as with a blood relative. Right after Brooke's death, all I could think was that the poor child lacked any true kin."

"Is that why you reached out to Lily's father?"

I nod again. "I know that you and Brooke and your single parent group disagree, but I think every child deserves to know both parents. And after Brooke died, well, I didn't think it was right for Lily to be orphaned if she still had a living father. I don't care what those donor clinics say, blood is thicker than water."

Quinn pulls her brows in a puzzled frown. "I've never understood what that's supposed to mean. People adopt children and love them as much as their own all the time."

"Yes," I allow, "but that's a freely made choice. When someone who's not family takes in a child because of an emergency or a sense of duty, the child doesn't always remain the priority."

"Nothing could ever alter my love for Lily."

"I believe you," I say, "but not everyone has your sweet, loving nature. And oh, things can happen! Children get older and become belligerent. There can be accidents, disabilities, marriage and remarriage, other children—life has no guarantees. But blood relatives, more times than not, will take of care their own."

"I worried that you wanted Zack to have guardianship of Lily."

"I wanted him in the picture," I say. "A young girl needs a father to protect her."

Quinn's eyes seem to see right through me. "You seem to be speaking from experience. Did something happen to you, Miss Margaret?"

Memories start to surface, memories I've mostly managed to keep buried all these years. I try to swat them away with a flip of my wrist. "Oh, it was all a long time ago."

"Still, I'd love to hear your story."

"Another day, dear. There's something else I need to talk to you about right now. Someone came by. She was a casing . . . a caser . . ." I riffle through the pages of my notebook and finally find what I'm looking for. "A case manager. Miss Johnson."

Quinn nods. "She and I already spoke."

I look at my notes. "That's what she said. I'm supposed to be here for the rest of the week, and then they want to transfer me to an inpatient rehabilitation hospital for a month or so. There's one attached to this place that they recommend."

Quinn's head bobs. "I went over and looked at it. It's excellent."

There's more in my notes. I read it aloud. "She asked about plans for after my release. She said I probably won't ever be able to live by myself in my own house." This hits me afresh as I say it. Merciful heavens; I can't imagine going into a nursing home or assisted living facility.

My eyes get a little misty. Oh, dear—I don't want to cry; I don't believe in indulging in self-pity, but it's hard not to feel sorry for myself. "I'm worried about what happens when I get out of rehabilitation."

Quinn leans forward. "I'd love for you to move in with Lily and me."

I pause, unsure I'm understanding correctly. "Into your house?"

"Yes."

"Until I'm well enough to go home or to an assisted living center?"

"Well, Lily and I would love for it to be permanent. For it to be your new home." She gives a hopeful smile, like she's asking me for a favor. "I can turn the downstairs office into a bedroom. That's what it was originally. There's a bathroom with a tub and a walk-in shower, so you'd have your own quarters."

"Well, I . . ." I don't know what to think, much less say.

"Lily would love to have you live with us, and so would I." Her hazel eyes lock on mine. They're sincere and full of affection. "And if you're willing and able once you get better, you could be a big help with Lily and the new baby."

"Oh!" My heart feels like it's dancing. I clutch my chest. "Oh, Quinn, dear, I would love to help with Lily and the baby!" I hesitate. "But I don't want to impose."

"Are you kidding? You'd be helping me."

I never, ever want to be where I'm not wanted or in the way. "Perhaps I could move into Brooke's house."

"Brooke's house doesn't have a ground-floor bedroom or full bathroom, but if you want to live separately later when you're fully recovered, we can figure that out then." Quinn reaches out and takes my hand. "The key thing is, Lily and I would love for you to come live with us after you get out of rehab."

I wonder if she knows what a lifeline she's throwing me. There's a lot I don't recall, but I remember that Brooke had wanted to turn full guardianship over to Quinn when I turned eighty. Before my heart attack and fall, I'd been planning to fight it. Oh, thank God I didn't! That would have been a terrible mistake, one based on pride and my own personal history, history that has nothing to do with Quinn.

"That's a wonderful offer, dear," I tell her now. "I—I feel a little overwhelmed."

"Take your time and think about it." Quinn squeezes my hand. "But having you there to help with Lily and the baby would be the answer to my prayers."

I squeeze her fingers back, my eyes as full as my heart. More than anything, I want to be useful. Being needed gives meaning to life. "It's an answer to mine, as well." She looks a little blurry to me, but the warmth in her gaze shines through. "If you're sure you want me, the answer is yes."

CHAPTER FORTY-FOUR

Quinn

Friday, May 31

WHEN I WAS a child, our house was a cluttered mess and my mother never invited people over. I promised myself that when I grew up, I wouldn't live like that. I'd have a home I wasn't ashamed of, a home that was pretty and neat, a home where people were welcome.

It's a promise I've kept. Tonight the single parent group is here for an early dinner of pizza and salad. I won't be able to make the usual monthly meeting at the coffee shop tomorrow, so I offered to host it this evening. The adults are gathered around my dining room table while Mac's niece watches Lily, Sarah's twins, and Annie's son on the backyard deck.

"Thanks for getting us all together," Sarah says.

"Yeah!" Lauren nods, taking a bite of salad.

"And what a great idea to let the kids have their own dinner party outside," Annie adds.

I follow her gaze out the window. "Kylie's terrific with children."

"She is." Sarah dabs her mouth with her napkin. "I've hired her as a mother's helper for the summer, and she's amazing."

"Where's Mac?" Lauren asks.

"He's out of town on business again," Sarah says. "The MRI manufacturer hired him to train other technicians on a new piece of equipment. It's a lucrative side hustle for him to help pay legal bills for his brother. Kylie is staying with me."

"She's really coming out of her shell," Annie remarks.

"Yes." Sarah casts an affectionate gaze at the girl out the window. "She's blossoming. Mac is great with her. I think there was a lot of stress in her home, and it's been good for her to be in new surroundings."

Annie turns to me. "Okay, Quinn—tell us what we really want to know. How are things going with Zack?"

Hearing his name makes my heart gallop. "He and Lily are crazy about each other. But I'm a little worried she's getting too attached to him."

"It's impossible for a child to get too attached to a responsible parent," Sarah says. "Besides, I think this is forming a great foundation for the long term."

"The person I'm worried about getting too attached is you." Lauren gives me a sidelong smile.

Despite my best efforts, I feel my face heat. "He's married. He's completely off-limits."

"That doesn't mean he's not attractive," Lauren says. "*I've* got a crush on him, and I've only seen him once."

"Married people should automatically become unappealing to everyone but their spouse," Annie says. "It ought to be a law."

"Yeah. The moment they say, 'I do,' they should sprout horns and facial warts and lots of nose hair," Lauren says.

Everyone laughs.

I laugh, as well. I don't dare tell them how hard it's becoming to keep boundaries around my thoughts and feelings about Zack. The other night, when the two of us were in Lily's room taking turns reading to her, it occurred to me that everything my heart desires was right there in that bed. More and more, my mind meanders to places it shouldn't go. I don't want to examine these little lapses, because acknowledging them in any way seems to only make them more entrenched.

"Zack will be moving in a few weeks," I say. "I hope Lily doesn't feel abandoned when he leaves."

"Moving isn't the same as abandonment," Sarah says. "And Lily knows he's moving, right?"

"Yes. I just hate for her to experience another big loss," I say.

"Life is a series of gains and losses," Sarah says. "Having Zack in her life will be a big long-term gain."

Everyone murmurs consent.

"Have you seen his wife since Miss Margaret's birthday?" Lauren asks.

I shake my head. "She's been in Seattle, but she's coming back into town tonight. The four of us are going to the aquarium together tomorrow."

A knock sounds at the door. Ruffles barks. Everyone on the left side of the table cranes their necks to peer out the sidelight.

Annie turns back toward me, her eyes big. "It's Zack."

"He's just as good-looking as I remember." Lauren smiles and waves to him from her chair.

I can't see the front door from where I'm sitting, but my heart pounds ridiculously fast as I get up and cross the room to open it.

He's wearing a dark suit with a loosened tie and a big smile. "Sorry to interrupt," he says. "I just wanted to bring you this." He hands me a box.

I turn it to read the front label. "A fetal Doppler?"

He nods. "Like I told you the other night, I bought it when Jessica was pregnant. She was never far enough along to use it, so I never gave it to her; I just kept it hidden under some old tennis gear in the back of the closet."

"Oh."

"There's no point in taking it to Seattle." He lifts his shoulders. "Anyway, I want you to have it."

"Oh," I say again. I feel like an idiot with a limited vocabulary. "Well, um, thank you."

"You're welcome."

I step back. "Do you want to come in?"

"No, no. I don't want to interrupt your dinner."

"Come in and join us," Lauren calls. "There's plenty of pizza."

He leans in and grins. "Looks good, but I'm on my way to pick up Jessica at the airport. I just stopped by to drop something off."

"I appreciate it," I tell him. "This is very considerate."

"No problem. I'll see you tomorrow." He waves again to the women, who are all twisted in their seats and openly gawking. "Have a great evening," he calls, then turns and strolls off the porch.

I close the door and head back to the dining room.

"What did he bring you?" Lauren demands.

I turn the box and show the table.

"Oh, how thoughtful!" Annie exclaims.

"Yes," I say. I put the box on the sideboard.

"Well?" Lauren looks at me expectantly.

"Well, what?"

"What was that all about?"

"He just came by to drop this off," I say, sliding back into my chair at the table.

I don't want to tell them about watching the DVD of the baby's heartbeat with Zack. It was a moment I want to just tuck into my heart. It was too tender and intimate to share, like the details of lovemaking.

Not that I'm equating anything I've experienced with Zack to lovemaking, I sternly tell myself. I'm not. Not at all! But if I talk about it, it might sound like something is happening between us.

Which it's not. It can't. It won't. He's married.

I refuse to feel anything I'm not supposed to.

Control your thoughts and you control your feelings, all of the advice books say. Sometimes, I just want to stick my fingers in my ears and repeat *La la la la la la la*—or maybe throw the books against the wall.

Because how are you supposed to control your feelings when

you spend time with a smart, funny, kindhearted, good-looking, goose bump–inducing guy who is not only everything you ever wanted in a man, but also a loving father to the orphaned child you're mothering—and the bio dad of the baby whose heart is beating right under your own?

CHAPTER FORTY-FIVE

Zack

I WAIT JUST beyond the security checkpoint at the New Orleans Airport and watch the sea of travelers flowing through the concourse. I can tell a plane has just disembarked, because people are compressed together and swarming toward the exit like a school of fish. I spot Jessica immediately. She must have gone to the Seattle airport straight from a meeting; she's wearing a tailored black dress, and her hair is pulled back in a sophisticated twist. She looks chic and professional—like a woman who knows how to get things done. And she does, I think. She's the most efficient woman I know. She's pulling her rolling carry-on bag with one hand and checking her phone with the other.

I step toward her as she passes the checkpoint, but she's so focused on her phone that she nearly bumps into me. She jumps when I speak to her.

"Hi, babe."

She looks up, her dark eyes wide. "Zack!"

I can't tell for a moment if she's pleased to see me or not. We give each other a quick hug and a peck on the lips.

"What are you doing here?" she asks.

"I came to pick you up," I say. "I thought I'd surprise you."

"You did. I was just calling an Uber."

I reach for her bag. She surrenders the handle to me. "How was your flight?" I ask.

"Good. Uneventful. I finished a couple of reports on the way." She shifts her large purse to her other shoulder. "How are your cases going?"

"They're coming along. The pro bono case has hit a bit of a snag, though."

"You can pass that off to Greg or someone, though, if it drags past your work for the firm, right?"

I shake my head. "I want to see it through."

Her attitude toward my pro bono work has always bothered me. I occasionally take on cases involving disadvantaged young people who've been arrested on nonviolent charges. I usually talk the DA into reducing or dropping the charges, or letting the kid work out some kind of repayment plan. Jessica acts as if the work doesn't matter as much as my other cases because I do it for free. I feel like it's even more important because a kid's future is on the line. In the interests of keeping the peace, I change the subject. "So you're here until Wednesday, right?"

She nods. "This is my 'say good-bye, pack everything up, last time I actually live in New Orleans' trip."

"Maybe this visit will make you want to reconsider that," I say.

She looks away. "My replacement here has all but been hired. I'm meeting with the candidate Monday to talk with him about the position and weigh in on whether or not I think he can do the job."

"So you still have a chance to keep it," I press.

Her lips flatten, the way they do when she's not pleased. "I'm loving everything about the regional position. And my family is so happy and excited that we're going to be living near them." She steps onto the escalator that leads down to the airport exit. "I know you understand the importance of family."

Why do I feel like she's playing a trump card? I follow her, propping the carry-on bag on the stair behind us. "I hoped you'd keep an open mind through the weekend."

She gives me what I think of as her professional smile. "I think it's very open-minded of me to agree to spend time with Lily and Quinn tomorrow. What's the plan?"

"I thought we'd go to the aquarium."

"For the morning or the afternoon?"

"Midmorning to midafternoon."

She sighs. "Okay."

Hey, I'm not asking you to watch a public execution, I nearly say, but don't.

We step off the escalator. "As I mentioned on the phone, a therapist friend of Quinn's thinks it's important that we all spend time together so that you can get to know them and they can get to know you."

She nods. "For when they visit. How often do you think that'll happen?"

Hell. She's pretending to be a good sport, but she's completely locked in on living in Seattle. "Probably once or twice a year. Then I'll try to get back here three or four times a year. I'd like to see the kids every two months or so."

She looks like she swallowed something sour. "That's a lot of back-and-forth. And we'll be paying for everyone's airfare?"

I haven't really thought of it. "Yeah, probably."

"That'll be a huge expense. And with the cost of housing on the West Coast and donor IVF . . ."

I refuse to talk about IVF. "So it's settled," I say teasingly. "We should just stay here."

"Not funny, Zack."

Great, just great. We're off to a terrific start. I glance at my watch and wonder what Quinn and Lily are doing right now. Lily's supposed to be asleep by eight, but I bet Quinn is still reading her stories. I almost say something to Jess about it, but I know the information won't be welcome.

I search my mind for something safe to talk about. She's never been all that interested in my work, and I don't dare talk about Quinn, Lily, the baby, or Margaret. I don't want to ask about Jessica's family, because she told me on the phone how upset they were to learn about my donor family. If I ask about her new position, she'll make it sound like nirvana.

Hell, I can talk to a stranger about more topics than I dare broach with my own wife.

I push open the door, and the humid New Orleans air settles over us.

"Christ, it's hot," she says. "Thank God I don't have to endure another New Orleans summer."

Was she always this negative, or am I just looking for things to criticize? That wasn't my intention. I came to the airport to pick her up so we could spend more time together. I know the situation has been difficult for her; she looks strained and tense and miserable. Hell, that's how I feel, too. We seem further apart now that we're in the same city than we did when she was in Seattle.

We clearly need to patch things up, but she isn't even trying, and I'm running out of ideas.

CHAPTER FORTY-SIX

Jessica

Saturday, June 1

HOW ARE THINGS going? My sister texts around ten the next morning.

Not great, I text back. I feel stressed and edgy, and a headache is starting to pulse around the edges of my scalp. Things have been difficult with Zack from the moment he surprised me at the airport. They didn't get any better when we got to his car and I saw a child seat fitted into the back. I've had trouble coming up with anything to say to him, and from the long, uncomfortable silences, I surmise he feels the same way. It's like we're both encased in armor and we can't really touch each other. Not even in bed—at least, not in an emotional way.

Can you talk?

No. We're in the car, on the way to pick up Zack's little family for an outing to the aquarium.

OMG! You agreed to that?

Yeah, I text.

Good luck! Keep me posted.

I put down my phone.

Zack brakes for a stoplight and glances over. "Everything okay?"

"Yeah. Just my sister."

"How's she doing these days?"

"Good."

"And her family?"

"All good. The kids are getting so big, it's unbelievable. Danielle can be our sitter when we have a baby."

He doesn't say anything. Every time I've brought up the topic of a baby, I get no response.

"I found an awesome fertility doctor in Seattle," I tell him. "She's had amazing success with tough cases, and she's booked three months out. I've already made us an appointment."

His face gets that stony look I've come to dread. "Jessica . . ."

My stomach plummets. Oh, God—it's never good when he says my name like that. I force a light tone into my voice. "What?"

"I'm not ready to dive back into that again."

"The appointment is three months away. Surely you'll be ready by then."

"We'll just be getting settled and starting new jobs. It sounds like you'll be super busy and traveling even more than you thought, and my job will require some travel, too."

"So what are you saying? That you don't want me to have a baby? Because I have to tell you, having a baby myself is the only way I can picture coping with this whole second-family situation you've got going here."

"A situation that *you* . . ." He brakes abruptly for a stop sign, takes a deep breath, and rubs his temple. He turns to me, his expression contrite. "Sorry. I don't want to be like that."

I mentally finish his thought—*A situation I created by going behind his back.* He's right. *My bad, my fault.*

He reaches for my hand as he proceeds through the intersection. "Let's just take it one day at a time, all right? Today, I'd like you to get to know Lily and Quinn. Let's just relax and have a good time together."

I look out the car window and sigh. He's avoiding talking about having a baby with me because he doesn't want to do it. I can read that clearly enough; what I can't read is whether the reluctance is temporary or permanent. Either way, it won't make it any easier to get through the day.

"Here we are," Zack says, pulling in front of a large, white, two-story Victorian. We're in a charming part of uptown, a section where I once thought Zack and I might live when we had a family.

"Nice house," I say. "Her business must be doing well."

"It is. But she bought the place for an amazing price because it was in terrible shape—a hoarder had lived here. Then she got deals renovating it because she used contractors she hires for her clients."

It bothers me that he knows these kinds of details about Quinn's life. Hell, it bothers me that he knows her, period.

He wants so badly for me to like her, but every fiber of my being rebels against it. She has his child and is pregnant with his baby, while I'm the infertile wife. What woman wouldn't hate being in this position? I probably hate it more than most; I've always despised settling for second place.

My thoughts fly back to a conversation I had with my mother a couple of days ago. Before I left her house, Mom had pulled me into her bedroom and sat me down on her bed. "Do you want to divorce Zack, honey? Because your father and I will support you, if that's what you decide. Zack is wonderful in many ways, but this is not what you bargained for. No one would blame you."

Having my mother mention the *D* word made the idea . . . what? More palatable, somehow. More like a positive solution, less like a failure.

Not that I need my parents' permission to make major life decisions; I'm way beyond that—aren't I? Of course I am. My sister would disagree, but what does she know? Most adults still want their parents' approval; there's nothing really wrong with that. Still, having Mom be the one to mention divorce sort of gave me absolution to pursue it.

I decided to investigate my options. The following day, I asked Brett for the name and number of his divorce attorney. I made a call, and the attorney returned it. He answered most of my questions over the phone.

In the state of Washington, only one party needs to be a resident in order to file for divorce. Residency doesn't require living there for a certain number of months; if you have a Washington driver's license and address, you're all set.

The attorney emailed me the paperwork. If I decide to file, all I have to do is fill out the forms, and he'll put together the official document. He'll hire a process server in Louisiana to deliver a divorce notice to Zack, then—bam! Three months later, it can all be over.

I like having this option in my back pocket. I leased Brett's rental condo, then visited a Department of Licensing office and got my Washington driver's license. I'll need them anyway, since I'm moving there. No harm in getting a jump on things.

I know Zack believes that marriage is a lifelong proposition and that he wants to make things work, but then, he's a natural negotiator. He chose his career because he believes people can adjust and compromise until everyone's happy.

I'm more of a realist. I'm not a fan of compromises, because neither party gets what they really want. It might be a solution for some people, but others—like me—are just not willing to settle. On the plane ride here, I took Brett's advice and seriously considered staying in New Orleans. I made a list of pros and cons—or at least, I tried to. I could only come up with one pro: it would make Zack happy. The con list went on and on. My bottom line: I'm not willing to do it.

I'm here today to see if I can accept life with Quinn, Lily, and the baby in the picture, or if it's time to cut my losses. I don't want Zack to move to Seattle if the situation is intolerable. That wouldn't be fair to him, and I truly care about him.

But I can't tell Zack any of this. If he knew I was even thinking about divorce, it would irreparably harm his perception of me.

And I like being married to Zack. Except for my infertility, his newly discovered donor family, the fact that we barely have sex anymore, and the way we can't talk to each other about anything important, our marriage is wonderful.

I nearly laugh out loud at the ridiculousness of my reasoning. Our marriage has the *potential* for wonderful, I mentally amend. We've had some wonderful times in the past. And we did have sex last night. It wasn't epic sex—I didn't feel emotionally connected to him, I had trouble getting my head into it, and I faked an orgasm so he'd just go ahead and finish—but sex happened, so that goes into the plus column.

Or maybe it goes in the minus column, because I felt lonelier afterward than I did before.

I gather up my purse and take my time getting out of the car. Zack comes around and puts his hand on the small of my back as we walk up the sidewalk to the door. I used to love that little gesture; I used to think it was masculine and chivalrous and possessive in a sexy, thrilling way, but now I just feel like he's steering me to an unwanted fate.

A high-pitched, little-dog yap sounds the minute we reach the porch, then Lily's face appears in the sidelight by the door.

"He's here!" Her yell is muted by the glass. She bounces up and down like a dribbled basketball. I remember Zack saying she'd literally jumped for joy at the zoo. That's exactly what she's doing at the sight of Zack. My chest feels like tight rubber bands are stretched around it.

Quinn opens the door, and the sunshine spills in on her. I'm struck all over again with how attractive she is.

"Hello!" Her smile is warm, and even though I don't want to like her, it's hard not to. Zack bends down and scoops up Lily. Lily throws her arms around him and kisses his cheek. His smile is wider and more genuine than any expression I've seen on his face since I got here. The bands around my chest squeeze tighter.

"So nice to see you again, Jessica," Quinn says, holding out her hand to me.

I take it. "Nice to see you, too," I lie. We shake hands, then I step into her home. It's as put together as her store, with a cool 1950s or '60s vibe. It smells like banana bread. "You have a beautiful place."

"Thanks."

"This is Miss Jessica," Zack tells Lily as he puts her down on the floor.

"I 'member. She's the sad lady."

"What?" Zack asks.

"She looked really sad at the hospital."

"Well, I'm very happy I get to go to the aquarium with you today," I manage. I hold out my hand, and Lily solemnly pumps it up and down. "I'm Zack's wife," I add, because he didn't.

Lily doesn't seem to register the comment. Zack straightens, and Lily grabs his hand as soon as she finishes shaking mine.

"Let me get my purse and I'll be ready to go." Quinn heads into the living area, and I peer into the dining room, taking in the midcentury table, the Telstar light, the tall-backed modern chairs. The only thing that seems out of place is a vaguely familiar box that says *Fetal Doppler* on the credenza. My heart contracts again. Quinn doesn't look pregnant, but then, she's still in the first trimester.

She comes back and smiles at Lily. "Do you need to run to the bathroom one last time, sweetie?"

"No," Lily says. She's still holding Zack's hand.

"Are you sure?" Quinn asks.

Lily shifts from foot to foot, considering her options. "Be right back," she tells Zack, and races around the corner.

Quinn and Zack exchange a smile, like doting parents. Quinn's gaze moves to me, as if she's trying to include me in the moment, but I still feel like a third wheel. "Anyone want a bottle of water for the road?" she asks, gesturing toward the kitchen.

"No, thanks," Zack says.

I hold up my hand. "I'm good."

"I'll grab one for Lily," she says, heading for the fridge.

Lily whips around the corner. "I'm back!"

Quinn smooths Lily's hair, the gesture unself-conscious and motherly. "I guess we'd better take my car."

"We can take mine," Zack says. "I bought a safety seat."

Quinn's eyebrows rise, and her mouth curves in a surprised smile. "You did?"

Zack nods. "I made a note of the brand and model you have, and I got one just like it."

"Well—wonderful!" She looks at me. "He's amazing, isn't he?"

"Yeah." The word feels like a hard rock in my throat. It isn't easy, hearing the woman who's carrying my husband's child tell me how great he is. "Yeah, he's terrific."

THE AUDUBON AQUARIUM of the Americas is right along the Mississippi riverfront. We watch a towboat push a dozen barges upstream, then Lily grabs Zack's hand. "I can't wait to see the penguins!" She tugs us toward the building. "They're on the second floor. An' that's where they have the birds you can feed, too. But first we'll go by the sharks an' the turtles."

"You really know your way around this place," I say. I'm trying my best to interact with Lily. Quinn asked me lots of questions about my work on the drive over—I'm sure she was trying to help me feel included, which I appreciate—but all of Lily's comments were aimed at Zack or Quinn.

"Lily's mom had an annual membership here," Zack tells me as we walk inside.

"Yeah," Lily says, once again grabbing his hand. "An' we had mem'erships to the zoo and the bug place, too. For all the Au-budon places."

"It's pronounced Au-du-bon," Quinn gently corrects. "But it's great that you know the name."

Lily nods. "An' I know they're named after a famous man who knew all 'bout birds an' painted bootiful pictures of them."

I smile. "You're a very smart little girl."

"Thank you," Lily says. "Grams says I'm jus' like Mommy."

"Yes, you are. And your mommy was very, very smart." Quinn smiles over at Zack. "Your daddy's no dummy, either."

It's small and petty of me, I know—but I feel left out and a little competitive. *I'm* accustomed to being acknowledged as the smart one.

"Daddy saved Grams's life. Did you know that?" Lily asks me.

My throat knots at the word *Daddy*. I curl my fingernails into my palm, hard. "Yes, I heard about it."

We've been strolling to the right, and we're now in front of the Gulf of Mexico exhibit. I want to walk beside Zack and hold his hand, but Lily is already doing that. They stop in front of an enormous aquarium featuring a scaled-down offshore oil rig. Sharks, schools of fish, and stingrays swim by both overhead and at eye level.

"Ooh, look!" Lily points. "A turtle! Like Franklin!"

"Who's Franklin?" I ask.

"He's prob'bly the mos' famous turtle in the whole world," Lily says. "He's got lots of books written 'bout him."

"What about Yertle?" Zack asks.

Lily ponders this for a moment. "Yertle's famous, too, but not as famous as Franklin. There's only one Yertle book. An' this turtle looks like Franklin 'cause he has a fat head."

Quinn and Zack exchange a gaze and laugh. I feel like a complete outsider. When did Zack learn so much about children's literature? When did he learn so much about children, period?

"Come on, Daddy! I wanna show you the penguins." Lily tugs Zack's hand and pulls him toward the stairs.

Quinn and I follow behind.

"Have you been to the aquarium before?" Quinn asks me.

"A few times," I say. "Zack and I came here once, and I've attended a couple of after-hours events."

"It's a gorgeous venue for a reception or a banquet," Quinn says, "but there's nothing like experiencing it with a child."

"That's true of life in general, isn't it?"

Her smile is warm and genuine. "Absolutely!"

We take the bend of the stairs in silence. "Lily is adorable," I say.

"She is, isn't she?"

"You and her mother must have been really close."

She nods. "I can't believe how much I miss her."

"How is Lily doing with the whole grief thing?"

"Most of the time, amazingly well."

"You're really good with her," I say as we reach the top of the stairs. I can't believe I'm complimenting her. I've thought of her as my nemesis ever since I first found out about her, and learning she's pregnant with Zack's child raised my rancor to a whole new level. It's bewildering to discover that the woman who's wrecking my life is so warm and likable.

Quinn lifts her shoulders. "I was there when Lily was born. I've always loved her."

It shows, I think. I'm about to say it when Lily turns toward us.

"Auntie Quinn! Miss Jess'ca! Come see these silly penguins!" Lily calls. She's maybe four feet away from us, standing in front of the glass wall with Zack.

We walk over, and everyone laughs at the penguins frolicking on the rocks.

"I can walk like one," Lily says, waddling with her arms held down straight like wings.

"Me, too," Quinn says, doing the same.

To my surprise, Zack joins in. I've never seen him act silly in public before. *This is how he'd be with our children*, I think. I always knew he'd be a good father, but I never knew he'd be so free and easy and fun-loving. He marches around with his legs stiff, his head jutted out, his eyes wide and unblinking, his mouth puckered like a beak.

He's hysterical.

He's adorable.

He's breaking my heart into little bleeding pieces.

I watch him cavort with Lily and this lovely woman who's carrying his child, and I think, *He belongs with them.*

The thought makes it hard to draw a breath.

No, I think. *He's my husband. Mine. He belongs with me, and I should be having his baby.*

I swallow around a painful lump in my throat and again dig my fingernails into my palm. Anxiety is swirling in my chest and starting to roar in my head. I have to do something; I can't just stand here and watch this, or I'll fly apart.

"Look at the funny family, Mommy!" a boy about Lily's age says, pointing at Quinn, Zack, and Lily.

He sees them as a family. The whole world probably does, because . . .

Hell. They are.

This is too much to take, I think, my heart rate spiking. *I need to get out of here.*

And then I see a man taking pictures of his wife and children with the penguins in the background, and all of a sudden, I'm inspired. That's what I need to do—focus on a task. I pull out my phone, turn on the camera setting, and start clicking photos.

There—that's better. I now have a role: I'm the group photographer. When viewed through the little window on my phone camera, the situation is cut down to size. I can choose what to shoot and how to shoot it. I can save or delete the photos. I can make choices instead of just being dragged along.

Taking pictures gives me the one thing I've never been able to do without: control.

CHAPTER FORTY-SEVEN

Quinn

I WAS ANXIOUS about spending the day at the aquarium with Zack's wife, but things are going a lot better than I feared. Jessica is friendly and sweet to Lily, and although I wouldn't call her manner toward me exactly warm, she's cordial and polite. Most importantly, she and Zack aren't holding hands or nuzzling or exhibiting a lot of PDA. This, I realize, had been my biggest worry. I don't want to examine why.

At the penguin exhibit, Jessica starts taking photos of Lily, and that role seems to put her more at ease. It occurs to me that Jessica is what Brooke used to call a task-oriented person.

After the penguins, we go to Parakeet Pointe, an enclosed outdoor area filled with trees, perches, and parakeets. We buy Lily little wooden sticks covered with peanut butter and birdseed, and she shrieks with delight as birds land on her hands and arms and head. Jessica takes lots of photos, and I'm grateful that she forwards some of them to my phone.

After a bathroom stop and thorough hand washing, we head to the aquarium food court. We've just placed an order of salads and sandwiches at the Aqua Grill when a woman stops beside us with a baby carriage. I can't help but peer in. A baby dressed in a baseball onesie gazes up with somber blue-gray eyes. He's mostly bald, with a little tuft of brown hair.

"Oh, he's adorable!" I exclaim. "How old is he?"

"Nearly three months."

I see a toddler hiding behind the woman's legs. He looks maybe two and a half. I want to make sure he gets an equal amount of attention, so I smile at him. "And you're the older brother?"

He shyly bobs his head up and down.

"I bet you're a really good one."

Again, he nods.

"I'm going to be a big sister!" Lily proclaims with a proud smile.

"Is that right?" The woman grins at Lily, then at me.

I touch my belly, feeling self-conscious. "It's still early days."

"Well, congratulations!" She turns back to Lily. "I'm sure you'll be a big help to your mommy."

"She's my auntie Quinn. My mommy's dead."

The woman's smile dissolves. "Oh! Oh, honey—I'm so, so sorry!"

"Auntie Quinn is like my mommy now." She turns to me. "Can I call you Mommy?"

"I, um . . ." My heart swells, but my brain is flummoxed. I would love that, but it's too soon. I wouldn't feel right, and Miss Margaret would be crushed.

"Y'all have a great day," the woman says, obviously eager to flee.

"You, too." I tell her. I look at Lily. "Let's go sit down, okay?" I lead her to a table by the window. Zack and Jessica follow.

"I really need a mommy," Lily says, her eyes glistening with tears.

"I know, honey. Come here and get a huddle." It's a term Brooke used, a cross between a hug and a cuddle. I hold out my arms and she climbs into my lap. "I'm here for you in every way your mommy was. I love you and I'll take care of you and always be there for you."

"So can I call you Mommy?"

"I would love that. But don't you want to wait a little while?"

"Why?"

"Well, your mother hasn't been gone all that long."

"I thought she was dead."

"She is, honey."

"But you just said 'gone.'"

"I meant dead. People sometimes say 'gone' instead of 'dead' because the word 'dead' is so sad."

"Oh." Her little body deflates. "She's dead gone."

"Yes, sweetie."

"An' she can't come back, 'cause she's in heaven."

"That's right."

"But I need a mommy here. And you're it now, right?"

I feel a sting at the back of my eyes. "Absolutely."

"So why can't I call you that?"

I hesitate. "I don't want your grams to feel like we've forgotten your mom. How about you call me Mommy Quinn for a little while, and later we can shorten it?"

"Yes!" She pumps her fist in the air. "So now we're a fam'ly! Me an' Mommy Quinn an' Daddy an' Grams an' the new baby!"

"Don't forget Miss Jessica," I say, painfully aware of her across the table, watching us. "She's your stepmother."

"My what?"

"She's your daddy's wife, so that means she's your stepmom."

"What did she step on?"

My heart, I think. *I hate that Zack's married.* I'm so dismayed by the thought that I can't come up with an answer. Fortunately, Zack and Jessica both laugh.

"She didn't step on anything, sweetie," I finally manage. "It's just what you call a lady who's married to your father but isn't your mother. She steps in and acts like a mom when you visit her."

"But I don' know her."

"You'll get to know her. And maybe she'll give you a little brother or sister, too," I add.

"An' they'll live with us?"

"No, they'll live in Washington, but they'll come visit us and maybe we'll go there to see them," I explain.

The man at the grill calls our number. "There's our food," Zack says.

I'm relieved that the conversation is interrupted, but my stomach is a tangle of emotions, and my appetite has fled.

CHAPTER FORTY-EIGHT

Zack

LILY FALLS ASLEEP in her safety seat on the way home, her head listing to the side. In the rearview mirror, I see Quinn brush a strand of hair from Lily's mouth. The tender little gesture makes me smile. "It was a busy day," I say.

"Yes, it was," Quinn replies.

"I think Lily had fun," Jessica remarks.

"She had a ball. I did, too." Quinn smiles at me in the rearview mirror. "It was nice spending the day with you two."

"Likewise," Zack says.

Jessica bobs her head.

Quinn covers her mouth and yawns. "Excuse me," she says, giving a sheepish grin. "Lily's not the only one who needs an afternoon nap these days."

"I remember pregnancy fatigue," Jessica says, her expression wistful. "But then, I was only pregnant for a week."

"Zack told me," Quinn says softly. "I'm so, so sorry for your loss."

An awkward pause dangles between the two women. I feel like I should fill it, but I don't know what to say.

"Have you heard your baby's heartbeat?" Jessica asks Quinn.

"Yes. I had an ultrasound, and the doctor gave me a DVD of it. Zack watched it."

"Really?" I can feel her gaze on me. "He didn't tell me."

I glance over at her. Her eyes are sad and full of reproach. Aw, jeez—I just can't win. I didn't tell her because I knew it would hurt her, but not telling her is just as bad.

Quinn leans toward the front seat. "Listen, Jessica—I can only imagine how hard this situation is on you. I mean, it's been hard on all of us—I wanted to have an anonymous donor, obviously, and so did Brooke, so having Zack show up was, well, extremely jarring, but . . ."

"I don't think you can compare your situation to mine," Jessica says, a little sharply.

"No, of course not. And that's where I was headed. I know this must be extremely difficult for you, and I just want to say that I appreciate the way you've been so gracious and generous with Zack's time. It means the world to Lily."

"Lily is a wonderful child."

"Yes, she is."

The sound of her name or maybe the turning of the car makes Lily stir. "Are we home yet?"

"Nearly," I say. "I just pulled onto your street."

"Will you stay the night again, Daddy?"

"'Again'?" Jessica fixes me with a laser-like stare.

"That only happened because you were sick," I tell Lily.

"Well, can we have a sleepover?"

"No, honey," I say. "I need to sleep at my place."

"With me," Jessica adds. Unnecessarily, I think.

"Well, maybe you can get in bed with Mommy Quinn and me again, and read me a bedtime story. You've done that lots of times."

In the rearview mirror, I see Quinn's face flame. I avoid looking at Jess, even though I can feel her glare burning a hole through me. "Not tonight."

"Why not?"

"Well, Jessica's in town, so I'll spend the evening with her."

"But I'm your little girl!"

"Yes, and I enjoyed spending the day with you." I pull into Quinn's driveway.

"We're home! Do you think Ruffles will be glad to see us?" Quinn asks Lily.

"Yes!" Mercifully, Lily goes along with the change of subject. "She'll be so glad she'll do her wiggle dance."

"Is that like the penguin walk?" I ask.

Her dimple flashes. "No, silly!"

I laugh and climb out of the car to hug Lily good-bye. Jessica gets out, too.

"Would you like to come in?" Quinn asks.

"No, thanks. We'd better be going," Jessica says.

The two women exchange a stiff hug. Jessica leans down and kisses Lily, and Quinn gives me an awkward embrace.

"Talk to you soon!" I call as I climb into the car. Jessica is already back in the passenger seat, her face like a summer squall.

I start the engine and back out of the driveway. "Before you say anything, let me explain."

"Oh, please do."

"I told you Lily had a stomach bug."

"You neglected to mention you spent the night."

I put the car into drive and head down the street. "About one in the morning, I told Quinn I'd stay up with Lily and she should go to bed. She was exhausted, and I was worried about her getting sick herself since she's pregnant. I slept in the living room with Lily."

Jessica huffs out a harsh breath, then sits silent for a moment, her arms crossed. "So what was all that about being in bed with Lily and Quinn?"

"The next evening, I dropped by after work to see how Lily was."

"Hold it right there." She raises her hands. "You 'dropped by'?" She makes air quotes with her fingers. "You couldn't have just called?"

"She's a little girl, Jess! Phone calls aren't the same as a visit. Besides, I wanted to see her."

"Of course you did."

I ignore her icy tone and turn the car onto Magazine. "Lily asked me to read her a bedtime story. She crawled into her bed—

it's big; double- or queen-sized or something—and I got on one side of her, and Quinn got on the other. We each read three little picture books, then we listened to her prayers. It was perfectly innocent."

"And you've done this multiple times?"

"Well, yeah."

"If it was so innocent, why didn't you tell me about it?"

"Probably because I didn't want to go through a scene like this."

She blows out a disgruntled sigh. "And watching the DVD of Quinn's ultrasound? When did you do that?"

"One evening after Lily was in bed."

"So you stay and talk with Quinn after Lily's asleep?"

"Sometimes. Not for very long." Even to my ears, my voice sounds defensive.

Tears spring to her eyes. "I wanted to watch our baby's ultrasound with you." Her voice is jagged as broken glass. It cuts my heart to hear it.

"I know, Jess," I say softly. "That's why I didn't tell you."

We drive in silence for a moment. "Was it amazing? Seeing the ultrasound, I mean."

"You couldn't really see anything."

I feel her looking at me. "You're not a very good liar."

"Seriously, you couldn't see much."

"But you heard the heartbeat?"

I nod.

Her head sinks back against the headrest. "God."

She knows I hate it when she uses the word like a curse. "It put me in mind of him, yes."

"Oh, Zack!" She puts her elbow on the car door, then rests her head in her hand. I know she's crying.

I don't know how to console her. I can't think of anything that will make this better for her, other than saying, *Let's try for a baby with a donor egg,* and I won't do that. I don't want to have a donor child with her just because she's learned I already have one—not to mention another on the way. Insecurity, jealousy, and revenge are not good reasons to have a baby.

And then there's another factor, one I hate to acknowledge, but it's there all the same: every baby needs a loving home, and this marriage doesn't feel like one.

CHAPTER FORTY-NINE

Zack

Sunday, June 2

I DIDN'T CHEAT on my wife at church, but I come home feeling like I did.

I left her a note: *Decided to go to church.* It's not something I do all that often, but I go every now and then, and I usually do it on my own because Jessica's not big on organized religion.

Instead of going to my usual Presbyterian place of worship, I went to the Methodist church where Lily goes to Sunday school and Quinn volunteers in the nursery—the church where Lily was baptized, and where Quinn will no doubt have our baby christened.

I told myself I wanted to see the building, to be able to picture them going there when I was in Seattle. But the truth is, I wanted to see them, period.

When I arrived, I discovered the church is large, the Sunday school rooms are in a different section of the building than the sanctuary, and there are three separate worship times. I was keenly disappointed to realize I was unlikely to see them unless I set out on a deliberate search. I restrained myself. I attended the worship service and told myself it was for the best that I hadn't encountered them.

But then, in the narthex, I spotted Quinn in a summery floral dress. Lily was beside her, wearing a white dress with yellow daisies appliquéd or embroidered or something around the neck. Lily saw me before Quinn did. "Daddy!" she exclaimed.

The amount of joy in that single word made it sound as if I were a veteran returning from a long war. People turned and grinned as Lily ran toward me.

I'm not much for scenes, and Lily was creating one. And yet—how wonderful to have someone so thrilled to see you! Quinn smiled widely, too.

I picked up Lily but kept my eyes on Quinn. The fact that she seemed happy at my unexpected appearance pleased me far more than it should have.

We talked for only a few minutes—the conversation involved me giving a lame explanation for why I was there, and Lily showing me pages she'd colored in Sunday school of Moses parting the Red Sea. I would have gladly sat through another sermon just to be with them, but I knew Jessica was waiting for me at home.

"Hello," I call now as I walk through the door of the condo. I can see she's been busy; boxes sit by the door, each marked *Bathroom*, *Closet*, or *Bedroom*.

I hear noises from the hallway between the guest and master bedrooms, so I know she's home—close enough that she should be able to hear me.

"Hi, Jess," I call again.

Silence.

Uh-oh. This isn't good. Guilt has me wondering how she could possibly know I went to Quinn's church this morning.

I walk into the bedroom and discover that she's wearing noise-canceling earphones as she packs her suitcase on the far side of the bed. She takes off the headphones as I wave. "Hey," I say.

"Hey, yourself." Her voice sounds raw and her eyes are red, as if she's been crying.

I tense, every muscle on high alert. "What's going on?"

She jerkily folds a silk blouse and sets it in her suitcase. "While I was cleaning out the closet, I discovered that the fetal Doppler you bought a couple of years ago is gone. And I saw . . ." She straightens and looks at me, her eyes both hurt and accusatory. "I saw one just like it at Quinn's house yesterday."

Oh, hell! "I—I didn't know you were aware I'd bought that. Why didn't you ever say anything?"

"Because I hoped that I'd get pregnant again, and you'd give it to me, and that we'd be able to . . ." Her voice breaks.

I feel terrible, just terrible—as if I've injured her in a car accident or something. "I'm so sorry, Jess. It was just sitting there, and I didn't think you knew about it, and Quinn—"

She holds up her hands, stopping me. "No need to explain. I get it." The words are sharp, but it's the sad resignation in her eyes that cuts me to the quick. "Quinn is having your baby, and I'm not."

I don't know what to say. I start to move toward her to comfort her, but she stays me with a shake of her head. I stand there, gutted.

"I just can't deal with this, Zack." She looks down at the suitcase, sighs, and briefly closes her eyes. "No; the truth is, I don't *want* to deal with it." She draws in a breath, and when she looks at me, her gaze is sure and steady. "I want out."

"What?"

"I want a divorce."

She's just being melodramatic, I think. *She's saying this to shake me up*. "Jessica, you're upset. You don't mean that."

"Yes, I do. I really, truly, sincerely do. I'm done."

"This isn't something to decide in haste. We should go to counseling."

She shakes her head. "I've given this a lot of thought. Counseling won't change the situation." She puts her hands on her hips. "The situation is this, Zack: I didn't sign up to watch you co-parent another woman's children. I don't want that in my life. Besides, we're not really a couple anymore. We want entirely different things. We don't even want to live in the same city. So let's just cut our losses and call it a day."

I'm on one side of the bed, and she's on the other. I stare across the mattress where we've slept and made love for the last three years. "Look, I know it's been hard on you, finding out about Lily and Quinn and the baby. And maybe I wasn't as sympathetic or involved or whatever as I should have been with your infertility procedures. I'm sorry for anything I've done or haven't done that's made you feel bad. But you don't throw away a marriage just because something happens that you don't like."

"This is way beyond something I don't like." She picks up the remaining folded clothes on the bed and puts them in the suitcase. "This would have been a deal breaker if I'd known about it before I married you. This is a circumstance I refuse to live with."

"Jessica, you're overly emotional right now. Why don't you take some time and we'll talk later."

"I'm *not* overly emotional. I'm an appropriate degree of emotional. And I'm tired of taking time and talking later, only to get another knife in the heart." Her voice quakes, but her tone is solid steel. "Besides, there's nothing to talk about. You don't really want to move, and I refuse to stay."

"We can work this out," I say. I truly believe this. I negotiate things for a living.

"I'm not willing to try." She fixes me with her *I'm done* look, a look that says further discussion is futile. "The truth is, Zack, I don't love you enough to take this on."

The words pour over me like a bucket of ice, chilling my blood, coldly echoing in my head. *I don't love you enough to take this on.* "You don't mean that," I say.

"I do. I'm sorry."

Later, I'll realize the regret in her eyes should have convinced me.

"It makes sense to settle this now," she says. "There's no point in you leaving your job and moving to Seattle." She snaps her suitcase closed and hoists it to the floor. She picks up her purse from the bedroom chair and pulls it on her shoulder.

I realize she's about to walk out the door. "Wait. Where are you going?" She can't be leaving town; she has an important meeting in the morning, plus the hotel staff is giving her a going-away party the following afternoon.

"I'm staying at the hotel tonight."

This strikes me as a fatal blow. If she stays at the hotel, everyone in her corporation will know by morning that she's got marriage problems.

"You don't have to do that! I can find a place to stay tonight, and you can stay here," I say.

"I've already got it set up. The hotel will comp my room."

Of course they will. That isn't the issue.

The issue is that she's already made up her mind. *I don't love you enough to take this on.* She wants out, and she doesn't care if the whole world knows it.

CHAPTER FIFTY

Jessica

Wednesday, June 5

BRETT IS DRIVING me to a dealership to see about leasing a car on Wednesday afternoon when my phone rings. I ease it out of my purse and look at the screen. Every muscle in my body tightens as if I'm braced for impact.

Brett pulls his eyes from the road and quirks up an eyebrow. "Is it him?"

I nod.

"You want me to pull over so you can get out and talk in private?"

"No. No, it's okay."

"What the hell, Jess?" Zack says the moment I answer.

I draw in a steadying breath. "I guess this means you were served."

"At my office? Are you *kidding* me?"

I feel a twinge. I knew that would embarrass him, but it was the only address where I could be certain that the server would find him. "Does it look like a joke?" It's a stupid comment, but it's all I can think of to say.

"No, damn it. There's nothing freakin' funny about it. When did you have all this prepared?"

"I told you it wasn't a hasty decision."

"You didn't tell me you'd already had the fucking papers drawn up!"

The f-bomb jars me. Not because I'm sensitive to bad language, but because I can count on one hand the number of occasions I've heard Zack use it the entire time I've known him. "I didn't," I say. "But I consulted an attorney before my last trip back to New Orleans. I wanted to know all my options."

"Must have been one hell of a consult."

"He emailed me the paperwork in case I decided to file. I filled it out on the plane last night and sent it to him. All he had to do was drop the info onto boilerplate divorce papers."

This must placate him, because Zack is silent for a moment. I hear him breathe. I can picture how he looks right now—his dark eyebrows scrunched in a scowl, his lips pressed together, his eyes blue-hot with hurt and anger. My heart aches.

"I told him to draw up an even split of things, taking into consideration what each of us brought into the marriage. Look through the papers and see if you think it's fair."

"Oh, I'll go over it, all right. Rest assured of that." Silence beats through the phone, then his tone softens. "So you're sure about this, Jess? You don't want to talk about it?"

"I don't think there's anything left to say."

"I guess not. I suppose these papers say it all."

Tears pool in my eyes. He's waiting for me to say something, but I've got nothing.

This—this right here—is why I filed. This distance, this silence. The divorce is as much about that as it is about Lily and the baby and Quinn. I can talk to Brett and my sister—hell, even my mother, with all of her heavy expectations of me—more easily than I can talk to Zack.

"Well, I'll be in touch," he says.

"Okay."

"Okay. Bye."

He hangs up before I can say another word.

"Are you all right?" Brett asks.

"Yeah." I wipe my eyes. "It's just hard."

"It's supposed to be."

I look at him. "Do you think I'm doing the right thing?"

"It's not for me to say."

"There was no point in dragging it out," I say. "I didn't want him to quit his job and move out here just for me when he really wants to be in Louisiana."

"True." He glances at me. "That's definitely a consideration." He pulls into the parking lot of the dealership. "I haven't heard you say anything about love."

"No." I look out the window. "Although I still do. A part of me might always love him. He's a great guy—a really good, decent, do-the-right-thing kind of man." A better man than I am a woman. The thought is sobering. "I don't think we brought out the best in each other, though. I hated what I was doing to him. And I hated the person I was becoming in our marriage." I twist toward Brett. "How about you? Do you still love Sue Anne?"

"Yeah. But now it's more like affection than 'capital *L*' love. It took me a while to sort it all out. At first, it just felt like a huge loss." He turns into a parking spot. "I was so used to her being there every single day."

"Well, Zack and I have already worked through that part."

He gives a small smile. "That's true."

"And I have a new big job to focus on, and he has Lily and Quinn . . . and the baby." I choke a little on the last word.

"It'll be okay." He looks over and covers my hand with his. "And for what it's worth—which is zip, because it's your marriage and your life and I'm just an outside observer—yeah. I do think you're doing the right thing."

"Thanks."

He gives my hand a little squeeze, then lifts his to turn off the car engine. But I feel the imprint of his warm palm on my skin for a long time after he moves it away.

CHAPTER FIFTY-ONE

Quinn

LILY IS SEATED at the vanity in her bedroom on Wednesday morning while I fix her hair. She's decided she wants to wear it parted on the side and fastened with a barrette shaped like a butterfly. "Is Daddy coming over today?"

I put down the brush and pick up a comb. "I don't know, honey." I haven't heard from Zack since we saw him on Saturday, and I'm a little disconcerted by how much I miss him. I tell myself I need to get used to it; after all, he's moving across the country. Still, I find myself thinking about him all the time. I wonder if he's thinking about us.

"Is the sad lady still with him?"

"Miss Jessica? I think she went back to Seattle yesterday."

"You should call him," Lily says.

"Oh, I don't want to bother him."

"He won't be bothered."

I section off some of her golden hair to put in the barrette. "Well, he might be, so I don't want to do it."

"Can I call him?"

I think about it; I actually do. But my phone number would show up on his screen and he'd know I'd punched the buttons. He'd think I put Lily up to it.

Or maybe he wouldn't. But then again, he might.

Why am I overthinking this so much? It's not a good idea. Neither Lily nor I need to get used to having Zack around all the time. He's moving.

He's married.

"No," I say, angling in the barrette. "He's at work and he's busy."

"Mommy was never too busy for me. An' you're not, either. I bet Daddy's the same."

"We'd be interrupting an important meeting," I say, although I have no proof.

"Well, maybe we can call him after work."

"Maybe." I can't get the barrette's clasp to fasten. I reinsert it and try again.

"Is that a real 'maybe' or a no 'maybe'? Because there are two different kinds."

"You're such a smarty-pants!" I laugh, finally getting the barrette to snap.

"A good smarty-pants, or a bad smarty-pants?"

"Both!" I say, making a dive for her. I swoop her up in a giggling hug.

I NEVER TAKE clients to my storage space. It's air-conditioned—that's a necessity with the New Orleans heat and humidity so that upholstered items don't get moldy and delicate woods don't get warped—but I always bring items to the store, because I understand the importance of setting. Today, however, I'm breaking my own rules. I'm pressed for time, the client is young and chill, and the upholstered spoon-back chairs I want to show her are at the very front of the storage unit.

I've just raised the garage-like door and pointed out the chairs when my phone buzzes. My heart skips when I see Zack's number. It's out of character for him to call instead of text. "Excuse me a moment," I murmur, and step into the hall to take the call.

"Do you have a moment to talk?" he asks.

"I'm with a client now," I say. "But do you want to come by and see Lily this evening?"

"Sure. What time?"

"If you can make it around six thirty, you can join us for shrimp étouffée." I'd doubled the recipe and frozen half the last time I made it, and I'd pulled it out of the freezer this morning to thaw in the fridge.

"Sounds great."

"See you then," I say, thinking the call is at an end.

"There's, uh, something I need to tell you," Zack says. "Probably without Lily around."

"All right. Do you want me to call you back, or do you want to just talk after Lily goes to bed?"

"I'll tell you quickly now, and we can talk more later."

"Okay."

"Jessica—well, she's filed for divorce."

"Oh!" The word comes out fast and startled.

"That was my reaction, too." His tone is sardonic. "Anyway, I'm staying here. In New Orleans, I mean. I'm not moving to Seattle."

I'm shocked. I don't know what to say, so I don't say anything.

"We need to talk about how much you do or don't want to have me in your life," he continues. "In Lily's life, I mean—and the baby's." He pauses. "And in yours, too."

"Yes." My voice comes out oddly breathless.

"Come to think of it . . . maybe it's better if I don't come to dinner. Until this week, I've been seeing Lily a lot because I was trying to forge a relationship before I relocated, but now that I'm staying here . . ." He draws a breath. "Well, I don't want her to think I'll be around all the time if that's not how it's going to be."

"No, come to dinner. She's been wanting to see you." *And I have, too.*

I hang up, feeling dazed. *Divorced.* Zack is going to be single! My heart starts to dance against my ribs.

Stop it, I tell myself. *Get a grip.* Just because his marriage is unraveling doesn't mean he and I will end up together. Didn't Brooke always warn me that fairy-tale endings only happen in children's books and Disney movies? When something seems too good to be true, it usually is.

Still, my mind is fizzing with the possibility that he and I could . . .

Stop it! Look at the facts, I advise myself. *He'll need time to get over a broken marriage, and you don't want to be a rebound romance.*

Besides, he's the father of Lily and my baby. If we get involved and it doesn't work out, it will affect them for a long, long time. Far better not to start anything than to risk having them go through anything like I experienced as a child.

Manage your expectations and you'll manage your disappointments. I'd read the advice in the *Reparenting Your Inner Child* book before I even knew I was pregnant, then again in a parenting guide this morning. The topic had been potty training, but it seems applicable all the same.

And just last night I'd read something else that fits this situation: *Everything requires money, time, or energy. Evaluate the costs before you set your heart on anything.*

"What's the cost?" the client calls to me from the storage room.

It's a sign, I think. The universe is warning me not to get overly invested in a personal relationship with Zack. "There, um, should be a tag on the bottom," I say.

If only, I think, *potential relationships came with price tags, as well.*

"THIS LOOKS DELICIOUS," Zack says as he spoons the étouffée on top of the rice on his plate. I've gone to some trouble with dinner—salad, whole-wheat rolls, and green beans, as well as the rice and étouffée—but I'm downplaying the effort by having us eat in the kitchen, with everything in bowls on the table. Zack and I have large glasses of iced tea on our green print placemats, and Lily has a cup of milk.

"I love it when we all eat together, jus' like a real fam'ly!" Lily exclaims.

"There are all kinds of families," I say, putting some green beans on Lily's plate.

She takes a gulp of milk. “I mean like Alicia’s fam’ly, where they all live together.”

I butter a roll for Lily. “Yes, well, our family is different.”

“Yeah, I know.” Her voice sounds despondent. “I wish you didn’ have to move away, Daddy.”

He glances at me, then settles his gaze on Lily. “Well, it’s looking like I won’t.”

“What?” An ear-to-ear smile brightens her face. “You’re gonna stay?”

“Yes.” He looks at me. “I talked with the partners at my law firm, and I’m staying on.”

“So I can see you every day?” Lily breathlessly asks.

“Probably not every day, but a lot more often than if I lived in Seattle.”

“Yay!” Lily cheers, bouncing up and down in her chair.

Ruffles gets into the act and barks.

“Settle down there, little missy,” Zack says to the dog, then grins at Lily. “You, too. And one of you needs to put your napkin on your lap.”

Lily giggles and immediately whisks it off the table.

I adore the light, humorous way Zack offers parental instruction to Lily. *He’s a wonderful father*, I think. My thoughts scramble all over each other, like crabs trying to climb out of a bucket. *He’s just wonderful, period. He’s kind, he’s smart, he’s funny, he’s attractive. So attractive! Aw, hell, who am I kidding? He’s sexy as hell! He’s exactly the kind of man I’ve always hoped to . . .*

He’s looking at me, and I realize he’s waiting for me to eat before he does. I feel my face heat. *Stick a fork in it, Quinn.* I spear a cherry tomato and force myself to chew.

LILY PRATTLES THROUGHOUT the meal about everything we can do together now that Zack is staying in town. I steer the conversation away from her plans for family outings by asking about her day at preschool. She's learning where foods come from, so she starts asking about everything on her plate. She asks how rice grows. She asks about shrimp—she remembers seeing some at the aquarium—and Zack tells her how they're caught. She talks about lettuce, and remembers how her mother grew some in a pot in the backyard.

"My mommy's house is right down the street," she tells Zack as we finish eating.

"Yes, I know. I was there when your grams fell."

"I wanted to go see if Mommy is still there, but Grams said she wasn't, an' she thought it would make me sad."

I draw in my breath. I remember the conversation.

"I know why she said that. It was 'cause I was so sad when I stayed there with her before the fun'ral," Lily says. She looks at me. "You an' Ruffles came back here, but I stayed there with Grams, an' I could hear her cryin' at night."

I put my hand on my chest. I didn't know this.

"I tol' Alicia, an' she said maybe it was my mommy, 'cause she doesn' think old peoples cry." Lily takes a slurp of milk. "I asked Alicia if she's ever seen my mommy there 'cause she drives by the house all the time, but she says no."

I look at Zack, then back at Lily, my heart heavy. I thought we were beyond this. "Your mommy's in heaven, honey."

"I know. But I thought maybe she talked to God an' he let her come back."

"It doesn't work that way, honey."

"I knew you'd say that." She turns her eyes on me, as blue and clear as the Caribbean. "But would it be okay if we go check?"

I don't know how to answer. I look at Zack.

He meets my gaze, then lifts an eyebrow. "Hey—weren't you supposed to call Sarah?"

I give him a grateful smile. "Oh, right—I was!" I push back my chair. "Excuse me a moment. We'll talk more about this when I come back."

Zack nods and gives me a secret thumbs-up. "Lily and I will clean up."

I go into my office and call Sarah. "Sorry to interrupt you at dinnertime," I say.

"That was an hour ago," she says. I hear loud toddler shrieks in the background. "This is letting-the-heathens-unleash-their-limitless-energy-outside time."

I laugh, then explain about Lily wanting to visit Brooke's house. I remind her that the therapist in Alexandria had cautioned that it might confuse Lily to return there.

"I think Lily's a lot further along in the grief and recovery process than that therapist thought," Sarah says. "It's very common for bereaved children to fantasize that their loved one is in the last place they saw them alive."

"Really?"

"Yes. And anyway, now that Lily's living just a block away instead of in Alexandria, it's natural that she'd want to go back. So yes, I definitely think you should take her. It'll help her get some closure."

"That's what I thought, too, but I wanted to get a professional's opinion."

"I think your instincts about Lily are solid and right," Sarah says. "You need to start trusting them."

"Thanks, Sarah." I hesitate. "There's one more thing I'd like some professional advice about."

"Let me guess. Zack?"

"How did you know?"

"Just a feeling." I can hear the smile in her voice. "What's up?"

"Jessica's divorcing him. He's staying here in New Orleans."

"Get out!"

"I'm serious."

"Wow. I figured they were having some troubles, but . . . wow!"

"Yeah. Zack wants to discuss how much—or how little—I want

him in Lily's and the baby's lives. And mine, as well. What do you advise?"

"Oh, Quinn, honey—you're the only one who can answer that."

"But what's best for Lily and the baby?"

"The closer the relationship children have with both parents, the better. That's all I can tell you."

"So . . . what do you think? Weekly? Every other week? Twice a week? Every other day?"

"You need to figure out what works for both of you," she says. "Relationships are like most things in life; it's usually a good idea to start slowly, see how things go, and adjust as necessary."

"Thanks, Sarah."

"No problem. By the way, my advice for you is the same as for Lily. Start slow."

Is my crush on Zack so obvious? "I—I don't know what you're talking about."

"The hell you don't," she laughs.

We say our good-byes and I head back into the kitchen, where Zack has cleared the table and put the dishes in the dishwasher. Lily has pulled all of the plastic storage containers out of the bottom cabinet and spread them on the floor, stacking them to build a tower.

"I'm helping Daddy put away the leftovers," she announces proudly, carefully placing yet another container atop the rest.

"For the whole neighborhood, apparently," Zack says.

"I see."

"He wanted to know where to find the 'tainers, and I showed him," she says.

"That was very helpful."

"I like helpin'."

"Well, then, would you please take Ruffles in the backyard and get her to run around? She needs some exercise."

"Okay. Come on, Ruffs." The little dog trots over. Lily hesitates and looks at up me. "But what about goin' to see Mommy?"

I crouch down to her level so I can look her in the eye. "Your mommy is dead, sweetheart. If she were alive, she'd be right here with you. She's not in your old house."

Her eyes fill with tears. "But I want her to be. I wished for it so much!"

"I know, darling girl. But there are some things in life we just can't change. If you want to go to your old house and look around, though, we can do that."

Her face immediately perks up. "Really?"

"Yes. Go play with Ruffles and let us finish cleaning the kitchen, and then we'll walk over."

Lily and Ruffles bound out the door. I look at Zack, and he reaches out a hand to pull me to my feet. I take it, and the warmth of his palm makes goose bumps travel all the way up my arm.

"Sarah thought it was a good idea?" he asks.

I nod. "She said it might bring some closure."

"Do you want to go alone with Lily?"

"No. I want you to come, too." The words fly out fast—too fast. I'd just assumed he'd be with us. "If—if you don't mind, that is."

"No, I want to. I just didn't want to intrude."

I shake my head. "I-I'd like the company. And I think Lily would, too." I spoon the leftover rice into a plastic container. "You have a way of lifting her spirits."

And mine, as well. The realization of how much I've begun to count on his steady, reassuring presence alarms me, especially now that he's going to stay in New Orleans. I know better than to rely too much on a man. I know better than to build up fairy-tale endings in my mind.

And yet, being around Zack makes it hard for my heart to remember all of its hard-learned lessons.

CHAPTER FIFTY-TWO

Zack

I BREATHE IN the scent of freshly cut grass, jasmine, and magnolia blossoms as we walk over to Brooke's house together. We pass neighbors on their porches, who nod and call hello. Quinn smiles and responds, and Lily waves.

As we draw near, I see that the lawn of Brooke's house is mowed and edged. It occurs to me that Quinn is probably responsible. "Are you handling the upkeep on the place?"

Quinn nods. "I kept the lawn service, and I had the cleaning lady come by yesterday to keep things dusted."

On top of caring for Lily, seeing to Margaret, and running her own business while in the not-always-feeling-great throes of early pregnancy, she's managing the details of her late friend's estate. My admiration for Quinn just grows and grows.

She leads us to the back door. Lily grips my hand as Quinn unlocks it. The kitchen smells like furniture polish and Windex as we step inside. Lily releases my hand and wanders around the granite island.

"I don't know what Miss Margaret wants to do with the place now," Quinn tells me. "She said something about moving here if she recovers enough, but I don't think it's feasible. All of the bedrooms and full baths are on the second story."

"Maybe I could buy it," I find myself saying. "Or at least lease it. I'll need a place to live now that I'm staying in New Orleans, because the condo's sold and I have to be out in three weeks."

"I bet Miss Margaret would be open to a short-term lease," Quinn says.

"That would be awesome," I say. "If Lily's okay with me living here."

But Lily isn't listening. She's staring at the stainless steel door of the refrigerator. "All of my art is gone!"

"Yes, honey," Quinn says softly. "Your grams and I took down all the personal items to get the house ready to sell, remember?"

Lily's shoulders slump.

I search my mind for a way to cheer her up. "You had some happy times here, huh?" I ask.

Lily nods.

"Maybe you can show me around and tell me about the things you used to do in the different rooms."

The suggestion immediately brightens her. "Okay." She holds out her arms and spins around. "This is the kitchen. It's where we cooked and ate."

"Did Quinn come over a lot?"

Lily nods. "She always came to the back door. Mos' ever'one else came to the front. That's over here." She shows me the door where I first met Quinn. "An' this is the livin' room, where we would play games an' watch movies an' read."

"It's very nice. I like how you can see the kitchen from there."

"Mommy said Quinn got the builders to tear down some walls." She skips into the dining room. "This is where we ate when Mommy had parties."

"It's really pretty."

Lily nods. "Mommy said Quinn found the furn'ture an' did the core."

"Decor," Quinn says gently.

"I really like it," I say.

"There's a bathroom underneath the stairs, but it's little. It's where we used to have my potty chair, 'fore I was a big girl. An' here's the way upstairs."

She starts up the staircase, then stops and cranes her head up at the wall. "Hey, all the pitchers are gone!"

"Yes," Quinn says. "We took them down so people looking at the house could imagine themselves living here. They're all packed up and stored for later."

"What kinds of pictures were they?" I ask.

"People ones," Lily says as she continues climbing the stairs. "Photos of me an' Mommy, an' Mommy an' Quinn, an' Mommy an' me an' Grams an' Quinn, an' gran'parents I never gots to meet, an' things like that."

"I'd like to see them someday."

"I have a photo album I can show you," Quinn says. "And Miss Margaret has lots of photos we'll bring from Alexandria."

"This was the gues' room," Lily says, pointing to the left. "This is where Grams would sleep when she came to visit."

"And where I would sleep before I moved here from Atlanta," Quinn says.

"And this is Mommy's room." Lily walks across the hall and stops. Her voice cracks, as if she's about to cry. "Hey—her pitchers and joolry boxes and pretty things all dis'peared!"

"Your grams and I packed them up," Quinn says gently. "We saved them for you for when you're bigger."

Lily opens the closet door. "Where's all her clothes?"

"Your grams and I cleared them out." Quinn's voice, too, has a slight quaver. She surreptitiously wipes her face.

Lily steps into the master bathroom. The countertop is completely clear except for a box of tissues. She opens the cabinet under the vanity and finds it empty as well. Tears stream down her face. "Everythin's all gone."

"Yes, sweetie." Quinn follows her in. I stand outside the bathroom, but I can see their reflections in the large framed mirror over the sink. Quinn kneels down and hugs the child. Lily's arms curl around Quinn's neck, and she cries into Quinn's hair.

My throat grows tight. I stand there, feeling awkward and useless. I ache to comfort them, but the loss is theirs, and this moment is, too. My arms feel long and unwieldy, and my heart thuds like a flat tire.

After a long moment, Quinn gets a tissue and dabs Lily's face. Lily sniffs, then wanders back into the bedroom. While Quinn uses a tissue herself, Lily kneels down, lifts the dust ruffle, and peers under the bed. She stands up, crosses the room, and opens a dresser drawer. Again, it's empty.

"Can you show me your room?" I ask.

Lily nods. She takes my hand and leads me across the hall.

"Oh, my," I say. "We must have taken a wrong turn. It looks like we left the house and stepped into a royal palace."

She grins. "No, we're in my room."

"Well, then, you must be a princess or a fairy, because this looks like the kind of place where a fairy princess would sleep."

"You're silly." Her smile fades as she looks around. "But it looks all naked! My books an' stuffed an'mals are missing." She opens her closet. "An' my clothes, and my toys!" Her bottom lip trembles.

"You have some of them at my place." Quinn has silently entered the bedroom behind us. "And the rest are in Alexandria, remember? Grams's friends packed up some of your things and sent them to us, and we'll go get the rest when Grams is better."

Lily turns around slowly. "This is my room an' my house, but it's not the same at all."

"No," Quinn says. "It's not the same."

"An' Mommy's not here."

"No, sweetie."

"That's 'cause she's dead, right?"

"Yes, honey. But your memories of her and the love you shared will always be with you."

"Yeah. But it's not the same."

"No, it's not."

Lily plops down on her bed, her legs dangling over, her slight shoulders rounded. Quinn sits down beside her and embraces her. They stay like that a long while, then Lily looks up. "I'm tired. Can we go home now?"

Tears well in Quinn's eyes. She tenderly places her hand on the child's head. "That's a great idea."

The significance of the moment is not lost on me. Home means Quinn's place now. Together they walk down the stairs, Quinn's arm around Lily. I follow, my heart feeling as soft as Lily's teddy bear.

As we trudge back through the neighborhood in the fading light, I realize I haven't once, all evening, thought about the fact that my wife has filed for divorce.

CHAPTER FIFTY-THREE

Quinn

Friday, June 7

TWO DAYS LATER, I'm at the shop conferring with Terri about the furnishings for a client's living room when I get a text from Zack.

Can you meet me for lunch at Bayona at 12:30?

My first thought is to say no. Ever since I learned he's getting divorced and staying in New Orleans, I've felt off balance. We didn't settle anything the night we went to Brooke's home; by the time Lily was bathed and tucked into bed, I was too exhausted to deal with how this news changes everything.

And yet, it does.

Terri looks at me, her eyebrows raised. I realize I'm standing frozen, staring at my phone. I turn it toward her so that she can read it.

"Say yes!" she urges. "You're headed to the French Quarter this afternoon anyway to drop off the bergères for the Franklin project at the upholsterer, right? And you two need some time to talk without Lily listening to every word."

She's right. I text back that I'll meet him.

At twelve thirty, I step through the iron gate into the lushly planted brick courtyard of the restaurant. Zack is waiting for me just inside the door. We're led through the quaint Creole cottage and seated by the window on Dauphine Street.

"This is lovely," I say.

"I thought it would be quiet," he says as we settle at the table.

We make small talk and place our orders—the apple and blue

cheese salad with grilled shrimp for me, a house salad and smoked duck for Zack. When the waiter leaves our table, Zack leans forward. "We never got a chance to really talk the other evening."

I nod. "Thanks for going with us back to Lily's old home."

"Glad I could be there. I hope to be around to help with lots of things in the future."

My heart stutters. I decide to directly address the elephant in the room. "I was surprised to hear that you and Jessica are splitting up."

"Me, too. I knew that things weren't great between us, but I didn't know she wanted to call it quits."

"I'm so sorry. Are you okay?"

"Yeah." He fingers the stem on his water glass for a moment. "Better than okay, actually. I told my sister on the phone last night that I feel like a terrible husband, because the truth is, I don't feel all that bad." He lifts the glass and takes a sip. "She said I probably need to talk to a therapist."

"Sarah can recommend someone."

"I may ask her for a name in a week or two. But right now, I'm just relieved I get to stay in New Orleans."

"Yeah?"

He nods. "I tried to talk Jessica into staying here a while back, but she wouldn't even consider it."

"I guess that's understandable," I say.

"Yeah, I suppose. But that's not why she's divorcing me. I mean, I was still planning to move to Seattle. I'd told her I would, and I believe in keeping my word. My father always said your word is who you are."

"So what's the reason for the divorce?"

"It's complicated."

"Is it Lily and the baby?"

"It's lots of things, but the bottom line is she doesn't want to be married to me anymore." He puts down the glass. "Anyway, now that we're splitting and I'm staying, I'm making new arrangements.

I have things lined out at work, and I notified the Seattle firm that I'm not moving. So the next order of business is you."

My heart thumps hard. "You mean Lily and the baby."

"Yes, and you." He looks me in the eye. My pulse rate irrationally soars. "I know you didn't sign up to have a father in the picture, but here I am. And, well, here I'm going to stay." He leans forward. "I don't want to impose on you, and I'm not saying I should see them every day, but I want to be as much a part of the children's lives as you'll let me be."

I don't really know what to say, so I don't say anything.

"The other night you mentioned the possibility of me leasing Brooke's house." He pauses as the waiter brings us iced teas. "I went by the hospital and talked to Margaret about it this morning."

I raise my eyebrows. "Wow. You didn't waste any time."

"I don't have a lot of time. The new owners take possession of my condo in three weeks."

"What did Margaret say?"

"She loved the idea." Zack smiles. "She's more than happy to lease it to me, fully furnished, for nine months. After that, well, we'll see."

"Wow," I say, trying to process what this means.

"This way I'll just be two blocks away. With Margaret and Lily living with you and a baby on the way, you're likely to need some help."

The concept thrills me. But wait—it shouldn't, should it? All my internal alarm systems should be flashing red. This is not taking things slowly as Sarah advised! "I'm planning on hiring some help when the baby comes," I tell him. "Brooke had a nanny who stayed with Lily while she was at work, and I plan to do the same thing. And Margaret will have a home nurse with her for much of the day, at least at first."

"Great. And I'll be nearby for backup."

My expression must give away my worries.

His brow furrows. "This was your suggestion, but you look kind of upset. Did you change your mind about it?"

No. Yes! I don't want to become too accustomed to you. "I, um, just don't want Lily to become dependent on you," I say, because it seems to cite Lily.

"Why not? I'm not going anywhere," he says. "I'm staying in New Orleans, and I'll be in her life from here on out. And the baby's, too. I think this is a win-win situation."

For everyone but me. What if I get too attached to him, and he gets involved with someone else and leaves?

Or, even worse—what if he gets involved with someone else, and doesn't? My stomach sinks at the thought.

"There's nothing to worry about, Quinn." He places his hand over mine on the table. "I'm not going to abandon Lily or the baby."

I both love and hate that he gets me. It's great to have someone who understands; it's terrifying that it's the man I'm falling for.

Oh, God—am I falling for Zack?

I force myself to smile. "You're right. I'm probably being paranoid. If you're going to be here, well, you might as well be nearby. But we need to talk to Lily and make sure she's okay with you living in her old house."

"Sure." He nods. "And while we're on the subject of me helping out, I want to help you with expenses, too."

I balk at the idea. I don't want him to have that kind of sway over me. "There's no need. Brooke set up a generous monthly trust fund to pay for Lily's care."

"Yes, but what about the baby? You said you're planning to hire a nanny."

"I've budgeted for that," I say. "I planned on being a single mother."

"And you still will be. That's no reason for me not to help."

My feelings are too confused to sort through this issue at the moment. "Let's talk about this later," I say.

"Okay. Sure. No rush." He gives me a smile. "There's one other matter I need to discuss with you, and then I'll be done with serious topics."

I brace myself.

"My sister warned me against being the good-time parent. She said Lily needs to do chores and errands and everyday boring things with me as well as fun stuff."

I smile. "I like the sound of your sister."

"Oh, you'll love her. And she'll love you, as well."

I feel a little thrill at the thought of getting to know his family. It's *Lily's* family, I tell myself. Lily's, and the baby's.

"I volunteer once a month with a group that builds backyard vegetable gardens for low-income citizens," he continues. "I was wondering if you'd both like to come help next Saturday."

Thank God—an easy decision! "Sure," I say with a smile. "I don't think this counts as a non-fun activity, though. Lily loves planting things."

"Just about anything can be fun if you do it with the right people."

"Oh, I beg to differ," I say. "I don't think a root canal could ever be fun. Or a colonoscopy."

He grins. "Have some experience with those, do you?"

"No. Nor do I want any."

His dimple deepens. "Well, no worries. I don't have either of those on the family agenda."

Family. He used the word *family*, as if that's what we are!

I can't help it. I beam at him, my heart so full it feels like it's spilling over. We sit there, just smiling at each other, until the server brings our meals.

As we eat, we talk about his work, my work, Lily, Saints football, what we're reading, music, a new exhibit at the New Orleans Museum of Art, charitable projects we're involved in, and movies. It turns out we have a lot in common. Our conversation is easy and fun and free-flowing. I feel lighter and happier than I've felt in months.

"This is the last week of your first trimester, right?" Zack says as we finish our meals.

I'm surprised he's kept track. "That's true."

"That's a big milestone." He picks up his iced tea glass and holds it out. "Here's to you and our baby."

Our baby. The words make goose bumps rise on my arms. I grin like a moron and clink my glass against his. I feel giddy, as if I've drunk champagne instead of iced tea.

As the plates are cleared, I excuse myself from the table and go to the ladies' room so I can have a serious talk with myself.

"Get a grip, girl," I whisper to myself in the mirror as I wash my hands.

Having Zack stay in New Orleans will undoubtedly be wonderful for Lily. It'll be wonderful for the baby, and wonderful for Margaret.

But what about me? I don't want to get involved with a man who ticks off every item on my things-to-avoid-so-I-don't-make-the-same-mistake-again list:

Not ready for a relationship—check.

On the rebound—check.

Is someone I must continue to interact with if things don't work out—check, check, and double check.

It's not wise for me to fall for Zack, not wise at all—and yet my heart already seems to have stepped off the ledge.

CHAPTER FIFTY-FOUR

Margaret

Tuesday, June 11

QUINN HELPED ME move to the rehabilitation hospital yesterday. It was just a wheelchair ride away, but it's in a whole separate building, so I got to go outside for the first time since my accident.

Oh, how glorious to be outdoors! I swear, I was like a puppy hanging its head out of a car window. The sky overhead was blue, but clouds hung heavy in the west, and the air smelled like rain and possibilities. It was the first time I'd felt like anything good could happen in a while. Since Brooke's death, I suppose.

This new building is definitely a medical facility, but it feels a lot less like a hospital than the one I just left. Good heavens, but they work you like a field hand here! I've had all kinds of therapy and activities of daily living and who knows what else.

It's now four o'clock and I'm finally back in my room, sipping from an enormous water bottle, when Quinn walks in. She kisses me on the cheek and sits in a chair beside mine, smiling. "You look like you've been working out."

"Worked over is more like it." I blot my upper lip with the end of the sweat towel looped around my neck. "I'm just getting back from cardiopulmonary therapy."

"What does that involve?"

"Well, among other things, lifting weights."

"Sounds like a good way to build up your strength."

"I'm sure that's true, but back in my day, weightlifting was strictly for men. A woman lifting barbells would have been considered unfeminine." I take another sip of water. "My father used to say, 'Men know women are the stronger sex, but they still don't want a girl to beat them at arm wrestling.'"

Quinn laughs. "Were you and your father close?"

"Oh, yes. I trailed around after him like the scent of his Old Spice." I can almost smell it as I remember him. "I helped out in his locksmith shop whenever I could. I learned the names of all his tools and handed them to him like a nurse handing scalpels to a surgeon."

Quinn smiles. "What was he like?"

"He was kind," I say. "He loved me and my little sister, and oh, he loved my mama. I thought he was going to die himself when Mama passed away of cancer."

"How old were you?"

"I had just turned ten, and my sister was eight." I feel my eyes grow moist. "She was in terrible pain at the end, but she was worried about us, not herself. One of the last things Mama told Papa was that she wanted him to marry again. She wanted Junie and me to have a mother. She said, 'You can do a lot of things for them, but you can't teach them to be ladies.'"

"Did he remarry?"

I nod. "About a year later. Mama Betsy was a widow with two girls of her own who were a little older than me."

"What was she like?"

The years seem to roll back, like a window shade going up. Instead of pulling it down as I always have, I decide to look at the past straight on.

"Mama Betsy was a pretty little thing with real nice manners," I say, "but she didn't like to deal with anything unpleasant. She favored her daughters, but Papa favored us, so things weren't too bad. But then, when I was fourteen, Papa died; he just keeled over of a heart attack while installing the locks on the new bank."

"Oh, how terrible!" Quinn murmurs.

I nod. "I thought the world had ended when Mama died, but it hadn't, not really. When Papa was gone, though—well, that's when the floor was yanked out from under us.

"Mama Betsy didn't know what to do about anything. Why, I had to make all the decisions about Papa's burial. I called my aunt Kathy—she was Papa's sister who lived in St. Louis, who'd stayed with me and Junie when Mama was sick—but she was in poor health, and couldn't even come for the funeral.

"It turned out Papa had left most of his assets, including the house, in a trust for Junie and me. Mama Betsy and the girls could continue to live there on the condition that she kept us and cared for us. Papa had arranged for her to receive a monthly allowance to pay for our care until we were of age, so we stayed where we were, but things were very different.

"Without Papa there to stop them, her daughters started raiding Junie's and my closet and taking our things. One day when everyone was out, I got Papa's toolbox and a dead bolt, and I installed it on our bedroom door. Her girls tattled on me—told their mother I was ruining the house—but I said it was mine to ruin.

"Well, that must have gotten Mama Betsy to thinking she'd best prepare for the future, because a few months later, she married an oilfield supervisor who had a teenage son. Oh, that boy was a hellion! He learned quick as the devil to leave Mama Betsy's precious daughters alone, but oh, he'd harass Junie and me something fierce. He'd grab us and flip up our skirts—he was just indecent.

"Mama Betsy did nothing about it and her husband, Mr. Earl, would just laugh. Half the time Mr. Earl wasn't home anyway; he'd spend days at a time away at work. We kept our bedroom door locked when we weren't in it and every night while we slept.

"Good thing we did, too, because lo and behold, a few months later, Mama Betsy's younger daughter turned up pregnant. I thought for sure the son was responsible—but the oldest girl, she piped up and said it was Mr. Earl. Said he'd been in her bed, too. Mama Betsy refused to believe her. Said she was a liar."

"Oh, no!" Quinn says.

"The boy was sent to live with one of Mr. Earl's relatives, and both girls were sent to Alabama to a home for wayward girls. A month after they were sent away, Mama Betsy was at a Wednesday night church meeting and Mr. Earl was supposed to be away overnight in the oil patch. I came home from the library, and I heard Junie screaming from the bathroom.

"I ran in, and Mr. Earl had Junie on the floor, as naked as the day she was born. I broke a glass bottle of bubble bath over his head and knocked him out cold. I thought for a moment I might have killed him, but at the time, I didn't even care."

"Oh, Miss Margaret!" Quinn's eyes are full, and her hand covers her mouth.

"I got there before he'd raped Junie, thank God, but she was a blubbering mess. He'd grabbed her out the tub, snatching her by her hair. A chunk of it lay on the floor."

I close my eyes, but I can still see it in my memory. I draw a steadying breath and continue. "I got Junie dressed—which wasn't easy; her teeth were chattering and she was shaking like a leaf in a storm—and threw a few clothes in a bag. We went to a friend's house. I told the mother what had happened and showed her Junie's head and the bruises on her arm. She said come in, she'd doctor it up—but then her husband said they couldn't get involved, that it wasn't their business, that it was our family matter. When I explained that we didn't have any real family, they let Junie and me stay the night, but we had to leave in the morning. Back then, I didn't think of calling the police, and no one suggested it; it was just too shameful."

"That's awful!" Quinn's voice is low and horrified.

"Yes, it was, but that's how things were back then. The next day, I tried to phone my aunt Kathy again, and learned she'd died. So I went to the library and tried to look up a home for orphaned girls, thinking I'd find us a place to go. I needed the librarian's help, so I made up a cockamamie story about researching a school paper, but Mrs. Clemmons saw right through me. Before I knew it, I'd blurted out the truth. She took us under her wing, bless her heart, and used her research skills to start looking into the situation." She was the reason I later decided to become a librarian myself.

Quinn takes my hand. I clutch it and continue talking. "She called up Mama's old friends and acquaintances—that's the advantage of a small town, where everyone knows everyone else—and asked if they knew anything about any of Mama's out-of-town relatives. Someone remembered a male cousin from Baton Rouge who'd come to visit Mama towards the end. Mrs. Clemmons telephoned every man in Baton Rouge with Mama's maiden name and finally found my uncle Ted. I didn't remember ever meeting him, but he and his wife, Opal, agreed to take in Junie and me. 'Blood looks after blood,' he said."

I fall silent for a moment. "Junie and I lived with them until we went off to college. Uncle Ted gave me away at my wedding, and I cared for Aunt Opal in my home the last year of her life."

Quinn's eyes brim with tears. "No wonder you were so intent on finding Lily's father."

"I know how vulnerable a child can be with no family."

Quinn folds her other hand on top of mine. I squeeze it. "I suffered terrible guilt all my life that I hadn't protected Junie by looking for a blood relative right away. I didn't want to make the same mistake with Lily."

"You had nothing to feel guilty about, Miss Margaret." Quinn's voice is full of conviction. "You couldn't have known what was going to happen. Besides, you were just a child yourself."

"I see that now. But for many, many years, I blamed myself." I look out the window and watch cars drive by on Jefferson Highway. "Shame and guilt sometimes haunt the wrong people."

"That's so true. Especially children."

We sit in silence for a moment.

"Whatever happened to Mr. Earl?" she asks.

I lift my shoulders. "He left town and never came back. I found out years later that one of the people Mrs. Clemmons called was the police chief. I believe that's what prompted his sudden departure."

"And Mama Betsy?"

"She moved about a month later. Took all the furniture in the house, which wasn't hers to take, but I suppose that was a small price for getting her out of our lives. I heard she married a man in Jackson."

The door swings open. A fresh-faced nurse's aide smiles at me. "Mrs. Moore, it's time for your group exercise class."

"Oh, fiddle! I thought I was through for the day."

"I promise it's not too strenuous. Besides, you'll get to meet some other patients, then you'll all have dinner together."

Quinn kisses my cheek. "Thank you so much for sharing your story."

"I never told Brooke about that. Never told her mother, either."

"Well, I think you're heroic and brave and a true inspiration. I'm so glad you told me." She touches the top of my head for a moment. It feels like a motherly touch—or maybe a blessing. "Good night. I love you!"

"I love you, too." We've never exchanged those words before, but I mean them with all my heart. I watch Quinn leave, and my gaze lingers on the door after it closes behind her.

"You're fortunate to have such a devoted granddaughter," the aide says.

I have no intention of correcting her. "Yes," I say. "Yes, indeed I am."

CHAPTER FIFTY-FIVE

Zack

Wednesday, June 12

WHILE LILY AND Alicia play tag outside, Quinn tells me about her visit with Margaret yesterday afternoon. We're in the kitchen, watching the girls through the windows and fixing dinner together. The tale makes me freeze in the middle of chopping yellow squash. "No wonder Margaret went on that donor site to find me," I say.

Quinn nods. "All those comments about blood relatives make sense now."

"Poor Margaret, feeling responsible for her sister's assault all these years." I attack the squash as if it's responsible. "Whatever happened to Junie?"

"I asked Margaret about her this afternoon." Quinn slides a baking dish of seasoned chicken pieces into the oven. "She said Junie became an elementary school principal, then died of pneumonia in her late fifties. She never married, never even dated, apparently. Margaret said Junie kind of 'lost her spark' after the assault. She didn't want to do anything but study and work."

There ought to be a special place in hell for men like Mr. Earl. I aggressively chop a tomato. "That monster scarred both sisters for life."

Quinn somberly nods. "That's what childhood trauma does." She gazes out the window at the two little girls laughing and racing around the backyard. "Losing a parent is a trauma, too. That's why it's so important to make Lily feel loved and secure."

"You're doing a really good job of that."

"You are, too." She meets my gaze, her eyes soft. "You know, I didn't want you in the picture at first, but you've turned out to be a wonderful addition to our lives."

The words mean more to me than she can know. "The feeling's mutual."

The air grows charged as we look at each other. She breaks the spell by turning, opening a cabinet, and taking out a bowl. "We need to talk to Lily about you moving into her old house."

"Yeah."

"Let's do that as soon as Alicia leaves."

The back door bursts open. Lily and Alicia bound inside, panting like puppies. "We're dyin' of thirst! Can we get some water?"

"Absolutely." Quinn smiles, opening another cabinet and taking down two glasses.

TWENTY MINUTES LATER, Alicia's father pulls into the drive. Quinn waves through the kitchen window as Alicia scrambles into her safety seat and her father buckles her in. "We want to talk to you about something," Quinn says as Lily comes inside. "Let's go sit on the sofa for a moment."

We traipse to the living room, and Lily plops down between us.

Quinn draws a deep breath. "You know how your old house is just sitting there empty?"

"Yeah," Lily says, her voice downcast. "I hoped Mommy was there, but she isn't." She climbs into Quinn's lap and sucks her thumb. "An' a whole lot of stuff is gone."

Quinn holds her for a moment, just rubbing her back. "That's because your grams was planning to sell it. Houses are meant to be lived in and cared for."

"I don' like the idea of other people livin' there."

"Well, what if it's someone you really like?"

"Like who?"

"Well, since your daddy is staying in New Orleans instead of moving to Seattle, he needs a new place to live. So what would you think of him moving in there for a while?"

Lily pulls her thumb out of her mouth, turns her head, and looks at me. I can practically see the wheels turning in her brain as she ponders the idea.

"I promise I'll take really good care of it and not scribble on the walls or anything," I say.

She giggles.

"I think it would be nice to have Mr. Zack living so close," Quinn says. "And I like the idea of him living there instead of strangers."

"I like that, too!" Lily scrambles off Quinn's lap and scampers into mine. "So you'll be close 'nough you can walk over an' see us?"

"That's right."

"So you can come tuck me in every night?"

"Probably not every night, but it'll be nice to be nearby."

"We wanted to make sure you were okay with the idea," Quinn says.

"I think it's fab-oo-lous!" Lily wraps her arms around my neck.

I hug her back. "You're the one who's fabulous." I glance over at Quinn. "And your mommy Quinn is pretty fabulous, too."

Ruffles barks and jumps up on the sofa, not wanting to miss out on the action.

Lily giggles. "She wants you to say she's fab-oo-lous, too."

I pet the furry creature's head. "You're all right for a dog."

"No!" Lily laughs. "Fab-oo-lous!"

"Okay, okay. Every female living in this house is absolutely fabulous."

Over Lily's shoulder, I see Quinn smiling. I give her a thumbs-up, and she returns the gesture.

I love how she handled the conversation, how gentle yet honest she was with Lily. I already thought she was amazing, but the more I'm around her, the more I find to admire.

ON SATURDAY, I dump yet another bag of topsoil in the just-built raised garden bed, then wipe my brow. It's hot as blazes. Across from me, Quinn and another volunteer are spreading the soil with rakes. It occurs to me that having a pregnant woman out in the summer heat might not have been my brightest idea.

"Are you feeling okay?" I ask.

"I'm fine."

"You should have stayed home and rested this morning."

"I wanted to come. I enjoy gardening, and I love the idea of helping out." She grins over at Lily, who's lying on top of a stack of soil bags. "But it looks like somebody else needed extra rest."

"I'm not restin'," Lily says. "I'm huggin' the Dirt Mother."

"Huh?" I say.

"Mommy said the Dirt Mother grows plants an' animals an' people, an' we need to give her lots of love."

"Oh—Mother Earth!" Quinn says with a laugh. "Yes, Lily—that's absolutely right. Your mommy talked a lot about Mother Earth and how we need to take care of her."

"Yeah," Lily says. "So I was givin' her a hug."

I look at Quinn and we exchange a smile, but my throat grows kind of thick. What a funny, loving, pure-hearted little creature Lily is!

She stands up, her pigtails bouncing. The front of both her T-shirt and shorts are covered with soil. She tries to dust them off, but her efforts are foiled by the mud-caked garden gloves she's wearing.

"Oh, honey, you're smearing dirt all over your clothes!" says a white-haired volunteer approaching with a flat of seedlings.

"It's okay," Lily says. "These are the get-dirty kind of clothes. Mommy Quinn says clothes can be washed and they shouldn' get in the way of livin' life."

A male volunteer with a neatly trimmed gray-and-black beard laughs. "I like the way she thinks."

"I do, too," Lily says, her face serious.

"I do, three," I chime in.

Quinn laughs and gives the woman a smile. "All I can say is thank goodness for washable safety seat covers and wet wipes."

This is one of the things I really like about Quinn: she finds the sunny side of every situation. Whenever I'm with her, well, I'm always just where I want to be, and whatever we're doing is just what I want to be doing.

"I'll dig the holes, and you can carefully place the little plants in," Quinn says to Lily.

"I'll help you dig," says the volunteer with the beard.

My role in this endeavor has been building the beds, hauling supplies, and doing all the heavy lifting, but that part's nearly finished. "I'll pull the plants out of the flats," I say. I carefully remove a pepper seedling, being sure to leave the roots intact.

"Can I name them?" Lily asks.

Quinn smiles. "Sure."

"Okay." Lily points to the plant I just removed. "This one's Petunia."

The bearded man laughs. "You're going to name a pepper plant Petunia? Aren't you worried it'll grow flowers instead of peppers?"

"No." She gives him a serious look. "It knows what it is. My name is Lily, but I know I'm a little girl."

He laughs, then shake his head. "I can't argue with that."

"Where does she even come up with this stuff?" I ask Quinn later, when the planting is finished, Lily has scampered off to play tag with the residents' children, and we're gathering up the tools. 'The plant knows what it is.' That's pretty deep!"

"I think she gets it from you."

"Get out!"

"Did you see the serious expression on her face when she said it?"

"Like she was giving it a whole lot of thought?"

Quinn nods. "You get that exact same look sometimes."

I pick up a rake, and we head for the car. "Like when?"

"Well . . . when you were watching the YouTube video on how to change out the doors for Margaret's bedroom." She gives me a playful grin. "And when you were trying to decide if you'd have the pineapple or mango snow cone."

"Hey, that snow cone decision was momentous."

"Did you jus' say somethin' 'bout snow cones?" Lily asks, appearing at my elbow. "Are we gonna go get some?"

Quinn grins at me. "As Margaret would say, 'Little pitchers have big ears.'"

"What does that mean?" Lily asks.

"It's an old-timey saying," Quinn replies.

"It means Mommy Quinn wants to get a pitcher of snow cones," I say. "And she wants us to pour them in her ear."

Quinn gives me a teasing faux slap, and Lily laughs. "You're silly!"

The sun filters through the leaves of the oak tree in the front yard, dappling their blond hair with light, and I suddenly realize I'm happy—all in, to-the-bone happy. This child and this woman are giving me something my heart has longed for, something I've missed, something I'd hoped to find in my marriage, but never did—the sense of being at home whenever I'm with them, wherever that might be.

CHAPTER FIFTY-SIX

Quinn

Saturday, July 6

I'M THE LAST one to arrive at the Java Hut for the July meeting of the single parent group. The place looks the same, with the exception of the artwork on the wall. A large new painting hangs over the table where we always gather. It's titled *Love Is a Leap of Faith* and features two valentine-like hearts holding hands, legs bent, ready to jump over a chasm. My gaze locks on the chasm, which looks dangerously wide and deep. If those two hearts had a child and an unborn baby relying on them, would they still choose to jump?

"Sorry I'm late," I say as I join the group with my glass of iced tea.

"No worries. We're just getting started, and Mac is speaking first," Annie says.

Everyone looks at him expectantly.

His face flushes. "Well, Kylie is doing much better. She still refuses to visit her parents in prison, but she's writing real letters to them and she doesn't spend every waking moment in her room. And she loves working as a mother's helper for Sarah."

"She's wonderful with the boys," Sarah says.

"She's got a real knack with kids," Annie agrees.

He nods, then sits there silently, as if he has nothing more to say.

"Don't you have some personal news to share?" Sarah prompts.

"Oh!" His ears look like they could burst into flames at any moment. "I'm, uh—well, Sarah and I are . . ." He darts a glance at her, and the redness spreads to his neck. "Well, we're, um, kind of dating."

"Oh, Mac—Sarah—that's so wonderful!" everyone murmurs. I smile at Sarah; she already told me this during one of our frequent phone calls.

Mac puts his hand over Sarah's and gives a bashful grin. "I've liked her for a long time, but I was afraid she didn't feel the same, and I worried I would mess up our friendship."

"I kept telling you to ask her out," Annie says.

"Yeah, but I didn't want to ruin things," Mac says.

"So how did you two move beyond the Friend Zone?" Lauren asks.

"I asked him out," Sarah says. "I actually used the word 'date.' He waited so long to answer I was sure he was going to say no."

"I was tongue-tied," he says. "I couldn't believe such a great woman wanted to go out with an old curmudgeon like me."

"You're not a curmudgeon." Sarah eyes him fondly. "You're kind and caring and smart. And you have a highly evolved view of gender roles."

"What do your kids think?" Annie asks.

"The twins are crazy about Mac," Sarah says.

"And Kylie adores Sarah," Mac says. "She wants to be a therapist like her when she grows up."

Lauren puts her hand over her heart. "You guys are precious together!"

Sarah's face grows pink. "So what's going on with you, Lauren?"

She puts her hands on the table and leans forward. "I'm applying to be an adoptive parent."

Everyone murmurs with excitement.

"It's a lengthy process," Lauren says. "I have to go through a home study and background check."

"You'll breeze through that," I say.

"Are you planning to adopt an infant or an older child?" Sarah asks.

"I'm looking into all the options," Lauren says. "They warn you up front that it's not easy, it can take a long time, and you might get your heart broken."

"Any child would be fortunate to have you as a mom," Annie says.

"Thanks, Annie. I've just made the decision, so I have a long way to go."

"It's exciting that you've started the process!" Sarah says.

Lauren nods. "I'll keep you posted each step of the way." She turns to Annie. "So what's going on with you?"

"Not much. Work. Caring for my boy." She hesitates. "There's one thing that's kind of new, but it probably won't come to anything. I don't know if I should even mention it."

"You should," I prompt.

"Yeah. Tell us!" Lauren urges.

"Well . . . I'm planning to go to my high school reunion in Mississippi. Did I tell you all that my old high school boyfriend has been texting me and contacting me on Facebook?"

"You most certainly did not!" I say.

"We've been corresponding for a while," Annie says. She suddenly looks shy. "He's been widowed for two years. He doesn't have any children, but he'd love to."

"Why didn't you tell us about him?" Lauren asks.

"I didn't want to build it into a big thing if it wasn't. But now . . ."

"Now you're going to see him at the reunion," Sarah says.

"Yes. So we'll see."

"That's awesome!" Lauren says.

Annie smiles. "It adds a little extra zing to life. But if it doesn't work out, life is still good."

"I love your attitude, Annie," Sarah says.

"Thanks." Annie turns to me. "And how about you, Quinn?"

Everyone looks at me expectantly.

"I have four pieces of news. First of all, I'm officially in the second trimester. I went to the doctor for my monthly checkup a couple of weeks ago, and everything is going as it should. I'll get another ultrasound at the next checkup that should tell me the baby's sex."

Annie claps. "Oh, how wonderful!"

Everyone smiles and congratulates me.

"Secondly, Miss Margaret is doing really well. It looks like she's going to get to come home next Friday. So I'd like to have a 'welcome home' dinner for her, and I want all of you to come."

"How fun!"

"I'll be there with bells on!"

"I'll text everybody the details as soon as her release date is certain," I say. My heart is warmed by the smiling faces of these dear friends. "As for my third piece of news . . ." I pause and draw a deep breath. "Zack's wife served him with divorce papers, and he's not moving to Seattle after all. He's staying here in New Orleans."

"You're kidding!" Lauren gasps.

"Oh my!" Annie exclaims.

Oh my, indeed. I nod.

"But there's a fourth piece of news: Zack is moving into Brooke's old house this weekend."

I explain the chain of events amid more exclamations.

"I've swapped out the furniture in Brooke's bedroom with some from my shop to give it a more masculine look," I say. "And I changed out a lot of the accessories to make it more reflective of his tastes."

"And Lily's okay with this?" Annie asks.

I nod. "She's excited. She loves the idea of having him nearby. She helped me pick out new pillows and lamps, and drew some pictures for him that I've framed."

"So Zack is getting divorced." Lauren shoots me a speculative glance. "That means he's single." She waggles her eyebrows suggestively.

"He will be soon."

"You're planning to jump on that, right?"

I shake my head and laugh, but my heart skips a little. "Oh, Lauren, it's way too soon to think along those lines."

"Oh, please." She rolls her eyes. "Don't tell me it hasn't crossed your mind."

My face heats, which means I'm blushing. "I'm trying not to go there," I say. "A relationship with Zack is loaded with problems."

"Like what?" Mac asks.

"For starters, I don't want to be a rebound romance."

"How much time does it usually take for someone to be ready for a new relationship after a divorce?" Annie turns to Sarah.

Sarah lifts her shoulders. "It varies a lot."

"Well, the divorce isn't the only issue," I say. "I want a man who wants me for myself, not just because I have his children."

"I understand that." Annie nods.

"And children raise the stakes," I say. "They make it even more important that their parents have a rock-solid relationship—*if* they have a relationship."

"Yes." Annie's head bobs vigorously. "I entirely agree."

"The last thing I want is for my children to have parents who aren't really in love."

"It's good to be cautious," Lauren says, "but you also want to be happy."

"Good point," Annie says. "Look at it this way: if you'd met Zack online or at a business function or in some way that didn't involve Lily and your baby, you'd be interested in him, wouldn't you?"

What red-blooded woman wouldn't? "I might," I say cautiously, "if he were completely divorced and emotionally available. But he's neither of those things right now."

"But he will be." Annie smiles encouragingly. "Just take things slow and easy."

"That's what I told her," Sarah says.

"That's always good advice," I agree. Some form of the suggestion is written in every self-help book I've ever read, and it seems to apply to just about every situation.

Now, if I could just figure out how to convey *slow and easy* to my pulse rate whenever Zack is around.

CHAPTER FIFTY-SEVEN

Jessica

"GO, PETEY!" I jump with excitement in the viewing stand as the little boy smacks the softball with the bat and races to first base. I hold my breath until his foot is on the base marker.

"Wahoo!'" I yell, clapping. "Way to go!" I turn to Brett. "Did you see that? He was amazing!"

"I saw, I saw. If my shirt had buttons, they'd be popping off with Papa pride." His eyes are warm as he smiles at me. He bends down and gives me a hard kiss.

I'm a little shocked. He's never kissed me before. It wasn't a particularly romantic kiss, yet it wasn't platonic, either. It's the kind of happy-moment celebration kiss you might give someone you've kissed a lot. I don't object—in fact, I feel sparks, and my lips still tingle from it—but I'm a little taken aback.

It's a couple's kind of kiss, and I still feel coupled with Zack.

"What was that for?" I ask.

"You're just so adorable, cheering for my son like that."

My heart thumps erratically. "He's a great kid. And that was an amazing hit."

Brett nods. "He is, and it was."

"He let the boy on third base run to home plate!"

"I know."

"I never knew a ball game could be so exciting."

He laughs. "I've never seen you so enthusiastic before. I love this side of you."

My pulse hops and quickens.

He grins at me. "I have to say, you seem really fond of Petey for a woman who doesn't want to date a man with children."

"*Didn't* want to. Past tense," I correct. "That was before I married Zack. I didn't say I felt that way now." *He said* date. *Are we dating?* I feel my face flush. "Besides, Petey's a special case." I've spent some time with him and Brett over the last few weeks, and the boy has stolen my heart. Just last Saturday, Petey, Brett, and I went to the Pacific Science Center. Petey was fascinated by all the exhibits and asked questions throughout the planetarium show. I love his inquisitive nature and his no-BS personality.

Brett smiles. "And me?"

That kiss still burns on my lips. "You're a special case, too." Our eyes meet, and a current runs between us. It's more than attraction; I feel an emotional pull. But I know I need to tell him the truth. "I love spending time with you, but I'm not thinking of this as a date. It's too soon after my split from Zack."

"That's completely understandable," he says. "And I apologize if I was out of line. The last thing I want to do is make you uncomfortable."

"Oh, I'm not uncomfortable. And I'm not disinterested." I smile, and he grins back—a sexy grin that gives me another electric zap. "I'm just not ready." I hesitate, then spill what's on my mind. "I guess I don't feel like things have fully ended with Zack."

"I guess I'm not surprised."

"You're not?"

He shakes his head. "Not really. It takes some time for your head and your heart to sync up. But I'm also wondering . . ."

"What?"

His gaze connects with mine—really connects, in a way I haven't felt with Zack in a long, long time. He rubs his jaw. "I hate to say this because it goes against my personal interests, but I wonder if you need to go back and have a heart-to-heart talk with Zack."

"There's no point. We're in an irreconcilable situation."

"Maybe so, but you walked out and filed for divorce without really talking things through."

I stare at the ball field, where the coach for the opposing team is changing out the pitcher.

"I made a couple of pathetic last-ditch attempts with Sue Anne, and as bad as it felt at the time, it's been important in the long run to know I did everything I could," he says.

"You tried to patch things up, even though she was seeing another man?" I look a few bleacher rows forward and to the right, where she and her fiancé are sitting. I have to say, Sue Anne and Brett seem to have a friendly relationship. When we arrived, she and Brett greeted each other with a kiss, and the two men shook hands. Sue Anne even seemed genuinely glad to see me.

He nods. "For Petey's sake, I felt like I had to try. And in the end, knowing I'd done all I could gave me peace of mind and closure."

Another little boy is up at home plate. His freckled face is puckered in concentration as he holds the bat near his shoulder. The ball soars toward him. He swings so hard he spins around, missing it by a mile.

"Shake it off," shouts a man in the stands—probably his father. "Just put it behind you."

"I like that man's philosophy better," I say.

Brett grins. "That's great advice for softball. Probably not so great for ending a marriage."

"So you think I should try to patch things up with Zack?"

"I'm not saying that. I just think that you owe it to yourselves and your marriage—or at least to the memory you'll have of your marriage in the future—to sit down face-to-face and talk. You'll never regret having an honest conversation, but you might regret not having one."

His words resonate deep inside, in the place I recognize unwanted truths—a place I've ignored for too long. "Peace of mind and closure sound pretty good," I say.

"You only get those by living out your values."

Hell—my values have been centered on achievements and milestones, on trying to look and feel successful. I've been so focused on pushing toward the next goal, and then the next, that I haven't seriously considered what success really means.

What *are* my values? Underneath all the external stuff, what really matters? What kind of person, deep down, do I want to be?

Someone who treats others the way I want to be treated, I realize. Someone who follows the Golden Rule.

I mentally apply it to my situation with Zack, and my spirits plummet still further. If the shoe were on the other foot, I would have hated being served divorce papers at work without any real notice. Chagrin spreads through me.

Values. What a damned inconvenient thing to learn at this point in my life!

"Hell," I mutter. "I think you might be right."

"Of course I am."

"How did you get so smart?"

"Oh, I've always been the guy with all the answers." He gives a self-deprecating grin. "If you don't believe me, just ask Sue Anne."

CHAPTER FIFTY-EIGHT

Quinn

Monday, July 8

IS DADDY COMING over tonight?" Lily asks as soon as I pick her and Alicia up at preschool. It's a question she asks every day.

"As a matter of fact, he is. He's going to grill us dinner."

"Hamburgers?" she asks, her face hopeful.

"Nope. Chicken, corn on the cob, and zucchini."

"Yay!" Lily says. "Sounds yummy!"

I grin. I could tell her Zack is fixing snake innards and wombat gizzards and she'd probably be thrilled. Lily has rapidly turned into a real Daddy's girl.

I worry a little about it. Zack and I have still never addressed the question of how often he should see Lily; instead, we've fallen into a pattern where it almost feels like we're playing house. Ever since he moved into Brooke's home last week, he calls every day to check on us and comes by nearly as often. He plays with Lily outside and gives me time to rest, because pregnancy fatigue hits me hard in the early evening. He entertains Lily with yo-yo tricks and is teaching her the basics on a toddler-friendly yo-yo, which no doubt makes Brooke smile in heaven. He usually eats dinner with us; sometimes, like tonight, he cooks.

He helps out around the house, too. He runs errands and sweeps the kitchen, and last weekend he replaced the glass-paneled French doors in the downstairs office with solid wood ones to turn it into a bedroom for Margaret.

He's become such a regular part of our lives that Lily remarks on his absence when he's not there to tuck her in bed. The other night when Zack was on one side of her and I was on the other, she said, "I love it when you're here, Daddy, because I like being Lucky Pierre."

I thought Zack would fall off the bed. "Where on earth did you hear that?"

"From a boy at school. He said it's what his daddy calls someone in the middle."

"Oh. I see." He tried hard not to laugh and failed. His attempt to hide it by pretending to cough made me laugh, which made him laugh harder, which made Ruffles start barking. Lily laughed, too, although she had no idea what was funny.

The more time Lily and I spend with Zack, the more attached we're both becoming to him. I'm concerned that Lily is getting too accustomed to his frequent visits.

I'm concerned that I look forward to them too much. I'm concerned that I'm feeling more and more attracted to him.

I know it's too soon and probably not a good idea, but I don't really know how to stop.

"G'NIGHT, DADDY." LILY reaches up and hugs Zack's neck.

"Good night, Lily-kins." He kisses her cheek.

"G'night, Mommy Quinn."

"Good night, precious girl." I give her a warm embrace and press my lips to her forehead. She snuggles up to Sugar Bear, and I tuck them both under the covers. "Sleep tight!"

Zack grins at me as we turn out the light and leave the room, closing the door behind us.

"Every time we put her to bed, I want to wake her up and talk to her some more."

"I know what you mean," I say, my heart full. "I never knew I could love anyone so much."

He nods and his gaze locks with mine. A lot more than our eyes seem to be communicating. I put my hand on my stomach as he follows me down the stairs.

"How's the other little one treating you?"

"Pretty well," I say. "I still keep the crackers handy, but I've noticed a big improvement."

"Have you tried the fetal Doppler?"

"Not yet," I say. "The box says 'as early as twelve weeks,' but if you read further, it says twenty weeks is the norm. It might still be too early."

"If you like, we can give it a try," he says. "I brought batteries." He motions to the kitchen counter, where he'd placed them after emptying the grocery bag he'd brought.

"Okay. Sure." I go into the dining room and retrieve the box containing the device. He opens it at the kitchen island, puts in the batteries, and then studies the instructions, his expression serious. I wish his serious face weren't so seriously sexy. It makes my heart race and my palms sweat.

"It says you need to lie down, then we need to put this gel on your lower stomach." He holds up a bottle that came in the box. "Then we'll slide this gizmo around until hopefully we find a heartbeat."

"It's a lot like what my obstetrician uses," I say. Except the transducer on this machine is disconcertingly shaped like a penis, the instructions call it a probe, and the man I have an embarrassing crush on is going to use it on me.

We go into the living room and I lie down on the sofa. My heart jackhammers in my chest as I pull up my T-shirt and adjust my yoga pants to a modest bikini position. Zack kneels beside me and opens the lid on the bottle of gel. The thought of him rubbing it on my naked belly makes me quake.

It evidently gives him pause, as well. "Maybe you should do this."

I take the bottle, pour some gel in my hand, and smear it on my slightly swollen stomach. He turns on the device, then gently places the probe at my navel.

The jolt of contact makes me jump. I'm hyperaware of how

close he is; I can smell the starch of his shirt and the faint male scent of him. I feel a buzz of electricity that has nothing to do with the batteries in the Doppler and everything to do with him.

He moves the probe against my skin, his face again set in that sexy-serious expression. A loud *wop wop wop* sounds through the machine. "I think I found it!" he says.

"I think that's my heart," I tell him.

"It's really fast."

I try to shrug, but the gesture doesn't really work lying down. "I'm excited to hear the baby's heartbeat."

Liar. I'm excited that Zack is so close to me, doing something so intimate.

He checks the instructions, then tries again, once again catching my traitorously fast heartbeat.

"It's too early," I say, after he makes a few more excruciatingly sensual passes below my navel. "We should wait a few more weeks."

"Yeah," he says, turning off the machine.

I start to sit up.

"Wait," he says. "I'll get you a paper towel."

I lie there, my heart still drumming. He returns, reaches out as if he were about to wipe my tummy, and then hesitates. Our eyes meet, and goose bumps cover my skin.

"You should probably do this," he says, handing me the towel.

I don't trust my voice. I nod, wipe off the gel, and sit up.

"Well," he says.

"Yeah. Well," I inanely echo.

"I, um, should probably go," he says. I nod and walk him to the door.

I lean against it after I close it behind him, my heart racing, my knees weak. *Nothing actually happened*, I tell myself.

And yet, I'm pretty sure something did.

CHAPTER FIFTY-NINE

Zack

Thursday, July 11

THE NIGHT BEFORE Margaret is due to come home, Quinn and I are sitting on the porch swing in Quinn's backyard, watching fireflies, after tucking Lily into bed. The screen door is open so we can hear Lily if she needs us.

The swing rhythmically creaks, in sync with the thrumming music of cicadas and tree frogs. "You asked me a while ago if I'd put you down as Lily's guardian in my will if anything happened to me," Quinn says. "I called my attorney, and he's done that. I'll have him send you a copy of the paperwork."

My chest feels tight. "Thanks," I say. "That means a lot."

"Well, you mean a lot to Lily."

"I'm crazy about her." *I'm crazy about you, too.* It would be wrong to say the words, and yet they're there, burning on my tongue.

Quinn's gaze is warm on my face. "I'm really glad Margaret found you."

My heart thumps against my rib cage. "Me, too."

"Even though it cost you your marriage?"

"It didn't," I say.

She looks at me quizzically. I want to explain more—to tell her that the marriage was already in trouble, that Jessica and I had never really felt like home to each other—but it's too soon. I'm still married, and it's not right to talk about that yet. Besides, there's something I need to tell her about Jessica that's been weighing on my mind all evening.

Quinn changes the subject before I get a chance. "I'm so excited about Margaret coming home tomorrow!"

"I'm sure she's excited, too. What can I do to help?"

"Could you possibly get here around five thirty to watch Lily while I pick up Margaret? She wants to complete her group exercise class before she leaves rehab."

"Sure."

"Great. That way you can let in everyone for the party."

"No problem." The swing creaks. "I'll have to leave the party a little early, though."

"Oh, no! How come?"

I hesitate, then just blurt it out. "Jessica is coming into town to talk."

Quinn looks away, but not before I see the hurt in her eyes.

"She wanted to meet me for dinner, but I told her you were throwing Margaret a 'welcome home' party and I couldn't make it."

Her feet drag the deck, stopping the swing. "You can skip the dinner if you want." Her voice is soft. "I'm sure Margaret will understand."

"No. I don't want to miss it. That's why I told Jess we'd talk afterward." I'm trying to convey that I'm prioritizing spending time with her, Lily, and Margaret over spending time with Jessica, but I don't think it's right to flat out say that. I don't know why Jess is coming to New Orleans or what she wants to talk about. All I know is that I'm dreading it.

"Okay. Sure. Well, it's getting late." Quinn abruptly gets out of the swing, making it sway crookedly. "I'm tired, and tomorrow's a big day." She heads for the door.

I rise from the swing, as well. "I'll, uh, just go out the back gate."

"Okay." The screen door squeals as she opens it and steps through it. "Good night." Her voice sounds funny, as though she's choking back tears.

I want to say something more, but I don't know what that would be. "Good night," I call, but the screen door is banging shut, and the heavy wooden door is closing right behind it. I hear the definitive click of the lock.

I stand there for a moment, hating that I upset her, hating that I didn't come up with anything reassuring to say, hating my own ridiculously acute disappointment that she didn't give me a good night hug.

But can I blame her? The mention of Jessica was like tossing a cup of cold water on us both.

Damn it. In the last few weeks, things have shifted between Quinn and me. We're getting close. There's a lot between us, and it's not just because of Lily and the baby. There's chemistry and emotion and respect and humor and shared interests and a sense of just generally being in sync. It's physical, it's emotional, it's mental, and it's spiritual.

And yet, I'm still a married man. I'm in the process of divorce, but I'm not free. I'm in no position to say or do anything yet. It's too soon. I shouldn't be having these thoughts, much less these feelings, about Quinn.

I push through the wooden gate and step out onto the sidewalk. A streetlight on the corner shines brightly, but the night seems a lot darker out here than it did a few minutes ago in Quinn's backyard.

CHAPTER SIXTY

Margaret

Friday, July 12

"TODAY'S THE DAY, Mrs. Moore." An aide with short auburn hair smiles as she hands me a stack of papers attached to a clipboard. I'm sitting in the chair in my room, opposite the door, wearing pants, a coral top, and a necklace Quinn gave me for my birthday. "You're finally going home!"

"Yes," I say. I smile because she expects it, but inside, I'm full of trepidation.

It's not exactly home I'm going to, is it? I'm going to live with Quinn—and, of course, Lily and the new baby, when he or she arrives.

I've come to think of Quinn as family, but still, it's worrisome. It reminds me of going to live with Mama Betsy, then later with Uncle Ted and Aunt Opal. Why, even moving in with my beloved husband, Henry, had been unnerving at first. There are always doubts and questions. *What if we don't get along? What if they don't like the way I do things? What if they think I'm in the way?* I have no reason to think Quinn will see me as a burden—after all, I'll be paying my own expenses, I've arranged transportation for all of my outpatient therapy sessions, and as I get healthier, I'll be helping her and a part-time nanny with Lily and the baby—but it's a concern I have, all the same. No matter how old you get, you never outgrow your childhood issues. I'm eighty years old, and I still worry about being unwanted.

Ah, well. Moving in with Quinn and Lily is the perfect solution for now. If it doesn't work out, I'll move somewhere else. That's the upside of having some life experience; you know nothing lasts forever. Of course, that's the downside, too.

I have to admit, the prospect of making a major change at my age is terrifying. But then, hasn't change always been scary? Yes, yes, it has. Change is frightening at every age. The fear of the unknown scares us all.

The antidote to fear, I've learned, is faith. I'm so fortunate to have that. Faith lets me trust that God is good and in control, that I'm loved and have love to give, and that even if I make a bad decision or a mistake, it's never so bad that some good can't come out of it. I've made it through every bad day I've had so far, haven't I?

Yes. Yes, I have. And I've learned that blessings, large and small, are hidden for us in every situation, even the ones that hurt. Every ending is the beginning of something new.

This whole episode with my heart attack and broken hip is an example. I've grown closer to Quinn, Lily has ended up where she belongs, and Zack has become a part of Lily's life. I'm recovering amazingly well. In fact, I'm something of a miracle, the nurses tell me. The doctor, too; he said he was afraid I was going to have permanent brain damage, and my brain is mostly fine these days.

Mostly, but not entirely. I'm not as sharp as I once was; my short-term memory has a lot of holes in it. But I'm okay with that; I'll trade a little short-term memory loss for having gotten a glimpse of the beautiful, peaceful light where my loved ones and love itself await. That little glimpse broadened and brightened my perspective.

Love is what matters. Love is what lasts. Love is the thing to look for in every situation, because it's always there. If it's hard to see, well, it probably just means I need to be the one to offer it first.

I look through the hospital release papers, pick up the pen attached to the clipboard, and sign my name. I check my watch and realize that my trepidation has turned into anticipation.

Quinn will be here soon, and together we'll start a new beginning.

CHAPTER SIXTY-ONE

Quinn

"SURPRISE!" LILY YELLS as I escort Miss Margaret through the front door of my house.

Sarah, Mac, Lauren, Annie, Terri, Zack, and Lily are crowded into the foyer, along with Kylie, Annie's son, and Sarah's two toddlers.

"Welcome home!" Annie and Lauren say in unison.

"Happy homecoming!" Sarah chimes in.

"Oh, my!" Margaret says, gripping the handles of her walker. "I didn't expect anything like this!"

"We're all so glad that you're coming home that we wanted to help celebrate," Sarah says.

"This is wonderful!" Margaret looks around and beams. "Thank you so much!"

I'd warned Margaret that Lily and Zack would be waiting at the house to welcome her home, and that Lily had planned a surprise. I figured that an eighty-year-old woman who'd just had a heart attack needed a heads-up. I also knew she'd want to be dressed in something nice and wearing lipstick. I didn't tell her about the other people, but as we walked up to the front of the house, I'd reminded her, "Brace yourself for Lily's surprise."

"Welcome home, Grams," Lily says, rushing forward, then stopping a short distance in front of the walker. She's been taught that she can't grab and hug her grandmother like she used to, at least until her hip more fully heals, so Lily bobs up and down on her toes and blows kisses with both hands. "Are you surprised?"

"Very much so." Margaret's smile warms my heart. "Let me get seated so I can give you a hug."

"Right this way." The crowd clears as I lead her into the living room to a chair with strong arms. She carefully maneuvers her walker and sits down. Lily runs over and hugs her, then the rest of the group comes by and greets her.

"I'll get her bag from the car," Zack says after giving Margaret a hug and a kiss on the cheek.

"He's so thoughtful!" Annie remarks when she sees him bringing in her suitcase a moment later.

"Yes." I try not to actively think about his meeting with Jessica later this evening, although it kept me awake much of last night and has had my stomach in a tangle all day. I put my hand on my just-barely-a-baby bump, smooth the fabric of my navy polka-dot dress, and head into the kitchen to get Margaret a drink.

Sarah has already beaten me to it. She hands me a glass of sparkling water for myself, as well. "We've got dinner ready and everything under control," she says. "Go sit with Margaret and relax."

I do. At length we gather around the table in the dining room, which I'd set last night. I deliberately seat Zack at the far end so I don't have to make conversation.

"Oh, everything looks delicious!" Margaret exclaims.

"Lauren made the salad and fixed the green beans, Sarah baked the lasagna, and Annie prepared the strawberry trifle," I say.

"You all have been so good to me," Margaret says, her eyes full of gratitude.

"Well, we're adopting you as our collective grandmother," Lauren says. "Brooke always talked about how warm and wise you are, and she was right."

Margaret's eyes are moist, but she raises her eyebrows. "Me, wise? Why, you young folks run laps around my tired old brain."

Sarah raises her glass. "To you, Margaret. To your loving heart, your wise ways, and your bright spirit."

"Hear, hear!" Annie says.

"Amen," I say.

We all clink glasses and drink to Margaret. She beams, then

wipes her cheeks with her napkin. It's a delightful evening, except for the tension I feel around Zack. *Don't let negative interactions with others carry over to your home life*, I'd read in one of the parenting books. I determinedly try to put that into practice tonight.

Lily and the other children eat in the kitchen with Kylie, then go upstairs to play. Everyone lingers at the table, chattering, laughing, and teasing.

At length, Lily comes downstairs. "Grams, have you seen the bedroom we fixed for you?"

"Not yet, dear," Margaret replies.

"Oh, let's show her!" Lauren claps her hands. "I can't wait to see her reaction!"

I'm suddenly a little nervous. I want so badly for Margaret to like her room and to feel at home. But I don't want her to feel put on the spot; I want her to feel complete ownership of her space. "Would you rather see it later, when you're alone?"

"Why, no, dear," she says. "I watched a lot of HGTV while I was laid up. Let's have a big reveal!"

Everyone laughs and scoots back their chairs.

"We can bring your furniture from Alexandria and use that, if you prefer," I tell her as she rises from the chair and grips her walker. "I just pulled a few things I had at the store and in storage that I thought you might like, but nothing has to be permanent."

We all head to the bedroom, and Lily opens the door. "Ta-da!" she announces.

Margaret steps inside and everyone crowds behind her. I'm gratified to hear a little gasp. "Oh, my," Margaret says.

"What do you think?" Lauren asks.

"It's magnificent," Margaret proclaims. She moves to the bureau, pushing her walker in front of her, and looks at the photos I've placed there. She turns to me, her eyes wide. "How did you get these photos?"

"I asked your pastor's wife to send me the pictures in your bedroom, along with some of your clothes and personal items."

"How wonderful. How very thoughtful!"

"Great touch, Quinn," Annie says.

Margaret slowly moves around the room, admiring the four-poster bed, the colorful pillows, the cream duvet, the dresser, the bedside tables.

"It's just lovely," Margaret says.

"Daddy changed out the glass doors to give you priv'cy," Lily chimes in.

"Well, isn't he handier than a pocket on a shirt!"

Zack laughs. "I've been called a lot of things, but I believe that's a first." He glances at his watch. "Sorry to leave such fine company, but I have to go."

My chest constricts.

"You can't go yet!" Lily exclaims. "I need you to tuck me in an' read me bedtime stories."

"I have to meet someone," he says. "But I bet your grams can help Quinn do it."

"But I wanted all three of you!"

"I don't think we'd all fit in one bed," Zack says.

The group laughs. Lauren comically raises her eyebrows.

"Will I see you tomorrow?" Lily asked.

"Probably not," I tell her, before he has a chance to respond.

"Why not?" Lily frowns.

"Well, Miss Jessica's in town," I say. "And Zack has been spending an awful lot of time over here lately. I'm sure he has other things he needs to do."

He shoots me a puzzled look. "I'll call you tomorrow."

I nod. "Or the day after."

"Tomorrow." His tone is definitive. He thanks everyone for the dinner, bends down and gives Lily a kiss, straightens and pecks Miss Margaret's cheek, and then turns and gives me hug. Is it more of a hug than usual, or am I imagining things? "We'll talk tomorrow," he repeats in my ear. I blink back the tears that suddenly pool in my eyes.

LILY RUNS BACK upstairs to play with the other children.

"His wife is back?" Annie murmurs to me as she helps carry empty dessert plates from the table into the kitchen.

"Yes."

Her eyes are concerned as she scrapes them over the garbage disposal. "Don't tell me she's changed her mind about the divorce!"

I blow out a sigh. "I'm not sure what's going on. Yesterday we were talking, and I told him I was glad Margaret had found him. He said he was, too. I asked, 'Even if it cost you your marriage?' and he said, 'It didn't.'"

"That probably just means there were other problems in paradise." She hands me a scraped plate.

"That's what I thought at first, but later, he told me Jessica was coming to town and he had to leave the party early to meet her."

"This late?"

I lift my shoulders. "She wanted to have dinner with him, but he didn't want to miss this."

"That's a good sign."

"I need to stop looking for good signs." The plate clatters as I place it in the dishwasher.

"What do you mean?"

"Oh, Annie—I'm in over my head with Zack."

"That seems pretty natural under the circumstances."

"Yes, but I don't think it's healthy. And I'm completely at odds with myself on this. The commonsense side of me says we'll be sharing these children for the rest of our lives and they need parents who have a comfortable, friendly, non–emotionally fraught relationship. On the other hand, I've already fallen hard, and I'm afraid it's one-sided."

"Not a chance. I saw the way he looked at you at dinner." She hands me another plate.

Her words make my heart soar. I try to rein it in. *This is exactly the sort of thing you can't let yourself read things into*, I tell myself. "He's still married, and Jessica came back to talk to him." I put the plate in the dishwasher.

"She filed for divorce, Quinn."

"People can change their minds. Even if this visit changes nothing and the divorce goes through, I don't want to be a rebound."

She passes me another dish. "He doesn't seem like the type to do that."

"Above all, I don't want to start something that won't last. I don't want Lily or the baby to get hurt." I put the plate in the dishwasher.

"I don't think he does, either, Quinn. He's a great guy."

She goes into the dining room to gather more dishes. She's right. Zack is a good man—a wonderful man, exactly the kind of man I've always dreamed of finding.

Which is why I need to be careful. He's the kind of man who might think getting involved with the mother of his children is the right thing to do, even if he doesn't love me. I want to be loved, just for me. I don't want to repeat my past mistakes; I always wind up in relationships where I'm way more emotionally invested than my partner. Brooke thought it started with my father, and she's probably right.

Case in point: tonight. I'm falling in love, and what is Zack doing? Having drinks with his wife.

Annie comes back into the kitchen carrying more dishes.

"If he gets back with Jessica, will he move to Seattle, or will he convince her to move back here?" I wonder aloud. I don't know which option would be worse.

"Quinn, you're getting all worked up over things that are unlikely to happen."

"Are they? She flew all the way from Seattle to talk to him," I say. "Whichever way it goes, I need to establish some serious boundaries."

Annie hands me another scraped plate. "For his visits, or your feelings?"

"Both." But I don't believe I'll do it even as I say it.

AFTER EVERYONE LEAVES, I give Lily her bath and get her ready for bed. Because Margaret can't manage the stairs, we go back down and Lily climbs into Margaret's bed. Margaret and I get on either side of her, and we both read her two stories.

Lily wraps her arms around Margaret's neck. "I'm so glad you're here, Grams. I've missed you!"

"I've missed you, too, sweetheart." Margaret runs her age-spotted fingers through Lily's soft hair, then plants a kiss on her forehead.

My eyes grow misty. I want to take a mental snapshot of this moment, to remember it and treasure it. My heart overflows with love for Lily and Margaret—for what they mean to each other, for what they mean to me. *This is what matters*, I tell myself, *this right here.* Instead of worrying about Zack and Jessica and things that are beyond my control, I need to focus on the blessings right in front of me. And I will, I resolve. I will.

"Margaret, I'm so glad you're here," I say, kissing the top of her head. I step back and put my hand on Lily's shoulder. "Okay, Lily-kins, let's go upstairs."

"You got that from Daddy! That's what he calls me," she says as she hops off Margaret's bed.

That's true, I realize with a little pang.

"I believe I'm going to call it a day," Margaret says.

"Do you need any help with anything?"

"No, Quinn, dear. Annie unpacked my suitcase and showed me where everything is. I can manage all by myself."

I nod. "I'm leaving a night-light on in the hall and in your bathroom."

"That's perfect. I'll be just fine." She hugs me. "Thank you so much for all you've done. You've made me feel right at home."

"Good, because this *is* your home."

"I feel so blessed to have you and Lily as my family."

"Why, thank you, Margaret." My heart warms with delight. "I feel the same way. And I don't think I've ever gotten a nicer compliment."

"I don't think I've ever given one," she says.

I smile as I go upstairs. The feeling of warmth stays with me as I read yet another story to Lily, hear her prayers, and then go into the master bath to take a shower.

I have a lot to be grateful for, I think as I take off my shoes and dress. I have a loving family, just as I've always wanted: Margaret and Lily and the baby on the way. And whatever happens with Zack, well, he's a blessing, too.

I turn on the shower to let the water warm, then take off my bra. And then, as I step out of my undies, I see something that stops my heart and changes everything: a bright red stain.

CHAPTER SIXTY-TWO

Jessica

I DON'T WANT *to be here.* The thought forms in my head as I walk up the porch of my husband's new home, and for a moment, I seriously consider turning around, jumping in my rental car, and driving back to the hotel on Canal Street.

But if I do, I'll have to live with the knowledge that I walked out on my marriage without ever sitting down and talking things through. For the rest of my life, I will know that I cut and ran when things got tough. I can spin it in ways that paint me as the wronged party, but deep down, I'll always know the truth. And there's another hard truth I'm here to face: Zack is one of the finest men I've ever known, and a part of me is still in love with him. I can't move on unless I know there's no hope for our marriage.

I raise my hand and knock before I lose my nerve. The sound reverberates among the evening hum of cicadas and tree frogs.

Zack opens his door. He's wearing his inscrutable courtroom face.

"Hello." I give him what I hope is a warm smile and step forward to embrace him.

"Hi, Jess." He returns my hug, but it's a distant one. He kisses my cheek, but it's not particularly warm. It's certainly not a lover's kiss. Well, I didn't expect that or even necessarily want it, but I miss it all the same.

I step inside and look around, determined to keep my attitude positive and my energy upbeat.

"Oh, wow—what a great house!"

"Yeah. It was Brooke's and Lily's."

I feel a little stab in my heart. Good God, but he's enmeshed with those women.

"It's only a couple of blocks from Quinn's place," he says.

"How convenient." Even to my ears, the comment sounds snarky.

"Yeah, it is. What did you want to talk about?"

"Can we sit down?" We're standing in the foyer, the front door still open behind us.

"Sure." He closes the door and gestures to the living room.

I sit on the sofa, thinking he'll sit beside me. Instead, he sits in one of the chairs in front of the fireplace.

I cross my legs at the ankle and fold my hands in my lap, trying to look contrite and demure. I *am* contrite, I genuinely am, but my sister says I never really look sorry for anything. "Well, for starters, I want to apologize for how I handled things. I acted unilaterally, and a marriage is supposed to be a partnership. I'm sorry."

"Apology accepted. Is that all?"

"No, it's not." My mouth is dry, the way it gets before a big presentation. "I-I'd like to talk to you about the things we should have discussed."

"The property division is fine."

He's been beyond fair, going above and beyond what I'd asked. He's shipped all our furniture to Seattle, and he's had the closing company send me a check for half the proceeds from the sale of the condo. He'd owned the place before we married, so he had a lot more invested. All the same, he held nothing back.

That's how he was in our relationship: he held nothing back. The thought stabs my heart, because I can't say the same.

"I wasn't talking about property," I say. "I was talking about whether or not we should split up."

He turns his hands palm up. "If you want to divorce me, I don't see anything left to talk about."

"You'd suggested marriage counseling earlier. I was wrong to just dismiss it."

He lifts his shoulders. "It's all water under the bridge."

"Zack, I don't want to walk away from our marriage without feeling like we tried."

"Are you willing to move back to New Orleans?"

"No, but . . ."

He raises his hand and cuts me off. "I won't move to Washington. I have Lily and another baby on the way here, and I want to be part of their lives. I've worked things out with my old firm and told the Seattle law office that I'm staying put."

"But you could make it work if you tried. The children could visit us in Seattle, and you could come back and see them here. I'm sure the Seattle firm still wants you." I angle toward him, and pull out the words I'd formulated on the flight. "You always said that marriage was a sacred vow, and that you didn't believe in breaking it."

"You're the one who filed for divorce."

"Maybe I acted too swiftly. I've had time to think, and, well . . ." Tears swell in my eyes. "I miss the way we used to be together. I don't think I'll ever be as happy as I was when we were first married. Remember how wonderful those first few months were?"

"Yeah. I remember." His gaze meets mine. "But, Jess—things haven't been wonderful for a long, long while."

"They were once."

He blows out a long sigh. "A lot of things were wonderful once. I remember getting a puppy on my eighth birthday. I remember turning sixteen and getting my driver's license. Just because you remember things, Jess, doesn't mean you can get those moments back."

Desperation squeezes my chest. The thing is, I can't tell if it's because I truly want to mend my marriage or because I hate to lose. "What would it take for you to want to try again?"

"Are you willing to live in New Orleans?"

"I—I can't."

"You mean you won't."

He's right. It's not really about my job; I could find another position. What I'm not willing to do is live here and share him with Quinn and the children. "Maybe I'd consider it if you'd agree to try for a baby with a donor egg," I say.

He shakes his head. "Having a baby is no way to fix a broken marriage."

The word *broken* sounds like *failure* to me. I ignore it and push on. "Well, maybe we could try online counseling and see if we can negotiate something."

He shakes his head. "Unless you're willing to move back, there's nothing to negotiate."

"But you agreed to move to Washington with me. That's why I accepted the job."

"That was before I learned I had a child here, and another one on the way." His gaze is direct and serious and chillingly decisive. "It was also before you said you don't love me enough to deal with my donor family. As far as I'm concerned, that drove a stake through the heart of this marriage."

"I was upset. I was wrong to say that."

"If that's how you feel and that's what you think, then I needed to know it."

I have no response. He's right. I ask the question that's burning in my heart. "Is it just the children, or are you involved with Quinn?"

"She's carrying my baby, and she's the guardian—the mom, really—of Lily. But nothing romantic has happened between us, if that's what you're asking."

"Are you attracted to her?"

"I've honored my marriage vows to you, Jess." His expression is unreadable. "I could ask you the same thing about your Realtor-builder guy, but the truth is, I don't really care."

I feel like I've been slapped. He doesn't care if I'm involved with another man?

His phone buzzes. He looks at the number. "Excuse me. I need to take this." He stands and strides into the other room, but I can hear him on the phone.

"Hey, Quinn," he says. "What's up?" His voice is warmer, kinder, softer. It's a jarring shift from the way he just sounded talking to me.

"A little or a lot?" His tone has changed again. Now he sounds wound up and worried.

"Is there pain?" He pauses to listen. "Did you call the doctor? Hang tight. I'll be right over."

He strides back into the room. "Sorry, Jess. I've got to go."

"Is something wrong with Lily?"

"No."

"Margaret?"

"No. It's Quinn."

"What's happened?"

"She's bleeding." He drags his hand down his face. "She's afraid she's having a miscarriage."

CHAPTER SIXTY-THREE

Jessica

"OH, GOD!" I whisper.

Later, I'm proud that my first reaction is sympathy. After all, wouldn't it be best for me if Quinn were to lose the baby? Surely this is a sign I'm becoming a better person.

But I'm not thinking of that at the moment. At the moment, the heartbreak of my own miscarriage is crashing in on me all over again, and I wouldn't wish that on anyone. "I'm so sorry, Zack," I murmur. "I hate for anyone to lose a baby."

He nods, a brief acknowledgment of my concern. "I need to get over there."

"Of course. My rental car is blocking yours in—I'll drive you."

We head out of the house and into the black Maxima. I back out of the driveway. "Go left to the intersection, then take a right," he tells me.

"What did her doctor say?"

"She got the answering service. She's waiting for a call back." He points to the lovely two-story house I remember from our aquarium outing. "It's right here." He opens the passenger door the moment I brake by the curb. "Thanks."

I kill the engine. "I'm coming in with you."

"No, I don't think . . ."

I raise my hand. "There are no cars, which means everyone's gone home from the party. Someone needs to stay with Lily and Margaret if you have to take Quinn to the hospital. If I'm not needed, I'll just leave."

"Okay." He nods. "Thanks."

I follow him through a gate into the backyard. He knows where the spare key is hidden—in a magnetic container attached to the garden hose holder. "She said to let myself in," he says. "Margaret and Lily are already in bed."

He fits the key into a door off the brick-paved patio. We step into the large kitchen and cross to the living area. I follow Zack to the staircase, and faintly hear Quinn's voice from the second floor. It sounds as if she's on the phone. "I'll wait down here," I say.

Zack nods and bounds upstairs. I stand at the bottom for a bit, trying to make out what Quinn is saying, then decide to climb to the landing, where the staircase takes a turn. I can hear Quinn more clearly from this vantage. I sit on the step just below the turn, out of sight, and listen.

"Yes, he just got here," I hear Quinn say. She's silent a moment. "Okay." She pauses again. "All right. Thank you."

"Was that the doctor?" Zack asks.

I hear no response, so she must have nodded.

"What did she say?"

"She's out of town—she was calling from Destin."

Zack and I took a trip to Destin a couple of years ago. It's a popular beach spot in Florida, about four hours from New Orleans.

"She said there's not a lot to do for an early second trimester miscarriage." Quinn's voice quavers. "Bed rest is the only medical treatment that's recommended."

"What about going to the hospital?" Zack asks.

"She said I can go to the emergency room and get a standard ultrasound, but they don't send patients to the obstetrics floor unless they're twenty weeks or more."

"I can take you to the ER if that's what you want to do. Jess came with me so she could stay here with Margaret and Lily."

"Oh! That was kind of her."

"Yeah, it was. So do you want to go to the ER?"

"Oh, Zack—I don't know. Dr. Mercer said the ultrasound

would be done by an ER doctor, not an obstetrician, and there's a chance the machine won't pick up the heartbeat even if everything is all right. She said I should come into her office first thing on Monday."

"I'll accompany you to that," Zack says. His voice is so gentle that my heart cracks a little. "Do you want to try the fetal Doppler again?"

Oh, so they've tried it before—together, apparently. My stomach tenses into a clump of nerves.

"No. I'm afraid it's still too early, and I'll just worry all the more." Her voice breaks. "I want this baby so much. And Lily's so excited about being a big sister. She's had so many losses, and this will break her heart. And Margaret's."

"Mine, too," Zack says.

The lump in my stomach tightens and hardens.

"Really?" Quinn's voice is soft and surprised and filled with something that sounds like wonder.

"Yeah."

"Your life would have fewer complications without it."

"Having fewer complications doesn't always make life better."

"It would help your marriage."

"That's not an issue," Zack says.

He might mean our marriage isn't an issue that affects this problem, but deep down, I know he means more. He means our marriage is dead, over, beyond resuscitation. I've known it in my gut for a while now—that's why I filed for divorce, after all. Our talk tonight confirmed it, but hearing him say it aloud still hits me hard.

What he says next deals an even harsher blow.

"I want you to have my baby."

The words I've longed to hear from him, he's saying to another woman. I clutch my stomach and rock back and forth.

There was a time when he felt that way about me. But then, things changed. *No,* I self-correct; *I changed.* After the second or third failed IVF procedure, I stopped focusing on creating a family and started obsessing on whether another woman had had his child. I ruined everything loving and good between us with competitiveness and jealousy and bitterness over an imaginary contest.

Zack doesn't love me anymore, and it's all my fault.

"We'll do everything we can to save this pregnancy," he tells Quinn, "but if it's not meant to be, well, we'll try again. I'll help you give Lily a brother or sister."

"You will?"

"Yeah." I imagine her hugging him, or him hugging her. Hell—it would be reciprocal, wouldn't it? Whoever started it, the other would respond. I realize I'm clutching my chest with one hand, and the other is over my mouth.

"So what's the final verdict on the ER?" he asks.

"Let's go," she says.

"All right! Where are your shoes?"

I take that as a cue to scramble downstairs. I'm sitting on the sofa when Zack and Quinn come down a moment later. She's wearing yoga pants, a loose gray T-shirt, and flip-flops. He's wearing a grim, worried expression.

"Thank you so much for coming over and staying with Lily and Margaret," Quinn tells me.

"No problem," I say. My throat feels so tight it's a little hard to get the words out.

"If Lily wakes up, just tell her I'm out with Zack and you're babysitting, okay?" Quinn says. "There's no point in worrying her."

"Sure. What about Margaret?"

"If she wakes up, you can tell her everything."

I nod. "Good luck."

"Thanks, Jess." Zack's worried frown momentarily softens. It's the kindest, most personal look he's given me all evening.

Quinn hands him her car keys. Zack opens the kitchen door, puts his hand on the small of her back, and gently guides her out.

That's the moment I know, truly know, that Zack and I are

over. It wasn't when he said our marriage wasn't an issue; it wasn't when he offered to help Quinn give Lily a sibling; it wasn't even when he told her he wanted her to have his baby.

It was the moment he put his hand on the small of her back, as if she was treasured and cherished . . . and his.

CHAPTER SIXTY-FOUR

Quinn

WE WAIT MORE than an hour in the ER before we're called to an examination room. Once there, we wait most of another hour for a physician to see us, then another twenty minutes for an ultrasound machine to be wheeled in.

The doctor, a round-faced man about my age with dark, curly hair, squirts cold gel on my belly. "All right. Let's take a look and see what's going on."

He moves the transducer over my stomach. Zack stands beside me. I'm terrified. I've been googling *miscarriages* on my phone the whole time we've been waiting. Now that I'm about to find out if that's what's happening, I'm shaking like Ruffles on the way to the vet. I reach out my hand, and Zack takes it. Both of us stare at the blurry gray screen. The room is silent except for the sound of our breathing. The silence goes on and on, and dread unfurls in my belly. It's so very, very quiet.

Too quiet.

"Shouldn't we at least hear *my* heartbeat?" I ask.

"Oh, right." The doctor lifts the transducer from my stomach, turns, and adjusts the machine. He gives a sheepish laugh. "It sometimes helps to turn on the sound."

I'm not in the mood for jokes, and he isn't inspiring confidence in his abilities. He puts the transducer back on my belly, and the hard, fast drum of my pulse fills the room. "Calm down, there, Mom," he says. "Stress isn't good for your baby."

There ought to be a law against a man my own age calling me

Mom. I hadn't realized I'd tightened my grip on Zack's hand until he squeezes mine back.

The doctor moves the transducer, and then—*Eureka! Hallelujah!*—I hear the fast, galloping *swish swish swish* I've been praying for.

"Chamber music!" Zack says.

"That's the baby's heartbeat," the doctor corrects, as if he believes Zack has actually mistaken the sound for a string quartet. "And there he is." He points at a small blob in a dark area of the screen. "You can see him right there."

I strain, but I can't make sense of what I'm seeing.

"Is he okay?" Zack asks.

The doctor nods. "Looks great. There's his head, and there are his arms and legs." He then turns to the machine, adjusts a knob and zooms in, making the image larger. "He's waving at you."

Suddenly, I see the movement of a tiny limb. My heart turns over. "I see it!"

"Yep. You'll be able to feel that in a few weeks."

I stare at the screen, transfixed. It's not a clear picture of an obvious baby, but I think I see the profile of a face. The doctor moves the transducer, and I lose perspective.

"Is it a 'he' for sure, or are you using the word as a catchall pronoun?" Zack ask.

"Sorry—I tend to call every fetus 'he' because I have a son," he says apologetically. "I can't determine the sex on this machine. It's not very high resolution; it's more for finding gallstones than making fetal videos. Your obstetrician can tell you that in a few weeks."

"Any idea what's causing the bleeding?" I ask.

He slowly moves the transducer and scans the screen. "There's nothing visible. My guess is it's a small subchorionic bleed or hematoma."

"What's that?" I ask.

"Sometimes a little blood will leak out of a blood vessel between the uterus and the placenta—the vessels are expanding and carrying a lot of blood during pregnancy. Most often it's not a big deal and will self-correct." He stops moving the transducer, puts some markers on the screen, and fiddles with some knobs. "Looks like you're about eighteen weeks along."

"That's right," I say. "What happens if the bleeding doesn't stop?"

"Well, then, the pregnancy could be at risk, but there's no indication that's the case."

I suddenly see the flailing of a limb. "He's kicking!"

"Wow," Zack murmurs.

The doctor grins. "Looks like he's going for a field goal."

We watch for moment, then he removes the transducer and turns off the machine. "Take it easy over the weekend. Stay in bed as much as possible, try not to worry, and see your obstetrician on Monday." He hands me some tissues. "Everything looks really good."

"Oh, thank heavens!" I feel like I can finally take a full breath. A heady sense of relief chases through my veins. "That's great news."

"The best," Zack says. He's still holding my hand, and he squeezes it.

My heart squeezes as well.

The doctor makes some notes on his computer. I wipe the gel off my belly, adjust my clothes, and sit up. The doctor shakes our hands and wishes us luck.

Zack helps me off the examination table. "Let's get you home."

Home—where his wife is waiting for us. The thought dampens my happiness, but I smile and nod.

The checkout procedure spares me from having to make small talk. I sit by the ER door as Zack pulls my car around. It's raining outside. He parks under the portico, gets out, and opens the door for me.

"It was worth a three-hour wait to hear that everything looks good," he says as he climbs in and fastens his seat belt.

"Yes." I have less than complete confidence in the ER doctor's obstetrics expertise, but it was reassuring to see the baby move and hear the heartbeat. I feel emotional and drained and on the verge of tears. As Miss Margaret would say, I'm on the Edge of Wetness.

I lean back against the headrest. The situation is truly soap opera material. Everyone at the hospital thought Zack and I were a couple, when in reality, his wife is at my house, babysitting the child he had with my best friend. "You should probably text Jessica that we're on the way."

"I already did."

So he, too, was thinking of her. Fat raindrops hit the windshield.

He turns on the wipers as he drives out of the covered entrance. "She texted back that she hasn't heard a peep from Lily or Margaret."

"That's a relief."

"Yeah." He turns onto Jefferson Highway. "If it's okay with you, I'd like to sleep in your guest room tonight so I can hear if you need anything."

"Oh, you don't have to do that. After all, Jess just got here, and you and she . . . you probably want . . ." Oh, God. What am I trying to say? My eyes fill and my face burns.

He glances over at me. "Jess is staying at the hotel. Nothing has changed about our divorce."

My heart skips a beat, then pounds hard. Joy neurons fire in my brain. I tamp them down. *You can't keep doing this*, I think. *You need to level out all these ups and downs. It's not healthy for your baby.* "I—I thought you two might be getting back together."

"No. Our marriage is over. The truth is, it's been over for a long while, but neither of us wanted to admit it. It'll be final in about a month and a half."

"That fast?"

He nods. "Washington is a very efficient state for uncontested divorces."

"I'm sorry." I sit there for a moment, watching the wipers slash back and forth. Under a streetlamp up ahead, I see a food truck parked against a building. As we drive by, I read the name on it: *Spill the Beans.*

Goose bumps rise on my arms. It's a sign; I'm sure of it. I angle toward Zack, and words start pouring out of my mouth. "Actually, I'm not. I'm not sorry about your divorce at all. I just said that because it seemed appropriate."

He laughs. "I love that about you—how up-front and outspoken you are."

"I'm not. At least, not always."

"No?"

"No. I haven't told you how terrified I am of you."

"Of *me*?"

I nod. "I don't want you to break Lily's or the baby's heart or . . ." *What are you doing?* I ignore my censoring brain, and words just spew straight from my heart. "Or mine."

"What are you talking about?"

"I don't want to get used to having you in my life, and talking to you all the time, and being around you and feeling . . . feeling . . ."

"What?"

I draw in a deep breath and shake my head. "I just think we should put some parameters on how much you're around. It would be healthy if we had some distance. I don't want any of us to get too used to you spending so much time with us."

"Why not?"

"I don't want to get hurt, and I don't want you to hurt Lily, or the baby." My voice cracks. "If . . . if the baby makes it."

"Hey." He reaches over and takes my hand. "Hey, the doctor said things looked good."

"Yes, as far as he could tell. But he admitted he couldn't tell much. He didn't know for sure why I'm bleeding. Until I see Dr. Mercer on Monday, I'm worried."

"I'm here for you."

"Didn't you just hear me? That worries me, too."

"Quinn." He glances over. "I'm not going anywhere."

"Maybe you should."

He pulls the car into the empty parking lot of a closed strip mall and shifts the gear into park. He takes off his seat belt, angles toward me, and puts his arm over the back of my seat. His forehead furrows. "What the hell are you talking about?"

I throw up my hands. "I got close to you and I let Lily get close to you because we thought you were moving. I thought there was a limited amount of time to bond. But now you're staying, and you're all entangled in our lives, and I should have established solid guidelines to keep us all from getting overinvolved, but it was just so *nice* that I didn't *want* to set any boundaries, and now I just feel . . ." I blow out a hard sigh and search for the word. "Vulnerable. Like I'm relying on you too much and getting too attached. And this whole thing tonight with Jessica made me realize how tenuous everything is. I have a history of getting involved in lopsided relationships with emotionally unavailable men, and . . . well, now the stakes are a lot higher because it's just not me who stands to get hurt. So I think we should back things off."

"I think that's a terrible idea."

"Easy for you to say!"

"Look, Quinn—it's too early and I'm in no position to make any big proclamations, but let me repeat what I just said: I'm not going anywhere. I care for you and Lily and the baby. I care deeply. And I never, ever want to hurt any of you." He draws a breath. His hand moves down from the back of my seat and rests on the back of my head. It stays there for a moment, and then he moves it away. "It's too early to be telling you this, but I have feelings for you that go way beyond what's currently appropriate."

I find it hard to breathe. My heart flutters as if it's sprouted wings, but I'm afraid they're penguin wings—useless little flaps that will never let me fly.

"It's more than just Lily and the baby," he says. "I think about you all the time. I think about your smile, your laugh, your crazy, psychic goose bumps—which I'm now getting, too, by the way. Apparently they're contagious."

My lip gives a funny twitch when I grin. Oh, God—can it be? Does he really mean . . .

"For the next few months, I'd like us to continue as friends," he says. "I'd like to see you and Lily every day or every other day—whatever you think is best. I'd like to spend time with you and get to know you better, and let you get to know me. And then, after the divorce is final, I'd like to date you. I want to take you to dinner and the movies and out to listen to music. We can take things as slow as you'd like. I'm not in a rush. I've got all the time in the world. Because what I really want, what I've always really wanted, is to have the kind of relationship that my parents had—where trust was as easy as breathing and they were equally crazy about each other and love not only flowed between them, but spilled out to everyone else around them. I think you and I can have that together. In fact, I think we're both further along the road to that than either of us is ready to admit."

I can scarcely see him—partly because it's dark and partly because there's a neon light blinking behind him, but mainly because my eyes are filled with tears. The wing stubs on my heart are growing now, growing and sprouting feathers.

"I'm willing to wait as long as it takes," he says. "Does that sound like something you could consider?"

It strikes me that this is one of life's brightest moments—like the sun at high noon on a cloudless day. It's a waterfall moment, a moment too full to be contained, a moment that can't help but spill over from now into the future. It's a moment that doesn't need a corroborating sign; it's a life-marking moment that will forever separate my life into "before" and "after."

It's one of those moments when words are inadequate, but a response is required all the same.

"Yeah," I say. "I think that's something I could consider."

He grins at me. "Well, then—let's go home."

EPILOGUE

Margaret

Two Years Later

"LILY HAS A little something planned for you, Miss Margaret," Quinn says as she pulls her car into the drive. It's my eighty-second birthday, and Quinn just treated me to a manicure and pedicure at a lovely salon on Magazine. "I thought I'd better tell you so you won't be too startled when the door opens."

"Lily's planned a little something, huh?" I smile. "All by her little lonesome?"

Quinn gives a sheepish smile. It's another surprise party, of course—and if the cars lining the street are any indication, it's a big one. I swear, these people throw so many surprise parties it would be a surprise if they didn't. Every time, though, Quinn tips me off.

I remember a time when Quinn didn't like surprises. She said she'd had enough in her childhood to last a whole lifetime.

Brooke, however, always loved the unexpected. She thought the element of surprise added to the fun. I suppose Quinn picked that up from Brooke. I know Lily certainly did.

Isn't it funny, how the ways of those we love rub off on us? Why, we're always influencing each other, whether we know it or not.

A lot has happened in the past two years. My hip has healed, and I'm getting around nearly as well as I could before. I'm still living with Quinn—well, with Quinn and Zack and Lily and baby

Violet Brooke and that little dog Ruffles. Quinn has scaled back her work schedule—her assistant Terri has become a partner in her company and they've hired two new assistants—but she still needs a hand with Lily and Violet, especially now that Violet's walking and starting to talk. As for Lily . . . I can't believe how quickly she's grown! She starts kindergarten in the fall, but she's been reading for over a year. She loves to read simple picture books to little Violet. She's amazingly smart, just like her mother.

It seems impossible that Brooke has been gone for two years, yet I know she has, because the thought of her now brings more gratitude than grief. I feel blessed to have had her as a granddaughter, and I'm so grateful that she brought Lily and Quinn and baby Violet into my life.

After that scare in her second trimester, Quinn had a normal-pregnancy, and beautiful little Violet arrived right on schedule. Quinn and Zack were married six months later. It seems like they've been married longer, because he's spent all his free time at Quinn's house ever since I've been around to witness it. I've never seen a couple more in love with each other and their children.

They had a lovely wedding, simple but elegant, at their church. There were no bridesmaids or groomsmen—just Lily as the flower girl, adorable in a cream-colored dress with a wide satin bow. Quinn was breathtaking in a beaded organza gown. The way Zack looked at her made me tear up; it was the same heart-in-the-eyes look that my dear Henry used give me. Zack still looks at her that way, across the kitchen or at the dining table—and I catch her gazing at him with the same adoration. Why, the other night, I saw them dancing together in the kitchen, with the lights out and no music I could hear.

Their wedding reception was a fun-filled affair on the *Creole Queen* riverboat, paddling up and down the Mississippi River. Zack's sister and her husband were there, along with all of Zack and Quinn's friends and, of course, the single parent group.

I'm sure that group is here for this party. Quinn still gets together with them every month, although hardly anyone is single anymore. Sarah and Mac are living together, Annie is married to a former high school friend she reconnected with at her high school reunion, and Lauren is engaged to the chef at the hospital where she works and is in the process of finalizing the adoption of an adorable special needs child.

As for Quinn and Zack—well, I have to think that searching for Lily's father was a bit of divine inspiration on my part, because that's a match that couldn't have been made anywhere but in heaven.

And now Quinn's pregnant with another baby. It's supposed to be a secret, but I've noticed her purse is full of crackers again, she's not drinking wine and sometimes she looks a little green around the gills. I may be old, but I'm not blind.

Brooke must be doing her happy dance up in heaven at how things are going down here. I feel so blessed that I got to see her and my other loved ones when my heart stopped. Some people would say I hallucinated or that my brain misfired or some such, but I know what I know.

And when you think about it, it all makes perfect sense. Everything is basically energy. It's a scientific fact that energy never disappears; it only changes form. What contains more energy than love? It's the most powerful force in the world.

Things even turned out well for Zack's first wife—who, ironically, was responsible for bringing Zack into our lives. He heard through a mutual friend that she'd married a man she knew in high school, and that they'd had a baby together through an IVF procedure. He and Quinn sent them a note of congratulations.

Quinn and I stop at the front door. "All right, Miss Margaret. Forewarned is forearmed." Quinn smiles at me. "Are you ready?"

I am. I'm ready for whatever comes next. Which, in the immediate future, is sure to be cake, champagne, loving friends, and family.

"Yes, dear." I tingle with anticipation as she opens the door, eager for the moment when everyone shouts, "Surprise!"

Because it's all a surprise, every single moment.

Author's Note

I LOVE TO write about situations that change people, and nothing changes a person's life like becoming a parent. Everything is reordered: your time, your priorities, your hopes, your fears, your goals, your finances, your sleep schedule. (Did I mention your sleep schedule?) As the mom of two daughters, I've found parenthood to be heart-warming, messy, hilarious, terrifying, joyful, harrowing, exhilarating, daunting, baffling, and rewarding. Sometimes it can be all those things in a single day! Having a child expands your heart and takes you to a whole new level of love. Parenthood is one of life's most challenging, meaningful, and beautiful journeys.

What if you yearn to have a child, but you haven't found the right partner? What if you discover you have a physical problem that makes it difficult or impossible to conceive a child? What if you have no problem, but your partner does—or vice versa? How does that affect a relationship? And what about sperm or egg donors?

I first started thinking about all these things years ago when I used to drive past a fertility center en route to my daughters' preschool. I'd watch the people going in and out, and I wondered about their stories. When my editor, Kate Seaver, expressed an interest in a novel about a single mother by choice, my imagination was primed and ready. I think I'd been incubating this story for years.

The characters in this novel are fictional, but the issues they face are real. I wanted to portray the procedures accurately, so I did a lot of research into fertility treatments, clinics, and legalities in Louisiana. One of the things I learned is that bioethical and law literature often refer to the field of reproductive technology as "The Wild, Wild West." Regulations vary by state, and legislation hasn't kept up with technology, leaving a lot of gray area. Many issues—such as whether or not leftover purchased vials of frozen sperm are transferable or refundable, and if so, what are the requirements and procedures for record-keeping—are addressed in the contracts between the involved parties and the fertility center or cryobank. For the purposes of this story, Brooke's contract with a fictional fertility center allows her to give the remainder of the frozen sperm she owns to Quinn.

Another gray area is anonymity. I read many articles stating that in this age of genetic testing, anonymity can no longer be guaranteed. Several national and international registries exist to connect donor siblings, recipients, and donors. For the sake of this story, I created a fictional registry. I also created a fictional single parent group, although those, too, are thriving in most cities.

Reproductive technology is changing, but one thing remains the same: the importance and impact of family. All of us are shaped by our families of origin. Pope John XXIII said, "The family is the first essential cell of human society."

Whether we grew up in a happy family or not, we're all hardwired to want one. We ache to belong, to connect, to be part of a tribe. We long to be surrounded by people who will love, support, and accept us no matter what—people who will root for us, pick us up when we fall, forgive our failings, and rejoice in our victories.

The writer Richard Bach said, "The bond that links your true family is not one of blood, but of respect and joy in each other's lives."

One of the truths I hope this book illustrates is that there are many different ways to create a family—a band of people whose love for one another transcends bad choices, physical limitations, and differing beliefs. Writing this novel gave me a renewed appreciation for the loved ones in my life. I hope that reading it does the same for you.

Acknowledgments

SPECIAL THANKS TO my amazingly talented editor, Kate Seaver, for giving me the magical four-word idea that spawned this novel: *single mother by choice.* Kate also has my gratitude for coming up with the title. Thank you, Kate, for all your wisdom, insights, guidance, and hard work!

She Gets That from Me

ROBIN WELLS

Questions for Discussion

1. Quinn says that early childhood experiences affect people permanently. Discuss how early family experiences shape the following characters: Zack, Quinn, Brett, Jessica, Margaret, and Lily. How did your childhood affect you?

2. Margaret thinks that every child deserves to know both biological parents. What do you think? Is this always true?

3. Discuss the ways some of the different characters in this book—Margaret, Quinn, Lily, Jessica, Zack, and Brett—had different definitions and expectations of family.

4. Some of the characters in the book decide to be single parents. What unique challenges do they face compared to parents who have a partner to help them? How were these parents able to succeed in the face of these additional demands? What do you think are qualities essential to being a good parent?

5. Discuss how the following characters grew and changed during the course of the book: Quinn, Jessica, Zack, and Margaret.

6. Brett tells Jessica that peace of mind comes only from living out your values. Is he right? Jessica realizes she'd focused on hitting goals and had never given much thought to values. What kind of values matter in life? What are yours?

7. Margaret reflects on how people are constantly affecting and influencing the lives of those close to us, whether we know it or not. What are some ways the characters in the book influenced each other's lives? Can you think of a trait you possess that you got from a relative or friend?

8. Margaret believes that blood is thicker than water. What do you think? Do genetic connections make the strongest family ties?

Photo by Arden Wells

Robin Wells was an advertising and public relations executive before becoming a full-time writer. She always dreamed of writing novels—a dream inspired by a grandmother who told "hot tales" and parents who were both librarians. Her books have won the RWA Golden Heart, two National Readers' Choice Awards, the HOLT Medallion, and numerous other awards. She and her husband now live in Texas and are the parents of two grown daughters.